Cathy Kelly is a number 1 bestselling author. She worked as a journalist before becoming a novelist, and has published fourteen bestselling books. She is also an ambassador for UNICEF in Ireland. She lives in Wicklow with her husband and two sons.

To find out more about Cathy and her novels, her events and to read her blog, visit her website at www.cathykelly.com, follow her on Twitter @cathykellybooks or find her on Facebook. She would love to hear from you.

Praise for Cathy Kelly:

'Her skill at dealing with the complexities of modern life, marriage and families is put to good effect as she teases out the secrets of her characters'          *Choice*

'An upbeat and diverting tale skillfully told . . . Kelly knows what her readers want and consistently delivers'
*Sunday Independent*

'Entertaining, moving and as vivid as a screenplay – presents a picture of the lives of Irish women which, like all good fiction, brings the truth into sharp relief'          *Irish Independent*

'A tear-pricking writer, capable of making you care about her characters'          *Daily Mail*

'Warm and delightful'          *New Woman*

# CATHY KELLY

## *Past Secrets*

HARPER

*Harper*
an imprint of HarperCollins*Publishers*
77–85 Fulham Palace Road,
Hammersmith, London W6 8JB

www.harpercollins.co.uk

This paperback edition 2012
1

First published in Great Britain
by HarperCollins 2006

Copyright © Cathy Kelly 2006

Cathy Kelly asserts the moral right to
be identified as the author of this work

A catalogue record for this book is
available from the British Library

ISBN 978-0-00-793688-5

Printed and bound in Great Britain by
Clays Ltd, St Ives plc

**MIX**
Paper from
responsible sources
FSC® C007454

*For Laura, Naomi and Emer*

# CHAPTER ONE

If a road could look welcoming, then Summer Street had both arms out and the kettle boiling.

Christie Devlin had lived halfway up the street for exactly thirty years in a small but exquisite red-bricked house that gleamed like a jewel in a necklace of pretty coloured stones.

Summer Street itself was curved and ran for half a mile from the crossroads where the café sat opposite a house which had once been a strawberry-ice-cream shade and was now a faded dusky pink.

From the moment Christie had seen the graceful curve of the street, where maple trees arched like kindly aunties over the pavement, she'd known: this was the place she and James could raise their family.

Those thirty years had gone in a flash, Christie thought on this beautiful late-April morning as she went about her chores, tidying, dusting, sweeping and wiping.

Today the sun streamed in through the windows, the house seemed filled with quiet contentment and Christie didn't have to go to work. She loved her job as an art teacher at St Ursula's secondary school, but she'd cut back her hours recently and was relishing the extra free time.

Her dogs, Tilly and Rocket, miniature dachshunds who had clearly been imperial majesties in a previous life, were sleeping off their morning walk on the cool of the kitchen tiles. The radio was playing quietly in the background and the old steel percolator was making the rattling death throes that signalled the coffee was nearly ready. All should have been right with Christie's world.

And it was – except for a niggling feeling of disquiet. It had been simmering in her subconscious since she'd awoken at six to the joyous chorus of birdsong outside her bedroom window.

'Happy Anniversary,' James had murmured sleepily when the alarm went off at a quarter past and he rolled over in the bed to cuddle her, to find Tilly squashed between them. The dogs were supposed to sleep on their corduroy bean-bags on the floor, but Tilly adored the comfortable little hollow in the duvet between her master and mistress. James lifted the outraged dog and settled her at his other side, then moved closer to Christie. 'Thirty years today since we moved in. And I still haven't finished flooring the attic.'

Christie, wide awake and grappling with the intense feeling that something, somewhere, was wrong, had to laugh. Everything was so normal. She must be imagining the gloom.

'I expect the floor to be finished this weekend,' she said in the voice that could still the most unruly class in St Ursula's. Not that she had ever had much trouble with unruly students. Christie's love of art was magical and intense, and transferred itself to most of her pupils.

'Please, no, Mrs Devlin,' begged James, in mock-schoolboy tones. 'I don't have the energy. Besides, the dog keeps eating my homework.'

Panting, Tilly clambered back defiantly and tried to make her cosy nest in between them again.

'The dog would definitely eat the homework in this house,' James added.

2

Christie took hold of Tilly's warm velvety body and cuddled her, crooning softly.

'I think you love those dogs more than you love the rest of us,' he teased.

'Of course I do,' she teased back. Christie had seen him talking adoringly to Tilly and Rocket when he didn't think anyone noticed. James was tall, manly and had a heart as soft as butter.

'Children grow up and don't want cuddles, but dogs are puppies for ever,' she added, tickling Tilly gently in her furry armpits. 'And let's face it, you don't run around my feet yelping with delight when I get home from work, do you?'

'I never knew that's what you wanted.' He made a few exploratory barking noises. 'If I do, will you whisper sweet nothings to me?' Christie looked at her husband. His hair was no longer a blond thatch. It was sandy grey and thinning, and he had as many fine lines around his face as she had, but James could still make Christie smile on the inside.

'I might,' she said.

From the bedroom floor, Rocket whimpered, wanting to be included in the fun.

James got out of bed and scooped her on to the duvet beside her mistress, whereupon Rocket began to smother Christie in kisses.

'I hope I get to come back as one of your dogs in my next life,' he remarked, heading to the bathroom for his shower.

Christie shivered. 'Don't even speak like that,' she said, but she was talking to a closed door.

Thirty years in this house. How had the time passed so quickly?

'I love it,' she'd told James that first day, as she stood, pregnant with their second child, Shane, outside number 34, a house they could only afford because it required what the estate agent hilariously described as 'a wee bit of renovating'.

3

'You're sure you don't prefer the mock-Tudor heap seven streets over?' asked James, holding tightly to little Ethan's hand. At the grand old age of three and a quarter, Ethan's current favourite hobbies included trampolining on his bed and wriggling out of his parents' grasp to fling himself in danger's path.

Christie had arched a dark eyebrow at her husband.

The heap's front garden had been tarmacked while the back garden contained two fierce dogs who hadn't responded when Christie instinctively reached out her hand. There was a sinister brick-sized hole in one of the upstairs windows and when James had casually asked the estate agent why there was no gun turret complete with AK47 peeking out, Christie had had to smother her laughter.

'Call me old-fashioned,' she told James, 'but I somehow prefer Summer Street and this house.'

Despite the obvious dilapidation, the very bricks of number 34 seemed to glow with warmth, and the stained-glass oriel window over the graceful arched porch was in its original condition.

From where they stood, the Devlin family could see the Summer Street Café with its aqua-and-white-striped awning and paintwork. On the pavement outside stood white bistro chairs and three small tables covered with flowered sea-blue tablecloths that looked as if they'd been transported from a Sorrento balcony.

On the same side of the street as the café there were terraced houses; then a couple of slender detached houses squeezed in; eight small railway cottages, their classic fascia boards traced with delicate carvings; then a series of redbricks including theirs; five 1930s bungalows and, finally, a handful of one-storey-over-basements. The other side of Summer Street was lined with more terraced houses and cottages, along with a tiny park: two neatly kept acres with a colonnaded bandstand, an old railway pavilion and a minuscule fountain much loved by the pigeons who couldn't bear to poop anywhere else.

The maple trees that lined the street were flanked by colourful border plants, while even the doors to the dizzying variety of houses were painted strong bright shades: cerulean blues, poinsettia scarlets, honeyed ambers.

Christie would always remember how James had responded when she'd said she loved the house. He'd put the hand that wasn't holding on to Ethan around hers and squeezed.

'Then we've got to have it,' he'd said.

They hadn't even looked inside.

When Christie told astonished people afterwards that they'd decided to buy 34 Summer Street without crossing the threshold, she'd explained that you knew when you were in the right place. Homes were about more than actual walls.

'You can't go far wrong with a well-built redbrick,' James's brother said sagely, put out by all this talk of feelings.

And indeed, the house was beautifully proportioned even though it was sadly down at heel, like a genteel lady who'd fallen on hard times but still polished the doorstep every morning even when she could barely afford milk for her tea.

But James and Christie knew it was more than decent proportions or the welcoming width of the copper-coloured front door that had made up their mind. Christie had simply known it was the home for them and James had learned to trust his wife's instincts.

When she, James and Ethan moved in a month later, they were the proud owners of a ramshackle four-bedroom pile with one bathroom, nothing resembling a usable kitchen and a butterfly sanctuary for a garden.

In those days, there was no three-storey apartment block at the bottom of the street and no unneighbourly huffing about parking since most families were lucky to own just one car. But it was also before the park was given the primary-coloured playground equipment where small children roared with both delight and temper, depending on how the arguments were going over whose go it was on the slide.

Christie used to take Ethan and Shane to the park to play. Now, she walked Rocket and Tilly along the neatly trimmed pathways. Her two beautiful granddaughters, Sasha and Fifi, had been wheeled into the park in their buggies, and Sasha, now two and a half, loved hurling herself at the fountain as if she was about to leap in. Just like her dad, Christie thought fondly.

Ethan had always had so much energy. He'd thrown himself into life at full tilt from his very first breath. And he'd adored Summer Street.

'We'd better get the mower out,' James had observed that first day as Ethan ran into the garden, whooping with excitement, his blond head almost disappearing in the long, wild grass. The van they had rented to move their belongings was parked on the drive and a few friends were due round to help shift all the heavy stuff. But for the moment, the small family were alone. 'It's like a jungle out there.'

'It's like a jungle in here too,' Christie had said wryly, looking up at the corner of the kitchen where a particularly murky black bit of wall stood out amid the peeling cat-sick-yellow plaster. 'Please tell me there wasn't that much mould on the walls when we viewed. We should have got the infectious diseases people to survey the house instead of an architect.'

'You think we'll be eaten in our beds by a noxious house fungus?'

Christie smiled affectionately at her husband, who'd given their son both his blond hair and sunny disposition. The pride of finally owning their own house shone in James's eyes, noxious fungus notwithstanding.

'Probably. Now, are you going to rescue Ethan, or am I to

shift my five-months-pregnant bulk out after him?' Tall and normally slender, she'd carried Ethan easily with a neat little basketball of a bump that was unnoticeable from behind. This time round, her slender figure was a distant memory and she felt like a giant stretch-marked pudding, equally enormous whichever angle she was viewed from.

Her sister Ana reckoned it was second baby syndrome, where all the muscles gave up the ghost. But Christie knew that her inexplicable cravings for huge bowls of deep-fried banana with ice cream hadn't helped.

'I'll go and rescue him, o Massive One,' James said, laying a hand on her swollen belly. 'I don't want you so tired out that you don't have the energy to christen the house with me tonight.' He grinned suggestively.

A laugh exploded out of Christie. The exhaustion of pregnancy meant she was asleep by nine most nights and not even a vat of aphrodisiacs could rouse her. But then she relented, seeing the look of hope on her husband's face.

'Back massage first,' she bargained. Why her back should be an erogenous zone, Christie didn't know. But feeling James's supple hands kneading away her aches always got her in the mood for love.

'Deal.'

The upside of living in such a wreck of a house was that Christie didn't have to worry about Ethan crayoning on the walls, though he was an intrepid mountaineer so she spent much of her time rescuing him from various pieces of the second-hand furniture which was all they could afford. The downside of the house was that it seemed to take for ever before the damp was banished and they could eat a meal without a bit of ceiling falling on to their plates.

Now, a lifetime later, Ethan was thirty-three, Shane was almost thirty and Christie was a grandmother twice over.

The long dark hair she'd worn in a loose ponytail all those years ago was now cut to jaw length and waved, its cool silvery white highlighting the warmth of her olive skin and dark, winged eyebrows.

She still wore a delicate flick of eyeliner, which gave her eyes a magical tilt at each olive green corner, but had swapped the block of cake eyeliner she'd grown up with for a modern miracle liner pen. She liked embracing new things, believing that living too much in the past made a person look their age.

The kitchen wasn't showing its age, either. Currently on its third incarnation, it had been decorated in brightly coloured chic, then antique pine and was now showcasing modern maple. Many woman-hours of hard work had turned the garden into a honeytrap for lazy bees, which moved from one variety of lavender to another in the height of summer.

Now, in the last days of April, the old French rose that Christie had been nurturing to sweep over the pergola had produced its first decent crop of antique white flowers with a musky, amber scent. Her garden was so sheltered that her roses bloomed at least a month before they should and she could smell their fragrance from the open window as she stood rinsing the breakfast dishes at the sink.

Scrubbing at some stubborn crumbs of toast glued to a white plate, Christie tried to rationalise the niggling anxiety in her head.

Anniversaries brought up old memories, that was all it was, surely.

Christie had been so lucky these past thirty years. Blessed, almost. There had only been that one time in her married life when it had all nearly gone wrong, and, like catching a falling glass before it hit the floor, Christie had averted the disaster. There was a tiny crack left behind from that time, but nobody except Christie could see it. That couldn't trouble her now, could it?

No, she decided firmly, as she slotted the clean plate into the drying rack. That was all in the past.

She knew she was blessed. James was as good a husband as he'd been when she married him. Better, in fact. They'd grown closer as they'd grown older, not apart, like so many others did. Christie knew plenty of people her own age who'd stayed married and had nothing to show for it except spite and old wedding photos. They bitched and bickered and made everyone around them uncomfortable. Why bother? Christie wondered.

Wouldn't it be better to be happy on your own instead of coupled off in sheer misery? She liked to think that if she and James fell out, God forbid, they could end it with dignity and move on.

'I bet you wouldn't,' her sister Ana had pointed out mischievously once, at the end of one long night on the small terrace in the garden when the wineglasses were empty and the conversation had turned to what-ifs.

'There wouldn't be a bit of dignity involved. I bet you'd stab James with your secateurs one night, bury him under the rhubarb and act delighted when it turned out to be a good crop!'

'Ah, Ana,' said James, feigning hurt. 'Christie would never do that.' He paused for effect, looking round the garden his wife adored. 'The lilac tree needs fertilising, not the rhubarb. That's where she'd bury me.'

'You're both wrong,' said Christie amiably, reaching out to clasp her brother-in-law Rick's hand. 'I'm going to bury James right here, under the flagstones, then Rick and I are going to run off into the sunset together.'

'As long as I get this house,' Ana said, getting to her feet, 'the pair of you can do what you want.'

It was a beautiful house, Christie knew. One of the loveliest on Summer Street. Christie's artistic talent had made it just as beautiful inside as outside.

'If Mum and Dad could see this place,' Ana said wistfully as the sisters hugged goodbye in the hall where Christie had black-and-white photos of the family hung alongside six watercolour paintings of irises of the kind that she used to sell to make money during the early days of paying the Summer Street house mortgage.

'Dad would hate it,' laughed Christie easily. 'Too arty farty, he'd say.'

'Ah, he wouldn't,' protested Ana, who at fifty-four was the younger by six years. 'He'd love it, for all that it's nothing like the house in Kilshandra.'

Kilshandra was where they'd grown up, a small town on the east coast that was never a destination, always a place cars drove past en route to somewhere else.

'No, it's not like Kilshandra,' Christie murmured and the fact that it was nothing like her old home was one of the best things about it.

Thinking of the past made the anxiety tweak again. She didn't want to think about the past, Christie thought with irritation. Get out of my head. She'd spoken out loud, she realised, as the dogs looked up at her in alarm.

The dishes done, she poured a cup of coffee to take into the garden while she went through her list for the day. She had groceries to buy, bills to pay, some letters to post, a whole page of the by-the-phone notepad filled with calls to return . . . and then she felt the strange yet familiar ripple of unease move through her. Like a thundercloud shimmering in a blue sky, threatening a noisy downpour. This time it wasn't a mild flicker of anxiety: it was a full-scale alert.

Christie dropped her china cup on the flagstones. Both Rocket and Tilly yelped in distress, whisking around their mistress's feet, their matching brown eyes anxious. *We didn't do it, we didn't do it.*

Automatically, Christie shepherded them away from the broken china.

'You'll cut your paws,' she said gently, and shooed them safely into the kitchen. Dustpan in hand, she went outside again and began to sweep up.

Her whole life, Christie had been able to see things that other people couldn't. It was a strange, dreamy gift: never available on demand and never there for Christie to sort out her own problems. But when she least expected it, the truth came to her, a little tremor of knowing that told her what was in another person's heart.

As a child, she'd thought everyone could do it. But there was no one in her deeply religious home whom she could ask. Something warned her that people might not like it. Her father prayed to centuries-dead saints when things went wrong, ignoring them when all was well, but he disapproved of the local girls having their fortunes told and hated the Gypsies' gift of sight with a vengeance. Her mother never ventured any opinion without first consulting her husband. Opinions that Father didn't approve of meant his black rage engulfed the house. So Christie had learned to be a quiet, watchful child. Her six elder brothers and her baby sister made enough noise for nobody to notice her, anyhow. And as she grew older and realised that her gift wasn't run of the mill, she was glad she'd kept it quiet.

How could she tell people she'd known the McGoverns' barn was going to burn down, or that Mr McGovern himself had set fire to it for the insurance money?

The first time she even hinted at her gift was when she was nineteen and her best friend, Sarah, had thought Ted, handsome with smiling eyes and a blankly chiselled face like Steve McQueen, was the man for her.

11

'He loves me, he wants to marry me,' said Sarah with the passion of being nineteen and in love.

'I just have this feeling that he's not being entirely honest with you. There's something a bit two-faced about him,' Christie had said. It was a flash of knowing that Ted didn't love Sarah and that there was someone else Ted made promises to.

'I don't believe it,' said Sarah angrily.

Christie noted the anger: there was a lot of truth in the cliché about shooting the messenger.

It transpired that Ted had indeed been seeing another girl, one whose family had money, not like Sarah or Christie, who came from a world of hand-me-down clothes and making do.

'How did you know?' asked Sarah when her heart was broken.

'It sort of came to me,' Christie said, which was the only way she could explain it.

The closer the person was to her, the fuzzier it became. For herself, she could never see anything. Which was probably as it should be. Except that today, for the first time ever, she'd had a horrible feeling that the premonition of gloom was for herself.

In the pretty kitchen with its bunches of herbs hanging from the ceiling, a place where Christie always felt perfectly happy, panic now filled her. Her family. Something awful must be about to happen to them and she had to stop it. Yet, the feeling had never been like this before. She'd never, ever seen any harm coming to her sons or James.

There was the day thirteen-year-old Shane had broken his collarbone falling from a tree, and Christie had been on a school trip to a gallery, explaining the gift of Jack B. Yeats to twenty schoolgirls.

When the frantic St Ursula's secretary had finally reached Christie, she'd cursed her own inability to see what mattered.

12

How could she not have seen her own son in pain? What use was her gift if it only worked for other people?

This morning, within ten minutes, Christie had phoned her two sons to say a cheery hello, she was thinking about them and her horoscope had said she was going to have an unfortunate day, and she thought it might extend to them, so not to walk under any ladders.

Finally, Christie phoned James, whom she'd only said goodbye to two hours before as he headed off to the train station for a meeting in Cork.

'Is everything all right, Christie?' he asked carefully.

'Fine,' she said, not wanting to transmit the intensity of her fear to him. 'I felt a bit spooked, that's all. It's thundery here.' Which wasn't true. The sky was as blue and clear as the single oval sapphire in her antique engagement ring. 'I love you, James,' she added, which was entirely true. And then the signal on his mobile phone went, the connection was severed and Christie was left with her feeling of terror still beating a tattoo in her chest.

She left a message on her husband's mobile phone: 'I'm fine. Off shopping now, phone me later and tell me if you're able to get the earlier train. I love you. Bye.'

James worked for a government environmental agency and had worked his way up the ranks so he now held a senior position. He travelled round the country a lot, and Christie worried that the endless trips were getting too much for him. But James, still fired up wanting to be busy and to make sure that everything was done properly, loved it.

By ten, Christie was on her way along Summer Street with her shopping bags in her hand, trying to put the fear out of her mind. On the three days a week when she worked at St Ursula's, she turned left when she walked out of her garden gate. Today, she'd turned right in the direction of the Summer Street Café.

It was a pleasant time of day, with not much traffic. The stressed morning drivers were at their offices and Summer Street belonged to the locals again. Many of Christie's original neighbours were gone, but there were some who'd lived on the street nearly as long as the Devlin family.

Like the Maguires, Dennis and Una, possessors of a series of clapped-out cars and gloriously oblivious to the outrage of their current next-door neighbour who clearly felt that a car with that many dents in its paintwork should not be parked beside her gleaming BMW. The Maguires had one daughter, Maggie: a good kid, Christie recalled. Tall, shy, always polite, hiding her prettiness behind a heavy veil of carroty red curls as if she needed a retreat from the world. She'd never been in Christie's art classes but, like many of the girls on Summer Street, she'd had a crush on Shane. Lots of girls had. It was that combination of tousled blond hair and a slightly cheeky smile. He was a few months older than Maggie – extraordinary that they could both be thirty now – and indifferent to her pubescent longing.

'Just say hello to her,' Christie said, exasperated that Shane couldn't see that even a few words from her idol would make a difference to this shy girl.

'Ah, Mum, she'll only think I like her. Get real, would you?'

'What does that mean?' demanded his mother. 'Get real? I am being real. I'm saying show a bit of kindness, Shane. It doesn't cost you anything, does it?' Her voice had risen up the scale.

'OK,' he muttered, realising his mother was off on her high horse about how goodness and kindness filled your soul with happiness. It was a sweet idea and all, but it didn't work with girls, did it? 'I'll say hi, right?'

'And be nice.'

'Should I propose as well?'

Maggie lived in Galway now and Christie hadn't seen her for ages.

But the adult Maggie had lived up to the early promise Christie had seen in her. She was truly stunning-looking, her hair darkened to glossy auburn, her face a perfect oval with silvery cobalt-blue eyes, wide expressive lips and the translucent skin of the pure redhead. Yet she didn't appear to be aware of her beauty. Rather the opposite, in fact. Christie sensed that Maggie Maguire was still hiding her real self.

'She's doing so well,' Una Maguire said every time Christie asked. All those years ago, Una had been red-haired, too, but now the red was a faded strawberry with fine threads of grey. She was still beautiful, though, with the fine-boned face her daughter had inherited. 'Maggie's going out with this fabulous man. He's a lecturer in the college and she's in the library research department now. They're made for each other. Living together for three years and they have a beautiful apartment off Eyre Square. No sign of them getting married, but young people don't bother with that these days.'

'No, they don't,' agreed Christie easily, who understood quite plainly that Una longed with all her heart for her only child to be settled down with a husband and children.

They'd gone on their separate ways, Christie sure that Una had no notion of what she'd really seen in Una's heart.

Along with learning about her odd gift, Christie had learned that mostly people didn't want you to know their deepest, darkest secrets. So she kept her insights to herself unless she was asked.

Ten yards ahead of her, Amber Reid shot out of her gate at number 18, long tawny-gold hair bouncing in the telltale manner of the newly washed. Amber was seventeen, in her final year at St Ursula's and undoubtedly one of the stars of Christie's class.

Amber could capture anyone or anything with her pencil,

although her particular gift was for buttery oil landscapes, wild moody places with strange houses that looked like no houses on earth. Even in a large class, Amber stood out because she was so sparky and alive.

An unfashionable pocket Venus shape, with softly curved limbs and a small, plumply rounded face, her only truly beautiful feature was that pair of magnetic pewter eyes, with the ring of deepest amber around the pupils. She'd never have been picked as one of the school's beauties, the languorous leggy girls with chiselled cheekbones. Yet Amber's vivaciousness and the intelligence of those eyes gave her an attractiveness that few of the teenage beauty queens could match. And the artist in Christie could see the girl's sex appeal, an intangible charm that a photographer might not capture but an artist would.

Christie knew that unless St Ursula's had been evacuated for some strange reason that morning, Amber should be in school. And yet here she was, trip-trapping along in achingly high heels and a colourful flippy skirt that flowed out over her hips – unlike the institutional grey school uniform skirt that jutted out in an unflattering A-line. Amber was holding a mobile phone to her ear and Christie could just overhear.

'I'm just leaving now. Has anyone noticed I'm not there? MacVitie's not got her knickers in a twist over the absence of her best student?'

Mrs MacVitie was the maths teacher and Christie doubted that Amber, who was typically left-brained and hopeless at maths, was her best student. Favourite, perhaps, because it was hard to resist Amber, who always paid attention in class and was a polite, diligent student. But not best.

She must be speaking to Ella O'Brien, to whom she was joined at the hip, and Ella obviously told her that no, the St Ursula's bloodhounds had not been alerted.

'Sweet. If anyone asks, you think I was sick yesterday and

it must have got worse. I phoned in earlier and told the school secretary I was sick but, just in case, you back me up and say I'm puking like mad. It's true,' Amber laughed. 'I'm sick of school, right?'

Christie wondered if Faye, Amber's mother, knew what her daughter was up to.

Faye Reid was a widow, a quiet, businesslike figure who'd never missed a school meeting and was utterly involved in her daughter's life. Even though they lived on the same street, Christie didn't see much of Faye. She kept herself to herself, head down, rushing everywhere, clad in conservative navy suits and low-heeled shoes, with a briefcase by her side. There was such a contrast between the butterfly beauty of Amber who had the best of everything and caught people's eyes, and her mother, who always appeared to be rushing to or from work, trying hard to keep the mortgage paid and food on the table. A person didn't need Christie's gift of intuition to see that Faye's life had been one of sacrifices.

'She's one of the most gifted students I've ever taught,' Christie had told Faye two years before, shortly after Amber arrived in her class. 'Any art college in the world would love to have her.'

And Faye's face had lit up. Christie had never seen a smile transform a person so much. Faye was defiantly plain beside her daughter, overweight to Amber's curved sexiness and with her brown hair pulled severely back into a knot that only someone with the bones of a supermodel could get away with. Faye Reid didn't have the supermodel bones. But when she smiled that rare smile, she suddenly had all the charm of her daughter and Christie caught herself wondering why a woman like Faye, who could only be forty, lived such a quiet life. No man had ever been seen kissing Faye a wistful goodbye on the doorstep. Her clothes, the discreet earrings and low shoes that screamed comfort – they were like armour.

It was as if Faye had deliberately turned her back on youthful sexiness and hidden behind a façade of plain clothes.

Christie wondered if she could see more . . . but suddenly, it was as if Faye Reid had abruptly closed herself off and Christie could see nothing but the woman in front of her.

'Thanks, Mrs Devlin,' Faye said. 'That's what I think too, but I love her so much, I thought I was totally biased. Every parent thinks their kid is Mozart or Picasso, don't they?'

'Not all,' replied Christie grimly, thinking of some of the parents she'd met over the years with no belief in their kids whatsoever.

Her comment apparently touched a chord with Faye and the smile vanished to be replaced by her more usual, sombre expression. 'Yeah, you're right,' she said, nodding. 'There are always a few who don't appreciate their kids. Nothing that twenty years of psychotherapy wouldn't cure.'

Up ahead, Amber said a cheery 'byee' into her phone. Christie knew that the correct teacher response at this point would be to catch up with her and ask what she was doing out of school. But suddenly Amber broke into a run, high heels notwithstanding, and was gone down the street before Christie could move.

Christie shrugged. Amber was a good student, hardly a serial absentee. She and Ella had never been part of the school's wilder cliques and had both managed to move from adolescence to young womanhood without any noticeable bursts of rebellious behaviour.

There might be a perfectly good reason for her absence today. And Christie herself knew that you could learn plenty of things outside school as well as in.

When she'd been young, she hadn't done everything by the book either.

Yet again, Christie thought about the past and the places she'd lived. The house in Kilshandra with bitterness and

18

misery engrained into the wallpaper so that she'd barely been able to wait till she was old enough to leave. The bedsit on Dunville Avenue where she'd met so many friends and learned that she didn't have to hide her gift. And Summer Street, where all the best things in her life had happened.

She could remember what the young Christie had looked like when she'd moved to Summer Street – long dark hair drawn back in a loose ponytail, always in jeans and T-shirts – and she could remember how lucky she'd been, with a kind husband, enough money so they weren't in debt, with one beautiful, healthy child and another on the way. Yes, the years on Summer Street were the ones she liked to remember.

But there were other times she'd like to forget.

The strange feeling came through her again and despite the warmth of the morning, Christie shivered.

# CHAPTER TWO

Amber Reid was concentrating so fiercely on getting to the bus stop in time that she hadn't noticed Mrs Devlin walking along Summer Street behind her. This was despite her intention to watch out for anyone who might sneak to her mother about her appearance out of uniform on a school day.

'We're going on a field trip,' Amber had planned to say blithely should the need arise, though the final-year students at St Ursula's didn't have time for field trips this close to the all-important state exams. And even if they did, what sort of field trip would require her best high heels – Oxfam spindly sandals revitalised with bronze paint – a sliver of a silk camisole and a flippy skirt, all topped off with the curious and fabulous silver tiger's-eye pendant she'd recently found buried in her mother's bottom drawer? The pendant was a mystery. She'd never seen her mum wear it. Faye dressed in boring suits and was resolutely against making the best of herself, no matter what Amber said. The pendant was so not 'her'. Amber was still wondering where her mother had come by such a thing. She didn't like to ask, because Mum would be hurt that she had been snooping. But it was odd of her to keep it hidden because they shared everything.

Well, not everything. Amber felt a splinter of guilt pierce her happy little cocoon. Today was a secret she couldn't share with her mother. It wasn't the first time she had concealed something. Mum was so square, so protective, that on the rare occasion that Amber had done anything outside her mother's rigid code of what was acceptable, she'd had to fib a little. But the current secret was certainly the biggest.

Ella had phoned just as Amber slammed the front door behind her.

'Ring me later and tell me how you got on, won't you?' Ella begged.

'Promise.'

'Wish I was bunking off,' Ella grumbled. 'I've history in ten minutes and I haven't finished my bloody essay on the Civil War.'

'Sorry, I did mine and I could have lent it to you so you could use some of my ideas,' Amber apologised. She loved history and the words flowed effortlessly from her pen to the page. Although how she'd written her essay last night was largely a mystery, as she'd been consumed with excitement thinking about today.

When she'd said goodbye to Ella, she broke into a run so as to race past the Summer Street Café in case of neighbours lurking within.

A minute later, she was at the bus stop on Jasmine Row, just in time to catch the 10.05 bus into the city, and Karl.

Karl. She whispered his name to herself as she gazed dreamily out of the windows on the top deck. Karl and Amber. Amber and Karl.

It sounded just right, like they were destined to be together.

Destiny had never been a concept Amber had held much faith in up to now. Just a few weeks away from her eighteenth birthday, and a month from the hated exams, she felt that she was in charge of her own life.

So she'd only been half paying attention when Ella read their horoscopes that fateful Friday at lunch. Horoscopes were fun but hardly to be relied on. Mum always insisted that Amber was responsible for herself and that life should not be lived on the word of what some astrologer had dreamed up for that day.

Mum was firm that Amber should never follow the crowd or do anything just because of someone else's opinion or because 'everyone else is doing it'. It was a lesson Amber had followed very well up to now.

'Crap for Aries, as usual,' muttered Ella, reading hers quickly. '"Rethink your options but don't let your enthusiasm wane." What does that mean? Why doesn't it ever give us hints on what's coming up in the maths paper? Now that would really be seeing the future.'

They were eating lunch on the gym roof – strictly forbidden but the current cool spot for sixth years – plotting their weekend and how to fit exam study in around at least one trip to the shopping centre to flip through rails of clothes they couldn't afford. All study and no play made you go mad, Ella insisted.

'Yours is better. "Single Taureans are going to find love and passion. Expect sparks to fly this weekend."'

'Sparks at the football club disco?' Amber roared with laughter at the very ridiculousness of this idea. It was the same big gang of people she'd known all her life and you couldn't get excited about a bunch of guys you'd watched grow up. Where was the mystique or the romance of that?

'Patrick?'

'Too nice. He'd want to walk along with his hand in your jeans pocket and yours in his and discuss the engagement party. Gross.'

'Greg's cute.'

'He called me Chubby Face once. No way.' Growing three

inches taller in the past year meant Amber had gone from being childishly plump to womanly and voluptuous. The addition of honeyed streaks in her rich brown hair meant that all the boys who'd previously talked to her like a clever younger sister suddenly sat up and took notice.

This new power over guys was heady and Amber was still testing it, gently. But she wanted to go somewhere more exciting than the football club disco to do so. Somewhere, beyond the confines of Summer Street, the football club disco and St Ursula's was Life with a capital L: pulsing, exciting, waiting for her.

'You're getting so choosy,' said Ella. 'You fancied Greg last year.'

'That was last year.'

'Should I get more highlights?' asked Ella, pulling forward a bit of the long, streaky blonde hair that was almost mandatory in sixth year and examining it critically. 'Your highlights look great but mine have gone all dull and yellowy.'

'Use the special shampoo for blondes,' said Amber.

'It costs a fortune. I bet your mum buys it for you. Mine wouldn't.' Ella was indignant. Because there were only the two of them, Amber's mum bought her everything she wanted, while Ella's, with three older sons as well, could hardly do the same thing.

'I'll give you some of my shampoo,' offered Amber. She knew how lucky she was and always shared any goodies with Ella. That's what best friends were for. 'Now, tomorrow night.' The pewter eyes gleamed. 'Not the football club disco, please.'

'Well . . .' Ella began. 'We could try something different.'

'. . . Something bad . . .' Amber shivered deliciously. 'Let's try to get into a grown-up club. Come on, in a few months, we'll have left school and we'll be the only people in our class to have never done anything interesting, Ella. Everyone else has gone to clubs they're not supposed to be able to get into, except us because we're the sensible ones. I'm fed up being sensible.'

Sensible was nice when you were thirteen and adored by all the teachers, but less so when you were nearly eighteen. The girls who never had their homework done and never got top marks in exams seemed to be having all the fun now, which seemed like an unequal division of spoils.

'Me too,' Ella breathed. 'And I've just thought how we can do it.'

Amber's eyes glittered. 'How?'

This feeling of dissatisfaction had in fact been incubating for weeks. Fed up with studying for exams and stifled by the pressure-cooker atmosphere at school, they felt the need to do something wild and rebellious for the first time ever, but their options were limited.

Most of their pocket money went on clothes or their mobile phone top-up cards, so they had little cash left over for wild behaviour.

Smoking was considered cool by some of the older girls, who insisted that it kept them thin, but cigarettes were too expensive to be more than a rare treat. Alcohol was easily available, like hash and ecstasy, but Amber's mother had a nose like an airport sniffer dog and could smell badness anywhere, so coming home drunk or stoned was hardly an option. Faye would have had a fit and grounded her for a month, not to mention being hurt by her daughter's behaviour, which would, in turn, make Amber feel bad for failing her beloved mother.

And that was the crux of the matter: their family unit was just two. Two people who adored each other, two people who'd gone through it all together, who protected each other from the world. But sometimes, that could be a burden too.

At least Ella had three brothers who could share living up to their parents' expectations: Amber had the weight of her mother's hopes and dreams resting squarely on her shoulders alone. And unlike Ella's parents, who seemed to understand that their kids eventually tested their wings and flew the nest, Faye Reid still seemed to think that she and Amber would be together for ever.

'What's the plan?' Amber asked now. 'Where are we going? Nowhere round here, surely? There's nothing but boring pubs.'

'Exactly. So forget about round here.' Ella grinned excitedly. 'Marco's going into town to a club tomorrow night, and if we went with him, we could get in without being carded.'

Marco was Ella's middle brother and they both realised he was their best bet for an illegal excursion. Her eldest brother wouldn't dream of taking two schoolgirls into a city night-club, while her youngest brother was too square to go at all. But twenty-three-year-old Marco, who had his own late-night show on a small radio station and went to all the coolest places, just might be persuaded to take them with him.

'Where?' asked Amber.

'Highway Seven.'

'That's twenty-ones and over.' It was hopeless. Doormen were up to speed on the best fake IDs. Amber and Ella didn't even have fake IDs. All the best clubs were over twenty-ones only. They'd be busted before they got in the door.

'Yeah, but there's a gig on there tomorrow night, some new band Marco's going to check out for his show,' Ella explained. 'He'll be on the guest list and he'll be going in the back door of the club, so the bouncer will let him in no hassle, and if we're with him . . .'

'. . . We'll waltz right in,' laughed Amber gleefully. 'You are one clever chick, Ella O'Brien. But how do we get Marco to take us in the first place?'

'Bribery and corruption.' Ella had thought it all out. 'We'll twist his arm this evening after school.'

Marco looked a lot like Ella: dark eyes, pale skin and the

same dark hair as she'd had before she discovered peroxide. Easy-going to a fault, he wasn't keen on taking his little sister and her friend out with him.

'In your dreams,' he said.

'Mum would go mental if she knew you'd had that huge party in the house when the rest of us were in Kerry at Christmas,' Ella said, all wide-eyed innocence. 'The one where the neighbours called the police. You'd be chopped liver if she ever found out. You know what she's like about not upsetting the neighbours . . .'

'How did you hear about that?' demanded Marco and then slapped his forehead and groaned. 'You didn't know, did you? You were just guessing.'

'Oh, Marco, we knew about the party,' Amber said, exasperated. 'We were only guessing about the police, but we found some guy's coat under Ella's bed, along with a lot of empty Heineken cans and a condom.'

Marco blanched.

'It's not as if Ella put the beer cans there. We never drink beer. We prefer wine or vodka,' she added, hoping to sound worldly-wise.

'Can't you go out with your own friends?' Marco begged, not even commenting on the wine or vodka remark. It seemed like only last week his sister and her friend had been sobbing their hearts out over guinea pig funerals in the back garden and winning badges for Guides.

'Think of it as community service for deeds previously unpunished,' Amber pointed out. 'We won't be any trouble. Once we're in the club, you can forget about us. We can look after ourselves.'

'OK, you're nearly eighteen and you know everything, right?' he said sarcastically.

'I've a yellow belt in karate,' Amber said, assuming what she hoped was a karate stance, though it was years since she'd set foot on a dojo. Her mother's insistence on self-defence lessons had been fun when she'd been ten, less so when she hit puberty.

Marco sighed. 'Close combat is not the answer to all situations in life. The most dangerous guys in the club probably won't ask you to arm wrestle, Amber. Understand?' He looked at both girls as sternly as he could. 'I don't want to have to come home at two in the morning and tell Mum and Dad that I've lost you two. Or worse, tell your mother, Amber. She'd rip me limb from limb.'

Amber's mother had always made Marco a bit nervous. There was something steely in Mrs Reid's gaze, as if she was warning him that she had his measure.

'We're not kids,' growled Amber. 'We're coming. It's no skin off your nose. You only have to get us in.'

'Well, you'll have to watch your drinks,' sighed Marco, knowing when he was beaten. 'There are guys out there who'll slip a date rape drug in your glass and, well . . . you don't have any experience. You don't know the half of it.'

'You're a wonderful brother.' Ella gave him a hug.

'This is a one-off deal,' Marco insisted. 'OK? And you've got to behave yourselves.'

'Of course,' said Amber, who had absolutely no intention of behaving herself. She could do that in the football club.

The truly difficult part of the plan was lying to her mother about where she and Ella were going that night. They decided that, because of Faye's ultra-vigilance, they'd stay at Ella's that night after their alleged trip to the disco. Having gone through it all before, Ella's parents were definitely more relaxed about their daughter's behaviour.

'Mum will check we're home, but if I put pillows in the beds, she'll think we're there,' Ella said.

Amber thought of how her mum never slept until Amber was back after an evening out. How many nights had they

27

sat up on Amber's bed on her return, Mum listening as Amber recounted her triumphs and disasters?

Then, she brushed the feeling of guilt away. It was only because Mum was so protective that she had to lie. She wasn't a kid any more. She didn't want to hurt Mum's feelings but she had to move on and Mum must be made to understand that.

Getting into Highway Seven worked precisely as Ella had predicted, although Amber only felt her breathing come right when they were deep inside the club, far from the stern eye of the doorman. In spite of her outward nonchalance, she was nervous. She and Ella might have sunbathed on the forbidden gym roof and smoked a few illicit cigarettes, but they were strictly homework-on-time girls in other respects. This was breaking into new territory, both exciting and scary at the same time.

Dark, moody and almost vibrating with bass-deep music, the club was crowded with bodies, perfume and a sweet smell that Amber knew was marijuana because even the football club wasn't trouble-free.

'Er ... what do you want to do now?' asked Marco, wondering how he'd got lumbered with this situation. Thankfully, the two girls looked old enough to fit in, but hey, they were still his little sister and her friend. He had a bad vibe about the whole thing.

'We're fine,' Amber said airily.

'Yeah, you go off with your mates. We're cool,' Ella added, matching her friend's unconcerned look.

Marco shrugged, but he looked relieved. 'If you're sure ...'

'We're sure.' Both girls nodded.

Amber scanned her surroundings idly, her body moving gently to the music. Ella adopted the same laid-back hauteur.

Marco was no match for them. He was fooled.

'Text me if you need me,' he said, then turned and was swallowed up by the crowd.

On their own, Amber and Ella clutched each other and shrieked, all pretence at being cool gone. Nobody heard them over the pumping beat. 'We're here,' they screeched and did their own little war dance.

'Loos,' gasped Amber, taking Ella by the hand.

In the toilets, they re-adopted adult cool while Amber applied a line of smoky kohl around the rims of her eyes like she'd seen in a magazine. The effect was startling: her beautiful eyes seemed larger and more hypnotic than ever.

'You really do look twenty-one,' sighed Ella, pausing in the act of applying another coat of sticky lip gloss.

A woman rinsing her hands at the next basin glanced at them.

'Thanks!' said Amber. 'I'm actually thirty-two but my plastic surgeon is a miracle worker.'

The woman left in a hurry and they creased over laughing again, high on their own daring.

They had enough money to order one drink each, which they'd have to make last all night, and they stood at the bar, nursing their vodkas, trying to look as if they'd been here a million times before and were bored with it all.

Behind her calm façade, Amber was enthralled, watching everyone, envying them the way they all seemed to fit in.

In a corner cordoned off by velvet rope sat a dozen people drinking champagne. All beautiful, having the time of their lives, utterly at home. One slender brunette in faded, sequin-decorated jeans was holding court, talking and laughing, while everyone else watched her with evident fascination. In that one second, Amber longed to be just like her: part of the scene instead of watching enviously from the sidelines.

Then, one of the guys saw her watching them, a guy with dark cropped hair and stubble that was probably five o'clock

29

shadow at ten in the morning. His gaze was so intense Amber looked away in embarrassment. Shit, how gauche to be caught staring hungrily like a schoolgirl.

She did her best to stare anywhere else, but she really wanted to look back at the guy and drink him in. She'd never felt that connection before, that instant buzz from another human being, the feeling that she knew him.

But who was she kidding? He was probably only staring at her because it was obvious she and Ella were out of place. She'd thought they looked old enough but perhaps they didn't and the guy was wondering what a kid was doing there.

'Nobody's bothering to chat us up,' moaned Ella beside her.

'It's early yet,' said Amber with more enthusiasm than she felt. Perhaps Marco had been right and they should have gone out with their own friends, but the football club would seem so tame after this. After him.

'Are you lost?' said a low voice.

Amber swivelled round. The dark, crop-haired man stood beside her, staring at her with intense blue eyes. Every nerve in her body quivered into alertness, though she tried to stay calm.

'Lost? No.' She shrugged, hopelessly trying to adopt the laid-back aura of the brunette in the VIP section.

'You weren't looking for someone?' he asked. His voice was soft and deep, a man's voice, not a boy's.

Amber shook her head.

'I thought you were looking for me,' he added, 'and you've found me.'

Amber just stared at him, concentrating on breathing.

Chat-up lines for her usually consisted of the guy asking what class she was in at school. This approach was wildly different. Amber felt her spine lengthen, some new instinct making her stand up straighter, yet slightly closer to him.

30

'I wasn't looking for you,' she said, nonchalant. How was she doing this? She'd never spoken this way before, like a heroine from a film. 'I was watching people. I'm an artist: I like watching people.'

'You draw them, then?'

Amazingly, he didn't spot that she was making this up as she went along. Buoyed up, Amber lowered her eyelids and gave him a sultry gaze she'd rehearsed in her bedroom in front of the faded line of her childhood teddy bears.

'If I like the shape of them and the look of them, I might draw them,' she replied coolly.

'And me? Do you like the look of me?' he asked.

It was noisy, so he'd moved till he was very close to her and, despite the gloom of the club, she could see that his face was moulded like a beautiful Renaissance statue: a straight, proud nose, flaring cheekbones, a finely planed forehead and a mouth so sensitive it would take a sculptor months to get right. Tightly cropped brown hair and a filament-thin cotton shirt flattened against his lean body took him into the modern era, but otherwise, he was like the historical princes of art that Amber had grown up admiring.

'I like the look of you very much,' she breathed, not bothering to be cool any more.

And he smiled at her, revealing an endearing dimple on one side of his mouth and perfect white teeth. Amber forgot about everything else in the world except this fabulous man. She wanted to touch him, kiss him, feel him wrap his arms around her and press his body against hers for ever. This, she thought, was love at first sight.

Karl was in a band, he told her. She introduced him to Ella and he led them over to the VIP area.

Ella squeezed Amber's hand in delight as they were ushered past the velvet rope, but Amber was too engrossed in Karl to sense Ella's message of 'Wow! Look where we are now!'

Some of Karl's as yet unsigned band were among the group. The rest, the ones who'd undoubtedly got everyone into the VIP area in the first place, were a band with an album that had just been released, the ones Marco had come to hear.

'The Kebabs, of course I've heard of you! My brother came to hear you play. Tell me, you do, like tours and stuff?' asked Ella, fascinated, as she was handed a glass of champagne.

As Ella listened to stories of life on the road, Amber barely heard a word. She was conscious only of Karl sitting beside her, with an arm loosely around the back of her seat, his leg casually close to hers.

She didn't want to hear about anyone else, only Karl.

'What do you do in your band?'

'I am the band,' Karl shrugged as if it was obvious. 'I write the songs, I sing, I play lead guitar. The band is me.'

'You're an artist too.' She smiled and took his hand, tracing the lines on it with sensitive fingers. 'I could paint you.'

'I could write a song about you,' Karl said, touching her face with his other hand.

Their faces were inches apart now, Karl was drinking in every inch of her, his eyes travelling from her tawny hair, past the softness of her jaw down to the firm, high curve of her breasts highlighted in the tight little T-shirt she'd borrowed from Ella.

'You're so sexy,' he whispered. His eyes roamed lower, past her waist to the rounded curve of her hips and along her jean-clad legs. For once, Amber didn't bother trying to lift one thigh up so her leg looked thinner. There was no mistaking the fact that Karl liked her the way she was, and that was headier than any alcohol she could have drunk.

'Get a room!' shouted someone to them, and everyone creased up laughing.

Amber and Karl didn't hear the jest or the insistent throbbing of the club music: they were locked into their own beat, aqua eyes in a lean face staring fiercely into grey-and-amber eyes in a gently rounded one, the red stain on each of Amber's cheeks owing nothing to her make-up.

They moved at the same time, Karl's arms winding around Amber's waist, her hands spreading out to feel the heat of his torso through the thin shirt. Before her fingers had a chance to revel in the fine muscles of his back, his mouth met hers and they were kissing. It was unlike any kiss Amber had experienced: Karl's tongue snaked into her mouth with practised ease, banishing the memory of every St Bernard slobber of a French kiss she'd ever had before. They melted against each other, his hands cupping her face, her hands raking through his hair. The heat of their bodies burned through their clothes. And long afterwards, when Amber was again capable of thinking, she realised that this was what love was all about.

As the morning bus lurched along into the city, Amber sat on the top deck in her finery and thought of how much had changed in the past two weeks. She had been a kid then, but now she was an adult.

An adult with an adult relationship. Or at least, she'd be properly having an adult relationship soon. Today, she was meeting Karl to take him home where they'd have the place to themselves all day. There was no privacy in the poky flat he shared with five other musicians. In her bedroom on Summer Street, there would be as much privacy as they needed. Briefly, Amber thought of how she'd explain it all to her mother if she arrived home early from work. She could imagine Faye's horrified face, and how hurt she'd be to have been lied to. But Amber flicked the thought away. She'd worry about that later. Everyone had secrets, didn't they?

# CHAPTER THREE

Twice a week for the past six months, Faye Reid had taken an early lunch and walked a mile to the swimming pool complex near her office. The brisk walk past the mirror-windowed buildings of the docklands was soothing. Striding along the pavement, away from the incessant phones and the beehive drone of the busy recruitment company where she worked, she listened to music, watched seagulls swoop and dive towards the river, and relaxed.

Today, she had Billie Holiday on her portable CD player. Billie's golden voice told of men who'd left and Faye thought how wonderful it was that, no matter how many times she heard Billie, it always sounded as if the guy had just that second gone, the screen door still banging behind him.

Music talked to Faye. Sound was the most evocative sense for her and the first few bars of a song on the radio could take her right back to where she'd been when she'd first heard it. She herself had a softly husky singing voice that few people had ever heard and could repeat a melody after only hearing it once. When she'd been Amber's age, she'd always been singing but she rarely did now.

For music could be a curse too. There were still some

songs she couldn't listen to, songs that would break her heart because of the memories they brought to life.

Billie Holiday songs thankfully, for all their pain, didn't fit into that category.

'It's lovely and everything, but it's kind of depressing, Mum,' Amber had pointed out the previous weekend about her mother's love of exquisitely melancholy jazz.

'Some of it is,' Faye agreed, trying to see things from her daughter's point of view. It was an unseasonably warm Saturday for the end of April and they'd spent the afternoon in the garden, Amber keen to start a dusting of golden tan on her face.

With the iron discipline Faye brought to every area of her life, the housework in the Reid household was always up to date. But when it came to gardening, she didn't know weed from plant. Occasionally, she wished she was more like Christie Devlin who'd created an exquisite all-white garden at the front of her house. Faye had never seen Christie's back garden, had never seen the inside of the Devlins' house, actually, because they barely knew each other in spite of living mere doors apart for ten years, but she'd have bet that it was just as beautiful, with frothy roses and trailing blooms that flourished under Christie's magic hands.

On this particular Saturday, Faye wore a tired pale-pink polo shirt over cheap loose-fit jeans that did nothing for her shape, and was trying to uproot any weeds she could identify. It all looked weedy to her. Surely that big thing that looked strangely like a marijuana plant couldn't be a flower? Although since she'd thrown those packets of wildflower seeds every which way last year, it was hard to tell. That would be a fine advert for sensible single parenthood, wouldn't it: a hash plant in Faye Reid's garden.

She grinned. If there was any illegal vegetation in her garden, nobody would cast aspersions on the arch-conservative Mrs

Reid, the very model of a career-minded widow with an equally model teenage daughter. Faye had worked very hard to reach that place in the local psyche. She'd learned that a single woman bringing up a child needed to be beyond reproach. Nobody would ever have cause to accuse her of trying to steal their husband or of letting her daughter run wild.

'I like songs like "Respect",' Amber went on. She was lying on her tummy on a rug on the lawn, her feet in the air and a school book propped up in front of her. 'Not sad ones where everyone's depressed, like no guy will ever look at them again 'cos they messed it up the first time.'

Faye paused in her weeding.

'You've got to remember, Amber, that the old jazz and rhythm-and-blues songs are from another age, when life was different and women didn't have the same opportunities we have today,' she said, wiping her hands on her jeans so she could clip a few strands of light-brown hair back. Faye didn't bother with her hair much: shoulder length, wavy and undyed for many years, it got washed, tied back firmly and treated to conditioner when she had the time, which wasn't often.

'They didn't have contraception, any hope of equal pay or equal rights in lots of things. So it might sound depressing to you now,' she explained, 'but they were brave. I think they were feminists in their own time because they sang when it wasn't considered a decent job for women. They didn't have what we have now. Girl power hadn't been invented then.'

'Yeah, I know that, but why do all the women hang around waiting for the lover man to turn up?' Amber wanted to know, abandoning her book with a speed that showed she hadn't been that engrossed in revising maths equations. 'The women do all the waiting in these songs and in the old movies. If a guy doesn't respect you, he's going to walk all over you. They're waiting for him to make it right. It's so passive. You don't need girl power to see that.'

'You and Ella have got to stop reading the therapist's sections in women's magazines,' Faye groaned, but she was smiling. 'I thought you were going to study art, not psychotherapy.'

'Ha ha. All I'm saying is that some people want to be rescued and that's, like, not going to happen.' Amber's small face was determined, her chin lifted to signify that life would have to take her on her terms, and not the other way round. Faye felt the familiar clammy grip of a mother's anxiety on her heart. Amber was full of energy and hope, for all her careful studying of women's magazines' problem pages.

What if one day, despite all Faye's efforts at protecting her daughter, someone or something destroyed that energy and hope?

'My little suffragette.'

Amber looked pleased. 'I like to think so,' she said, 'only I'm the modern version. No chaining yourself to the railings involved. I'm glad it's different now.'

Faye said nothing. It was hard to tell a seventeen-year-old with her whole life ahead of her that heartache and loss crossed every century, women's rights notwithstanding. She sat back on her heels, tired from gardening. If only she could wave a wand and conjure up a lovely garden: then she'd take care of it. But creating it was another matter.

Her house was one of the smallest on Summer Street, the first of the eight railway cottages lined up in a terrace like an illustration in a Victorian picturebook. The painted front doors – theirs was teal blue – carved fascia boards and perfectly square windows were like something a child would draw.

Most of the cottages had been extended at the back. Faye's extension had made the kitchen bigger, creating a T-shaped upstairs attic bedroom for Amber, and taking the already tiny garden down to shoebox size. It had a small block of mossy lawn, flower beds on either side and a rackety garden shed at the bottom.

'I can't imagine Gran waiting for a man to fix what was wrong,' Amber added, 'and she grew up when it was different. I mean, she takes the car to get it fixed, not Stan. She's a real role model. I tell all the girls in school about her and they think she's amazing. They think you're amazing too, Mum, because you don't take crap from anyone.'

'No,' said Faye, ignoring the use of the word crap and wondering if that would be her only epitaph. *Here lies Faye Reid, who never took crap from anyone.* It wasn't what she'd hoped she'd be remembered for when she was younger, but it certainly fitted now. When she'd been Amber's age, she'd wanted to be thought of as exciting and glamorous, a mysterious woman loved by many men. Teenage dreams were funny in retrospect, weren't they? She'd bet that Amber would never imagine that her mother could think like that. Before Amber had been born, Faye had been a very different person altogether, not the cautious, dowdy mother she'd become.

'Nor does Gran,' Amber went on. 'And not everyone her age is like that. Ella's grandmother makes them all run round after her like headless chickens since she had her heart operation. Ella's terrified her grandmother is going to end up living with them. She says they'll all have to be on drugs to cope. I'm glad Gran's not like that.'

Faye's widowed mother, Josie, had got married again a few years previously to a widower who understood that his new wife had got too used to the independence of almost twenty years of being on her own to ever be under a man's thumb again. A retired teacher with boundless patience, Stan was a calm breeze to Josie's cyclone of activity. Josie ran her local meals on wheels, while Stan was the Martha to her Mary.

'Your gran was on her own for a long time so she had to learn to take care of herself,' Faye said absently.

'Like you.'

'Yes, like me.'

'I was thinking.' Amber swung her legs back and forth. 'About Dad being dead and Granddad being dead, and now Gran is married to Stan and, well . . . When you go to heaven, how do they work it out if you've had more than one husband? I mean, if Stan dies and then Gran dies, who does she live with in heaven – Granddad or Stan? It's a problem, isn't it? They never talked about that in religion classes. Just that we'd all be happy but how?'

'Your gran's probably not planning on shuffling off to meet her maker just yet,' Faye said, startled.

'I know, I can't stand the thought of her not being here.' Amber shuddered. She was very close to her grandmother. 'But how does it work? Like if you met someone and Dad's up there waiting for you. He's still only in his late twenties, and then you come and you're this old lady, but you've got another husband who's waiting too, because women live longer than men, so he's there first. Do you see what I mean? Reincarnation sounds better,' she added, 'because then you're not all going to be in heaven at the same time. It makes more sense.'

Faye had a sinking feeling in the pit of her stomach, the same feeling she always had when Amber talked about her father. The long-dead and beloved dad who was reduced to a photo in a frame, a misty figure who never did anything wrong, never shouted or discussed tidying up her bedroom. Never said no to a mobile phone or the purchase of a mini-skirt of belt-like proportions. The dead could do no wrong.

'I hope Dad's waiting for you in heaven, though. That's nice. I like to think of that.' Amber smiled. 'For your sake, really. So you can be together again, like in *Titanic*. Although the woman in that was really old at the end, and then when she joined them all on the ship, she was young and back being Kate Winslet. Which was a bit convenient, wasn't it? Does that mean you get to be at your best in heaven, like twenty-one, even if you're very ancient and falling apart when you die? I think it's a bit too convenient.'

Faye breathed an inward sigh of relief at this rapid turn in the conversation. It meant she didn't need to discuss the concept of Amber's father waiting patiently for her in heaven. Not that he'd have waited. Patience had never been one of his virtues.

It was because saying he was there already would be a lie and now that Amber was older, it was getting harder and harder to lie. Adults lied to children all the time, little white ones for their own good. But time had turned Faye's white lie into a giant black one and now she couldn't stomach repeating it any more.

'I think the whole problem with heaven is that nobody really knows anything about it,' she said, copping out. 'You're supposed to believe even though you don't know.'

Amber grimaced.

'That's what the whole faith thing is about,' Faye added, feeling she was on shaky ground here. 'Believing when you don't know for sure.' Like you've always believed me, she thought guiltily. 'You could ask Stan. He studied theology.'

'The thing is, you have one person who's right for you, your soul mate, the one who's waiting for you,' Amber said. 'But if they die, how can you meet another soul mate? There's only going to be one person who makes you feel complete, who you can't wait to see and talk to, right? Isn't there? People say that, anyway,' Amber added hurriedly. She bent her head to her book again.

A few more minutes passed by and Faye tugged listlessly at a couple of weedy plants, obsessing over her daughter's vision of her dad happily waiting in heaven for Faye to turn up. Amber never needed to know, did she?

'Ella said something totally crazy the other day, Mum.' Amber broke the silence.

'She said that maybe you have to pretend not to be independent and that's what men like. That's crap, isn't it? Why should you pretend? I told her, Ella, you have to be you.' Amber was earnest, sounding like a much-married matron explaining the ways of the world to a teenage bride.

'That doesn't sound like Ella.' Faye knew her daughter's best friend as if she were her own daughter. Like Amber, Ella was clever, sweet, responsible and had never caused a moment's trouble in her life. 'What's come over her?'

'Giovanni's new girlfriend, that's who,' Amber went on. 'Dannii. With two i's and little hearts over each of them. The hearts are very important. She's messing up Ella's head and saying that the reason Ella and me don't have boyfriends is because we're too clever and too independent and guys don't like that.' Amber snorted dismissively.

Giovanni was Ella's youngest brother and Faye had heard about this new girlfriend enough times for alarm bells to tinkle gently. Giovanni was in his second year in college, handsome like all Ella's half-Italian family, and Faye knew Amber had a mild crush on him, despite the fact that she said he was boring. The appearance of an actual steady girl-friend was certainly a catalyst for Amber to realise this. Faye wouldn't have minded if her daughter's first serious boyfriend was someone like Giovanni: someone she knew all about and approved of.

'Dannii's OK-looking, I suppose,' Amber conceded, grudgingly, 'but she's a pain and she's round Ella's house all the time talking this crap. She's doing business studies, Mum, right, and when she's with Giovanni, she behaves like she's had her brain sucked out. You don't get into business studies in college if you're a moron, so I don't know who she's kidding. Well,' she added gloomily, 'Giovanni appears to be falling for it. Big dope. Dannii told Ella that Giovanni's a really hot guy. You can't say that to your boyfriend's little sister! *Your brother is so sexy*. Yeuch. That's disgusting. I can't stand her. She hasn't a clue about anything.'

Faye said nothing for a while. She gazed at her work so far. She'd definitely pulled up some genuine flowers along with the weeds. How was it that carefully planted flowers could be ripped up easily, while unwanted weeds needed incredible force to shift them?

'If you act stupid with a guy, he's only going out with you because of how you look,' Faye said eventually.

'Exactly what I said,' Amber pointed out. 'Oh, I suppose Ella was only thinking out loud. She couldn't act dumb, anyway. She's going to come top of our year in the exams.'

Talk of the exams made Amber stare wearily down at her maths book again. 'That's not love. Love is different. If any guy's only interested in what a girl's like on the outside, then he's not what you want, is he?'

It was half question, half statement.

'That's what I think,' Faye said decisively. This was safe ground: she'd been telling Amber to appreciate her worth all her life. 'If he doesn't love you for who you are, then he's not the right person for you. Have you and Ella met any hot guys?' she asked lightly. She'd love to ask if Amber thought she might fancy Giovanni.

'No,' said Amber hastily. If her mother hadn't been so busy being thankful at the change of subject, she might have noticed just how hastily Amber had spoken. But Faye didn't notice. She was pulling at weeds and she didn't see the hint of red on her daughter's cheeks.

'Summer Street is not exactly awash with hot men my age.' Amber fanned herself with her book as if the sun was responsible for the heat suffusing her complexion. 'Ella's road is just as bad. The whole neighbourhood's full of nerds and middle-aged men with beer bellies who suck them in when we walk past.'

Savage but accurate, Faye thought with a smothered laugh. Amber and Ella's teenage beauty made them a stunning pair, Amber all tawny hair and those spectacular eyes contrasting with Ella's flashing dark Italian looks. Though they'd never have believed it, they were gorgeous – a scary prospect when you were the mother of one of them. But Amber was so sensible. Faye had taught her well. How not to make mistakes, how not to be led by other people. Except, Faye thought, she'd never explained to her daughter how her mother knew these lessons were so important.

'The people from number 42 have sold up,' Faye said breezily. 'Who knows, a handsome father-son combo might have bought it.'

'Doubt it. But hey, if you're right, you could go out with the dad. Wouldn't that be great?' Amber was delighted. 'You could come home and tell me all about it. And I'd laugh and warn you not to let him get past first base on the first date!'

Faye grabbed a nettle by mistake and gasped with pain.

'Ouch. That was stupid,' she muttered lamely.

'It's a serious subject, Mum,' Amber said gravely. Just to show how serious, she sat up cross-legged and gazed at her mother, her face solemn. 'I know how much you've given up for me but I'm an adult now and you can have your life back. I'll be going to college. You need to do your own thing.'

The little speech sounded like one Amber had been working on for ages and Faye almost grabbed the nettle again for the comfort of physical pain against this shocking emotional stabbing sensation. She was meant to be urging Amber gently into the world, not the other way round.

Seventeen-year-olds were supposed to be too involved with their own problems to notice their mothers'. If Amber was urging her to get a social life, she must be a total basket case. Well, Faye's own mother thought so, too.

'Come on, Faye, don't bury yourself. You're not dead yet,'

Josie had said many years before, and it had triggered the one big row between them since before Amber was born.

'Leave me alone to live my life my way! You don't know what I want,' Faye had said furiously.

She'd never forgotten what her mother had said. Josie hadn't understood at all. This life with Amber wasn't being buried: it was living peacefully and contentedly without the interference of any man.

'I'm just saying think about it,' Amber went on. 'I'll be gone and I'll worry about you, Mum. I won't be here so much and you'll need to keep busy. And I don't mean doing overtime,' she added sternly. 'I mean having fun. Getting out. Going on dates. Grace would love to set you up on a blind date at one of her dinners, you know she would. Sure, you'd probably meet a few men you'd hate, but you never know, you might find romance.'

Lecture over, she went back to her maths book, leaving Faye feeling that their roles had been reversed. She'd been the one receiving the lecture on life from her daughter.

Amber's remarks had been running through Faye's head since Saturday afternoon.

Climbing the steps to the swimming pool complex, Faye wondered, was this all normal teenager stuff: get a life, Mum, because I'm going to and I don't want to worry about you. Or was there something else?

Faye went into the women's changing room, switched off her music and changed into her plain black swimsuit quickly. She did everything quickly and efficiently.

'Economical and precise,' Grace said, which was high praise indeed because Grace, Faye's boss in Little Island Recruitment, turned efficiency into an art form.

'Economical and precise or obsessional?' Faye wondered from time to time when she was interviewing in her office and saw candidates staring at her pristine desk with everything exactly at right angles to everything else. A cluttered desk meant a cluttered mind and Faye had never had time for a cluttered mind.

But didn't it signify an obsessional mind if you arranged all your paperclips to lie lengthwise in their compartment in the desk organiser?

She stowed her navy skirt suit in a locker and pulled on a swimhat. She never looked at herself in the mirror like some women in the changing room, anxiously making sure they didn't look awful in clinging Lycra or admiring a physique honed by laps.

At the age of forty, and carrying probably two stone more than she should, Faye was no fan of mirrors. They lied. You could be scarred to bits on the inside and look beautiful outside.

She walked out of the changing room, shivered under the cool shower for a moment, then slipped into the pool's medium-fast lane where she pushed off into the water.

The Olympic swimming selectors were unlikely to be calling on her any time soon, but over the last six months she'd worked her way up to swimming sixteen lengths each time and she knew she was getting faster, no matter how unprofessional her forward crawl. She felt more toned too but that wasn't the primary reason for the exercise.

What she loved about swimming was the solitude of the pool. Even if the lanes were full and every noise was amplified by the water, when her head was down and her body was slicing through the pool, she felt utter peace.

This was her time, time for Faye alone.

Six months previously, when she'd paid for the swimming complex membership, she'd realised it was the first time in seventeen years she'd indulged herself in something that didn't directly benefit Amber. Even the CD player she used was an old one that Amber had discarded when she'd saved up her pocket money for an iPod.

The money she'd spent on the membership fee could usefully have gone somewhere else. Amber would need a whole new expensive kit for art college, and there would surely be trips to galleries abroad. There never seemed to be enough money for all the things Faye thought Amber should have.

But the pool had called to her.

'I wish I was into swimming,' Grace had begun to say on the days that Faye took an early lunch.

Grace and her husband Neil ran the recruitment company together. Grace regularly said they couldn't have done it without Faye, and Neil, who actually worked very little, was smugly convinced its success was all down to him.

'Swimming sounds so easy, swim, swim and the weight falls off,' Grace had said.

Faye grinned, knowing that Grace liked the idea of exercise and the results that exercise provided but wasn't that keen on actually doing it.

'Is it better than running, do you think?' Grace went on. 'I'd quite like to run but I've weak ankles. Swimming could be the answer.'

'You'd get bored in a week,' Faye told her. Grace was a chataholic and got anxious if she hadn't had at least four friends phone her a day in between her hectic schedule of business calls. 'There's nothing sociable about swimming. You put your head into the water and plough on. You can't hear anyone and you can only see what's ahead of you.'

It was like praying, she often thought, although she didn't say that to Grace, who'd have thought she was abusing recreational pharmaceuticals. But it seemed like that to Faye – here it was only you and God as you moved porpoise-like through the water, nobody else.

46

'Really? No *Baywatch* male lifeguards?'

'I haven't noticed any,' Faye said drily.

'Well, who needs a *Baywatch* lifeguard anyway?' Grace said.

Which was, Faye knew, her way of moving on to another line of conversation. Because Grace, although happily married, had many fantasies about a muscle-bound hunk who'd adore her. It was strange when Faye, who'd been on her own for most of the past seventeen years, went out of her way not to notice men at all. She was with Billie Holiday on the whole men issue: they were too much trouble. And she'd learned that the hard way.

Lunchtimes could be busy in Little Island Recruitment because that was when staff from other offices got the opportunity to slope off, march into Little Island, relate the sad tale of their current employment and discuss the possibility of moving elsewhere where their talents would finally be appreciated. But today when Faye arrived back from her swim, damp-haired, pleasurably tired out and dressed in her old reliable M & S navy suit, reception was empty except for Jane behind the reception desk.

'Hi, Faye,' said Jane cheerily and held up a sheaf of pink call slips. 'I've got messages for you.'

The office was very high-tech and designed to impress. Nobody could fail to be dazzled by the glass lift, the stiletto-crunching black marble floors, or the enormous modern-art canvas that dominated the reception. Faye thought the picture looked like what two amorous whales might paint if they'd been covered in midnight-blue emulsion and left to thump around for a while on a massive canvas. But having an artistic daughter, she understood that this was probably not the effect the artist had anticipated.

'People are scared of modern art,' Grace said gleefully when the painting had first been hung.

'It can be intimidating,' Faye pointed out bluntly. 'But this one's a bit dull, to be honest.'

'Perhaps you're right,' sighed Grace. 'But it says we've arrived. We've come a long way from that awful dive of an office we started out in, remember.'

Faye remembered. Ten years ago, Faye had been broke after a series of dead-end jobs, and was desperately trying to get her foot on an employment ladder that didn't involve late-night bar work. She'd been so grateful to Grace for taking a chance on her in the fledgling recruitment business she had made sure Grace never regretted it. Nobody in Little Island worked harder than Faye. The two had forged a professional friendship that grew stronger every year.

'The ex-barmaid and the ex-banking queen, who'd have thought we'd make it?' Faye used to say, smiling. She didn't let many people past her barriers, but Grace was one of the few. What if Grace was a social butterfly, was married to the obnoxious Neil, and could air-kiss with the best of them? Despite all that, she was a real person. True, kind, honest. Faye trusted her, which made Grace part of a very small and exclusive club.

'You should say "ex-beverage administrator",' Grace chided. 'Besides, you should have been running that bar. If you'd had the childcare and the opportunity, you would have been.'

Grace knew Faye's history and how she'd worked in dead-end jobs so she could take care of Amber herself. She knew most of Faye's secrets, but not all.

Faye took her messages, walked past what was now dubbed 'Flipper Does Dallas', went up to her office and got ready for the afternoon meeting.

At three in the afternoon, on Mondays and Wednesdays, there was a staff meeting in Little Island Recruitment. Grace said it kept everyone in touch with what the whole company was doing.

They'd been holding it for nine years and it was a marvellous idea because it made every single member of staff feel both personally involved in the company and valued by it.

'We're only as good as our last job,' Grace would remind the staff at the meeting, where there was always a buzz of conversation, until the apple and cinnamon muffins came in. 'This is the think tank where we come up with ideas to improve what we do.'

The staff all believed the idea for the meeting had been Grace's. After all, she'd been a banking hotshot for years before starting up the agency, and could write a book on how to get ahead in life.

It could be called Who Moved My Emery Board? joked Kevin who was in charge of accounts. Grace's nails were things of beauty: ten glossy beige talons that clacked in a military tattoo on the conference-room desk when she was irritated.

Clack, clack, clack.

In fact, Faye had suggested the staff meeting shortly after she joined.

Grace felt that some benign presence had been on her side the day Faye walked into her life. Grace may have been the one with the financial acumen and the qualifications as long as her fake-tanned arms, but Faye was the one who'd made the agency work.

On this afternoon, nineteen members of staff sat around the conference table and worked their way through the agenda.

Today's meeting focused on the few sticky accounts where the jobs and the jobseekers didn't match. There were always a few. Little Island had an ever-growing client roster, with just three companies who created the problems, people for whom no applicant was good enough and who went through staff faster than Imelda Marcos went through shoe cream.

49

Chief among the difficult clients, known as VIPs, in-house code for Very Ignorant People, was William Brooks.

It was wiser to transfer a call from him by saying, 'It's Mr Brooks, one of our VIP clients,' and risk being overheard, than to say, 'It's that horrible bastard from Brooks FX Stockbroking on the phone and I'm not talking to him, so you'd better.'

William Brooks, the aforementioned company's managing director, was yet again looking for a personal assistant. This was his third search in six months, the previous two assistants having decided to leave his employment abruptly.

Little Island also supplied temps, and only that morning, Faye had been on the phone to Mr Brooks's current temp who said she was giving it a month more, 'Because the money's so good, Faye, but after that, I'm out of here. He's a pig. No, strike that. Unfair to pigs.'

'We have no PAs on our books that will do for him.' Philippa, who was responsible for Mr Brooks, scanned through the file wearily. 'Out of last week's interviews, we found two wonderful candidates and he doesn't like either of them. I don't know what he wants.'

'I do. He's after a Charlize Theron doppelgänger who can type, operate Excel and doesn't mind picking up his dry-cleaning or listening to his dirty jokes,' said Faye.

'If such a person existed, she wouldn't want to work for a fat, balding executive who goes through secretaries faster than I get through Silk Cut Ultra,' Philippa said with feeling. She hated William Brooks. The only person who seemed to be able to handle him was Faye, who somehow made William rein in the worst parts of his personality and who stared him down into submission. Philippa wished she could glare at men in the steely way Faye did. Mind you, the steely gaze seemed to scare guys off too, because in the years Philippa had known Faye, she'd never had a man around. She couldn't

50

imagine Faye with a guy, anyway. There was something about Faye, something about the look on her face when the computer repairman came in and flirted with everyone in the office, which suggested Faye was one of those women who had no interest in men.

'It's a prestigious account,' Faye pointed out gently. 'We've made a lot of money out of Brooks FX and having them as clients looks great on our prospectus. William is the fly in the ointment but it would be sensible to work with him.'

Recruitment was a delicate balance. Finding the right person for the right job didn't sound too hard in principle, but, as Faye had discovered during her ten years in the industry, it could be impossible in practice. The right person in the right job might suddenly realise that her boss (sweet on recruitment day) was a control freak who insisted on just two loo breaks a day, didn't allow hot drinks at the desk in case coffee spilled on the keyboard and thought that paying a salary meant he owned her, body and soul.

'The right PA for William Brooks exists,' Faye said. 'And we'll find her.'

'Only if someone comes up with a PA robot,' muttered Philippa. 'They won't complain if they get their bums pinched.'

'He's pinched somebody's bum?' This was news to Faye. Difficult clients were one thing, sexual harassment was another.

'Well . . .' Philippa squirmed. She wasn't supposed to say. The second assistant they'd placed with William had phoned her up in tears.

Faye looked grim. 'Tell me. Chapter and verse.'

Philippa told her and gained some satisfaction from the steely look on Faye's face.

'You'll talk to him?' Grace asked warily, also seeing the look.

'I'll talk to him,' Faye agreed.

The women around the table grinned at each other. Mr Brooks was about to be taken down a peg or two. If only they could witness it, but they wouldn't. Because Faye was so famously discreet.

After the meeting, Faye poured herself another coffee and shut the door to her sanctum.

She loved her job. Recruitment suited her perfectly because it was about placing the right person in the right job and to a woman who liked the towels in her airing cupboard folded just so and in the correct place, it was very satisfying indeed. People were not towels, but life might have been easier if they were.

Over the years, she'd discovered that the main skill was interviewing potential employees and working out whether a certain job and company would suit them. With no training whatsoever, Faye turned out to be a natural at it.

'It's like you can work out precisely what sort of person they are from just twenty questions,' Grace said admiringly.

'Yes, but you've got to know which twenty questions to ask,' Faye said. She was justifiably proud of her ability, if a little amused. It was odd being successful in business by seeing through people's façades to the character within, when the biggest problems in her private life had come from being unable to do just that.

'It's easy to suss people out when you're not involved with them,' she added. 'You might never have met them before but it's possible to gauge fairly soon whether someone is hard-working, easy-going, anxious, a team player, whatever.'

In the early days, they only recruited secretarial staff and the competition was vicious, but the combination of Faye's talent and Grace's business savvy meant the company took off. Then, there would have been no question of dropping difficult clients: they needed everyone they could get. But not any more, as William Brooks was about to find out. Recruitment was a small business where everybody knew everybody. Faye phoned a couple of her old colleagues, now with other agencies, and asked what the word was on William Brooks. Fifteen minutes later, she hung up the phone a lot wiser.

After a moment or two of deep thought, she dialled the number for Brooks FX. She was put straight through to Mr Brooks, probably because he thought she bore news of a suitable PA with the required Miss World physique.

'Well,' he snapped. 'Found anyone?'

'I'm not sure Little Island is the right recruitment agency for you,' Faye began blandly.

'What?' He was instantly wrong-footed, she knew. Few agencies could afford to turn down business.

'As you know, we work with Davidson's and Marshal McGregor.' She named the two biggest stockbroking firms in the country, both of which could buy and sell Brooks FX with the contents of their petty cash boxes. 'And we have excellent relationships with both those companies, but you do appear to have peculiar requirements, Mr Brooks.'

'I'm exacting, that's all,' he snapped. 'You've been sending me morons. Call yourselves a recruitment agency . . .'

'You're more than exacting,' Faye interrupted, feeling cold rage course through her. She'd planned to do this the official way, but it was clear that Brooks needed the unorthodox approach. 'Let's put it this way, Mr Brooks, if we were offering sports massages, I believe you'd be the client insulting our therapists by asking for a massage with a "happy ending".'

'What?' exploded out of him again, and Faye grinned to herself. 'Happy ending' was code for a massage with sexual services included, the sort only available in red-light districts.

'How dare you . . . ?'

Probably nobody had ever talked to William Brooks this

way. She knew his sort: a bully. And, importantly, she now knew some even less pleasant things about him.

'We have our reputation to consider too, Mr Brooks,' Faye went on, the vein of ice evident in her tone. 'And we've been hearing stories from the staff we've placed with you, stories that neither of us would like to hear repeated. You see, we place temps in the equality agency too, and with some of the city's top legal firms, and we can't have any hint of scandal associated with our company.'

'What are you implying?' he roared.

'We've placed a lot of staff with Wilson Brothers too,' Faye went on. 'They're one of our best customers and actually handle our legal affairs, so if there was any, shall we say, unpleasantness, we'd naturally go to them.'

This time, there was an audible indrawn breath at the other end of the phone.

Wilson Brothers was a law firm where the senior partner just happened to be William Brooks's father-in-law. The unspoken message was that Mr Wilson would be fascinated to learn of his son-in-law's fondness for touching up his assistants.

'How about we pretend we didn't have this conversation, Mr Brooks,' Faye went on, 'and we'll resume our search for a PA for you. However, if and when we do find one, I shall be in constant communication with her and I assure you, I expect any Little Island person to be treated with the utmost respect and dignity. I'm sure you agree that bullying and sexual harassment cases can be so messy and time-consuming?'

'Oh, yes,' blustered William Brooks but the fight had gone out of him. 'I'll talk to you again, Mrs Reid,' he muttered and hung up.

Result, thought Faye, leaning back in her chair, relieved. She knew that what she'd done was unethical and that Grace would have had a coronary had she overheard, but sometimes the unorthodox approach was required and this time, thankfully, it had worked. She'd never had a problem thinking outside the box when it came to business. And being tough was second nature to her now.

Some people thought it was being hard-nosed, but it wasn't: it was self-preservation.

She'd tried to instil that and a sense of personal power in Amber.

'You are responsible for you,' Faye used to repeat mantra-like. 'It's not clever to be led by other people or to do what you don't want to do, just to fit in. You have the power to do and be anything you want and to make your own choices. Believing in yourself and in your own power is one of the most important things in life.'

'Ella's mum says to behave like a little lady, not to hang around with rough boys in the park and that if a stranger tries to get you into a car, to scream,' Amber reported when she was younger and her friends thought Faye's 'be your own boss' mantra was cool. 'But Ella thinks your rules are better. I told her you were a feminist because you never let anyone walk all over you. It's because Dad's dead, I said. You had to be tougher because we were on our own.'

Faye spent an hour on paperwork, then returned her emails, by which time her eyes were weary from staring at the screen. She fetched another coffee, shut her office door firmly, kicked off her shoes and lay down on the couch for a few minutes. She was tired today. The reason still worried her. Amber had woken her up at three the night before, talking loudly to herself in her sleep, saying, 'No, I will not!' firmly.

Faye had stood at her daughter's door in case this middle-of-the-night conversation became a nightmare, but it didn't. Amber muttered 'no' a few more times before turning over and falling back into a silent sleep.

Amber had been prone to nightmares when she was a

small child and Faye, who couldn't bear to think of her darling lonely and frightened in her bed, would carry the pink-pyjama-clad little girl into her own room.

Having your baby sleep with you when you were a lonely, affection-starved single mother was probably against every bit of advice in the book, Faye knew. But she needed the comfort of her little daughter every bit as much as Amber needed her. The sweetness of that small body, energetic little limbs still padded with baby fat, gave Faye strength. No matter how tough life could be, she'd go on for Amber. Her daughter deserved the best and Faye would provide it, no matter what.

'Mama,' Amber would mutter in her lisping, babyish voice, and fall into a deeper sleep, taking up half the bed by lying sprawled sideways.

'Mama, how did I get here?' she'd say in wonder the next morning, delighted to wake up in her mother's bed. And Faye would cuddle her tightly and they'd giggle and tickle each other, and the nightmare would never be mentioned.

Now, Amber didn't have nightmares, just the odd restless night when she had a lot on her mind, like exams or last year's school play where she was in charge of painting the scenery and used to sit up in bed murmuring about more Prussian blue paint for the sky.

She was probably suffering from the most awful exam stress, Faye decided, as she sipped her coffee. There were only weeks to go, after all.

If there was anything else worrying her daughter, she'd know, wouldn't she?

Except that recently, she was beginning to think it was easier to understand total strangers searching for the perfect job than work out what was going on in her daughter's mind.

# CHAPTER FOUR

One hundred and fifty miles away, Maggie Maguire didn't know what impulse made her go home that afternoon instead of trekking off to the gym. Karma? Fate? Destiny twirling a lazy finger in the human world?

Unexpectedly getting off work early meant she could have had a rare meander around Galway's shops before taking her normal Wednesday evening Pilates class. But some unknown force made Maggie walk past Extreme Fitness, bypass the lure of the bohemian boutiques, and go home to the apartment she shared with Grey. A modest third-floor flat, it was her pride and joy, especially since she'd gone ahead and painted the tiny cloakroom's wall tiles a mesmerising Indian Ocean blue.

'You can't paint tiles,' Grey had said, lounging against the door of the cloakroom, barefoot and jean-clad, as Maggie sat on the floor and read the instructions on the tin. Grey had the sort of shape that lent itself to lounging: long, long legs, a lean torso and an elegance that made women stare, admiring the swept-back leonine hair, strong, patrician face and intelligent eyes that were the same colour as his name.

'You can. It says it right here.' Maggie peered at the instructions, her nose scrunched up. Her auburn hair was held up with a big clip, but bits still straggled wispily round her freckled face. Maggie could have used cement as a hair product and red wisps would still have escaped to curl around her face.

Grey said he loved her hair: it was unruly, wild, beautiful and unpredictable. Like her.

After five years together, Maggie believed him, even though his last three girlfriends before her had been Park Avenue-type blondes with sleek hair, sleek clothes, push-up bras and shoe collections organised by Polaroid. Maggie's shoe collection was organised by age: old cowboy boots at the back of the wardrobe, new ones at the front. Her clothes were rock chick rather than chic, faded Levi's being her must-have garment. Being boyishly slim, she didn't have enough boob to fit into a push-up bra. And nobody looking at her pale freckled face with the silvery cobalt-blue eyes that showed exactly what she was thinking could have imagined Maggie having even a grain of Park Avenue Princess hauteur.

Alas, she'd have loved to be such a creature: icily cool without a hair out of place, and could never see that her wild russet beauty and eyes that belonged to an ancient Celtic warrior queen were far rarer and more precious than high-maintenance blonde glamour.

'And this is the last bit of beige in the whole place. It's got to go,' she'd added, opening the tin of paint and breathing in, as if the salty tang of the sea would drift out, scenting the air with memories of a foreign beach.

They'd bought the apartment two years ago and the previous owners had been keen on beige, beige and more beige. It was like living in a can of mushroom soup, said Maggie, who'd grown up in a quirky house on Summer Street where her bedroom had been sky blue with stars on the midnight-blue ceiling. Dad had been going through his planetarium phase and the stars had been in their correct places too. Ursa Major and Ursa Minor would not be the wrong way round when Dennis Maguire was in charge.

The cloakroom in the Galway apartment was the last room Maggie had painstakingly redecorated. Now it was all cheery blues and whites, like a small beachside restaurant from their last holiday, a glorious, special-offer week in the Seychelles. Holidays had been off the agenda for the past few months as they were broke but Maggie had an almost physical longing for the feeling of sweltering sun toasting her skin while her toes wriggled in sand.

We need a break, she thought as she stepped out of the lift on to their floor. Sun, sand and no conversations with irritated students when they'd discovered that the very book they needed for that night's rush-job essay on Greco-Roman funerary practices wasn't in its place.

Grey was a politics lecturer and Maggie was one of six librarians in the vast, modern Coolidge College library, a job she loved because it allowed her mind to wander over many varied subjects from medicine to literature. The downside was that pre-exams the stress levels of the students went up and people who'd spent six months working on the formula for the perfect Long Island Iced Tea to fuel a party suddenly required actual research materials for their courses. And Maggie was the one they got mad at when the research material in question was booked out by someone else.

'But, like, I need it today,' a radiantly pretty brunette girl had said only that morning, slim fingers raking through her hair, which irritatingly made her look even better. What hair product did she use? Maggie wondered briefly but didn't ask.

Instead, she said, 'I'm really sorry but I can't help you. We've only two copies and they're both booked out every day for the next week. You've got to make arrangements in advance with some textbooks.'

'Well, thank you very much,' snapped the girl sarcastically.

'You've been a great help, I must say.' And she marched off in high dudgeon.

'You can't win 'em all,' commiserated her colleague Shona. 'Still, she's not like the back of a bus, so she can always sleep with her prof if the going gets tough.'

'Shona! That's so sexist. I thought you were reading *The Female Eunuch*?'

'I did and it's marvellous, but I'm on to the new Jackie Collins now. I know Germaine Greer wouldn't approve, but I'd have slept with my prof if it'd have improved my degree,' countered Shona wistfully. 'He was sex on legs, so it wouldn't have been a hardship.' Shona's degree had been in European Literature. 'When he talked about the Heart of Darkness that was in all of us, I swear, I felt a shiver run right down my spine into my knickers.'

Shona was, in fact, happily married but she was an irrepressible flirt and batted her eyelashes at every passing cute guy, despite many weary conversations with the head librarian about appropriate behaviour in the workplace. 'Just because I've eaten doesn't mean I can't look at the menu,' was her motto.

Fortunately her husband Paul, whom she adored and would never cheat on, was merely amused by all this.

'Professors don't have sex with students, except in the fevered imaginations of people like you,' Maggie retorted. 'Besides, she's in third-year history. Have you seen Prof Wolfowitz? Brilliant, yes. Beddable, no. He is totally bald except for that one eyebrow. Every time I see him, I want to pluck a few of the middle hairs out and give him two eyebrows instead of one.'

'Maggie, Maggie,' sighed Shona. 'The eyebrow is immaterial. Sleeping your way to success has precisely nothing to do with how good-looking the powerful person is. You may wear scuffed cowboy boots and a tough attitude, but you're Haven't-a-Clue Barbie at heart. You don't have a calculating bone in your body – apart from the one hot Dr Grey Stanley puts there, of course.' Shona laughed like a drain at her own joke.

Maggie groaned. She was used to Shona by now. They'd become fast friends from the moment they'd met on Maggie's first day in the library, where she discovered that her new friend's second degree subject was indubitably Teasing: Honours Module. Now Maggie leaned over and swatted Shona on the arm with her ruler. 'Brat.'

'Haven't-a-Clue Barbie.'

'Slapper.'

'Oh, thank you,' Shona said, pretending to preen. She was impossible to shock. 'Shona O'Slapper, I like that. Now, can you swap shifts with me? I know you're on till six tonight, but I'll do it and you can go early if you'll do tomorrow afternoon for me? You could spend another hour honing your body in Extreme Fatness,' she wheedled. Shona had accompanied Maggie to the gym once and hated it, hence the new name.

'Are you and Paul going out?' inquired Maggie.

'I'm providing a shoulder to cry on,' Shona informed her. 'Ross has broken up with Johann.' Ross was a hairdresser who lived in the apartment below Shona and Paul, providing the perfect opportunity for Shona's fag-haggery and giving Paul a chance to watch football on the television while she and Ross sat in the apartment below, rewatching old *Will & Grace* episodes and bitching happily.

'He's inconsolable, even though he whined all the time they were going out about how insensitive Johann was and how he didn't like Nureyev.' Nureyev was Ross's beloved pet, a lop-eared rabbit, who was spoiled beyond belief and had his own Vuitton bunny carrier as well as a purple velvet collar with his name spelled out in diamanté. He lived in luxury in Ross's Philippe Starck-style kitchen and was house-trained to

61

use a cat litter box. 'Nobody's ever truly gorgeous until they dump you, right? We're partying to get him over it.'

'On a Wednesday?'

'Woe's day, sweetie, as the ancient Danes would say. It's apt.'

'Who's looking after Nureyev?'

'We're going to leave the Discovery channel on for him. He loves all those shows about meerkats.'

Maggie was still laughing at the idea of the rabbit sulkily glued to the television when she got to her own front door and pulled out her keys.

The mortice lock was undone. Grey must have got home early, she thought with a smile. That was good, they could have a blissfully long evening together. Good call, Maguire, she thought as she let herself in. Sometimes a girl's gotta know when to miss stretching on a mat so she can stretch on a bed. And for all of his intellectual cool, Grey knew some pelvic contortions the Pilates teacher had never taught. It was funny though, Grey was supposed to be at a meeting – perhaps it had been cancelled?

'Shouldn't be too late, honey,' Grey had said on the phone earlier. 'You've got your class tonight so I'll pick up Thai food on the way home.' Grey believed in sharing cooking duties, although he preferred takeout to actual slaving and stirring with wooden spoons.

Inside the apartment, Maggie heard muted noises coming from the apartment's lone bedroom. Grey must be watching the TV, she thought, and, shedding her possessions as she went, handbag on to the floor, jacket on the couch, she crossed the small living room, went down the hall and pushed their bedroom door open.

The door was still swinging open when Maggie stopped on the threshold, frozen.

Grey was on the bed, naked and lying underneath a woman, also naked.

The woman's hair hung like a silken curtain, erotically half covering a lingerie-model body with a hand-span waist and high, perfect C-cup breasts.

Three mouths opened in surprise. Maggie twisted her head sideways to try to get the scene to make sense. It was like a clever illustration in a psychoanalyst's office, a bizarre, mind-bending scene designed to make you question everything you knew: what's wrong with this picture?

*Well, Doctor, that's our bed with our duvet tangled up on the floor, and my side table pretty much the way I left it this morning with a book open on it. And there's the photo of me and Grey outside the cathedral in Barcelona, but in the bed, there's this strange blonde girl with an unbelievable body arched over my boyfriend who has – well, had – an erection. And there really is no other explanation for this apart from the obvious.*

'Maggie, I'm so sorry, I never meant you to see, I wouldn't hurt you for anything,' Grey said urgently, wriggling out from under the blonde girl so fast that she squealed.

Maggie didn't answer him. She couldn't. She just stared in disbelief.

Politicians were supposed to be excellent at wriggling out of embarrassing situations. Perhaps Grey taught that, too, along with analysis of world power structures and globalisation.

Bile rose in Maggie's throat and she turned without a word and ran to the tiny cloakroom she'd decorated with such pride. Student. That girl had to be one of Grey's students. Someone who'd possibly stood in the college library and looked calculatingly at Maggie sitting at the research desk, pleased to realise that her rival was older. Perhaps wondering what Grey saw in thirty-year-old Maggie with her tangle of wild hair when he could have a twenty-one-year-old with a silken mane like a hair commercial, and a va-va-voom figure with the peach-bloom skin of youth.

Students were always getting crushes on Grey. The two of them joked about it, because it seemed so funny, despite Shona's stories. Grey was miles away from the image of a fusty academic with woolly hair, badly fitting jackets and mismatched socks. When they had first met, five years previously, when she was finding her feet in the city, Maggie herself had found it hard to believe he held a doctorate in political science. At a start-of-term college party, he'd stood out among the soberly dressed professorial types. He wore jeans, and, around his neck, a couple of narrow leather coils from which hung a piece of obsidian that glittered like his cloudy grey eyes. Maggie had heard of Dr Grey Stanley, a brilliant thinker who'd resisted attempts by various political leaders to advise their parties and who was the author of several widely read articles on the state of the country. Nobody had mentioned how jaw-droppingly handsome he was.

'Hey, Red,' he'd said, tangling long fingers in the tendrils of her auburn hair. 'Can I get you a glass of the vinegar that passes for wine round here?'

Maggie, tomboy extraordinaire whose shoulder-length hair was one of her few concessions to femininity, would normally have given the death glare to any strange guy who dared to touch her. But this man, all heat and masculinity so close to her, made it hard to breathe, never mind shoot murderous glares. She exhaled, suddenly glad she'd worn the black camisole that hung low on her small breasts, the fabric starkly dark against her milky white skin. Her skin was true redhead type, so white it was almost blue, she sometimes joked.

Grey stared at her as if milky white with a smattering of tiny freckles was his favourite colour combination. The party in a draughty hall on the Coolidge College campus was full of fascinating, clever people with IQs that went off the scale, and he'd chosen her. Even now, no matter how many times

64

Shona told her she was beautiful and that Grey Stanley was lucky to have her, Maggie shook her head in denial. It was the other way round, she knew.

'Maggie . . .'

As she slammed the cloakroom door shut and slid the lock, she heard Grey's anxious voice outside. He rarely called her Red any more. Red was the girl he'd fallen in love with, the feisty redhead who was fiercely independent, who needed nobody in her life, thank you very much. She was so different from the Park Avenue Princesses, she must have struck him as a challenge he couldn't resist. But five years of coupledom had surgically removed her independence and now, she realised, she had become like a tiger in a zoo: lazily captive and unable to survive in the wild.

She leaned over the toilet bowl and the cloudy remains of her lunchtime chicken wrap came up. Again and again, she retched until there was nothing left in her except loss and fear.

She was the old Maggie again, the one who hadn't yet learned to hide her anxiety under an armour of feistiness. Stupid Maggie who'd never imagined that Grey would cheat on her. Just like Stupid Maggie from years ago. It was a shock to feel like that again. She was so sure she'd left it all behind her. The memory of those years in St Ursula's, when her life had been one long torment of bullying, came to her. She'd had four years of hell at the hands of the bullies and it had marked her for ever. Now she was right back there – reeling from the shock, sick with fear.

When she could retch no more, she sank on to the floor. From this unusual vantage point, the bathroom had turned out well, she realised. The colours were so pretty and it was so carefully done. Even Grey had said so.

'You're wasted in the college library,' he'd laughed the day she finished it. 'You should have your own decorating business.

The Paint Queen: specialising in no-hope projects. Your dad could consult.' Grey had seen and admired the planetarium ceiling in her old bedroom in the house on Summer Street.

'Lovely,' he'd said and joked that her parents were sweetly eccentric despite their outwardly conservative appearance.

Grey's parents were both lawyers, now divorced. He'd grown up with money, antiques and housekeepers. She couldn't imagine his French-cuff-wearing father ever doing something as hands-on as painting stars on the ceiling for his son. Or his mother, she of the perfect blonde bob, professionally blow-dried twice a week, breathlessly explaining about winning €75 in the lottery and planning what she'd do with the money, the way Maggie's mum had.

'My parents are not eccentric,' Maggie had told Grey defensively. 'They're just enthusiastic, interested in things . . .'

'I know, honey.' Grey had been contrite. 'I love your mum and dad. They're great.'

But it occurred to her that Grey had been right. Her parents weren't worldly or astute. They were endlessly naïve, innocents abroad, and they'd brought her up to be just like them. Blindly trusting.

She put her head on her knees and tried not to think about anything. Numb the brain. Concentrate on a candle burning. Wasn't that the trick?

There was noise outside in the hall, muffled speech, the front door slamming. Grey's voice, low and anxious, saying: 'Maggie, come out, please. We should talk, honey.'

She didn't reply. He didn't try to open the door but she was glad it was locked. She had absolutely no idea of what she'd say to him if she saw him. There was silence for a while.

After half an hour, he returned, sounding harder this time, more lecturer than contrite boyfriend. 'I'm going out to get us some Thai takeout. You can't sit in there all night.'

'I can!' shrieked Maggie, roused to yell at him with an unaccustomed surge of temper. How dare he tell her what she could and couldn't do.

'You *can* stay in there all night,' Grey said patiently, in the voice he used to explain difficult concepts to stupid people at parties, 'if that's what you want to do, but you ought to come out and eat something. I won't be long.' The front door slammed again.

Gone to phone his nubile student, perhaps? To say that Maggie would get over it and then it would be business as usual.

*We'll have to use your place instead of mine.*

Grey mightn't like it so much if he had to bonk his lover in some grotty student digs, though. He liked the smooth crispness of clean sheets, a power shower and wooden floors where you could comfortably walk barefoot without wondering how many other zillions of people had walked barefoot on it before, shedding flakes of dry skin. He'd been brought up in luxury. Before she'd met Grey, Maggie had known nothing of the world of Egyptian cotton sheets with a 400-thread count. To her, sheets came in only two varieties: fitted and flat.

Maggie stuck her ear up against the door and listened. Nothing. She unlocked the door, came out and looked around the apartment, thinking that it no longer looked like the home of her dreams, only an identikit apartment trying hard to be elegant and different, but still looking exactly like its neighbours.

Everything she had achieved had been done on a budget, from the bargain basement African-inspired coffee table to the Moroccan silk cushion covers she'd bought on a street stall and which were now woolly with loose threads. Despite the kudos of being an ultra-clever doctor of studies whose lectures were always packed, Grey wasn't paid well.

The library paid less. But Maggie was used to not having money. She'd grown up that way. Making do, managing: they were the words she'd lived with as a child. There had been great happiness in her home, for all the lack of hard cash and the shiny new things some of the other girls had. Money wasn't important to her. Love, security, safety, happiness were. She'd tried so hard to make their home beautiful, the heart of their love. What a waste of time that had been.

Sinking down on the low couch, still numb, she wondered what she should do next. Storm off? Or wait for Grey so she could rage at him that since he'd cheated, he should be the one to go.

Maggie's Guide to Life didn't cover this one.

He'd tell her not to be stupid. She could almost hear him saying it, in measured tones that made any argument he laid out sound entirely plausible.

*Honestly, Maggie, listen to yourself. There's absolutely no point in being hasty. Think about this, don't give in to some primitive emotional response. It was just sex.*

Just sex. One of Grey's endlessly philosophising colleagues had probably written a paper on the subject: how *just sex* was occasionally justifiable. If the partner in question was away; if the potential bonkee was particularly gorgeous; if nobody would ever know.

Even with her eyes open, Maggie could still see Grey and the blonde on her bed, imagine it all: the blonde's moans of pleasure as she rose to orgasm; Grey saying: 'Oh baby, oh baby, that's so good.' The words he murmured to Maggie, her words. But they'd never be truly hers again.

Although there was nothing left inside her stomach, Maggie felt she might be sick again. No, she wouldn't wait for him to explain it to her. Grabbing her handbag from where she'd dropped it so happily what felt like a lifetime ago, she ran out of the apartment. If she was somewhere else, a place where every single ornament didn't remind her of Grey, she might be able to work out what she'd do next. A bus was coming down the road, the bus to Salthill where she could walk on the beach. Without hesitation she ran to the stop and got on.

# CHAPTER FIVE

On Summer Street, the sun had shifted in the afternoon sky. Christie Devlin's back garden was bathed in a golden glow that lit up the velvety roses and turned the cream-coloured trellises a glittering white. It was the sort of afternoon Christie loved.

James had phoned to say he'd caught an earlier train and should be home by seven instead of nine. The postman had arrived with a late-afternoon bounty of the gadget catalogues Christie loved to devour at night, picking out useful things she'd buy if she could afford them. The dogs, too tired of the heat to clamour for another walk, were content to lie in the shade of the kitchen door, dreaming happily, two sets of paws twitching.

Sitting on her tiny terrace with a cup of iced tea, Christie was supposed to be marking art history essays for tomorrow morning, but she couldn't concentrate.

The heat, the glory of her garden, James coming home early, none of it mattered. Nothing except the fear that sat hard and stone-like in the pit of her stomach, telling her there was something very wrong.

\*   \*   \*

In her kitchen seven houses away, Una Maguire was standing on a chair looking for a spare tin of baking powder in the larder cupboard beside the fridge. She'd decided to bake a Victoria sponge for the church fair and there had been only a scraping of powder in the old tin.

'Dennis, have you been at my cupboards again?' she yelled good-humouredly at her husband. It was a joke. As their daughter, Maggie, was well aware, Dennis Maguire barely knew how to open the cupboards in the kitchen and his only domestic duty was washing and drying. He never put away the dishes he'd dried. Una did that.

For years, it had been Maggie's job in the production line of washing and drying, but she was long gone with her own life, and the duty fell to Una again.

'Never touched them,' Dennis yelled back from the living room where he was putting the final touches to the model of a Spitfire that had taken two weeks to complete. The construction was entirely accurate: Dennis had checked in his *Jane's Aircraft Guide*.

'Don't believe you,' teased back Una, over-reaching past a pack of semolina because she was sure she'd seen the red metallic glint of the baking powder tin. With a swiftness that surprised her, the chair tilted, she lost her footing and fell to the floor, her left leg crumpling underneath her.

The pain was as shocking as it was instantaneous. Cruelly sharp, like a blade neatly inserted.

'Dennis,' whimpered Una, knowing that she'd done something serious. 'Dennis, come quickly.'

In the comfort of her bedroom at number 18 Summer Street, Amber Reid lay in her boyfriend's arms and heard the sound of the ambulance droning up the street to the Maguires' house. Amber had no interest in looking out the window to see what had happened. The world didn't exist outside the tangled sheets of her bed, still warm from their love-making.

'What are you thinking?' she asked Karl.

She couldn't help herself, even though every magazine she'd ever read said that this sort of question was a Bad Idea. She didn't think she was a needy person, but there was something about this intimate moment after lovemaking, that made her want to know. She'd been a physical part of Karl. She wanted to be inside his head too, inside for ever, always a part of him.

'Nothing. Except how beautiful you are.'

Karl shifted, laying his leg over hers, trapping her.

As fresh heat swelled in her belly, Amber realised that there was nothing more erotic than the feeling of naked skin against naked skin. Just lying there after the most incredible lovemaking was almost beyond description.

She ran questing fingers along his powerful chest, feeling the curve of his muscles, the sensitive nubs of his nipples, so different from hers.

She'd seen men's bodies before, but never fully naked except on a canvas or on a plinth carved from finest Carrara marble. And marble felt different from the warm, living beauty of a man's body beside hers, inside hers. Desire rushed through her veins again. Why had nobody told her love-making could be like this? All those talks about pregnancy, AIDS and being emotionally ready, nobody had said how utterly addictive it all was.

'We should get up,' Karl said. 'It's after six. Your mother will be home soon.'

Half six, Amber had said. Her mother ran her life on a strict schedule. Half six home, change out of her office suit by 6.35, dinner on the table – pre-prepared from the night before, obviously – by seven.

Amber used to love the comfort of their evening routine.

It made home seem like a refuge. No matter how much life changed in the outside world, her mother put dinner on the table at seven. But lately, Amber found herself telling Ella that when she moved out of home, she'd never have a schedule as rigid as her mother's as long as she lived. Life was about being a free spirit, not a slave to the clock or the powers of good kitchen cleaning products, or having to hear the oft-repeated phrase 'a good education and you can go anywhere, Amber'.

Right now, education suddenly seemed so boring. Her mother's view of life was stifling and there was no escape from it. And Mum would hate Karl, who was a free spirit, would hate his intrusion into their tightly run lives. It wouldn't be the two of them any more. It would be a different twosome, Amber decided firmly: her and Karl.

She slithered over until she was astride Karl, her long tawny mane a tangle over his lightly tanned shoulders. 'We don't have to get up,' she said, smiling. 'We've ages yet.'

There was so much they could do in that precious twenty minutes.

'And if my mother arrives home early, you can always hop out the back window and climb down the flat roof of the kitchen.'

Her mother was still paying off the credit union loan for the kitchen extension, a fact that often brought a worried look to her face.

Money: that was another subject Amber never wanted to worry about again, along with timetables and exams. Karl was going to be a famous musician and they'd have loads of money. Enough to pay off her mother's debts, enough to buy anything Amber wanted.

Just once, she'd love the thrill of shopping and never looking at the price tag. Wouldn't it be glorious to spend without worrying or feeling guilty over it?

'The neighbours will call the cops if they see a strange bloke hop out of your bedroom on to the kitchen roof and down the lane.' Karl put both hands around her waist and splayed his fingers.

Amber was proud of her tiny waist. She'd inherited her mother's hourglass figure, although, thank God, she hadn't inherited her total lack of interest in looking good. Her mother wouldn't have been seen dead in the clothes Amber wore: slivers of vintage fabric that barely covered her breasts, low-rise jeans that revealed more than a hint of bare skin. Mum just never bothered making herself look good or showing off her waist.

Amber arched her back as Karl's fingers moved up to cradle her ribcage. She didn't want him to go. They had plenty of time.

'Everyone's at work or cooking kids' dinners,' she said, feeling sympathy for anyone engaged in such boring duties. 'Nobody will see you.'

There was only one person on the street who might possibly know she had phoned in sick to school and might wonder at her having a strange guy in the house, and that was Mrs Devlin.

Amber approved of Christie Devlin, even if she was old and, therefore, should be totally wrinkly, boring and incapable of remembering what it was like to feel alive. For all Christie's silver hair, she had a way of looking at Amber that said she knew what was going on in the girl's head. Scary. Amber wondered if Christie would know by looking at her that Amber had just had the most incredible sex of her life.

Losing-her-virginity sex. She'd nearly done it eighteen months ago, with cute but dopey Liam, who was a friend of Ella's youngest brother. She'd called a halt to the proceedings just in time. Liam's hand was burrowing into her jeans and she'd realised that she was about to have sex with a guy just to see what it was like rather than because she would die then and there if she didn't.

A woman had the right to say no at any point, her mother had said in one of her talks about sex.

'Whaddya mean, you don't want to after all?' demanded Liam, who clearly didn't agree with Amber's mother on the whole issue of coitus interruptus.

'I mean no,' said Amber. 'No means no. Got it?'

And although Liam hadn't spoken to her since – not a big worry – she was glad she'd said no when she did. Imagine having to live your whole life knowing you'd lost your virginity to an ordinary guy like Liam when you could have the memory of a man like Karl Evans?

This was sex with a man of the world, a twenty-five-year-old man with a future. He was her future. She was going to travel the world with him and discover life, with a big L. She'd be eighteen in less than three weeks. She could do what she wanted then. Nobody could stop her.

'So you'll come with us?' he asked, returning to the subject they'd discussed earlier, before they'd fallen into bed. 'If we're going to work with a producer in New York, we'll be gone at least six months. I'd hate to be away from you. I couldn't bear that.'

'I'd hate to be away from you too,' Amber answered, stroking his skin with exploring fingers.

This was love. Pure contentment flowed through her veins. Karl was so crazy about her that he wanted her to travel with his band to America to record their album.

He needed her, he said. He'd been writing songs like a man possessed since they'd met. 'You're my muse,' he'd said.

And Amber, who'd been told all her life how talented and special she was, believed him. She and Karl: they were the twosome now.

As the ambulance carted Una Maguire and her frantic

husband Dennis off to hospital, Amber gazed at her lover with shining, besotted eyes and imagined all the wonderful times they'd have. Her mother would flip when she discovered Amber wasn't going to art college after all, but Amber was an adult now, wasn't she? She could do what she liked. That, surely, was the point of all those years of 'you have the power to do what you want' conversations. Amber would do what she wanted and although she hated hurting her mum, Faye would have to live with it.

Faye left work early so she could dash into the mini-market near home and pick up a few last-minute bits. They were out of basmati rice and she'd defrosted a home-cooked vegetarian korma the night before.

Ordinary rice wouldn't work, it had to be basmati.

Near the checkout, she dallied briefly by the ranks of magazines and papers. She loved the interior decoration magazines but they were all so expensive, so she didn't splash out very often. But she felt weary this evening, and the house felt lonely when Amber was upstairs at her desk bent over old exam papers. Faye could do with a treat. Finally choosing a magazine with a supplement on bedrooms, she looked down and her eye was caught by the lead story in the local free newspaper.

*Developer's Deal With Council: 25 Apartments in Summer St Park*

She picked it up and moved to the checkout.

'They must have got it wrong. They can't be talking about the park here, opposite my house?' she said to the cashier.

'That's the one,' the woman said, scanning the groceries. 'Shame to rip up that lovely little park. I don't know how they get away with that type of thing. There won't be a bit of green left around here if the developers get their way.'

'But it's tiny,' Faye protested. 'And surely nobody's allowed to buy an actual park?'

A queue appeared behind her and Faye was in too much of a rush to stop to read the story, so she stuffed the paper into the top of her grocery bag and left. In her car, she read it all quickly with mounting horror.

The pavilion in the park was falling down and the council had decided to sell it, and the half-acre of land that accompanied it, to a developer in return for the developer building another park and a community centre on a sliver of waste ground a mile away.

'We're not tearing up the park,' insisted a council spokesperson. 'The park is staying. The pavilion was never part of the park. People just thought it was. We've every right to sell it because we can't afford to renovate it and it's dangerous, besides. Summer Street will still have its park.'

Except that it will be half the size and have a dirty big apartment block cutting out the sun, Faye thought furiously.

She drove home angrily. Amber would be just as annoyed to hear about this, she loved that little park. Honestly, why did things have to change all the time?

The evening walkers were out in force when Maggie left the beach at Salthill and got the bus back into the city. The bus was only half full and she sat a few seats behind a group of schoolgirls still in uniform.

Half listening to their chatter, she stared listlessly out the window. She'd come to no conclusions because she couldn't think about Grey. Her mind refused to cooperate, racing off on ideas of its own. She had to work late the next evening instead of Shona. Were they out of coffee? Should she and

Grey go to see the new Pixar film? Anything was better than thinking about what had just happened.

From the depths of her handbag, her mobile phone rang. On auto-pilot, Maggie retrieved it, saw that her father was calling and clicked answer.

'Dad,' she said, managing to sound bright. Her entire world hadn't just crashed and burned, no. All was well. Faking happiness – wasn't that what communicating with your parents was all about?

'What's up, Dad?'

'Hello, love, it's your mum.'

Maggie's hand flew to her chest.

'She's in hospital, she's broken her leg.'

A breath Maggie didn't know she'd been holding was released. 'I thought you were going to tell me something terrible,' she whispered, cupping her forehead in one hand with relief.

'It is terrible,' he went on. 'Your mother insisted they did a bone density scan in the middle of it all, and it seems she's got osteoporosis. The doctor says he doesn't know why she hasn't broken bones before.' Her father had to stop talking for a moment and gulped. 'I don't know what to do, Maggie. You know how your mum copes with everything and all, but she's taking this badly. She keeps saying she's fine but she's been crying. Your mother crying.'

He sounded shocked. Una Maguire could see the silver lining in every cloud and had taught her daughter that a smile was easier to achieve than a frown. Mum never cried, except at films where a child was hurt or the dog died.

'Maggie, I know it's not fair but could you come home for a couple of days ... ?'

Maggie could imagine her father standing obediently outside the hospital entrance, not using his mobile phone inside as per the instructions on the hospital walls, even though nobody else obeyed them.

Dad, with his wide-open eyes, his few strands of hair and his endearing inability to deal with daily life to the extent that Maggie felt he ought to wear permanent L-plates. Dad, who'd never seen her mum cry over anything.

'I'll be home tomorrow,' she said. 'Don't worry about a thing.'

It was, after all, the solution to everything.

You're running away, said a voice in her head: a voice that sounded remarkably like Shona when she was in Dr Phil mode. Shona loved Dr Phil and felt that America's favourite television doctor's principles could be applied to every life situation.

Are you doing the right thing? Ask yourself that. Would you advise a friend in a similar situation to do what you're doing? Will running away solve your problem? Dr Phil asked all the right questions and so did Shona.

No, no and no. Maggie knew the answers. But Dr Phil hadn't the benefit of Maggie Maguire's Guide to Life.

Don't stuff your bra to make your A-cups look like B-cups. Boys won't get close enough to notice but nasty girls from school will. Nobody wants to be No-Tit Maguire for a whole month, as Maggie knew from experience.

Guys who say things like 'I've never met anyone like you' are not lying, exactly, but probably don't mean it the way you think they do.

Maggie had a new piece of advice to add to the Guide:

When in doubt, put your running shoes on. Nothing will improve but at least you don't have to stare your defeat in the face on a daily basis. And if you can't see it, surely it can't be there?

In a trendy little internet café close to the apartment, she ordered a latte and a session on the web. Flicking through flights to Dublin, she found one that left the following afternoon, giving her time to pack as well as to negotiate with the library for emergency leave. When she'd booked it, she knew there was only one more big task left: to go home and say goodbye to Grey.

*Goodbye Grey, I'm going and we're selling up so you'll have to take your jail bait somewhere else from now on.*

No, too bitter.

*Bye, Grey, I'm going home to Dublin for a while to think. You cheating son of a bitch.*

Again, too bitter.

Maybe she ought to stick at *Goodbye, Grey.*

When she got back to the apartment, Grey and the remains of a Thai meal were both in the living-room area. Maggie didn't feel even mildly hungry.

The words 'You lying, cheating bastard' ran round in her head like a washing machine on final spin.

'Hello,' she said. See, not bitter.

'Honey.' Grey leapt off the couch and went to touch her, but the frozen look in Maggie's eyes stopped him. They stood several feet apart, staring at each other, misery on both their faces.

'I am so sorry,' Grey said, and he sounded it.

He honestly was sorry. But sorry that he'd had sex with a stunning blonde student or sorry he'd been caught? Bastard.

'I love you. You might not believe that, but I do.'

'Then why did you do it?' Maggie asked. She hadn't meant to ask anything, had meant to tell him bluntly she was going home for a while. But the question had shot out of her mouth before she could stop it.

Grey's gaze didn't falter, she had to give him that. 'I don't know,' he said dismally. 'She was there, I could have her ...

80

it sounds dumb, but I still love you, Maggie. You're different, special.'

The spinning washing machine still kept rattling out 'lying, cheating bastard' as Maggie struggled to make sense of Grey's words. Her heart was broken and this was his sticking plaster?

'She was there? Is that your only excuse, Grey? She was bloody well there? If I'm so special, why would you even want to make love with someone else whether she was there or not? If I'm so special, then you wouldn't want to look crossways at another woman, never mind screw one in our bed. IN OUR BED!'

He looked taken aback at this. Maggie was not a shouter.

'It wasn't making love, it was sex. It's not what you and I have. That's . . .'

'Don't tell me,' she snapped, 'special.' Infidelity must have a previously undetected side effect of robbing people of their linguistic skills. Even Grey. She had never known Grey to run out of words before.

'I'm not explaining it correctly,' he began.

'Oh yes, you are, and it still doesn't make sense. You're the one who says he's logical, I'm supposed to be the klutzy one who forgets her bank card numbers and can't program her mobile phone.' Maggie knew her voice was rising but she couldn't help it. If Grey was tongue-tied, her word power was on 110 per cent. 'So how can you come up with such an illogical explanation? If I'm so different and special, you shouldn't want sex or love with anyone other than me. Simple. QED. That's what I thought I was getting when we moved in together: fidelity, monogamy, no threesomes. Did I miss the briefing where you said we'd sleep with other people? Or were you just lying through your teeth when you said that I was the sort of woman you wanted, not a pneumatic blonde like all your previous girlfriends?'

'I wasn't lying and I do believe in fidelity, really,' Grey

said helplessly. He sat on the edge of the armchair, running a hand through his hair. He had such long, sensitive fingers, like a pianist, fingers that could elicit a ready response from Maggie. He still looked handsome and desirable, with sexily rumpled hair as if he'd been so lost in his books he had forgotten to comb it. Maggie, who spent all her time surrounded by books, had always found this combination of brains and beauty utterly captivating. She could totally understand Ms Peachy Skin wanting to sleep with him. Grey was gorgeous, clever, and powerful within his sphere, all wrapped up in one package.

Just not faithful.

'I love you, Grey, I don't look at other men,' she said. 'I don't think about anyone else but you, I almost don't see anyone else but you. If there was anyone else there, if Brad Pitt and George Clooney and Wesley Snipes and anyone else you can think of were there for the taking, you know what?' She paused. 'I'd still say no.'

'I know, I'm sorry, so sorry.' The long piano-player's fingers ran through his hair again and for a flicker of an instant, Maggie thought of his hands running through the girl's hair in the throes of passion, twisting it and pulling gently like he did with Maggie.

'I love your hair,' he'd mutter when they were naked together. Maggie almost never cut it now. Grey loved its length lying tangled on the pillow as he hung over her, cradling her face before he kissed her. He thought she was feminine and sexy, things Maggie had never felt in her life until he'd come along and made her feel them. Now he'd taken all that away.

When her mother or Shona or other people said she was beautiful, she didn't believe them. They loved her, they were being kind to her. But when Grey said it, she had believed him. He made her beautiful because she glowed from being with him.

That he had so much power over her made her feel help-less now. Going back to the sort of woman he'd had before her made it a double betrayal – a blonde with curves that Maggie would never have. She felt so hurt that she wanted to hurt him too.

'You're lying. You're not sorry, only sorry I got home early and ruined it all. You screwed her. In. Our. Bed,' she said slowly. 'That's not love and respect.' She paused. 'Were there others?'

A strange look touched his face briefly, a look of sheer guilt, and it was gone so quickly that only someone who loved his face and knew it in every mood would have noticed. But Maggie was that person. She noticed.

'No,' he said. She didn't believe him.

The armchair seemed to rise up to greet her. Collapsing into it, she hugged her knees to her chest, a gesture that said 'keep out'.

There had been others, of that she was sure and she wasn't strong enough to hear about them. Her mother was ill, crying and not coping. Her father was asking for her help. Maggie's world was topsy-turvy.

'Just tell me, what's so hard about fidelity?' she whispered, afraid she knew the answer.

It had to be her fault. This confirmed what she'd known all along. She'd always felt lucky to have Grey, astonished that he was with her.

Someone like Grey could manage faithfulness with other people, with one of those icy blondes, but not with her. For one of those women, the right sort of wife for a man with a political future in front of him, he'd have got married. But Maggie obviously wasn't the right sort of wife for him. She was an experiment between the Carolyn Bessette Kennedy types, the trophy women. She wasn't worth giving up other women for. That was what this was all about.

The demons of anxiety and the self-doubt she'd grown up with rushed back howling into her mind and it was as if they'd never been away.

'I'm sorry, Maggie, I swear this will never happen again, never.' He looked up at her but Maggie was away in her head, remembering the years when she'd lived with a permanent clench of anxiety in her gut.

Sunday nights were the worst, when the weekend was careening to an end and Monday loomed, Monday with Sandra Brody and her taunting crew who'd made it their mission in life to destroy Maggie Maguire. Maggie had never done anything to them but that didn't appear to matter. Maggie was the chosen scapegoat. Daily verbal torture and cruel tricks were her punishment. The self-loathing – because it had to be her fault, hadn't it? – felt just like it did now.

'I'm sorry, Maggie,' Grey repeated. 'I don't know why I did it. I wouldn't hurt you for the world.'

'Really?' she asked with a bitter laugh. Why was he bothering to pretend? She'd prefer it if he told her the truth: that he loved her but just not enough. She wasn't quite good enough.

'You're different, Maggie,' Grey began and sat at her feet, pulling both her hands from around her knees, trying to make her hold him. 'I love you, I never meant to hurt you. I am so, so sorry. Can't you forgive me?'

She whisked her hands away, but he laid his dark head on her chair, pleading, imploring. It would be so easy to reach out and touch him, make it all go away and start again. Go on holiday, sell the apartment, move somewhere else, anything to paper over the crack. Maggie felt her fingers reach out, an inch away from brushing the softness of his hair.

Marriage – that would be the ultimate Band-Aid. A sign that they were together despite it all. Her mum would love it if she got married. Poor Mum, always hoping for the fairy-tale ending for her daughter. But Grey had never discussed marriage with her. Perhaps she wasn't worth that, either.

Maggie's hand stilled on its way to his hair. She could forgive Grey, she could forgive him almost anything. But then it would happen again. Other women, who'd work at the university and pity her, understanding that a prince like Grey wouldn't be satisfied with just one woman. That was the price a woman like Maggie had to pay to be with a man like Grey. Why hadn't she realised that there was a trade-off, a price?

She pulled her hand away. She couldn't pay that price.

Suddenly, her running shoes seemed very inviting. Even home, the confines of Summer Street where her life had never been storybook perfect, was better than this.

It was familiar, somewhere she could lick her wounds. Shona and Dr Phil were probably wrong about running away. Now, staying was the hard option and running was easy.

Christie had cooked a beautiful goulash by the time she heard James's key in the lock.

Goulash in honour of her dear Hungarian friend, Lenkya, who'd once said, 'You can kill a man or cure him in the kitchen.' This had been nearly forty years before, when Christie's culinary expertise extended to making porridge or boiling eggs.

'Cooking is the heart of the home and is the place where the woman is queen,' Lenkya pointed out in the husky Hungarian accent that would have made the phone book sound fascinating, should she ever want to recite it.

Lenkya had lived below Christie in a house on Dunville Avenue that contained a veritable warren of bedsits.

'If you can kill in the kitchen, I'll end up in the dock for murder,' Christie had said merrily.

She was dark-haired then and when she and Lenkya walked the half-mile to Ranelagh to buy groceries, people often mistook the two women with their flashing dark eyes, hand-span waists and lustrous curls for sisters.

'You should learn to cook,' said Lenkya, who could rustle up the tenderest stew from a handful of root vegetables, a scattering of herbs and a scraggy piece of meat. 'How have you never learned before this? In my country, women learn to look after themselves. I can grow vegetables, raise chickens, kill chickens, pouf –' She twisted both hands round an imaginary chicken's neck. 'Like that. If you are hungry, you soon learn.'

'My mother cooked for all of us, my father, my brothers and sister,' Christie told her. It was harder to explain the family dynamics which meant cooking was the only power her mother had ever had. Under Christie's father's thumb all the time, it was only when Maura was in front of her stove that she was in charge. If it was possible to kill or cure a man in the kitchen, Christie wondered how her mother had resisted the impulse to kill her overbearing husband.

James hadn't known Lenkya well, but he'd been benefiting from her cooking expertise ever since. Food was all about love, Christie knew now. Feeding your family, giving them chicken soup when they were sick, and apple cake to take away the bitterness in their mouth when they were lovelorn: that was how you could cure them. Love and healing flew out of her kitchen into her home. Her life was nothing like her poor mother's and she had no need of killing.

'Hello, Christie.' James put his arms round her and held her tightly. He smelled of the train, of dusty streets and other people's cigarette smoke. He looked, as he so often did these days, tired and in need of a long, long sleep.

'Hard day?' Christie took his briefcase and jacket, resisting the impulse to push him up to their room, tuck him into bed

86

and make him stay there until the exhausted look had gone from his face.

'Ah no, fine,' he said, removing his shoes and pulling on the old leather slippers he kept on the second step of the stairs. 'The trip takes it out of me, I don't know why. I'm sitting on the train half the day, not driving, so I should be in fine fettle.'

'Travelling is exhausting,' Christie insisted. 'There's a difference between sitting in your own armchair at home and sitting on a train at the mercy of leaves on the track, worrying about missing your meeting.'

'I'm hardly Donald Trump,' he joked.

'He has a limo, I'd say, so he's not at the mercy of the leaves.' Christie handed her husband a glass of iced tea. 'And someone else to drag his briefcase around after him. How did the meeting about the emissions go?'

'We're getting there. But one of the people was sick today, so there's a chance we'll have to go through it all again.'

'For heaven's sake,' exclaimed Christie. 'Surely if they're sick, they have to catch up with the rest of you, not the other way round.'

'You know how it works, love,' said James. 'For some people, the more meetings there are, the better. Then nothing actually gets done, but lots of minutes are typed up and the department's accounts' people are kept busy printing out expenses cheques for tea and coffee. Global warming won't kill the planet: bureaucracy will.'

He followed her into the kitchen and sat down on a low stool to pet the dogs, who'd been clamouring for love since he arrived.

He normally knelt on the floor to pet them, she knew. His hip must be bothering him again. Not that James would ever say so. Christie knew many women with husbands whose flu symptoms were always at least on a par with Ebola, if the patient was to be believed. She was the lone dissenting voice with a husband who never magnified his illness to the power of ten, which worried her because James could be having a heart attack in front of her and he'd probably say he had 'a bit of an ache' and that a moment sitting down would cure it. How could you look after a man like that?

'Now, what was that all about this morning?' he asked when Tilly's inner ears had been rubbed to her satisfaction and Rocket had snuffled wetly all over his shoes to establish that no other dogs had been admired that day.

'What was all what about this morning?' said Christie, feigning innocence.

'You know, the phone call when I'd only just left the house.'

'I was having an anxious day, that's all,' she relented. 'Sorry, I didn't mean to worry you but I had this awful feeling that something bad was going to happen to us.'

James pulled her over on to his knee and the dogs whimpered in outrage. This was their time for cuddling, not Christie's. Tilly stormed off to her bed to sulk.

'You can't take my weight on your hip . . .' Christie began. She knew it was stiff, she could see from the way he'd been walking that morning.

'Oh, shut up about my bloody hip, woman,' James said and held her tight. 'I love you, you daft creature, d'you know that? I love that you still worry about me.'

'Yes and I love you too, you daft man,' she replied. 'Even if your hip is aching and you won't mention it.'

'It's only a twinge.'

'I don't believe you. You'd be in agony, and you'd still say it was only a twinge. You're not impressing anybody with your stoicism,' she said crossly.

'It's not agony.'

'If your arthritis is playing up, it's not good to have me on your lap,' she said.

James laid his head against her cheek. 'The day I can't manage to have you on my lap,' he said, 'get them to shoot me.'

'They couldn't shoot you,' Christie murmured, hugging him. 'You're an endangered species.'

'Like the dodo?'

'The poor dodo's been and gone, sorry. You're more of a white tiger: rare and special.'

'You say the nicest things,' he replied, his lips close to her cheek.

'Impossible man,' sighed Christie, kissing him on the forehead and getting up. 'I made goulash.'

'Lenkya's recipe? Great, I love that.' James sat down at the table expectantly. 'Whatever happened to her? She hasn't been in touch for years, not since Ana was involved with that artist fellow and they were all here for the big exhibition in Dawson Street. Remember that? How many years ago is it?'

Christie opened her mouth but no sound came out. Fortunately the phone blistered into the silence and she leaped to answer it.

It was Jane from the Summer Street Café, with news that poor Una Maguire had been carted off in an ambulance after a fall.

'I knew you'd want to know,' said Jane, 'and that Dennis might not get round to telling people.' Which was a kind way of saying dear Dennis would be too flustered to brush his teeth and might need some hand-holding. Christie was good at that: calm in a crisis.

'I'll pop a note through their door telling him I'll drop in on Friday and to phone me if he needs anything before then,' Christie said and Jane hung up, knowing it was all taken care of now that Christie Devlin knew.

'Looks like your feeling of gloom was right after all,' James said as they sat down to their goulash. He'd opened a bottle of lusty red wine to go with the stew, even though it was only midweek, and they stuck pretty much to the wine only at weekends rule.

'Yes,' said Christie, thinking of the Maguires and how Dennis would cope with being the carer instead of the cared for. 'That must have been it, after all.'

But she wasn't telling the truth. Whatever dark cloud had moved over her head was still there, looming, promising bad things to come.

And James had mentioned 'that artist fellow' of Ana's, Carey Wolensky, who'd turned out to be one of the most famous painters of his generation. When James had carelessly referred to him, Christie had felt a shiver run right through her. She didn't believe in coincidence. Everything happened for a reason. There were tiny signs of the future everywhere and only the watchful spotted them. First her anxiousness, now this mention of a man she wanted to forget. Christie was scared to think of what it might all mean: her past coming back to haunt her. Why now?

90

# CHAPTER SIX

The next afternoon, Maggie's suitcases arrived together on the carousel. They looked shabby among some of the classier travellers' bags from the Galway to Dublin shuttle.

She hauled them off the belt with some difficulty, having murmured, 'No thanks, I'm fine,' to the man who'd leaped to offer to help the tall redhead in the trailing pale suede coat.

Her eyes were raw with crying and she kept her head down as she spoke, embarrassed by how she must look. The man probably felt sorry for her; thought she was one of those care in the community patients who rattled because of all the Xanax bottles in their pockets.

Maggie didn't need anyone feeling sorry for her today. She felt sorry enough for herself.

The first piece of luggage was the heaviest, a wardrobe-on-wheels affair that was fit to burst, only a bright purple strap preventing its internal organs splurging out over the concourse. An orange 'heavy item' sticker hung from the handle. The second was a hard candy-pink case that was a dead weight even when empty.

Grey used to joke that it had been cursed by so many

baggage people, it had probably developed magical powers itself.

'If our plane ever goes down, the pink case will be the only survivor, you wait and see,' he'd laugh.

Fresh misery assailed her at this thought of Grey and the fabulous holidays they had saved up for and shared before they'd bought the flat.

They'd never go away together again. Not when she'd be watching like a jailer every time he tipped a beautiful waitress or glanced at a woman on the beach. Only a fool would trust him again. Maggie was not going to be that fool. Last night she'd packed and said they'd talk later, trying to delay the inevitable argument in case she gave in.

'Would you like me to sleep on the couch?' Grey had asked, and she wanted to whisper: no, lie next to me and hold me. Tell me it'll be all right, it was a mistake, that you'll make it better.

'Yes, sleep on the couch,' she said, finding the strength from somewhere to say it.

*We'll try again, I know you love me,* her heart bleated.

But her head had to do the talking. Leaving this way was easier, because if she stopped and thought about actually losing him, about not sharing her life with him, Maggie was afraid she'd relent. And her head told her that staying would destroy her, in the end.

Gulping back a fresh batch of tears, she grabbed Cursed Candy Pink and shoved it on to the luggage trolley behind Wardrobe, ignoring the interested gaze of the man who'd tried to help her. She wished he'd stop *looking* at her. Honestly, what was wrong with people? Couldn't a person cry in public?

On top of the trolley, she dumped her handbag, a banana-shaped black leather thing that held everything, and cleverly deposited the most vital bits right at the bottom, thus deterring both purse-snatchers and Maggie from locating her money in shops.

She wheeled her trolley hopefully past the special mirrored section, holding her breath.

On those girls-only holidays to Greece, in the pre-Grey days, the others had always trooped through customs happily clinking contraband bottles of ouzo and Metaxa brandy, while she (the only one who'd actually read the customs bit of paper about only importing 200 fags and giving notice if they'd been loitering near goats) was the one to have to unpack her case in public.

Today, fortunately, the customs people behind their two-way mirrors resisted the impulse to go through Maggie's blameless luggage.

Then she was out into arrivals, into the spotlight, where hundreds of eager people scrutinised and rejected her as they searched for whichever special person they'd come to meet so they could wave their welcome home placards, wobble their helium balloons and scream 'hello!!!'

It brought home to Maggie that she had no special person any more. The person for whom she used to be special had cheated on her. God, it hurt.

Trying to look cool, as though she didn't care, she was thankful when her mobile rang and she could busy herself answering it.

'We're home from the hospital,' said her father happily. 'Where are you, love? Are you nearly here yet? Will I boil the kettle? Your mother can't wait to see you.'

Maggie felt the usual dual burst of affection and irritation reserved for conversations with her parents. The plane had only just landed, for heaven's sake. She'd already given Dad the details and told him to add another fifteen minutes for normal plane delays. Unless Clark Kent was bursting out of his Y-fronts in a telephone box nearby in order to whisk her off home at supersonic speed, she wouldn't reach Summer Street for another three quarters of an hour at least.

'Not quite, Dad,' she said, keeping her tone cheery. It was only because he cared. 'I've just come through arrivals.'

'Oh, right then. You'll be here in . . .'

'Less than an hour,' she said. 'See you then. Bye!'

She stuck the phone back in her jeans pocket and tried to ignore the feeling that the walls were closing in. She was back home. Back with nothing to show for five years away in Galway and the Maguire family clock – always at 'Where were you? Why didn't you phone? We were worried!' – was ticking once again.

Maggie manhandled all her worldly goods towards the door and the taxis. It was too late for the if-onlys but she went through them all the same – if only Grey hadn't screwed someone else, if only she hadn't witnessed it, if only he'd realised how much he loved her and pledged undying faithfulness instead of saying he couldn't help himself. If only she wasn't so stupid to fall for someone like him in the first place.

That's what it all came back to: her stupidity. An intelligent woman would have known that Grey, who could have had any woman, would one day stray. An intelligent woman would have got out before this happened. An intelligent woman would have made it calmly clear long beforehand that straying wasn't an option and that if he did, their relationship was over. For such a woman, Grey would have agreed.

But not for Maggie. For all that he'd said she was special, that he didn't want a pert blonde, he'd lied to her.

Now all she had to do was work out what to tell her parents. With luck, she'd have some peace on the ride home to adjust and get her story straight. They didn't need her in tears right now, with her mother in such distress.

\* \* \*

'. . . So you see, what the politicians don't realise is that if you have a system with toll roads, it's the people like myself who are paying for it . . .'

'Right, I see.'

The taxi driver's monologue was only stemmed by having to negotiate the tricky box junction just before St Kevin's Road. Since picking her up at the airport, he'd been talking at high speed about the price of property, chewing gum on car seats and now toll roads. Maggie hadn't felt able to interrupt. It would have been rude and in the grand scheme of things, there was no excuse to be rude, was there? Her mother's training had kicked in as usual.

Maggie was the one who got stuck with bores at parties, charity muggers in the street, and sweet bewildered people who wandered into the library for warmth and who ought to have been thrown out. She was too kind and too polite to say no or ignore people.

'That's what I said to that woman politician. I said: that's my opinion, Missus, and if you don't like it, don't get in my cab,' the taxi driver went on. 'Was I right to say it?' As with all the other questions he'd posed on the forty-minute trip, he didn't pause for a reply. 'I was right, you see. Nobody stands up to these people. Nobody.'

The taxi turned the corner, driving slowly past the Summer Street Café where people sat outside at the small tables, looking as if they hadn't a care in the world. Mum and Dad loved the café, loved the buzz of meeting people there. Mum would listen to all the gossip and pass it eagerly on to Maggie, forgetting that she'd lived away for five years and didn't know all the people they met.

Maggie, who didn't know all of the people in her Galway apartment block and clearly didn't know her boyfriend at all, had learned that the wild-eyed Mrs Johnson was off the sauce after failing the breathalyser test one night and losing her licence, that Amber Reid, the teenage girl who lived alone with her mother – lovely woman with a big job but never too busy to bake cakes for the Vincent de Paul fundraisers – was going to art college and would be a big star one day. Christie Devlin said she was a marvellous artist, and Christie would know, wouldn't she? Look at those lovely paintings Christie had done for Una's sixtieth. Maggie knew that the carrot cake muffins in the café were now sugar-free; oh, and she knew that Jane and Henry in the café had hired this lovely Chinese waitress.

'Xu her name is, although we call her Sue, because it's almost the same. Came all the way from China by herself, brave little thing, and not knowing anybody here. She'd put us to shame,' Mum had said. 'Learning English and working at the same time, and not knowing a sinner here. It must be terrible hard to leave your country and start again.'

Maggie loved the way her mother was so interested in people. Maggie used to be like that too, she realised, before she met Grey and became so wrapped up in him that she had no space or time left for anyone else. Yet how could she be totally involved with him and still not see the obvious? Love wasn't just blind, it was lobotomised.

In the back seat of the taxi, her thoughts miles away, Maggie realised they'd passed the third of Summer Street's maple trees and suddenly they were slowing down outside her house.

'Number forty-eight you said?' the driver asked.

'Yes, thanks,' she replied.

She scrabbled in her bag to pay him.

'Cheer up, gorgeous,' he said, beaming up at her from the window, 'it might never happen.'

True to form, Maggie managed a smile.

'See ya,' she said. There was no way she was going to tell him it had already happened.

She turned and stared at number 48. Home. It was one of the 1930s houses, white with dark beams painted on the front gable and diamond-paned windows. Part of the house was covered by the bronzed leaves of a Virginia creeper that had science fiction film capabilities to regrow no matter how often it was pruned back to the roots.

Maggie felt the years shrink away. Home made her feel not entirely like a child again but as if still under the influence of all the old childhood problems.

Her father met her at the gate, dressed up in his going-into-the-hospital outfit of navy blazer and tie, but still comfortingly familiar. When he put his arms around her, Maggie snuggled against him like the child she once was, even though he was shorter than her and as skinny as ever.

'It's so lovely to have you home,' he said. 'Thank you for coming. I know it's a lot to ask, but thank you.'

'How could I not come?' admonished Maggie, pulling away briskly. If she let her reserve drop, she'd sob her heart out. Better to be brusque and not give them a chance to ask after Grey. She'd tell them later, when she – and they – felt stronger.

'How's Mum?'

'Much better today.' Her father's face brightened. 'She got an awful shock, you know. It was all so quick. One minute we were here, the next, she'd passed out with the pain. I thought she was dead, Maggie,' he added, and he looked so forlorn that Maggie had to take a deep breath to steady herself.

'Where is she?'

'Where do you think?'

The kitchen at the back of the house was certainly the heart of the Maguire home. A cosy room which had been decorated at a time when there was no such concept in interior design as using too much pine, it was the room Maggie felt she'd grown up in.

Sitting in an armchair at the table (pine) with her plastered leg up on a kitchen chair (pine), watching the portable television that was perched on the *Little House on the Prairie* dresser (distressed pine), was Maggie's mother, Una.

As tall a woman as her daughter, she was just as slender but with faded red hair instead of Maggie's fiery curls. Their faces were very similar: perfect ovals with otherworldly cobalt-blue eyes and wide mouths that were always on the verge of a smile. But whereas Maggie's smile was tremulous, anxious, Una's was the all-encompassing beam of a woman who embraced life. Now Una sat listlessly in the chair, as if breaking her leg had taken the strength out of all her bones. Beside her was the crossword, nearly finished.

'I've left the hard ones for your father,' Una said, which was the standard and affectionate lie in the Maguire household.

Dennis was no good at crosswords. A champion at the Rubik's Cube, and deeply sorry when that had gone out of fashion, he was marvellous with gadgets, figures and magazine quizzes where you had to work out which tetrahedron was the odd one out.

But words defied him.

'What'll I say?' he used to beg Maggie when he had to write the only birthday card his wife didn't write for him.

'To Una, happy birthday, I love you so much, Dennis,' was Maggie's usual suggestion.

It was what she'd have liked written on a card to her. Grey, for all his eloquence, hadn't been much good at cards either, although Maggie had kept every single one he'd given her.

Mum hugged Maggie tightly, then somehow managed a final squeeze and whispered in her ear: 'We're so glad you're here, Bean.'

Bean or Beanpole was her nickname, so given because she'd been long and skinny as a child.

'Like a beanpole!' her cousin Elisabeth used to say joyfully.

Elisabeth, also tall but with Victoria's Secret model curves instead of Maggie's racehorse slenderness, was never called anything but Elisabeth.

While Dennis bustled off with Maggie's suitcases, Una told her daughter that the osteoporosis was advanced.

'They can't believe I haven't broken anything before,' she said finally. 'It's a bit of a miracle, and at my stage, I could end up breaking bones with just a knock against a bookcase.'

Maggie was shocked. 'Oh, Mum,' she said. 'That's terrible. Dad said it was osteoporosis but he never said it was that bad.'

They heard Dennis coming back.

'I don't want him to know everything,' her mother went on. 'It'd only worry him and what's the point of that?'

'He ought to know, Mum.'

'Ah, why? It won't be good for his heart if he's watching me every moment worrying about me. I'll be fine.'

Maggie's father came back into the kitchen.

'What'll we have for dinner?' said Una breezily. 'I can't wait for a decent meal. Your poor dad is doing his best but he can only do soup and rolls. How about a roast? I fancy beef.'

'Roast beef? Is there beef in the fridge?' Maggie asked.

Her mother looked blank. 'I don't know, love. I can't get near the fridge. But look. Or you could go to the shops. The car's there.'

At that instant, Maggie began to feel panicky. Everything was more serious than she'd thought.

Her father wasn't exactly one of life's copers. He'd never been able to cook, and viewed both the iron and washing machine as arcane specimens, beyond his ability. Her mother had done everything in the Maguire household.

And yet here she was, expecting Maggie, who had just arrived, to know what was in the fridge, not to mention to feel confident hopping into a car she had never driven before and going to the supermarket. Maggie had passed her driving test when she was a teenager but she'd never owned a car and could barely remember the difference between all the pedals.

Had breaking her leg broken something else in her mother too?

'Mum,' Maggie said, feeling horrendously guilty at not being able to do this simple thing in a family crisis, 'I can't drive. You know I can't.'

She looked into the fridge. There were several big chill-cabinet cartons of soup, half a pack of butter and eggs. Nothing else. 'We shop from day to day,' her father added helpfully. 'I'll stay with your mother.'

Maggie shut the fridge. She was in charge. She wondered how this had happened. She was not qualified for this. Her mother was the one who was in charge.

'You'll be able to go, won't you?' Una's voice quavered slightly.

With frightening clarity, Maggie saw that their roles had swapped. One cracked femur and she was the parent.

She had no option.

'I'll do a shop right now,' she said firmly. 'The mini supermarket will have everything we need. I'll walk.'

Speedi Shop on Jasmine Row had been open from dawn to dusk since Maggie had been in infant school. More expensive than the proper supermarket a mile away, it was always busy but there were never any long queues at the checkouts, mainly because Gretchen, the owner, didn't encourage chitchat. She was, however, an interrogator of Lubyanka standards and Maggie had always felt that Gretchen was terrifying. She didn't smile much and when she did, her forehead and face remained static, as if filled with Botox, although it was hard to imagine Gretchen spending the money on such a thing. Beauty, a bit like politeness, was a waste of time in Gretchen's book.

She was there behind the counter when Maggie arrived at the checkout, her basket spilling over with the makings of a roast dinner, shop-bought apple pie and ice cream for pudding.

'Maggie Maguire, a sight for sore eyes. Long time no see. I thought you were living in married bliss in Galway.'

Maggie translated this bit of faux politeness in her head: *fancy seeing you here, and is it true you're not married at all but still shacking up with some fellow who clearly won't marry you?*

'Home for a few days,' said Maggie, aiming for the happily unconcerned approach. Had Gretchen X-ray vision? Could she see that Maggie's man had cheated on her? It wouldn't surprise her if the answer was yes. 'And I'm not married, actually, I've a long-term partner.'

Translation: *I am a fulfilled woman who has made interesting life choices and wouldn't be bothered getting married when I could live the free life of a modern feminist unshackled by silly old wedding vows.*

'Right.' Gretchen nodded appraisingly and began to scan Maggie's groceries. 'You remember my Lorraine, don't you? You were in the same year in school. Lorraine's living in Nice, married to this gorgeous French pilot, Jacques, with three kids and a live-in nanny. You should see their house: Jacuzzi, pool, bidet in every en suite, the lot.' *I don't buy your story,* said her eyes. *Long-term partner, my backside. Now Lorraine, she's a success story. She has it all: fabulous husband, children, everything money can buy. She's not home with her tail between her legs at the age of thirty with no ring and no kids either.*

'How wonderful for her,' Maggie said, adding a large bar of chocolate to the basket to comfort herself. 'Lorraine always knew what she wanted, didn't she?' She snatched back her shopping and shoved it into a bag. *Lorraine was a hard-nosed little madam and she was always keen on self-improvement without doing any actual work. Like stealing other people's homework or hanging round with the class bullies.*

'Bye, Gretchen, have to rush.'

On her way home with the grocery bags weighing her down, Maggie passed the time by trying to remember who lived in the various houses on Summer Street. Many of them were still owned by the people who'd lived there when she was a child, like the Ryans, who bred Burmese cats and never minded the neighbourhood children coming in to coo over the latest batch of apricot-coloured kittens. Or sweet Mrs Sirhan, who'd looked eighty when Maggie had been small, and now must be unbelievably old, but still went for her constitutional every day, up the street into the café for a cup of Earl Grey with lemon.

There was a sign on the park gate: 'Save Our Park', written in shaky capitals on a bit of cardboard, and Maggie idly wondered what the park had to be saved from. But the sign-writer hadn't thought to add that bit of information. Rampaging aliens, perhaps? Or people who didn't scoop the dog poop?

The old railway pavilion was her favourite part of the park: she'd played in it many times during her childhood and it was easy to imagine it as a train station, with ladies in long dresses sobbing into their reticules as handsome men left them behind, sad stories behind every parting. There hadn't been a train that way for many years.

The train tracks were long gone, too. Maybe that was the lesson she needed to learn: nobody cared about the past. Her misery over Grey would mean nothing in a hundred years.

102

It was ten before Maggie managed to escape to bed and to her private misery. She'd left her mobile phone unanswered all day and when she finally checked there were seven *where are you?* texts from Shona, along with two missed calls and one *I am so sorry, please answer your phone* text from Grey.

Yeah, right, Maggie thought furiously, erasing it. One lousy text and a couple of phone calls. What an effort that must have been. Feeling angry with Grey was easier than giving in to feeling hopeless and alone. If she let go of the anger, she'd collapse under the weight of the loneliness.

She unwrapped the giant bar of milk chocolate she'd bought and dialled the only person in the world, apart from Shona, who might possibly understand: her cousin Elisabeth. Despite coming up with the nickname Bean, Elisabeth was one of Maggie's favourite people.

Elisabeth was tall, athletic, had been captain of the netball team and was wildly popular at her school, a fact that had often made Maggie wish they'd gone to the same one. She might have protected Maggie. She was now a booker in one of Seattle's top model agencies and incredibly, despite all these comparative riches, she was a nice person.

It was eight hours earlier in Seattle and Elisabeth was on her lunch break, sitting at her desk with her mouth full of nuts because she was still doing the low-carb thing.

'How are you doing?' asked Elisabeth in muffled tones.

'Oh, you know, fine. You heard about Mum's accident?'

'Yes, Dad told me.' Her father and Maggie's were brothers. 'You don't sound OK,' she added suspiciously.

Elisabeth picked up tones of voice like nobody else. Certainly nobody else in the Maguire family, who all had the intuition of celery. 'What's up?'

'I told you.'

'I mean what else?'

'You can hear something else in my voice?'

'I spend all my life on the phone to young models in foreign countries asking them how they are, did anybody hit on them and are they eating enough/drinking too much/taking coke/screwing the wrong people/screwing anybody. So yes, I can hear it in your voice,' insisted Elisabeth.

'I caught Grey in bed with another woman.'

Silence.

'Fuck.'

'I didn't know you were allowed to say that outside Ireland any more,' Maggie remarked, in an attempt at levity. 'Everyone on your side of the Atlantic nearly passes out when they hear it, when here, it's a cross between an adjective and an adverb, the sort of word we can't do without.'

'Desperate situations need desperate words,' said Elisabeth, then said 'fuck' again followed by, 'Fucking bastard.'

'My sentiments exactly.'

'Is he still alive?'

'He has all his teeth, yes,' Maggie said.

'And they're not on a chain around his neck?'

Maggie laughed and it was a proper laugh for the first time all day. Elisabeth was one of those people with the knack of making the unbearable slightly more bearable. With her listening, Maggie didn't feel like the only person on the planet to have been hurt like this before.

'No, they're still in his mouth. I did think about hitting him but he was attached to this blonde fourteen-year-old at the time . . .'

'A fourteen-year-old!' shrieked Elisabeth.

'Metaphorically speaking,' Maggie interrupted. 'She's probably twenty or twenty-one, actually. Gorgeous, from the angle I was looking from. Which was really a bummer. I mean, if she was ugly and wrinkly, I might manage to cope, but being cheated on with a possible centrefold doesn't do much for your self-confidence.'

'Oh, Maggie,' said Elisabeth and there was love and pity in her voice. She'd long since given up trying to boost Maggie's self-esteem, although having a beautiful cousin with a skewed vision of her gorgeousness was perfect training for working with stunning size six models who thought they were too fat and faced rejection every day. 'I wish I was there to give you a hug. What did you do?'

'Dad phoned about Mum, so I left to come here. Ran away, in other words, which is what I'm good at.'

'You haven't told them.'

'No. Couldn't face it.'

Maggie heard muffled noises at Elisabeth's end.

'Sorry, I've got to go. Call me tomorrow?'

'Sure.'

Maggie looked at her suitcases waiting patiently to be unpacked. It was hard to feel enthusiastic about moving back into her childhood bedroom. All she needed now was one of those big doll's heads that you put eye make-up on, her old Silver Brumby books, and she'd be eleven again.

She'd read so much as a child, losing herself in the world of books because the outside world was so cruel. And yet she hadn't learned as much as she'd thought she had: books taught you that it would work out right in the end. They never envisaged the possibility that the prince would betray you. They never pointed out that if you gave a man such ferocious power over your heart, he could destroy you in an instant.

She finished her bar of chocolate slowly.

If everything had been different, she'd have been at home now in her own flat with Grey.

Without closing her eyes, she could imagine herself there: sitting on their bed, talking about their day, all the little things that seemed mundane at the time and became painfully intimate and important when you could no longer share them. Like waking up in the night and feeling Grey's body, warm

105

and strong beside her in the bed. Like leaning past him at the bathroom sink to get to the toothpaste.

Like hanging his T-shirts on the radiators to dry. These things made up their life together. Now it was all gone. She felt betrayed, broken and utterly hollow inside.

She was back in her childhood bed with nothing to show for it.

# CHAPTER SEVEN

Mrs Devlin's art classes were different from any other lesson in the school, agreed all the girls in the sixth year. For a start, Mrs Devlin herself was not exactly your average teacher, although she was older than many of the others. Even her clothes bypassed normal teacher gear, whether she wore one of her long honey suede skirts and boots with a low-slung belt around her hips, or dressed down in Gap jeans and a man's shirt tied in a knot around the waist. Compared to Mrs Hipson, headmistress and lover of greige twinsets and pearlised lipstick, Mrs Devlin was at the cutting edge of bohemian chic.

Most of all, the girls agreed, it was her attitude that made her different. The other teachers seemed united in their plan to improve the students whether they wanted to be improved or not. But Mrs Devlin, without ever exactly saying so, seemed to believe that people improved themselves at their own rate.

So on May the 1st, with just weeks to go to the state exams and with the whole teaching body in a state of panic, Mrs Devlin's assignment to her sixth-year class was to 'forget about the exams for a moment and paint your vision of Maia, the ancient pagan goddess who gave her name to May and who was a goddess of both spring and fertility'.

'As today's the first of May, it's the perfect day for it.'

She stopped short of pointing out that the exam results probably wouldn't matter in a millennium. Not the way to win friends and influence people in a school. 'You've all been working so hard with your history of art,' Christie added as she perched on the corner of the desk at the top of the class. She rarely sat down at the desk during art practicals, preferring to walk around and talk to her students: a murmured bit of praise here, a smile there. 'I thought it might be nice to spend one hour of the day enjoying yourselves, reminding yourselves that art is about creativity and forgetting about studying.'

The class, who'd come from double English where they were re-butchering *The Catcher in the Rye* for exam revision, nodded wearily.

The most art they got to do these days involved colouring in their exam revision timetables with highlighter pens – generally a lot more fun than the revision itself.

'Maia is the oldest and most beautiful of the seven stars called the Seven Sisters, or the Pleiades,' Christie continued. 'The Pleiades are part of the constellation of Taurus, which is ruled over by Venus, for those of you interested in astrology. Maia is around five times larger than our sun.'

It was such a sunny morning that flecks of dust could be seen floating on shafts of light filtering in from the second-floor windows. St Ursula's was an old building, with decrepit sash windows and huge sills perfect for sitting on between classes and blowing forbidden cigarette smoke out into the netball court below.

'In art, spring is represented, as you know, by the sense of sensuality and passion,' Christie went on. 'Can anyone remember any artists who painted spring in such a way?'

'Botticelli,' said Amber Reid.

Christie nodded and wondered again what Amber had

been getting up to on Wednesday. The way she'd been dressed and the joy in her step made Christie damn sure that Amber had been on her way to some illicit activity.

'Yes, Amber, Botticelli is a good example. Remember, girls, artists didn't have television to give them ideas, or films. They looked at their world for inspiration and got it from nature. Keep that in mind during the exam, they were influenced by their times. By war, poverty, nature, religion. As we discussed in art history last week, religion is important as an influence on artists. Remember the puritanical Dutch schools with their hidden messages.

'Today's the pagan festival of Beltane, which is why May is called Bealtaine in Irish, and it's a celebration of spring, warmer days, blossoming nature and blossoming of people too. Of course, the Church wasn't too keen on pagan festivals, but they're part of our history too, so it's interesting to know about them. You paint, I'm here if you need me.'

The class were silent as they considered painting a fertility goddess. At St Ursula's in general, sexuality was given a wide berth by the teaching staff. Even in sex education classes, the concept of passion was diluted, with scientific words like 'zygote' giving students the impression that it was a miracle the human race had gone on for so long considering how boring procreation sounded.

'Is it true that Titian only painted women he'd gone to bed with?' asked Amber suddenly, her eyes glittering.

Christie had a sudden flash of knowledge: a picture of Amber and a dark, moodily dangerous young man came into her mind, entwined on a childhood bed doing grown-up things. Christie knew exactly what Amber had been up to the day before. She blazed with burgeoning sexuality. To embody Maia, Amber just needed to paint a self-portrait.

Christie felt a rush of pity for poor old Faye who probably hadn't a clue that her teenage daughter had just taken one

109

of the giant steps into womanhood. Having sons was definitely easier than daughters, she thought gladly. Sons were rarely left holding the baby.

'So I believe,' said Christie carefully. 'Paint, Amber,' she whispered, 'don't talk.'

'I swear Mrs Devlin'd bring in nude life models if she was let,' groaned Niamh to Amber. Niamh was struggling with art in general and was sorry she hadn't done home economics instead. How was she going to embody a fertility goddess? Couldn't they please do a still life instead – a couple of bananas or a nice simple apple?

'I wish she did bring in nude models,' said Amber, glaring at Niamh. 'It's impossible to learn to draw people properly with their clothes on.' At least in art college, she'd be able to study line drawing properly with nude models . . .

But she wasn't going, was she? She was going to New York with Karl, before the exams, and she had to tell her mother all this, and soon.

'It's not as if you haven't seen a man with no clothes on, Niamh,' added the girl on the other side of Amber with a wicked grin. 'You've been going out with Jonnie for a year now, don't tell me he's kept his boxers on all this time.'

It was Niamh's turn to grin. 'He's worth drawing, all right. And he's got a bigger you-know-what than all those Michelangelo statues!'

The back of the class dissolved into filthy giggles, but were sure Christie, who was walking sedately around the art room, couldn't have heard the remark.

Silvery-white hair was a fabulous disguise, Christie thought as she managed not to smile. Schoolgirls appeared to think that white-haired equalled deaf, which meant she overheard all manner of things she mightn't have heard otherwise. These girls probably would have been stunned to think that their esteemed art teacher had made the same jokes once, a lifetime

110

ago, when she was as young and when men's heads turned to look at her.

Young people always imagined that sex and passion had been invented by them. Christie fingered the gold and jasper scarab necklace that James had once bought for her in a market in Cairo, and smiled.

When you were over the age of sixty, if you hinted at a moment of wildness in your youth, people smiled benignly and imagined you meant a reckless time when you'd sat in a public bar and drank a pint of Guinness when such a thing was frowned upon. But she'd known plenty of passion. Still did. Being a stalwart of the local church didn't mean she was dead from the neck down, no matter what the youngsters thought.

That holiday in Cairo had been before the children were born, when she and James had been able to take advantage of a cheap week-long trip. They'd sighed with pleasure over the treasures of the Egyptian Museum by day, and lay in each other's arms in their shabby hotel by night with the overhead fan not quite doing its job.

Despite that, they'd made love every night, caught up in the sensuality of Cairo with its iconic sights, and the heady perfume of the spice markets.

The heat was an incredible aphrodisiac, James said, on the last night of their holiday, as he lay back against the pillows, sated, and watched his wife standing naked in the moonlight in front of the hotel-room mirror.

'Just as well we don't live here all the time, then,' Christie teased, admiring the necklace that lay between her full, high breasts. 'I love this,' she said, holding it tenderly. 'Thank you.'

'You do understand that I'll want to rip your clothes off every time you wear it?' he asked.

'Even in the supermarket?'

111

'We'd probably have to wait till we got to the car park,' he amended. 'Wouldn't want to bruise the avocados.'

'How about we introduce a one-hour rule? Once you notice the necklace, we have one hour to get to bed.'

James grinned lazily. 'Sounds good to me.'

No, she thought now, watching her class concentrating on their drawing boards: young people thought that old age was at best fifteen to twenty years older than they were, and reckoned your life was over once you hit forty. They'd learn one day.

Christie had no teaching in the period before lunch, so she headed for the staff room to mark the art history revision test the fifth years had handed in earlier. St Ursula's staff room was in the original, 1940s part of the school, surrounded by small classrooms with creaky wooden doors, crumbling parquet floors and thick walls that you couldn't hammer a nail into. The staff room itself was the biggest room in this section of the building and, in the fifteen years she'd worked in the school, Christie had decided it had a routine about it, an ebb and flow rather like a sea.

There was the calm of half past eight in the morning, when Christie sat at the long veneered table with its decoration of mug rings and drank green tea while she mentally prepared for the rest of the day.

By 8.45, the staff room would have filled up, the teachers all business, fuelling up on murderous coffee from the large catering tin.

By late afternoon, the tide had swept steadily out and no amount of coffee could raise the energy of the staff as the clock ticked on towards four and freedom.

Once, when an Italian teacher – Gianni, a man who looked as if he'd love to whip you off to bed and teach you how to roll your 'R's properly – had arrived to teach languages, there had been talk of buying a proper coffee-making machine.

112

'This ees muck, this coffee,' Gianni would say when he caught the rest of the teachers listlessly spooning brown dust into their mugs. 'If we had a proper machine, then you would have coffee worth dreenking.'

A coffee machine collection had been started, not to mention a few diets, but then Gianni had decided that he missed the Italian climate too much, and had gone home to Florence.

Christie, who'd been immune to Gianni's Paco Rabanne-scented charms and wasn't as heartbroken as the rest of them by his abrupt departure, suggested they buy a small television with the coffee machine fund.

'Not to watch junky soap operas on,' insisted Mr Sweetman, who taught English.

'What's wrong with soap operas?' demanded Mademoiselle Lennox, French.

'You're both so busy, you probably won't get to watch much but the lunchtime news,' Christie remarked gently and there was much muttering in agreement.

The news, yes, that's what they'd watch. Keeping in touch with current affairs was vital, Mr Sweetman agreed.

The television was now a much valued part of the room, with the channel screening *Who Wants to Be a Millionaire* repeats being the favourite. Mr Sweetman was currently top of the league having got to the quarter of a million question four times, with Mrs Jones, physics and applied maths, in second place.

Today, the TV was off, though, and only Christie and Liz, who taught home economics and biology, were there. Christie pulled the uninviting pile of essays towards her.

She'd only had two classes that morning, but she felt tired because she'd slept so badly, waking three times in the clammy grip of a cold sweat after nightmares, one particularly horrible one involving a sea of giant black spiders which burned people

113

they touched. She often had vivid dreams – the downside of her gift of intuition. But giant spiders? Very strange.

Eventually, she had stopped trying to sleep and did her best to lie quietly, eyes closed, amusing herself by imagining how useful the inside of her head might be to a roomful of psychiatrists.

Some people left their bodies to medical science – she might leave her brain because there was definitely something weird going on in there.

'Are you all right, love?' James had murmured drowsily at half five when Christie had given up on the psychiatrists, slipped out of bed and pulled on her jeans and a T-shirt.

'Fine, I'm fine. You go back to sleep, pet,' she'd replied, gently pulling the pale-blue sheet over his shoulders.

James's nightmares had to do with losing his job or not having money to buy food for his family. Christie had long ago decided that he could do without hearing about her horror movie versions. Now her eyes felt gritty with tiredness and the nagging sensation of doom was still there.

'Christie, how are you?' A voice interrupted her thoughts.

Liz, the other teacher, plonked herself and her 'You don't have to be mad to work here but it helps' mug down beside Christie and the untouched pile of essays.

'Busy?' she said, obviously hoping the answer would be no.

Liz was in her early thirties, attractive with dark curly hair, and had been a big hit with the pupils since she'd arrived at the school the previous September. She'd replaced eccentric Mrs Cuniffe who'd been at St Ursula's for over twenty years and refused to be in the same room as a microwave because of a story she'd heard about a man cooking his liver by accident. Eventually, this had made her position as home economics teacher untenable and Liz had arrived to take her place.

'I'm not really busy,' fibbed Christie. 'How are you?'

114

'Fine,' Liz began and stopped herself. 'Awful. Sorry.' Her eyes brimmed. 'I only wanted to say hello, not burst into tears.'

Christie reached into the tapestry bag that served as her briefcase, rifled a bit and came up with a pack of tissues.

It transpired that Liz was in love with a man who loved her back but felt it was all moving too fast, and perhaps they should see other people.

'He said he needs time,' wept Liz helplessly. 'We've been going out for a year. He's never mentioned this before, why does he need time? I don't know what to do, Christie. I love him. My sister says I should send him packing but she's never liked him. She thinks I'd be better off without him. He says we're still going to my brother's wedding as a couple, so it can't really be over, can it? What should I do?'

The hardest questions were often simplest, Christie thought. Stay and hope, or walk away to start again?

'I can't tell you what you should do, Liz,' she said gently. 'Only you know that.'

'But I don't.'

'Close your eyes and tell me what does it feel like in there?' Christie gestured at the place on Liz's chest where her heart resided.

Liz obediently closed her eyes and instantly her face lost some of its tension. Her shoulders slackened.

'I think it's over. He's being nice by saying he'll go to my brother's wedding with me and he thought it was all fun between us until I mentioned that I wanted a baby.' She snapped her eyelids open and stared at Christie in misery.

'Then it's over,' Christie said gently. She hadn't seen the future for Liz, she'd merely let Liz reach out and think the unthinkable herself.

'You're right. I was kidding myself, wasn't I? I think I always knew he wasn't in it for the long term,' Liz said sadly.

'I kidded myself because I wanted it so much. Looking back, I can see it all now and I should have done everything differently.'

'Looking backwards is a terrible thing,' Christie added, smiling. 'With the benefit of hindsight, there are lots of things we should have done and didn't, and vice versa. But we learn from them and do better next time.'

'You're being kind,' Liz whispered, getting up. 'I bet you've never been as stupid as me. You think before you act, Christie. I blunder along and convince myself that everything's fine when it's not. I only wish I could stop myself doing that. I wouldn't be in bits now if I did.' She bent to give Christie a small hug. 'You're very good for listening to me. I know why everyone says you're wise. You really are.'

The room was filling up again as lunchtime arrived. Liz took her cup and her folder and left Christie sitting at the table, frozen in thought.

For all the noise going on, all the chat about the third form's behaviour that morning and the traffic being a nightmare, Christie might as well have been sitting in a room all on her own. She heard nothing, except Liz's words. You think before you act, Christie.

Because there had been a few times when she'd acted before thinking, and one time in particular that haunted her. One stupid, awful thing she'd done and regretted ever since.

She thought she had put it out of her mind, filed in the memories best left forgotten box, and had tried to forgive herself ever since. And recently she had been thinking of it again and again and it was as red and raw as if it had all happened yesterday. How was it that she hadn't been wise then, when Ana had been involved with Carey Wolensky and the world had been a different place? And why did the memories of that time keep sneaking into her mind, so many years later? She simply didn't know.

116

Shane phoned her that afternoon as she walked home.

'Mum, I've something to tell you,' he said, after the how-are-yous.

Even in late-afternoon sun as she stopped on the footpath on Summer Street, Christie felt the shadow of fear over her again.

'Yes,' she said, dry-mouthed, thinking of all the terrible things that could happen to her beloved son.

'Janet's pregnant. We didn't want to tell anyone until she was three months gone and then, the other day, we thought she was having a miscarriage but she didn't and it's all fine.' Pride and joy sounded in every one of Shane's words.

It really was like having a great weight lifted from her. The fear fell away. 'Oh, Shane,' was all she could say. 'Oh, Shane, my love, I am so happy for you both.' She leaned weakly against a garden wall, her eyes focused on the park opposite where children played and dogs barked. Thank you, thank you, God, she prayed silently.

'That's the best news I've heard in a very long time,' she said. 'It's wonderful. I'm so happy for you both. How is Janet? Tell me everything.'

'Delighted, and so relieved after we thought she was going to lose the baby.'

Christie's mind flashed back. It was then the insight had started – something was about to go horribly wrong. She'd been right. Her grandchild had almost been lost from the world.

'She's had a scan, though, and everything's fine. You can see your third grandkid in a speckled black-and-white picture. We got one for you and Dad. Could we come over at the weekend and give it to you both?'

'I can't think of anything I'd like more.' Christie sighed with pure happiness. 'Shall I tell your father or did you want to phone him yourself?'

'I'll tell him.'

He sounded so like James at that moment: proud daddy-in-waiting, that Christie felt overwhelmed with the emotion of it all. She was so, so lucky.

'Let's have Ethan and Shelly and the girls over too, and maybe your Aunt Ana. Just a small family gathering on Sunday afternoon, not a party in case you think it's bad luck, but just us celebrating the baby getting this far. If you think Janet would like it?' Janet loved the Devlin family get-togethers but she might not be up to even a small one right now and Christie was never one to bulldoze.

'That'll have to be a few weeks away,' Shane said eagerly. 'We're going to a house-warming this weekend, and something else the next weekend, but I'm sure Janet would love a little party. It nearly killed us both not telling anyone. Well, Janet told her mum when she thought she was mis-carrying . . . I'm sorry, it's not that we were leaving you out, Mum . . .'

'Shane, you know me better than that,' Christie admonished. 'Girls tell their mothers more, it's the way of things. And I'd be some piece of work if that vexed me. Now, if we have the little party the Sunday after next, why don't you ask Janet's mum to come too?' she urged. Janet was an only child with a widowed mother. 'We'd love to have her here.'

'You're a star, Mum,' Shane said. 'Hey, you'll be up for babysitting, right?'

'Count me in,' Christie said fervently.

At home, humming happily as she thought about the good news, she spent an hour and a half cooking, then filled a basket with dishes for Una and Dennis Maguire. She hadn't heard yet that Maggie was home, and Dennis didn't know one end of the kitchen from the other. If it was left to him, the pair of them would starve. So Christie had made a huge stew, enough for two days, some chicken soup with her own home-made stock, and a dozen fat floury scones. Then she hurried up Summer Street to see Una.

'Christie, how lovely to see you,' said Una when Dennis led Christie into the kitchen.

'And you too.' Christie laid down the basket, pulled up a chair and sat beside her old friend, laying a comforting hand on Una's.

'This is terrible, Una. Such bad luck. How long will you be in plaster?'

'Six weeks,' said Dennis, hovering in the background anxiously. He was sorting out papers for recycling, a job his wife usually did efficiently, while he was getting in a muddle.

'Five and a bit now,' corrected Una. 'The doctors and nurses were lovely; said I'd be right as rain.'

This was clearly said for Dennis's benefit. Christie had felt the fragility of Una's bones as she'd touched her: instead of strength, she'd felt a spider's web of bone, fragile, tissue-thin. Christie had a sudden flash of the gleaming wheels of a wheel-chair in her mind and she hoped, as she often did when she saw something sad, that this was only one out of many possible futures. Her hand patted Una's in a gesture of under-standing and their eyes met in complicity.

'Dennis, you know, I believe I didn't shut the front door properly behind me,' Christie smiled at him. 'Perhaps you should check . . .'

'No bother,' he said, getting up. 'I have to put the rubbish out anyway and sort it out. It's the recycling collection next week instead of normal rubbish and I've got to tie up all the newspapers with string.'

'Is it *that* obvious I'm worse than I'm letting on?' Una said when he'd bustled off.

'Only to me,' Christie replied. 'What did they really say?'

'I wish I had your gift,' Una sighed. 'It must be great to know things, to see what's up ahead, although I don't know if I'd have liked to see this.' She looked morosely at her leg in its plaster cast.

'My gift?' asked Christie, genuinely surprised. She still rarely talked about what she could do. And she'd certainly never talked about it with Una. Not everyone approved of the concept of visions and she'd never wanted to be labelled a dotty old dear.

'You see things, don't you? My mother had a friend like you, she read the cards for us when I was younger.'

'I don't read cards,' Christie said. 'I think I had it engrained in me as a child that the Church didn't condone anything like that, but you're right, I do see things sometimes. Not so much the future, as what might be. I can't see for people close to me,' she added quickly, in case Una asked her what her future held. 'If I could see everything, I'd have seen that you knew!'

'You can see when people are lying, though?' Una asked perceptively.

Christie nodded. 'It's more intuition than anything,' she added, which wasn't entirely true. 'I knew you weren't as well as you said. What did the doctors say?'

'It's osteoporosis, quite advanced,' Una said. 'My mother had it, you see, so I pushed them to do a bone scan in the hospital, although they kept going on about how I could have it done later, and I insisted. Seems it's a miracle I haven't broken things before. I'm going to have to be careful now or I'll be like a mummy in a film, all bandages trailing after me.'

'How's Dennis coping?'

'Maggie's back, so she's looking after us both,' Una pointed out.

'And is she well?' asked Christie warmly.

'Great,' said Una with pride. 'She's just nipped off to get the papers and something for dinner. Although she needn't have bothered now you've come with food. She's so good to

120

us, you know, Christie. Dennis phoned her from the hospital on Wednesday and she was on a plane yesterday, quick as anything. She's a great girl. I just wish she'd settle down like your two lads. But you can't make them do what you want, can you? Still, she's happy and that's the main thing, isn't it?'

'Yes,' said Christie, resolving that now wasn't the moment to tell her friend the news about her daughter-in-law's pregnancy. 'Shall I make a fresh pot of tea?' she said, indicating the tea-cosied pot that sat on the table.

'Go on,' said Una. 'Milky tea is one way of getting more calcium into me. Far nicer than those awful tablets they have me on. You should have a bone scan done, you know. It's our age, unfortunately.'

'I know,' said Christie, rinsing the teapot and automatically tidying up around her. Dennis's newspapers caught her attention. There were Sunday supplements from weeks ago jumbled up with daily papers open at the crossword pages and she organised them neatly into a pile while she waited for the kettle to boil. Una was telling her about the hospital and the steam from the kettle was building as Christie threw the last paper lightly on to the heap. Before the newsprint landed, the small headline caught her eye:

*Polish Artist's First Irish Show in 25 Years*

Christie caught the countertop to stop herself swaying. It was only a small story and she pulled it towards her, hardly daring to read it. Carey Wolensky was coming to Ireland next month for an exhibition of his work, including his most famous paintings, the Dark Lady series.

*Much prized by the world's richest art collectors and quite unlike all his other work, the Dark Lady paintings are Wolensky's mysterious masterpieces.*

Before Christie could rip the story from the page, she heard Dennis come back.

'Christie, don't bother with those,' he said, scooping up the pile of papers. 'I'll put them out with the bins.'

He carried them off and Christie was left staring into the neat shrubbery of the Maguires' back garden, barely hearing what Una was saying. She was thinking of Carey Wolensky, her darling younger sister's one-time boyfriend, the man who'd almost destroyed everything. He was coming back into their world and, even now, he could devastate their lives.

Now, at last, Christie knew for sure what her feeling of doom had been about.

# CHAPTER EIGHT

Motherhood was harder than marriage, Grace realised, as she admired the art portfolio that Faye had just purchased, at great expense, for Amber's forthcoming eighteenth birthday. At least with marriage, you got time off for good behaviour and could duck out when the going got tough. But motherhood was never-ending and was clearly designed to make you a selfless person. Like when you spent more than a week's wages on something for your kid.

'She'll love it,' Grace said, thinking that if she ever bought anything of supple leather that expensive, it would be hanging off her arm right now with a discreet label inside proclaiming that it was handstitched lovingly by people at the Tod's leather goods factory. Still, that was Faye for you: the only exquisitely dressed thing in Faye's house was Amber. 'Any art student would kill for it.'

'Do you think so?' Faye asked anxiously.

She'd just spent a fortune buying the portfolio from the most expensive art shop in town because she wanted her darling Amber to have the very best of everything when she started art college.

Basically nothing more than a large wallet for transporting

drawings and paintings, it wasn't the most important bit of art college kit. Amber had an old plastic portfolio that could have done her perfectly well. But this large zippered folder was a thing of luxury and it would be nice for Amber to have a beautiful creamy leather one. Except, maybe Amber would have preferred a black leather one. Who knew? The fact that she'd once admired a cream leather one might mean nothing now.

She could have totally changed her mind, in the way she'd announced the night before that she might start having a quick dinner before Faye came home, so she could retreat to her room to study.

'If I eat earlier, I sleep better,' she explained.

'You've got to eat properly,' Faye had said, motherly hackles raised.

'Mum.' Amber dragged the single syllable out in exasperation. 'I'm not anorexic or bulimic or anything. I like to eat early, that's all.'

'OK,' agreed Faye, deflated.

It was mid-May, the exams were looming ever closer and it wouldn't be fair to complain that she missed mealtimes together, the only time the two of them could really talk these days. Amber was under a lot of strain, she looked tired too from all that studying, with violet circles under eyes that looked wildly alert.

Faye had never seen her work so hard, locked in her room for hours every evening, sometimes emerging pale at ten to say she was going to sleep and not to bother going in to say goodnight.

That was what worried Faye most: her daughter not wanting to talk to her. They'd been so close for so long, had managed to bypass most of the awfulness of adolescence, only to end up with this coolness between them over Amber's exams.

For the past few weeks, Amber had barely spoken to her

124

and seemed lost in her own world. Was she *that* worried about failing?

'I can see your mind whirring,' Grace warned, interpreting Faye's look incorrectly. 'Stop already. She'll like it, OK? If she doesn't, she's being . . .'

She'd nearly said *rude* but stopped. The childless should not criticise other people's children; that was the eleventh commandment and came right before the twelfth, which was not to criticise how other people put their own lives on hold for the said children. When she saw how Faye had given her life over to Amber, Grace felt glad that her own biological clock had never started the fabled ticking.

She'd known Faye for ten years and among all the things she'd learned about her – like the fact that Faye was incredibly clever, yet liked hiding her light under a bushel, and was the only single woman Grace knew who genuinely had no interest in finding a man – foremost was the fact that Amber was Faye's reason for living.

Surely that wasn't right. Were children supposed to be the only thing in a woman's life? Grace was sure her other friends with kids had more fulfilled lives than Faye.

'If she doesn't like it, it might be a fashion thing,' Grace amended, 'but the natural look is very chic.'

'I'm sure she'll love it,' Faye agreed, thinking that she no longer knew any such thing.

The catch on Amber's window had finally given in and broken. She'd jemmied it so many nights when she crept in well after midnight, pushing the window up and praying it wouldn't creak and wake her mother. Burglary must be easier than people thought: nobody had stopped her or even appeared to notice her late-night climbs in and out of her bedroom window.

'I don't know how you've got away with it,' Ella remarked. She and Amber walked to school together most days, although they were getting later and later, as Amber was finding it hard to drag herself out of bed.

'Your mum must be losing it if she hasn't noticed that you're not in your room at night. So,' Ella added, 'what did Mr Luverman do with you last night? Spill.'

'I wish you'd stop calling him that.' Amber didn't mind really, but she felt bad when Ella reminded her that she was deceiving her mother.

'Mr Luverman? I call him that 'cos he can take you places that nobody else can.'

'Ella, give it a rest.'

'OK, but I'm just jealous. Being a boring old student with no boyfriend and exams on the horizon, I have no sex life and I want to hear all about yours. I don't know how you're doing any revision at all. Are you?' Ella asked suspiciously.

'Of course,' Amber snapped.

She still hadn't told Ella that Karl had asked her to travel to America with him and the band. She didn't know why; it wasn't as if Ella would disapprove. They'd wanted to be daring, the opposite of sensible, and skipping the exams was just that. But she hadn't managed to say it yet.

It was Thursday evening, less than a week to go to Amber's eighteenth birthday, and less than three weeks to the exams. Faye paused in her driveway and looked across Summer Street to the park. There were no children running or scampering there now, but the evening dog walkers were out in force. She could see Christie Devlin in the distance, light and elegant as a ballerina, with those two cute little dogs skipping around her feet. Mr Coughlan, a very elderly gentleman who owned three pugs, was just in front, walking slowly with his nose in the air, just like his dogs with their squashed-up faces and airs of refinement. People did look like their dogs, Faye thought with a grin.

When Amber had been younger, Faye had spent many

hours in the park, overseeing five-a-side football matches or watching racing games. They'd both loved the park then, but now, well, Faye rarely went in there. There wasn't any time in her life for sitting in parks, she was always busy.

And yet now it was going to be ripped in half, she felt oddly angry.

Summer Street wouldn't be the same without the rackety old pavilion surrounded by its carpet of green. Faye knew it was crazy to mourn something she never used, but just because she didn't go into the park, didn't mean she didn't appreciate it.

If only she had the energy or the time to do something about it, to fight the council, to insist that they stop the deal. But that would involve going around the neighbours and getting names and signatures, drafting petitions, all sorts of work that Faye didn't have time for. Also, that job was for people who were good at chatting to strangers and Faye had lost that ability a long time ago. No, somebody else would be bound to start a campaign and she would add her name to the signatures. That'd be enough. Getting involved was always a mistake.

The house was quiet. Amber wasn't home yet. Probably at Ella's revising. Good, Faye thought. It gave her a chance to make a special dinner for the two of them. A pre-birthday dinner. She'd decided to give Amber the portfolio tonight instead of waiting until her birthday the following Wednesday, half hoping that the gift would have a magical effect on the coolness between them. And as an extra treat, she quickly rustled up some flapjacks. They used to be Amber's favourites years ago, and although they were such a childish food, she'd suddenly felt like making them. Feeding her daughter the love that Amber didn't seem to want any more.

Amber arrived after seven, laden down with her school books and looking, yet again, oddly alert and excited.

The portfolio lay at her place on the table, a giant package wrapped in gold paper, tied with narrow gold ribbon.

She stared at it in silence for a moment. A present? She'd planned to talk to her mother about Karl tonight, had spent ages with him to buoy herself up for this moment and now her mother had ruined it all with a gift. How could they have the conversation from hell now?

*Mum, I'm not going to do my exams because my boyfriend and his band have a development deal with a New York producer and I'm going with him because he needs me and I love him. Oh yeah, and thanks for the portfolio.*

'It's an early birthday present.'

Mum looked so thrilled with herself. And she'd made stupid flapjacks too. Kids' biscuits. That was what was wrong with Mum, Amber thought, guilt making her angry. She still treated Amber as if she was a kid.

*Don't stay up too late: you won't be able to get up for school.*

*Take a scarf in case it's cold.*

*I don't care if everyone else in the class is going, you're not.*

She meant well, but she'd never accept that Amber was an adult with adult desires and her own choices to make.

Amber knew with sudden certainty that there would be no easy way to tell her mother about Karl. The umbilical cord couldn't be stretched – only severed.

'Open it.' Faye couldn't understand why Amber hadn't launched herself on the gift and ripped it open, the way she used to do with presents.

Amber shot a tense look at her mother, then carefully opened the gift.

'Well, do you like it?'

Amber bit her lip. The portfolio was beautiful, and had cost her mother a fortune she didn't have. Worse, the treacherous

128

thought slipped into her mind of what she and Karl could have done with that money. It would have paid Amber's ticket to America. The band's fare would be covered by the production company but she and Karl had to come up with hers.

This present was so typical of her mother: spend what she didn't have just so Amber could have the best. It was so unnecessary. And it made Amber feel guiltier than ever.

'Of course I like it.' She managed to keep the irritation out of her voice.

'Really?'

Amber felt the tension coil in her.

'Really,' she said. 'It's lovely.' Lovely but totally bloody useless, since she wasn't going to art college and wouldn't need it. Not yet, anyhow. She could study art anywhere, any time. When she and Karl were settled, she'd do it. A gift like hers couldn't be lost.

'I thought you'd prefer the cream but we can change it if you'd prefer a black one,' Mum went on fondly.

The hands holding the portfolio tightened and Amber felt as if she was holding in a scream. Would her mother ever stop?

'Thank you, it's lovely,' she said, forcing the words out of somewhere. She pecked her mother on the cheek. 'I've so much work to do.'

'But what about dinner?'

'I'm not hungry. I ate at Ella's,' improvised Amber.

'Amber, I know you're worried about the exams . . .' began Faye, desperate to get her daughter talking.

The tension in Amber finally sprang free. 'The fucking exams aren't what this is all about!' she yelled. 'You don't understand, you don't understand anything!'

Faye's face was stricken. 'Amber, please, talk to me. We've always talked about everything. What's wrong?'

'I told you,' hissed Amber, 'you wouldn't understand. You've never done anything with your life, you've never taken a single risk. I'm different from you. I need space, not you hanging over me waiting and hoping for me to live my life the way you want!'

'I never wanted that.' Faye could hardly speak with the hurt. How could Amber accuse her of this, of expecting too much from her, when all she'd ever wanted was for Amber to be safe and not to have to go through what she had. 'I only ever wanted you to be happy.'

'No,' shot back Amber, and it was fear and guilt talking, making her say hateful things because she couldn't bear her mother looking at her with those huge wounded eyes. 'You wanted me to be happy in your way. The sensible, dull and boring way. That's not what I want. I don't want to end up like you.'

'Oh, darling, please, listen to me . . .'

'No, I won't listen to you any more, Mum. I'm an adult now and I've got my own life to lead, and so do you.' Amber paused, flushed with emotion. 'I can't be responsible for being here with you, you've got to move on and not stay stuck in the past, stuck remembering Dad. Being a widow shouldn't define your life.'

There, she'd said it: told her mother to move on. It wasn't quite how she'd meant to put it but it was a start. She wouldn't be around any more, she'd be away with Karl and even if she hadn't got round to saying that, she'd said the main part. They weren't a little family unit any more. She and Karl were the unit. Her mother had to be made to understand that.

Faye said nothing at all. She watched Amber as she tucked her present under her arm and left the kitchen, anything to be away from her mother's anxious face and the weight of her expectations.

Alone, surrounded by flapjacks, Amber's favourite feta and filo-pastry pie, and torn wrapping paper, Faye felt lost and unbearably hurt. What had she done wrong?

For once, she didn't bother to tidy up the kitchen, scrubbing with her own solution of bleach and water, eau de Faye, as she used to joke. The dinner sat untouched on the table and she walked, sleepwalked almost, to her bedroom.

It was a pretty room, feminine, luxurious in its way, a boudoir that nobody at Little Island would easily identify as hers.

Her office, with its clean surfaces, tables and chairs set at precise right angles, and the pot plant whose leaves she cleaned every week, was a far cry from this haven of soft fabrics. There was a luscious velvet throw in antique rose on the bed, and Tiffany-style lampshades that cast a soft burnished light.

Not knowing quite what else to do, Faye sat on the edge of her bed. She felt powerless. It was so long since she'd had that feeling and it flooded back into every vein as if it had never been away.

'What can I do now?' she said aloud. Inner strength could get you through anything. She'd trained herself to believe that and loved to read about other women who'd gone through pain to emerge stronger, tougher, untouchable. They were proof that she was in some kind of women's club. The We Screwed Up But Hey, We're Still Here Club.

But to do it, you needed that inner strength and hers was centred around one central core, Amber. Golden, loving, talented, funny Amber. Without Amber's love, that strength crumbled. And Amber had just cast herself off like a shard of ice shearing off an iceberg.

She sat on the bed for a long time, hearing Amber moving around upstairs, then the sound of music thumping through from the attic bedroom. The Scissor Sisters were playing, and

Faye managed a half-smile because to her they sounded like a classic seventies rock band, like one of her old vinyl records. She still had some of her old LPs. And the photos.

They were hidden in the big bottom drawer of Faye's 1930s wardrobe, under a bundle of spare sheets and a couple of elderly Foxford rugs. She got up and pulled open the drawer. *Spare pillowcases*, said the label on the box. Who'd open that? Faye had reasoned. Not even Amber, who rooted around in her mother's dressing table for make-up, would bother to look in there. Perhaps if Amber had known her mother had something to hide, she might have found it. But Faye knew that she'd managed to keep her secret very well.

What had her daughter called her? Sensible, dull and boring. Seventeen years of trying to become someone she wasn't had been very successful, it appeared.

She hadn't touched the box for years, but now she carried it over to the bed and, settling herself against her pillows, took off the lid.

On top of the pile of memories inside was a grainy colour photograph of a girl with wide, laughing eyes and tawny hair rippling around her shoulders. Very like Amber, in fact. She was sitting in the middle of a group of smiling people, captured mid-laugh, frozen in time. Behind them was a wall of leatherette from a curving banquette; in front of them, a bar table spread with bottles, glasses, cigarette packs, ashtrays.

Faye didn't remember the names of everyone in the picture, but she could hear the music that had been playing when Jimi had taken it – Led Zeppelin, something dark and moody, the mahogany darkness of 'Kashmir', perhaps.

She wondered where Jimi was now. Then, he'd been a sweet guy with spiky punk hair and a lost puppy-dog expression who hung around the fringes of the gang. He was probably unrecognisable now, working in a strait-laced office job with a tie, lace-up shoes and normal hair. But then, she was hardly recognisable herself.

Nobody looking at mumsy Faye Reid in her high street navy suit and her neat little earrings could imagine her as the girl in that picture, the one who'd been swaying sexily to the music moments before the photo had been taken.

When she moved the pile of photos, a faint scent of perfume rose from the box. YSL's heady Opium, she remembered. She closed her eyes, and it was as though she was there once more in her former life. She could almost smell the atmosphere of The Club. Smoke, marijuana, the full-bodied reek of Jack Daniel's, perfume and sweat. And excitement. The excitement of not knowing what might happen next.

The mixed-up girl she'd been then was no more, but Faye would never forget her.

That girl represented both the great tragedy and the triumph of her life, a former life she'd never been able to share with Amber.

Keeping it all a secret had been an obsession with Faye because if Amber knew, she'd never understand and their relationship would be destroyed. Except that somehow, her relationship with Amber was fracturing more every day anyway. Faye was beginning to wonder if things might be better if Amber actually knew the truth.

# CHAPTER NINE

*Hi Shona,*

    *How are you? Is all still well on your planet? I miss you, Paul and Ross and the fun we had.*

So much, Maggie thought. How come you only realised how great your friends were when they weren't around?

    *No news here at all. I am sitting in my bedroom at my dad's ancient laptop on Friday morning and I keep getting this weird feeling that it's a Sunday night and I've got school in the morning. If* Hart to Hart *was still on the telly, it'd be like nothing has changed.*
    *Did I ever tell you that I wanted to be Jennifer Hart? She was always so nice, so beautiful, had a rich husband and never had to do housework. I honestly thought that was an option when I was small: that one day I'd grow up to be her and I'd have a gorgeous Mercedes-driving husband who happened to be a multi-millionaire and my hair would look fantastic, auburn rather than carrot, and there'd be a Max around to do stuff. Where have all the millionaires gone? I might sign up to a class to find one.*

*Ooops, can't. I couldn't keep up the act: the long nails, the long blonde hair or the giggling at my chosen millionaire's stupid jokes – which is what all the magazines say is vital. I am also at a loss in the boob department. Millionaires seem to like women with tiny waists and big boobs who simper that they only eat grilled fish and nothing but nuts after six o'clock. My chest and my waist are the same size and I like a proper dinner, plus dessert and maybe a bar of chocolate or two after six. I would not fit in.*

*Anyway, I hate men. Except for Ross and Paul, and they don't count. And Dad. Nice men who don't hit on me don't count, either. Not that any men are hitting on me, Shona. So no mad phone calls about how I should put mascara on and wear flat shoes so I'm shorter than them because men like short women, OK? Summer Street is a date-free zone, like wildlife preserves where hunters can't go after ducks. Men around here are like my parents' friends, the nice dad sort who worry about when they're going to cut the hedge.*

*And when did men fling themselves at me anyway? Like, never.*

Elisabeth had been on the phone a lot from Seattle telling her to get out and get a life.

'Please don't say that the only way to get over a guy is to get under another one,' warned Maggie, which was what Ross had said to her on the phone, adding that if he left it too long between dates, both he and Nureyev got depressed.

Maggie got depressed just thinking about having sex with another man. That electric attraction she'd felt for Grey could hardly be found twice in a lifetime. All she wanted was him and she couldn't have him, mustn't have him.

'That's old-fashioned drivel about getting another man,'

Elisabeth said, 'and I'd never give advice like that. A man's the last thing you need. I mean go out with co-workers, friends. Go to galleries, take up charity work, try a new sport, have fun.'

Maggie didn't think she knew how to have fun any more.

*Don't know if the boss told you but they've let me extend my unpaid leave. After that, I have to put up or shut up. Get another job or come back. Don't know if I can face the college again.*

*Mum's librarian friend who gave me my first job years ago has asked me to do a few shifts in the local library as a huge favour. One of her people is pregnant and has had to go off early because of back pain. So I'm filling in and it's great, actually. Almost a relief, which sounds unkind to Mum and Dad, but you know what I mean.*

She hadn't worked in a public library for years and it was quite nice to get out of the house for a few hours, to escape from the claustrophobia of home.

*I'm in the children's department and I really like it, actually. The kids are gorgeous and no, I'm not broody, so don't even go there. Kids say the funniest things. They're so blunt, it's hilarious. Plus, I get to flick through the books I loved as a kid. I'm rereading the Narnia series. I can't believe I haven't read them for years.*

*Have you seen Grey? No, don't answer that. Yes, do. And as for that blonde piece, put a note on her file. 'Slept with librarian's long-term boyfriend' should do it. 'Known for ripping pages out of books' might be even better.*

*I don't know what her name is. Probably something*

*like Flower or Petal or Butterfly, stupid bitch. He must
still be with her. It's been two weeks and I haven't heard
anything from him since the first day. Some boyfriend
he turned out to be.*

*Not that I'm bitter. I am better off without him.
Love Maggie.*

She logged off. The last bit was untrue. She was bitter and
right now, no, she didn't feel better off without Grey.

Since she'd been home, her mother had perked up no end
having her daughter around, while Maggie herself felt
strangely adrift. She was living in the house she'd grown up
in with her parents – whom she loved, even if they did occasionally drive her mad – and yet the sense of belonging had
gone.

All the remaining remnants of her younger self – the furry
cushions on her bed, the Holly Hobbie dolls on the shelves
– only made her feel more alone, more isolated.

In this bedroom, she'd cried with misery over the hell of
school and dreamed of a wonderful future, where she would
be wise and successful. Now she was back, futureless and
feeling not a lot wiser.

'Bean!' her father yelled. 'We're going to the café for lattes
and paninis. It's the Friday-morning special. Want to come?'

Sense of belonging wasn't the only thing to change. When
had her parents started having lattes and paninis? What was
wrong with a coffee and a bun, which was what they used
to sell there. Home had moved on without her, Maggie
thought, almost childishly. It wasn't supposed to change. It
was supposed to stay exactly the same so she could come
back and refresh. Still, latte and panini was better than sitting
in her bedroom.

'OK, coming.' At least in the café, there couldn't be too
many probing questions about Grey.

Breakfast in the café ended in a cholesterol-inducing flurry at eleven when eggs done every which way came off the menu, and wraps, paninis and ciabatta bread sandwiches went on. Henry was painstakingly writing the day's lunch specials on the blackboard outside the café when the Maguires arrived, first Una, regal with her crutches, and then her people-in-waiting, Maggie and Dennis, bringing up the rear, carrying Una's handbag and a cushion so she could rest her leg on a hard chair.

'Henry, love, how are you?' asked Una.

Henry, a fatherly balding man in cords and a checked shirt, stopped writing to greet Una, who was one of his favourite customers.

'How's the poor leg?' he asked solicitously.

'Sore but what's the point of complaining?' said Una. 'If that's the worst thing that happens to me, won't I be fine?'

They went in and arranged themselves at a table by the window, Una swivelling herself until she was comfortable before handing her crutches to Maggie. Xu, the petite Chinese waitress, appeared with a silent smile and gave them menus. Maggie smiled hello back at her. There was something that fascinated her about Xu. Imagine coming all that way to a country where you knew nobody. Yet Xu didn't appear lonely or sad, just grateful for this chance of a new life in Ireland. Her life must have been hard before, Maggie surmised, but she didn't want to offend Xu by asking intrusive questions, so she settled, Maggie-style, for smiling a lot at her.

Henry finished working on the blackboard and came inside.

'Tell me, Henry, what's good today? We're trying to feed poor Maggie up or she'll go home to Galway and Grey will think we starved her here. Grey's her partner,' Una added in her version of sotto voce, which meant only half the street heard.

Maggie managed the required polite smile at this. Had her

138

mother always mentioned Grey this often or was it notice-able only now that he was gone?

'Great soup, wild mushroom,' said Henry, who had come in after them. 'Jane's trying out this new cookbook and herself and Xu were slaving away all morning at it.'

'Let's have that, then,' said Una. 'We love trying new things, don't we?'

She beamed at Maggie who was trying to make herself think cheerful thoughts so she could join in this happy family lunch instead of looking like a shrivelled old misery guts. But what was a cheerful thought?

Let's face it, she decided, she had better take the bull by the horns. It would be easier to tell the truth than to suffer endless public comments about how wonderful Grey was.

'Grey and I have split up,' she blurted out.

Her father immediately looked concerned and laid a hand on hers, while her mother bit her lip.

'Oh, Maggie, love,' Una sighed. 'I wish you'd told us before, you poor pet, instead of bottling it up. We love you.'

There it was: the most simple and most poignant thing any parent could say. They loved her and it didn't matter if she was single or about to be married to the planet's most eligible bachelor, they loved her.

'I didn't mean to cry,' she said, crying. Honestly, what was wrong with her? It was like being sixteen again, tearful at the drop of a hat. 'We broke up just before you had the acci-dent and I thought you had enough to deal with without my worries as well. I – well, he – it wasn't working.' She couldn't tell them about the blonde. It would be too humiliating.

'He wasn't good enough for you,' snapped her father, angry wolf circling his precious cub. 'Should have asked to marry you. I said that all along, didn't I, Una? What sort of a man goes out with a girl for five years and never wants to make an honest woman out of her?'

'Dennis,' warned his wife. 'This is not the time for recriminations.'

'Well, he never asked, did he? Marriage isn't that unfashionable now, lots of people are doing it, but it wasn't good enough for me bucko, no sirree . . .'

'Dennis!'

'Dad, Mum, it's OK. I'm OK about it all,' Maggie lied. 'Really, we both knew it wasn't working.' She was glad she hadn't mentioned Petal, or whatever her name was. Her normally mild-mannered father might run off to purchase a gun and remould Grey's intestinal tract with a bullet. Who could tell?

'You'd had enough of him?' asked Dad, suddenly concerned with getting a speck of dust from his eye. 'That's my girl. Dump him and move on, that's the ticket. You always knew how to take care of yourself.'

It was almost too much for Maggie. She'd never known how to take care of herself. She'd spent four years of hell in school for that very reason. But inexplicably her dad believed otherwise. She wasn't sure whether to laugh or sob. Did he and Mum not understand what sort of a mess of a person she really was?

The next morning, Maggie was on her knees in the library playhouse tidying up books when she heard her name called.

'Maggie!' Tina, the other librarian in the children's section, hissed urgently. 'You've got a visitor.'

It was hard for a tall person to squash down enough to get even half of themselves inside the library's red wooden kiddie zone, so Maggie figured that unless Bill Clinton was outside exuding charisma and charm, whoever it was could wait until she'd finished tidying up the picture books that small kids loved to take into the house.

'Maggie!' hissed Tina again.

'Keep your knickers on!' Maggie hissed back as she grabbed *The Very Hungry Caterpillar*, and instantly wished she'd said nothing. It had only taken one day of being under the watchful gaze of wide-eyed primary school kids for her to realise that children loved saying things to their parents like: 'The lady behind the desk said "crap", Mummy. That's a bad word. Is she going to get into trouble?'

Books still in her arms, she wriggled out of the small space and sat back on her knees. There were no kids in hearing range, thankfully. But standing beside Tina, who looked intrigued, was Grey, particularly drop-dead gorgeous in his serious business outfit of dark brown jacket, collar and tie. It was his meeting-with-the-boss outfit, and today, it seemed, Maggie merited boss treatment.

It was strange how easily she'd managed to forget the effect Grey's physical presence had on her. Away from him, it was simple to think him ordinary, a man who left beard scum in the bathroom sink, upturned his cereal bowl to drink the milk, and snored like an asthmatic pig in bed. Now that he was here, arrestingly handsome, her stomach flipped, remembering.

'Hello, Grey.'

'Hi, Maggie.'

They stared at each other. Maggie's instinct was to move to hug him until the picture flashed into her mind again: Grey and his blonde in their bed. Immediately, her stomach did the other sort of flip, the betrayed and devastated flip that completely neutralised the effect of his charisma.

'How are you?' he said. 'I've really missed you.'

For an instant, she forgot where they were: all she could think was that Grey was here to tell her that he loved her and that they should forget the past, she was the one for him. Then, reality reasserted itself. She was at work. Grey was saying these things in front of Tina, whose eyes were protruding so far it looked as if she was a rabbit with myxomatosis.

She imagined his face if the positions had been reversed and she'd accosted him in a tutorial. He'd have been furious.

This was not a game, Maggie thought darkly. It was her life and she wasn't going to be played with.

'Long time no see. What are you doing in Dublin?' Maggie asked evenly.

'I came to see you,' he replied. 'To bring you home.'

He hadn't spoken to her in two weeks and now he'd just turned up at her place of work and thought he could fix everything. How dare he?

Anger and heartache fought in Maggie's head and anger won.

'How did you know I was working here?' she asked.

'Paul told me. By mistake,' Grey added. 'He said Shona would kill him. And me,' Grey added, as if the possibility was ludicrous. Women never stayed angry with him for long, he was too charming. Able to charm them into bed, Maggie thought.

'I'm at work, Grey,' she said with a coolness she didn't know she possessed. 'I can't talk.'

'Later then?' he asked. 'Lunchtime?'

Maggie managed to keep her game face on. 'I'm busy at lunchtime,' she said with the air of someone with so many appointments she needed an assistant to keep her diary straight. The keep-'em-keen angel that was Shona hovered in her head, shrieking, *make him suffer, make him wait for you!*

She remembered Shona's advice when she had told her what had happened.

*If you go back to him, I'll never speak to you again! Don't ditch your principles just because you're crazy about him. You deserve better.*

Grey leaned against the end of the J–K shelf, graceful as

ever, long legs crossing at the ankles. Maggie could almost sense Tina sighing in appreciation, and she felt irritated again. Not for jealousy's sake but because Tina – who was twenty years older than Maggie and should know better – was falling into the same trap Maggie herself had tumbled into: believing that a stunning-looking man was a prize beyond rubies.

Only if he was faithful.

'When then?' And Grey looked straight into her eyes as if they were in a private room and he was able to caress her into agreeing to anything.

'After work. Half five.' Maggie felt jolted by how much she suddenly wanted him to hold her, despite it all.

'The Summer Street Café.' It was the only place she could think of and instantly regretted it. Just up the road from home and her parents might drop in, you never knew. Maggie couldn't cope with a scene, not now.

'That pretty little blue and white place on the corner?' Grey asked.

She remembered she'd taken him there once before when he'd visited her parents. It had felt like a royal tour, showing him where she'd grown up, wanting him to love it all and approve of it, and Grey had said he did, but she'd imagined he felt it all a bit provincial really. A street where everyone knew everyone else. The only street where Grey would like to know everyone was probably in a toney neighbourhood in Washington DC where world policies were discussed with under-secretaries at dinner parties, not gossip over muffins in a little café.

On that occasion, Maggie had lost count of the people who'd come up to them in the café and said, 'I haven't seen you for ages, Maggie,' and then, with unconcealed fascination: 'And who's this gentleman?'

'Yes. We'll only have half an hour but I'm sure that'll be long enough,' she said coolly.

He didn't respond to the barb.

'See you then.' He touched her arm gently as he left and Maggie closed her eyes in pain.

Tina took the books from Maggie's arms. She was at least a foot shorter than Maggie and favoured pale blue above all other clothes colours.

With books in her arms and a glint of pearl earrings peeking out behind a grey bob, she looked like the archetypal librarian. But Maggie knew she had a wicked sense of humour and could make the library staff room rock with laughter.

'There's a new hair salon up the road,' she said, eyeing Maggie's unwashed, tangled locks. 'You could take early lunch today. It's my turn, but I don't mind. I wasn't going anywhere.'

Maggie felt herself come back to earth and smiled at Tina.

'I need a hairdo?' she asked in mock surprise.

'It wouldn't hurt,' Tina said. 'Might make him wonder what you were doing for lunch and with whom.'

'I don't want him to think I got my hair done for him, though.'

'When did a man ever notice your hair?' Tina demanded. 'He'll think you're looking amazing without him, and you'll feel better if you're going to dump him and you look marvellous.'

'True,' sighed Maggie without much enthusiasm.

Tina shot her a gimlet-eyed look. 'You are going to dump him?'

Maggie nodded, and found herself confessing. 'I caught him with someone else. Younger, sexy, big boobs: your basic nightmare.'

'Well, you're hardly the hunchback of Notre Dame yourself,' Tina responded.

'Oh, I'm just thin,' Maggie said, exasperated. People who weren't thin always thought it was the be-all and end-all of looks. It wasn't. Sexy and curvy, and with skin that could be tanned and hair that could be tamed: *that* was something.

'Just thin, huh?' Tina came closer. 'Do yourself a favour, Maggie. I don't know where they've put the mirrors in your house, but there's a lot more to you than just thin. And if Romeo hasn't told you so, then you've got to dump him because he's a vampire sort of guy – sucks the life force right out of you and convinces you that you're ugly and useless.'

Maggie stared at her. She wanted to say that Tina was wrong, that Grey was the only one who'd made her feel sexy and gorgeous, and that his leaving her had taken it all away from her. But it would sound so silly.

All afternoon, after she got back from the hairdressers with tumbling glossy curls that made a gang of workmen on the road whoop and whistle at her, she thought about what Tina had said. And Shona. And Elisabeth.

You're worth more, they'd said. Grey didn't deserve you, they'd said. And she'd dismissed their advice because it was well-meaning girlfriend talk where people said the right thing to buoy up your spirits. It didn't have to be true. It was just verbal hugging. *We love you even if he doesn't.*

But for once, she tried to step outside herself and imagine if she was wrong. What if Grey wasn't good enough for her?

He'd never asked her to marry him, though they'd been going out for five years and it seemed like the next logical step. Even at Shona and Paul's wedding, where Maggie had been a bridesmaid and had caught the bouquet – well, Shona had flung it directly at her, so catching wasn't the operative word – even then, Grey hadn't held her hand tightly or looked at her in a manner that suggested it could be them next.

'Hasn't today been romantic?' she'd said that evening as they sat in the sunset on the hotel terrace, Grey handsome in his pale linen suit, Maggie like a wood nymph in hand-dyed green silk, with tiny creamy flowers woven into her hair.

'Must be costing them a small fortune,' Grey had remarked, sucking on his cigar. Shona's dad had passed round cigars after the toasts and Grey had insisted on going out to smoke it instantly. He looked like a character in a Scott Fitzgerald novel, Maggie thought, with love. His hair suited him swept back and he twirled the fat cigar expertly, savouring it. 'You could put a down payment on a fine house for what today's costing. Is it typically Irish, I wonder,' he added thoughtfully, 'this business of a huge, costly ceremony with everyone you know there? It's like our obsession with owning land. We can't just rent, we have to own. It's always the grand gesture. I could write a paper on it, what do you think?'

In the library, an entire year after the event, Maggie felt suddenly aflame with anger at what Grey had said. She'd been annoyed then, too, but hadn't said it, assuming Grey was just bored because he wasn't Shona's biggest fan – it was mutual – and wasn't as fired up with enthusiasm over the whole event as Maggie had been.

'It's nice to have everyone you care about watch you marry the person you love,' she'd said hopefully. Her mother would be in seventh heaven organising Maggie's wedding, and her father would probably spend months working on his speech, a speech that would be loving, respectful and would probably halt halfway through for Dad to wipe his eyes behind his glasses.

That's what she'd been thinking of at Shona and Paul's wedding, and bloody Grey had been thinking of another bloody paper. It wasn't that he wasn't clever enough to understand what Maggie had been getting at: he wasn't one of those academics who understood chaos theory but couldn't change a light bulb. Grey was savvy. He'd simply avoided a discussion about marriage because he wasn't interested in marrying her.

And she'd been so besotted, so terrified of frightening him

off, she'd let him get away with it. She'd shut up like a good girl.

Maggie wasn't sure which of them she was most angry with: herself or Grey.

She'd never seen Summer Street quite so busy as today, when at 5.28 she walked up to meet Grey at the café. Just when she wanted no one to notice them. 'Hello, Maggie!' Somebody waved across the road at her. Maggie felt cornered. A woman with grey-blonde hair, vaguely familiar. Maggie had no idea who it was.

'Hello,' she said brightly. 'How are you and . . . er, everyone?' Everyone was the fail-safe for when she couldn't remember if the person in question had a husband or children or a budgie menagerie.

'Oh, they're all fine,' said the woman. 'Fine. How are you? Your poor mother, I heard about her leg. I haven't dropped in to see her because I'm just so busy with the Guides.'

The Girl Guides! That was it, thought Maggie, delighted. Now she knew. Mrs Cooke, lived at the bottom of the road and was an outrageous busybody. It was a complete miracle that she hadn't been to the house already to see Mum's leg, pass comment on the furniture and circulate details of her visit.

'I'll call in now, though,' said Mrs Cooke with horrible intent.

'Well, she's not really having visitors today,' Maggie said hurriedly. 'She's tired, needs to sleep a lot really. It takes it out of a person when they break their leg.'

'Of course, I completely understand,' said Mrs Cooke. 'I'll drop in next week instead. She'll be feeling better then.' And she was gone.

By the time Maggie made it to the café, she had nodded, waved, smiled and recounted the story of her mother's leg

147

to two more people. So much for trying to meet Grey in a quiet place.

The café was the centre of the local universe and entirely the wrong place to meet a man whom your parents were hatching a plan to stab.

Not that the lovely Henry and Jane would breathe a word to Dennis and Una if Maggie had met King Kong himself and sat at one of the back tables, stroking his furry arms and discussing big buildings to climb. But someone else might blab.

It was in this frame of mind that Maggie shoved open the door of the café and looked around suspiciously. It came as a great relief to see that, apart from Grey, it was empty.

Grey had naturally got the best seat, at a slightly larger than normal table in the window. There he sat, looking gorgeous and relaxed, a black coffee in front of him along with a croissant that he had half nibbled and pushed away. How typically man-like, Maggie thought, irritably. He'd only eaten half the croissant and realised he didn't need the rest. A woman would have eaten it no matter what: she'd bought it – she'd eat it.

'Hello,' Maggie said, and plonked herself down in the seat opposite him. She was angry and nothing Grey could say would change it.

'Maggie,' said Henry, coming up before Grey could open his mouth. 'Can I get you anything?'

'Erm, ah, coffee, black,' she said stupidly, because she took milk and sugar.

'Anything to eat?'

'Muffin, erm, sugar-free.'

'Carrot or lemon or chocolate?' Henry asked politely.

It was as if her ability to speak had disappeared.

'Lemon,' she said finally.

So much for getting her hair blow-dried into tousled, artful curls at lunchtime. What use was looking glamorous and untouchable when she couldn't string two sentences together? Henry vanished and Grey and Maggie stared at each other.

'So,' she said.

'I'm really glad you came to meet me,' Grey said, looking the picture of penitence. 'I've missed you. You've no idea how much.' He reached across the table and grabbed her hand. Maggie pulled it away.

'Sorry. I shouldn't rush it,' he said.

'No,' she agreed.

They sat in silence.

'How have you been?' he asked.

'Fine.'

'You don't look fine.'

'Thanks for that vote of confidence,' she said sarcastically.

'I didn't mean it that way. You look beautiful.' He reached out again for her hand but thought better of it. 'You always look beautiful.'

'I thought you preferred blondes with big tits,' Maggie said, aiming for flippant and sounding desperately hurt instead.

Henry put a coffee in front of her and pretended he hadn't heard.

'You know, Henry, maybe you could put a bit of frothy stuff on the top of it, I changed my mind.'

'No problem.' Henry whisked it away. Thirty-five years in the café business meant he knew better than to question a woman's change of mind.

'I don't prefer blondes,' Grey said earnestly. 'I prefer women with wild red hair, and liquid blue eyes I can't stop thinking about . . .'

'Oh, Grey, stop it,' she said. 'That's crap. You were in bed with her. Nothing you can say can change that.'

'I know.'

149

'Let's talk about the apartment and what we're going to do with it,' she added. That was good, she was firm, in control. She would not turn into the old Maggie, desperate for approval.

'I'm not here to talk about the apartment. I'm here to make you come home.'

'I left two weeks ago, so it's taken you quite a long time to get here,' she said sharply.

'I was giving you time to think, time to get over being mad at me,' he said with such simple sincerity that she felt herself being pulled back in.

'I'm not mad, I'm hurt. Betrayed. Devastated,' she emphasised. 'Mad is what you get when you stub your toe. I loved you with all my heart for five years and you threw it back at me by taking another woman to bed in our apartment, so no, mad doesn't quite do that justice.'

'It was just a figure of speech,' he said, giving her that wry grin she adored.

Maggie felt herself being reeled in again, despite her plans to tell him it was all over. Because that's what she'd told herself she'd do, wasn't it?

Henry put the coffee down a second time.

'Is that all right for you, Maggie?' he asked.

'Yes, thank you, perfect,' she said.

Henry looked shrewdly from one to the other, smiled and walked back into the kitchen.

'You've every right to be angry with me,' Grey went on, as if they hadn't been interrupted. 'I didn't know what to do to make it better, that's the truth. I . . .' He hesitated. 'I know what you think, but nothing like this has ever happened before, I want you to believe that, Maggie. It was a stupid one-off thing and I can't forgive myself – that's why I haven't been in touch. I didn't think you'd even want to see me. I can understand how hard it is for you to forgive me but

150

please, we've got so much going for us. We can't throw it all away.'

'I didn't throw it all away – you did!' she breathed. 'You did.'

They both sat back in their chairs, a pair of gladiators wondering how to attack next.

Again, the moment on the terrace at Shona and Paul's wedding flashed through Maggie's mind. She hadn't been a strong modern woman and asked her boyfriend if he thought they should get married. She'd wittered on about how romantic the wedding was, waiting for him to say something, and then when he'd dodged the subject, she'd never mentioned it again. What a wimp.

'Why did you never want to get married?' she demanded suddenly. 'You knew I did. I hinted that I did. But you avoided the subject.'

'Well . . . I . . .' For once, Dr Grey Stanley was nonplussed.

Maggie watched him think. She could read his face like a book, or so she'd once believed – now she realised she was wrong. She hadn't read signs of his infidelity. Another certainty crumbled.

'You didn't want to get married, did you?' she said, looking down at her coffee.

'No,' he said. 'Truthfully, no. I thought we had everything already and that marriage would spoil it. Why fix what's not broken, right?'

'You're the one who broke it.'

He bowed his head, as if the weight of the pain was too much to bear. 'I can't tell you how sorry I am, Maggie. I miss you so much, I want you back, I should never have let you leave that morning. Everyone says I must be mad to have let you go, you're so stunning, beautiful, too good for me, they tell me.' And he laughed, but it was clear that some-body had indeed said that to him. And Maggie felt a surge

151

of pleasure that at least someone on campus had thought good of her.

'Is that why you're here? Because your colleagues think you should be with me instead of some beautiful little blonde?'

Grey looked up and stared at her with mystification. 'Beautiful? She's nothing compared to you. You've never had a clue how beautiful you are, Maggie. It's one of the most beguiling things about you. Most beautiful women are like stockbrokers, always bartering. Their presence costs. Presents, dinner, compliments. But not you. Even when you're sitting on the couch in your old jeans and that horrible cardigan you love, with your knees scrunched up, biting your cuticles watching a movie, you look like someone should be photographing you,' he added. 'I suppose I'm more used to the stockbroker beauties, they've got hard shells. They know their worth. But you don't.'

He reached out and took her hand now. 'Please come back to me. I do love you. Don't you believe me?'

'I believe you,' she said in a small voice, loving the feeling of his hand on hers. Her resolve to tell him it was over between them crumbled some more. 'But what does that mean, Grey? What does your loving me mean? I only want the sort of love that's not shared. I can't share you. That would kill me.'

'Let's get engaged,' he said eagerly. 'We'll set a date. Soon, let's get married soon. Please, can't you see that I'm serious?'

It sounded so seductive the way he put it. How easy it would be to go back to him. Familiarity lured her in. And marriage. Was this a proposal? If so, she would never have the face to tell people how she'd got engaged. Because her fiancé had had an affair . . .

'Now's not the time to talk about getting engaged,' she said firmly, taking her hand back.

But marriage. It was what she'd wanted ever since that day watching Shona and Paul make their vows.

There was one question she still had to ask.

'I know what you said, but I need to be certain: were there others?' She was sure she'd seen it in his eyes that night. A flash of guilt when she'd asked him if he'd slept with other women. Yet now, there was no guilt in his face, no sign that he had ever cheated before.

'I swear to you,' he said fervently, 'there has never been anyone else, Maggie. She came into my office and she was coming on to me and . . . I don't know, I felt flattered.' He hung his head, paused for a moment before looking up at her again, pleading. 'It's stupid, isn't it, stupid to be flattered by a student? She's just a kid and not even very bright. And I had you and you're so clever and brilliant and wonderful and a grown-up. Oh, I can't articulate all the things that you are, all the amazing things you are to me.'

In her head, Maggie computed that he was saying all the right things. But in her heart, she didn't care whether he was or not. He loved her, wanted her. That was what mattered. She needed him in her life.

'There was nobody else, ever?' she asked.

'No, never,' he said. 'I'll be honest, I was tempted. Some-times kids get a crush on lecturers. You know that, we've talked about how flattering it is. Come on, I'm nearly thirty-seven, I'm over the hill as far as these kids are concerned and it's hard to resist their attention. Who wouldn't be flattered? You know what I mean,' he pleaded, 'you've had the guys come into the library, smile at you and flirt. It turns you on a little bit and you feel good. But it doesn't mean anything. None of that takes away from the love that you feel for one person, and that one person is you, Maggie, I love you. I don't love some kid. She's nobody.'

'Which is worse,' Maggie said, all the hurt of seeing him in bed with that blonde nobody flooding back, crashing into her hopes of them being a couple again, 'that you think she

153

is a nobody or that you could have sex with someone you think is a nobody?'

He leaned back in his chair and his eyes glittered, the way they did when he was thinking. He was so clever. His mind could work on so many different levels and today Maggie could almost hear the cogs whirring.

'I didn't mean it like that,' he said. 'I don't think of women in that way.'

'Oh, for heaven's sake,' she interrupted, 'this is not a party political broadcast. I'm not a feminist voter you have to convince to come over to your side. I'm not worried about being politically correct when it comes to the person you fucked on our bed. I'm making the point that it says a lot about you when you can have sex with someone and then say they're nothing. I'd prefer it if you told me the truth.'

But she didn't really want to know the truth.

'You know what, this is a mistake,' she said wearily. She couldn't go back to him, not yet anyway. She needed more time to think about everything that had happened. 'You coming here. I was wrong. It's too soon. Maybe we should just talk on the phone or something. I'm not ready to see you and Mum's sick and . . . it's difficult.'

She had mused that afternoon in the library that two weeks was plenty of time to get over the fierce pain of his betrayal and talk sensibly but two weeks had turned out to be just a heartbeat after all. The agony was just as intense as it had been. She felt angry, hurt, stupid, so many conflicting emotions. She couldn't make a decision now.

'Let's talk about everything later. I'll come back to Galway soon and we can talk then.'

'No,' Grey said firmly. 'I want to talk to you now. I want to get it sorted out now. I can't go on living like this, with this uncertainty, wondering what's going to happen, wondering if you're going to come back to me.'

'Oh, so it's about you now, is it?' retorted Maggie furiously. 'You sleep around, wait two weeks to come to see me, then you have the audacity to say you were waiting for me to phone and you want to get it all sorted out and back to normal. Well, no thank you very much, Dr Stanley.'

'Please.' He grabbed one of her hands between both of his and his touch was electric.

'You shouldn't do that,' she said weakly, but she didn't mean it.

'I love you, Maggie,' he said. 'I'm going to go in a minute because I think that's what you want me to do, but I just want you to remember that I love you so, so much. Please remember that. I made a mistake, *one* mistake, don't crucify me for it, please. We're stronger than that. We're worth more than that.'

He stood up and leaned over the table and kissed her very gently on the lips. Almost against her will, Maggie found her head tilting up to get closer to him.

Then he moved away and stroked her cheek with exquisite gentleness.

'I love you,' he said. 'Please believe that.' And then he left.

Maggie stared back down into her coffee and stirred it. She added a couple more little packets of sugar and drank slowly, thinking. What on earth should she do?

Part of her desperately wanted to run out on to the street and call him back, to say that she couldn't live without him. But part of her was still too hurt to do that. His betrayal had broken something precious inside her and it could never be fixed.

No matter what, their relationship would never quite be the same. And, inside her, a voice relentlessly whispered: if they got back together, would Grey cheat on her again?

# CHAPTER TEN

The brass knocker shone, the doorstep was spotless and delicious scents of beeswax polish and home baking wafted from the hallway.

Faye loved the home she'd grown up in but there was something about walking back through the door that made her feel she'd failed her mother in some way. From this tiny council house, with a combination of her widow's pension and what she earned in her part-time job, her mother had put Faye and her brother, Miles, through college at a time when there weren't many kids on their street in third-level education.

The maze of houses in the vast Linden Estate had been a tough place to bring up children, riddled as it was with petty crime and the scourge of drugs.

But Josie Heffernan had managed to keep her children on the straight and narrow so that Faye could win a place at art college and Miles could achieve the school exam results he needed to study economics at Trinity.

Now Miles was a high-flyer in corporate banking, making good use of his mother's hard work. Although Faye regretted that they didn't make enough time to see each other very often, she knew he was a loving husband and father as well as a hard worker. He'd never gone off the rails in his life. But Faye still felt a twinge of guilt that she had wasted her early promise.

It was late on Sunday morning and the house was full of Josie's friends from St Michael's Church. Josie was what people called 'a pillar of the community' in the best sense of the phrase. She got involved with kindness and capability and really made a difference.

Today, as usual, her mother was holding court in the kitchen, with every seat in the place taken, the big stainless-steel teapot on the oilcloth, and the remains of some home-made scones on jammy plates.

'Hello, Faye,' said her mother, jumping up lithely. Josie was light on her feet. A small woman, like her daughter and her granddaughter, she didn't carry an ounce of spare fat because, as Amber accurately put it, 'Gran never sits down for long.'

Whether it was cleaning St Michael's, taking care of meals on wheels or working in a local daycare centre for disabled children, Josie gave it her all.

Stan Stack, Faye's stepfather, was reading the newspapers in the quiet of the tiny living room, although how he could concentrate with the laughs coming from the kitchen, Faye didn't know.

'When Father Sean said she could feed the baby in the church and she says "fair enough" and whips out a boob, I swear, I thought I'd laugh up a lung!' shrieked one woman, church perfect in a navy suit.

'Ah, Father Sean wouldn't mind, he's been on the missions and he's seen it all,' grinned Josie. 'He'd take that in his stride.' She loved Father Sean and called him the Under Boss, in that he answered to the Man Above.

'It wasn't the boob so much as the tattoo,' insisted the

navy-clad woman. '*Robbie 4Ever* in a heart. And the husband's called Tom. That's what got me.'

'Robbie Williams,' suggested one of the ladies thoughtfully over her scone. 'I do like him.'

'They can get them off with lasers nowadays.'

'Robbie Williams?'

'No, tattoos.'

More howling ensued.

Eventually, the visitors had had enough scones and tea, and took their leave. Mother and daughter were left alone in the kitchen. Without Josie's chatty, lively crew of friends, it seemed very quiet indeed.

'How's Amber?' asked Josie, making quick work of tidying up her kitchen.

'Fine,' Faye said.

Her mother said nothing but looked at Faye inquisitively.

'All right, she's not fine,' Faye gave in. Her mother would get the information out of her anyway. She might as well explain that Amber had been avoiding her since Thursday, using the excuse of studying to rush upstairs any time Faye tried to talk to her. 'She's moody and she wants to eat her dinner on her own instead of with me.'

Josie nodded.

'She shouted at me for going into her room the other night too, because I thought she was having a nightmare.' Faye could barely cope with how much it had hurt when Amber had sat up in bed and shouted at her, hissing that she needed some privacy. Faye was used to wandering into Amber's room any time, to chat to her daughter. Now she felt that she couldn't do that, either. 'She's cutting me off.'

'And you can see how it hurts,' finished Josie softly.

Shocked, Faye looked into her mother's face and saw remembered pain there. Nearly two decades ago, she'd caused Josie exactly the same hurt Amber was causing her, she realised. Yet her mother had never for a second betrayed how wounded she'd been. There had been no recriminations. Nothing but help when she'd needed it. Her mother was extraordinary, Faye realised, not for the first time.

'Is it a man?'

'She's not that into boys,' Faye said. 'You know what she and Ella are like: they run rings around Ella's brothers and they're dead set on getting into college. Modern girls are different, they're sorted, they know what they want and they won't let anyone or any man stop them.'

'If you're sure . . .' The rest of the sentence hung in the air.

'I'm sure,' Faye said. She'd know, wouldn't she?

'Where is she today?'

'Off at Ella's, studying. It's these bloody exams,' Faye went on. 'That's the problem. When they're over, everything will be fine again.'

'For sure,' said Josie. 'Myself and Stan were going to take the train out to Howth for a bit of lunch. Would you like to come?'

Faye smiled. 'I'd love to,' she said. After all, it wasn't as if she had anything else to do without Amber.


Sunshine, beautiful food and all the people she loved most in the world together – what could be better than that? thought Christie.

It was the Sunday of the celebration, the day the Devlin family celebrated the new life they'd nearly lost. Christie stood in her kitchen and thought of dear Lenkya's pronouncement on how you could kill or cure in the kitchen as she got ready to carry trays of food outside to the garden where her family sat, some in the full sun, some in the shade of the terrace. Dear Lenkya. She'd left Ireland many years ago and although they'd kept in touch for a long time, there came a

159

point when her letters stopped and Christie's ones were never replied to. Christie hoped she was happy wherever she was.

Today, in the same way Lenkya had woven comfort and friendship in her stews, Christie had put all her wisdom and love into her cooking to nourish her family every way she could. She wished and prayed happiness into every recipe, hoping that the ferocity of her love would provide a talisman for her sons, their wives and her born and unborn grand-children.

And hoping that this love could keep the feelings of danger away.

But no, Christie refused to think about Carey Wolensky. That man would not ruin today. This Sunday was for her family, a day of love, celebration and food.

There were tender chicken kebabs and bowls of chilled salad heaving with avocado, cherry tomatoes and honeydew melon. Baked potatoes laced with sour cream and chives sat with a dish of grilled rosemary-scented slivers of lamb, and Christie's own sliced tomato and fennel bread nestled in a basket with crusty white rolls.

'Are you cooking for the apocalypse?' James had teased the evening before when Christie missed her favourite TV show because she was up to her eyes in flour, baking, measuring and peering into the oven to see if the honey and poppy-seed cake had risen. 'I haven't ordered the nuclear shelter for the garden yet, but I can if you want. Although most people take cans of food with them . . .'

'I cook therefore I am,' Christie said serenely, spooning mixture into muffin cases.

Which was true. Cooking was therapy for her as well as an expression of love for her family and right now, she needed that spiritual nourishment.

James's hand snaked out towards the mixing bowl.

Christie laughed and let him take one finger's worth of dough, before slapping his hand away.

'People who tease me don't get fed,' she said.

'Are you making guacamole for me?' he asked, eyeing the avocados. James loved food and would eat most things, but his love for guacamole was legend in the Devlin family annals.

'Have I ever forgotten to make it for you?' Christie patted his cheek with a floury hand and went on with her spooning.

'No,' said James and put his arms around his wife for a kiss.

Who'd have thought guacamole would be the secret to love, Christie thought, closing her eyes and leaning back into his arms: on such strange things were marriages made.

'Mum, this is delicious,' sighed Ethan, sitting back in a striped deckchair, the dogs at his feet and a plate piled high on his lap.

'Yes,' murmured Janet, who was paler than usual, but had a light in her eyes that Christie had never seen there before. 'I like this eating for two thing.'

'It really kicks in at dessert,' Ethan's wife, Shelly, informed her sister-in-law. 'You don't think you can eat two entire pieces of cheesecake or two wedges of chocolate cake, but you can.'

Ethan and Shane, well trained by their mother, helped her tidy up so she could bring the desserts out.

'Thanks,' Shane said, kissing her affectionately on the cheek. 'This is a lovely party.'

It was getting so hot that the dogs came in to lie on the kitchen floor, panting in the heat.

James carried in the last of the buffet plates and stacked them in the dishwasher.

'I don't know if it's the wine talking, but today has made me think. We're very lucky, Christie, aren't we?' he said as he straightened up. 'We've got everything, a healthy family, each other, a few quid in the bank.'

161

'Hey, don't you think I know it?' replied Christie, smiling at her husband. She'd had a glass of wine too and finally felt the tension leave her. She must stop thinking about Carey Wolensky. After all, how could something from so long ago touch her now? 'I thank God every day for what we've got.'

From outside in the garden came the sounds of their family enjoying themselves. Sasha was shrieking as she chased around after balloons that Christie really hoped wouldn't get caught on the spiky thorns of her Madame Pompadour rose. Children always got so upset about balloons popping.

Christie didn't have to look out to know that Shane would be beaming from ear to ear, the proud look of the daddy to be. He'd had that look on his face all day and Christie could remember when James looked exactly the same. The pride of the family man.

'I say thanks every day too,' said James. 'But, you know,' he paused, 'do you ever worry that something will happen? That one of us will become ill, something random, something we can't do anything about.'

Christie stared at him. James was never maudlin, not even after a glass of wine. Instantly, she wondered what he knew, how he'd found out. Yet he couldn't know anything, could he?

'What do you mean?' she asked tightly.

'No, no, it's nothing,' James said. 'It's just . . . I don't know. It all seems so good. Sometimes I worry that it could all go horribly wrong and we could end up bitter and twisted.'

Christie's anxious eyes looked for some sign that he knew, but there was none. Perhaps it was just that her feeling spooked had transmitted itself to him.

'Is that all?' she said with relief. 'You're the least bitter and twisted person I know. Just because we're happy doesn't mean something has to come along and ruin it all.'

'Ah, it's nothing.' James brushed his melancholy thoughts

162

away. 'I'm just being stupid. It's probably the male menopause.'

'You're too old for the male menopause,' Christie teased. 'That was supposed to happen ages ago, when I went through mine. I didn't do too badly, I didn't run off with some handsome young stud.'

'If you had, I'd have bloody killed them,' James said, suddenly serious.

'Lucky no one fitted the job description at the time,' she teased, but felt sick inside. Why had she said that? How stupid. 'Seriously, you're safe enough, my love. What would I want with a young stud, when I have you?' Christie put her arms around James, and they kissed, sinking into an embrace that was familiar and reassuring, except that today Christie didn't feel reassured.

'OK, back to basics,' she said, leaning against him. 'What are we going to do, financially, for Shane and Janet? We've got to do something. They're totally broke and they have no idea how expensive babies are.'

'I was thinking about that too,' James said. 'We've got some savings. What are we keeping them for?'

Christie kissed him. 'You're a great father,' she said, thinking of how hard it had been to save that money.

'What are you two looking so thoughtful about?' said a voice. It was Ana wandering in with another empty wine bottle. 'This is a celebratory day,' she added a touch too merrily. 'We should be happy, celebrating.'

'We're just having a chat,' Christie said lightly. 'James, will you get another bottle out of the fridge and I'll sort out the cake? Ana, you could take out these little fairy cakes I've made for the children.' She'd spent ages doing them the night before: pretty-coloured iced cakes with little animal faces to tempt the toddlers' appetites.

'Delighted to help,' said Ana, slurring her words slightly.

Over her head, James and Christie exchanged a glance. Ana had never been used to drinking and after two glasses really needed to lie down in a darkened corner.

'Come on, Ana,' James said, putting his arm around his sister-in-law affectionately. 'I'll take the plate.'

Christie was left alone in the kitchen to sort out the cake. Looking out the window, she could see Ethan cuddling little Sasha. Shelly and Janet were engrossed in baby talk, while Janet's mother, Margery, threw a balloon up into the air for Fifi. James was smiling as he helped a giggling Ana to a comfy chair.

Christie watched her family and wished she could see the future when it mattered.

James was right, they had been lucky. But it was more than luck that had made their marriage so strong over the years. You didn't spend thirty-five years with somebody without wanting to kill them occasionally. Or even leave them.

There had been that time when the children were very young and she and James had drifted far apart, when work had taken over his life and Christie had been low on his list of priorities, but they'd got over that. Eventually.

They'd worked hard to get over their differences. There hadn't been many big rows in the Devlin family household. Having grown up with nervous tension as a constant backdrop, Christie hated rows. Her father's rantings had been enough to put her off arguments for life. James was easy-going and affectionate and had brought their children up to be the same. So yes, there had been hard work involved. All the same, they were lucky. Why was James suddenly worried that their luck was about to turn? Christie shivered despite the heat.

# CHAPTER ELEVEN

It was Sunday evening, one of the most important evenings ever for Karl and the band. Amber had escaped from Summer Street by telling her mother she was going to be studying late and not to bother her.

She'd left the radio on low in her room, closed the door, and hoped her mother had listened the night Amber had made her point about deserving a little privacy. That privacy meant keeping her mother away from her room so she could escape out to Karl. It also meant huge guilt over the deception.

Now, despite the two giant Southern Comforts Karl had bought her, Amber's mouth was dry and her heart was thudding. She prickled with nerves. She'd found the perfect position at the right side of the SnakePit stage, behind a giant light where there was a small box she could sit on and see perfectly, yet remain out of sight.

Huge cables trailed around her feet. The stage and backstage were both hives of activity as muscle-bound guys with tattooed biceps shifted amps and equipment, shouting to each other as they worked. Two men with radio headsets directed the backstage dance, snapping out directions, ticking off on clipboard lists. Everyone backstage at the venue appeared to have a role, from the various promoters' staff rushing round with laminates rattling off their chests to the bands themselves, cocooned in their dressing rooms to get ready.

'Give us a moment, kid?' Karl's newly appointed manager, Stevie, had said to Amber in the band's poky little room fifteen minutes previously. Before she'd been able to throw a questioning look at Karl to say how dare the man dismiss her like that, Stevie had hustled her out into the dimly lit corridor right behind the stage. Here, nobody seemed to know or care that she was Karl Evans's girlfriend and muse. Here, she was a blonde in jeans in a place that had seen a lot of blondes in jeans who were *with the band*. Amber had felt she might cry. This Sunday evening event was so important for Karl and, therefore, for her. A big showcase gig that horrible Stevie had got for them. Producers, heads of record companies, everyone who was anyone was going to be there to see the hot new bands. It was huge, but Amber, who felt she was irrevocably tied up with Karl and his future, had been sidelined.

Anxiously, she fiddled with the tiger's-eye pendant she'd found in her mother's drawer and which she wore on many of her trips with Karl. It had always comforted her before, making her think of Mum and home, where she was safe, treasured, much more than a hanger-on.

But since the terrible row on Thursday evening, when Mum had given her that stupid present, nothing had given her much comfort.

They'd had rows before, but never like that. Never with such words of bitterness and anger. Amber could hardly bear to think of what she'd said, but she couldn't back down and say sorry, because there was so much more to be said.

*Mum, I'm leaving with Karl and I won't be sitting my exams, won't be going to college.*

She'd done her best to avoid her mother all weekend,

166

muttering about having to study and not meeting Faye's eyes. She couldn't face it. The tension was killing her.

She hadn't told Karl about the row, either. He had been worrying so much about tonight he hadn't noticed how upset she was. And now he'd let Stevie throw her out of the dressing room, hadn't fought for her, hadn't sneaked out to see whether she was all right.

She hugged her knees up close to her chest, and laid her cheek on one knee. Hidden away here, safe and unseen, she'd be fine.

There were three bands before Karl's, and Amber listened, her eyes half closed in concentration, jealous of any sign of anyone better than him. And then they were on stage and her nerves returned in force.

Please let them be brilliant. Please let there be no bum notes. Don't let Karl fall apart from stage fright.

There were four of them in the band, Ceres: three other guys who were good-looking and good musicians, too, but Karl had been right when he'd told her that first night that he was the band. It was the simple truth. The magnetism he had offstage was magnified tenfold on it. Brooding and Byronic, he held the mike to his mouth with two hands, like a man might hold his lover's face cupped close to his own before kissing her lips.

*Now I've found you, I can't let you go*
*You're in my blood*
*In my dreams*
*Like a sleepwalker, I'll come back to you*
*My love*

It was the song he'd written for her.

'You inspired me,' he said softly after he'd played it to her one afternoon in the quiet of her bedroom when she should

167

have been at double history. Amber had listened with her heart singing along, because this was pure, true love: to be immortalised in song as the beloved of a man as gifted as Karl.

And it was all worth it, even putting up with nasty Stevie, who looked at her with appraising eyes as if she was a piece of meat he was bidding for at a market. He'd only known Karl for a week. Wait till he realised that Amber wasn't some bit of fluff, that she was part of Karl, then Stevie would change his attitude.

The last note of their three-song set finished, and Karl raised his hands in triumph at the crowd, who cheered wild approval.

They'd loved him and his band.

A huge grin split Amber's face as her lover turned to where she sat hidden and smiled that private, sexy smile he kept for her alone. He'd seen her! But just as quickly, he turned to his audience, still with her smile on his face, a smile of such languorous heat that people screamed. Then, applause ringing in his ears, he dragged himself away from the drug of the crowd's approval and stalked offstage, long-limbed, panther-like, utterly fuckable. He passed feet away from Amber's hiding place and never glanced her way. He hadn't seen her at all, she realised with a jolt. That private smile had not been for her, but for the thousand-strong crowd he'd held in the palm of his hand. It wasn't her smile any more: it was everybody's.

Amber snatched at her tiger's-eye pendant for comfort but there was none there.

An hour later in a small, late-night restaurant, Amber went to slide into the curved banquette seat beside Karl, but Stevie – stocky, slicked-back hair Stevie in his heavy leather jacket and chunky Tag Heuer watch – muscled in past her so subtly that only Amber felt the nastiness of the gesture.

'How's my best lead singer?' he said, grabbing Karl's shoulders in a matey manner.

'Walking on air,' replied Karl. 'That was some buzz in the SnakePit, wasn't it?'

'In two words, in-credible,' said Lew, the drummer, moving in to sit the other side of Karl, pulling his girlfriend, a shy girl called Katie, in after him.

'Amazing,' Kenny T, the keyboards man, pronounced, squashing up beside Katie.

'Total blast,' sighed Sydney, bass guitar. Sydney's girlfriend was away, so had missed their night of triumph. Syd had spent ages on the phone trying to describe how wonderful it had all been, and was now drinking himself into oblivion to make up for her absence. Syd settled in beside Stevie and then looked up at Amber, still standing beside the table, waiting for Karl to notice her and make space for her beside him.

But Karl didn't notice. He was wrapped up in Stevie and the flannel that spewed effortlessly from the manager's mouth.

Everyone wanted to sign the band.

They were the hottest ticket there. Stevie was so shallow, so fake, Amber thought.

Could nobody see it except for her? They were all in thrall to Stevie, laughing at his hopeless jokes. What do you call a drummer with no girlfriend? Homeless.

Lew, the drummer, laughed himself sick at that one, seeming not to realise that it was totally true in his case because Katie's teacher's salary supported him.

It was a horrible evening and Amber had never been so glad as when it ended and she and Karl were alone in the taxi.

'Will you stay the night? Please, this was so special. I want you here beside me when I wake up so I know it hasn't all been a dream.'

Karl's head was resting on her shoulder in the taxi, his breath still sweet with the orangey tang of the final glass of Cointreau. There had been endless drinks, champagne even. 'You better get used to it because it'll be premier cru all the way from now on,' Stevie had said, summoning waiters with a rude click of his fingers.

At least the waiters could see what he was like, filling his glass more slowly than anyone else's, glaring at him. She hoped they'd spat in his coffee.

'Stay,' repeated Karl sleepily.

Amber never stayed. Staying might mean her mother finding out that her bed wasn't slept in, that she hadn't been burning the midnight oil in her bedroom, studying diligently like the sensible schoolgirl she was supposed to be.

And then Karl's hands unbuttoned her jacket and reached into the cavern of her cleavage, expertly finding the exact place where the lacy strap of her bra gave a finger's-width access to the bare skin beneath.

She felt the liquid rush of desire hit her groin and moaned softly, moving closer. 'I want to be with you tonight, Amber. Please.' Suddenly, the words of the song he'd written for her came into her mind.

To hell with not wanting her mother to know. She'd have to know sometime. Karl was a part of Amber's life now, for ever.

'I'll stay,' she murmured back. 'Just try and stop me.'

Faye woke early the next morning. It was Monday and she hoped that a new week would bring peace between her and Amber. Her daughter was definitely avoiding her and, yesterday evening, had gone upstairs to study at six, saying she'd see her mother in the morning.

Faye had stood at the door before she went to bed, but she could still hear the low sound of the radio Amber always listened to when she worked, and she decided that interrupting the study might result in another argument.

Faye normally liked waking early and would get a cup of coffee and sit up in bed reading and thinking. But today, she was too restless to sit. She brewed coffee and decided to take a cup in to Amber both to wake her up and as a peace offering. Not that Faye felt she was the one who had to say sorry because Amber had been the one to fight.

But being a parent had taught her that getting over an argument was what mattered: not how you did it or who felt they'd won. You could be victorious or be happy was the child/parent mantra.

She knocked on Amber's door and then walked in, expecting to see the gloom of shut curtains and Amber, a sleepy lump, huddled in her bed.

But the curtains were open, so was the sash window and Amber's bed was patently unslept in. The radio hummed low in the background, set to Amber's favourite station. The room was cool from the window being open a long time and Faye realised that her daughter hadn't slept at home the night before.

Faye dropped the cup of coffee, didn't care that it spilled all over the floor.

'Oh Lord, what's happened?' she cried. 'Amber, where are you?'

She ran for her phone and dialled Amber's mobile but got nothing but the automated message asking her to leave a message.

'Amber, wherever you are, please phone me back, love, please. It was only an argument, that's all. I understand how stressed you are, just call. It's all OK.'

Faye had no idea what she should do next. She certainly couldn't go into work as normal with Amber missing. Panic had robbed her of her senses. Finally, she sank to her knees on the landing floor and prayed. Dear God, I know I haven't been around much lately after all I prayed to you when she was a baby, but find her for me, please, please, I beg you.

Ella's phone was off too. They could be together. That might be something, at least together they'd have each other. But if Amber was alone and unhappy, out there somewhere thinking her mother was furious with her . . .

Faye scrolled through her mobile directory, found the number for Ella's house and phoned. The fact that it was six forty-five in the morning was immaterial.

A male voice answered.

'Marco, it's Faye Reid. Is your mother or Ella there?'

'Hang on,' Marco said, catching the urgency in her clipped tone.

She heard muffled conversation and then Trina, Ella's mother, came on the line.

'Faye, it's Trina. What's wrong?'

'It's Amber, she's not here and her bed's not been slept in,' Faye said shakily. 'I can't get her on her phone. We had a row on Thursday, it was over nothing, you know how it is. But she's been avoiding me since then, barely said two words to me, and now, when I went in to wake her, she's gone. I'm sure she hasn't been home all night. Trina, is Ella there? Amber might have stayed with you, or Ella might know where Amber is.'

'Ella's here but I know that Amber isn't,' Trina said, doing her best to hide the instinctive relief that at least she knew where her daughter was. 'I had to wake Ella for school and Amber's not there. Hold on, I'll get Ella now.'

'Ask her,' Faye begged, 'ask her if she knows where Amber is, if they talked about the argument.'

It was several long minutes before a reluctant-sounding Ella said 'hello' into the phone.

'Ella, I know she'd talk to you if she was upset,' began Faye, her voice shaky. 'Just tell me where she's gone.'

'I can't, Mrs Reid,' Ella said slowly. 'I think I know who she's with but I don't know where exactly. I'm sorry – I shouldn't be telling you this, Amber should.'

'Tell her what?' demanded Trina's voice in the background. 'If you know anything about where Amber is, you better spill the beans now. Her poor mother is sick with worry.'

'She'll kill me if I do,' Ella hissed at her mother.

'I'll kill you if you don't,' Trina hissed back.

'Where is she?' demanded an anguished Faye.

Ella sighed. 'His name is Karl and he's in a band called Ceres. We met him in a club in town and they've been going out for a few weeks. She's probably at his flat. I don't know where it is, though, sorry.'

Two mothers made involuntary gasps of shock.

The phone rattled as it changed hands and Trina came back on the line.

'Faye, I'm so sorry. I had no idea,' she said. 'Is there anything I can do?'

'No, thanks,' said Faye, sure that Ella had already fled the scene to text the grisly news to Amber. *Your mother knows and you're up to your neck in it.* 'I'll leave a message on her phone and then, I'll have to wait until she decides to come home.'

Faye rang in sick. She couldn't cope with work with this huge issue unresolved. She was tidying the kitchen when Amber finally made it home at half eleven that morning, still in her going-out clothes, her eyes wary, her pale skin evidence of lack of sleep. And sex, Faye thought, horrified. Her baby had been out with some man having sex when she'd thought Amber was tucked up in bed.

'Tell me about this Karl,' said Faye grimly.

'I love him. I'm going to New York with him.' Amber snapped the words out in a voice that brooked no opposition. On the journey home, with both Ella's text and a phone message from her mother telling her that she knew about

173

Karl, she'd been caught between fear and fury. Her mother would not stop her seeing Karl. No way.

'You're what?' said Faye, disbelieving. 'Don't be ridiculous. You don't even know him, how can you love him and leave the country with him?'

'I know enough to know he's the man I love.' Amber spat it out.

'When did this happen?' This had to be a sick joke, a game that Ella and Amber had dreamed up.

'Last month. He's a musician, he's in a band. He's a songwriter, he's brilliant,' Amber said fiercely. 'I love him.'

'You love him? You can hardly know him. And what do you mean about going to New York with him?'

'I do love him and I do know him. Where do you think I've been every night for the past month?' hissed Amber. 'Not in my room, that's for sure.'

The kitchen suddenly seemed cold to Faye, even though it was sunny outside, as the enormity of what Amber had kept from her struck home. Nothing or no one in her past had ever made her feel so betrayed before, simply because she'd never loved anyone the way she loved her daughter.

'I can't believe you lied to me,' she said, then tried a different tack. 'Amber, you know this is crazy. You can't head off with a strange guy. You've got exams. You can't have been studying and you'll never pass . . .'

'I'm not doing the exams, didn't you hear me?' shouted her daughter. 'Don't you ever listen? I'm not going to college, I'm going away with Karl. You can't stop me, you know.' Amber realised her mother looked as if she'd been struck in the face. Well, it was her mother's fault – she never listened.

'You can't stop me,' she yelled again. 'I'm an adult. I don't want to go to college. You've always said an education was the most important thing in the world, well, you dropped out of college and you've done fine. I can paint any time I

174

want to, Mum. This is about living life now, something you've never understood.'

Faye thought of how she'd lived her life and the pain it had brought her and how the only good decent thing she'd felt she'd ever had was her life with Amber. Now it was disappearing in front of her eyes.

'Running away with some guy in a band isn't a life,' she said softly. 'You think it is but it isn't.' She took a deep breath. 'I know.'

'You don't know a thing about it,' yelled Amber.

'I've been there,' insisted Faye.

'Yeah right!'

Amber's gorgeous face was angry and bitter. She'd never looked at Faye like that before and it was crueller than all the words to see the fury and resentment in her eyes.

'How did all this happen?' Faye asked helplessly, knowing the question sounded stupid but not knowing how else to put it.

'It happened while you were trying to make me live the life you want me to live,' Amber said. 'I'm not that sort of person, Mum. You can't make me just like you.'

Faye choked back a bitter laugh. There were so many things she should have taught Amber. Things *she'd* had to learn the hard way, lessons she'd sworn her daughter would never need to learn.

Instead, she'd hoped she could keep Amber cocooned from the crazy wild world and wrap her up in mother love and domesticity. A good school, nice friends, cosy happy families – that would keep her safe. And she'd still failed.

'I'm going,' Amber said briskly, wanting to be out of there. 'I'm sorry. I don't mean to hurt you but I've got to live my own life and you've got to too. You can't live through me.'

'Is that what you think I've been doing?' asked her mother quietly.

'Isn't it?' Amber's face was the impetuous mask of youth. She knew everything and her mother knew nothing, right?

'I'll be in touch.'

'You can't go now.' Faye came to life and dragged herself to her feet. 'Don't be silly, I've got to meet this guy. And your exams are only a couple of weeks away, Amber. Think about what you're doing.'

'I have thought about it,' Amber said simply. 'And I'm going. There's nothing you can do about it. I'll be eighteen in two days. Old enough to vote, old enough for anything.'

'You can't leave now.' Her mother looked crazy, fluttery, uncertain, which was scary because that wasn't Mum.

'I'm sorry, I can't hang around. We'd just fight and you'd stop me seeing Karl.'

'Karl,' repeated her mother bitterly. 'Why can't I meet this Karl, then, if he's so fabulous? Or is he a down-and-out in a band of no-hopers?'

'He's amazing and I love him. He makes me feel alive.'

She couldn't bear anyone to criticise Karl, not even her mum. Especially not her mum. Her mum didn't understand, nobody did, not even Ella.

'I'm going to pack,' Amber said coldly. 'Don't bother running after me. I want to live my own life now and you can't stop me.'

Faye was silent, thinking of the many things she needed to tell Amber but couldn't. Because then she'd have to give up her secret and that was the one thing she could never, never do. Amber would hate her for it. Faye hated herself.

Amber ran upstairs to pack, trying to quickly work out what she needed in her new life: not the knick-knacks on the white chest of drawers, which she'd lovingly painted with butterflies one weekend, Mum varnishing the artwork

176

afterwards, saying how beautiful it was. Not all the good-girl clothes. But she'd take a lot of her stuff. She was moving out, after all. This wasn't just a holiday.

And she'd take the pendant. She'd take it because it was beautiful and it was a reminder of home. Not that she needed it but something of the past was good. God knows where her mother had got it in the first place. She couldn't imagine her mother wearing it, looking cool. What had she said: *I've been there*. Oh yeah, right.

As if her mother had ever done anything wild in her life.

Maggie was walking briskly past the railway cottages when she saw the woman standing at the gate of the first cottage, staring wild-eyed up the road, her face wet with tears. She was dressed in a plain navy suit with her hair tied neatly back, but there all vestiges of normality ended. Her face was distraught, as if she'd had the worst news ever and her world was crashing around her.

Maggie didn't know the woman's name, although she sort of recognised her, and for a nano-second, she wondered what the etiquette was for this situation.

'Are you all right?' she asked, stopping. To hell with etiquette. If the woman wanted to tell her to get lost, then that was fine too. But she just couldn't walk on by in the face of such human pain.

'No,' said the woman in a low moan, not even looking at Maggie. 'She's gone and I didn't try to stop her. I knew I couldn't and now she's gone and I don't know where. What am I going to do? I should have locked her in the house, made her stay, but I didn't.' She began to cry again, a low keening noise.

This was bad. Maggie looked around and saw the familiar figure of Christie Devlin on the other side of Summer Street walking her two small dogs back from the park. Christie

177

might know this woman and what to do, because Maggie sure as hell didn't.

'Mrs Devlin?' called Maggie. 'Mrs Devlin? Can you help? *Please.*'

Together, Maggie and Christie helped Faye into Christie's house where they sat her on an old soft armchair in the living room. Once Christie had established what had happened, she thought that Faye might be better off away from her own home and the scene of the row, where Amber's presence was everywhere. Maggie had located house keys and Faye's handbag in the Reids' kitchen, closed the door, and then the trio had walked to the Devlins' house, with the dogs following quietly, anxious at all the crying.

'I'm sorry, I'm sorry, but Amber, she's a good girl. You know,' Faye kept muttering over and over. 'She's run off, you see. With a man, someone I've never heard of before and have never met, and I didn't try to stop her. I let her go and I don't know where she's gone.'

'It's hard to stop someone when they've made their mind up,' Christie said gently. 'Amber certainly has a mind of her own, Faye, and she's an adult now. She's nearly eighteen, right? So legally, she's an adult, whether or not she is emotionally.'

'She's still a baby,' wailed Faye. 'She's nearly eighteen on the outside but she's so vulnerable on the inside and I've let her down because I never told her the truth. I thought she'd be better off not knowing and now she thinks I want her to be boring and have no fun, except it wasn't that. I wanted to protect her from what I went through.'

It was like watching a rock crumble, Christie thought compassionately. She hardly knew Faye Reid and, from the outside, nobody would have guessed that this outwardly together woman would ever react with such wild grief.

Christie knew that Amber was Faye's life and that the two were very close. But a man had come into the mix – that's

178

what Amber must have been up to the day Christie had spotted her skipping school, Christie remembered, and shook her head grimly. The result was the sort of relationship triangle that could never work and Christie felt sorry for the loser – Faye.

In spite of her exasperation at Amber for leaving her mother in such a way, Christie could see that running away from the scene of the emotional crime often seemed like the only option. It was what she herself had done, wasn't it?

'You stay with Faye,' she told Maggie now. 'I'll make tea, hot and sweet to give her energy.'

A faint grin lit up Maggie's face. 'Now I know why you and my mother are such friends, Mrs Devlin,' she said. 'She thinks tea is the answer to all life's problems too.'

'And shortbread biscuits,' Christie added wryly. 'Don't forget the biscuits. They might not be the answer but they help you back on your feet so you can deal with the pain. And don't call me Mrs Devlin. It makes me feel about a hundred when I'm not at school. I'm Christie.'

It wasn't like talking to someone of her mother's generation, Maggie thought when Christie had gone.

She could also see why her mother said Christie Devlin was sought by all in times of crisis: Una Maguire would have made the tea, all right, and then talked rapidly about anything to fill the air in case anyone started talking about what was really wrong. But Christie said little, and waited calmly and serenely in case Faye needed to talk. And she'd know when there was a deep, dark subject waiting to be brought up, Maggie thought with a flash of pain. She was thinking of herself as a teenager when the painful subjects had never been touched upon. If Christie had been her mother, she'd have seen the trouble Maggie was going through from the very first day she came home from school, shell-shocked at the naked hatred she'd encountered from the gang of bullies.

179

And she'd have sorted it all out, too. And Maggie might have become a different person, not anxious and insecure. She might have become the person she'd like to be.

'Are you all right, Maggie?' whispered Christie, coming back with the tea and laying a cool hand on the young woman's wrist.

Maggie nodded, flashing a smile. Christie thought that, with her flaming hair and wistful eyes, she looked more beautiful than Una had been when Christie met her thirty years ago. But Maggie was different from her mother in other ways, Christie realised. Una was a whirling free spirit, happy wherever she was, content in herself and her world. While Maggie was like a nervous deer, easily startled, unsure of herself, hopelessly unconfident.

Faye was not the only one here today with some secret past, Christie decided.

The hot, sweet tea did as hoped and stopped Faye crying, but she still looked bereft.

'I suppose you think I'm a hopeless mother,' she muttered to Christie. 'I didn't know what was going on under my own nose. Teachers always say they hear the real story from kids when the kids can't talk to their parents at home, but Amber did talk to me, she did.'

'I don't think you're a hopeless mother at all,' Christie said. 'I think you're a wonderful mum, and it's not an easy job, I know.' She gave a rueful laugh. 'You should try having two boys. They can challenge you, that's for sure. And there were lots of times – are lots of times still,' she corrected herself, thinking of Shane and news of the precious third grandchild on the way, 'when you think you know what's going on and really you haven't a clue. Any teacher who says otherwise doesn't know much about human nature.'

Faye nodded, sniffing.

'We were so close, you see, that's what's hard.' She turned

180

to Maggie. 'I know you don't really know me, but I know your parents and they'd tell you, Amber is a good girl.'

'Mum's said,' Maggie interrupted. 'She's a wonderful artist, right?'

'Right.' Faye looked so pleased and proud for a moment, before the realisation hit her again – Amber wasn't going to college to work on her great artistic ability. She was going off with that horrible man.

'Could we phone the police?' she asked suddenly.

Christie looked at Maggie, a look shot through with pity, before replying: 'They can't help much when the person is of age, you know. She can go where she wants, really. When's she eighteen?'

'On Wednesday,' said Faye.

'And she's taken her passport, I suppose. Has she got one?'

'Yes, but I didn't look. But how can she go to America without a visa or anything . . . Maybe she won't go if she can't get into the country?' Faye was hopeful.

'If he's in a band and they're going there for work, they might organise visas through the record company, with one for her too,' Maggie said, shrugging. 'With travel security so tight, they might get round it that way.'

There was a silence as Faye digested that bit of information. 'So she's really gone. After eighteen years, she's gone.' And she began to cry again, only this time they were the silent, body-wrenching sobs that were somehow more painful to hear than any noisy ones.

'Oh, Faye,' Maggie said in anguish, grabbing Faye's hand. 'She's a clever girl, everyone says so. She'll be able to look after herself and growing up with just the two of you, she'll have learned so much about taking care of herself. She'll be fine. This guy could be a wonderful guy after all. Think of all you've taught her and trust her.'

Faye's eyes, when she looked up, were hollow with pain.

'That's it, you see,' she said bleakly. 'I could have taught her so much but I didn't. I wanted to protect her. There's so much badness in the world, men who treat you like dirt and really don't care. I've been there, I've been down there. I'll never forget it. I never wanted my daughter to go through what I went through.'

'But you never told her what you saw and experienced, did you?' Christie asked intuitively.

'No,' Faye said. 'I never told her. I was ashamed of what I'd been and done, and thought if I could just keep her in this cosy world, then she'd never go down the same path as me.'

Christie could suddenly see everything. The old Faye Reid had gone, her façade was shed like an old skin and the real Faye sat there, a woman without all the answers for the first time in years.

'And that's just what she's done,' Faye finished. 'I've sent her off into the world not knowing the truth about anything that mattered because I wanted to protect her, and it turns out, I haven't protected her at all: I've left her completely unarmed.'

'Music,' Faye said, as she began to tell her story. 'That was my passion when I was a teenager. Music and stories about love. I spent every penny on records, and myself and Charlotte, my friend from school, read romance novels and dreamed. I loved the books with the clinches on the cover. You know the ones: there was a woman and a gorgeous man holding her to him, as if he'd never let her go.' Her eyes were misty, dreaming of that time.

'That's what I wanted. I wanted to be beautiful and adored. I wanted to be the woman in that picture with the man telling me I was too beautiful, too incredible for him to live without me. I grew up in a place called the Linden Estate, it's a council estate and not many dreams came true there. But there were ways of escape and I chose mine: I remember the first time Charlotte and I went out like grown-ups. I was in college then, and there were all these cool places to hang out. One in particular was on the quays. They had late-night live music. It was all red inside, dark red with smeared mirrors and shiny seats where you could sit for hours making your drink last,' she said. 'It wasn't like I'd thought it would be at first. There weren't people fighting over us, we were on the edges. Charlotte didn't like it much, but I did. And I wanted to fit in. I figured out that if you hung around long enough you'd become part of the scene and somehow I did. I was supposed to be working on my degree but I wasn't doing any work. I loved sitting and watching, learning about life but not out of a book.'

Faye's eyes were dreamy. They were the same as her daughter's: a luminous and magnetic pewter grey with that startling ring of amber around the inky black of the pupils, Christie realised. She could suddenly see the beauty of the young Faye, the girl who'd cared how she looked, with long streaked hair like her daughter's, a grown-up woman's body, and the heart of an eager young girl who'd wanted to be loved, to be part of something.

Christie reached out and took Faye's hand, but Faye didn't appear to notice. She was lost in remembering the past . . .

There was TJ, there was always TJ. In the outside world, there were no jobs then, people were leaving the country for London and New York looking for work, wearing their best suits and fine-tuning their résumés. But not TJ. He wasn't cutting his long, dark hair to get a boring job. He wore his in a ponytail and it suited his long, lean face with its soulful hollows. He wasn't a man from a romance novel, he wore a leather jacket instead of a white shirt, but his body was the same sinewy combination of muscle and energy, and there was passion in his soul and in his eyes. Faye had seen it, seen the way he looked at her, knew he wanted her.

There were a lot of them from her college hanging around The Club, and they all looked up to the older guys, the regulars like TJ, who'd seen it all and bought the ripped T-shirt. And she was a regular now, too, as much part of the place as the scent of stale smoke – cigarette and other kinds – in the air. The Club was like a second home to her.

'Silver, baby,' TJ said that night, 'they oughta have a picture of you over the door.'

He called her Silver, even though it wasn't her name. It was her new name, her club name, so it was what she was called now. She loved it. Her hair had long strands of platinum through the tawny golds and browns. Silver strands.

The music was low with an insistent bass. No matter what music was in fashion, The Club played rock – tonight, TJ's favourite, the Stones. Faye loved their music. Song after song, reaching into her heart and tearing it out. Every emotion was there: pain, love, sexual ecstasy, heartbreak, Mick's voice speaking directly to her.

TJ passed her the joint.

'Try this, Silver, you'll like it.'

His hand was around her shoulder, touching her breast through her thin T-shirt, a gesture of possession to all the other men around the booth. Telling them she was his, Faye thought with pride.

There was a moment before she took the first drag of the joint when she thought how odd it was – her, goody-two-shoes honours student, here in a smoky bar about to smoke hash. This was unlike anything she had envisaged before. And then, the moment passed, for the heady numbness soaked into her limbs.

TJ smiled, sipped more of his Jack Daniel's and smiled some more as he watched her get happy. When she was

184

happy, Faye got up and danced on her own, with TJ looking on from the back booth, his eyes hooded, watching her body undulate to the music.

That night, he sent Faye up to the bar to order drinks.

'Hi, Maria,' she said to the barmaid. 'Can I have four JDs, one Coke, and three double vodkas, no ice.'

Maria was forty, maybe older. She had dyed red hair, big brown eyes and a smoker's mouth with lots of lines. In her black jeans and teeny T-shirt, with the tattooed butterfly on her biceps, she didn't look like Faye's mother, but she spoke to her like a mother now.

'Honey, you shouldn't be here,' Maria said, expertly filling the drinks order. 'You're just a nice kid. What are you, nineteen, twenty? This place isn't for you.'

'Why not?' Faye asked, confused.

''Cos that man is using you, can't you see? They're laughing at you, honey.' Maria paused at the disbelieving look in Faye's eyes. 'I'm only trying to help. I hate to see you get tangled up in this world. Get out, while you can.'

'You're wrong,' Faye said. 'Nobody's using me.'

Maria moved closer to her. 'Honey, you know what they call you? Silver.'

'It's because of my hair,' Faye said, smiling, shaking her mane.

'No,' said Maria flatly. 'It's because TJ's the Lone Ranger. His horse was called Silver. It's because he rides you.'

'What's up, Silver?' TJ asked when she came back with the drinks. 'You don't look happy to see me.' He didn't like people's minds moving from him. Except when they were wasted, and even then, he'd keep his hand on her thigh possessively, reminding her of his presence.

'Nothing,' she said. She drank half of her vodka and leaned in against him to take the joint.

This was it, right? What else was there?

The next morning, there were so many of them lying around TJ's tiny flat, the usual assortment of bodies on the floor, the smell of dirty feet, sweat, cigarette smoke, who knew what else. Faye sat up in the bed. She was wearing her T-shirt and knickers but no jeans, and she couldn't really remember getting here. She hugged her knees up to herself in an attempt to get comfort. From somewhere she could hear 'Gimme Shelter' playing on the stereo, another song in the soundtrack to this life. This life, the life of being TJ's Silver.

She felt her skin crawl.

Faye had never liked herself much. Other people she liked. It was herself she had no time for.

She had been grateful to lose herself in this numbing new life with TJ and The Club. But now she saw it all with stunning clarity and she loathed who she'd become.

'Hey, Silver,' said one of the guys from the floor, opening an eye. 'How's it going?'

Silver. Everybody had known what it stood for except her. That's all she was: Silver, the Lone Ranger's ride, nothing more. Not a person. A ride. All the hopes and dreams of a young human being cruelly dismissed by one word.

She found her jeans at the end of the bed, pulled them on.

She bent down to put on her socks and winced. In the mirror, she saw the reason for the pain: there were bruises down her back, angry, livid marks.

Trawling back through the mental fog of the night before, she could remember her and TJ in the kitchen having sex up against the kitchen cabinets, with people everywhere, nobody noticing, nobody caring. Even now, she could feel the ridge of formica digging into her tender back. This was the great new world she was in, this was where she'd thought she was special.

A world of being treated like dirt by people who didn't care, who were looking for victims, people to use.

Faye didn't know where she got the strength but, somewhere deep inside her, she found courage. She gathered her stuff together. There wasn't much really, nothing to mark her presence there at all.

There was no sign of TJ. He was probably off with some other woman, poor cow. Faye felt sorry for her.

Nobody noticed as she slipped out and closed the door behind her.

'But I was pregnant,' she told Christie and Faye as they sat in Christie's beautiful room with the dogs at their feet. 'It must have happened that night, the night before I left. I worked it out. Him and me in the kitchen, up against the cabinets.' She wiped her eyes with a rough gesture. 'Pregnant and alone.' She laughed, mirthlessly. 'Because I was hardly going to find TJ and say, "Hi, Daddy, what sort of cot will we buy? Are you planning to be there at the birth?" I had to leave college because I was so unwell and couldn't cope. My mother was so good to me and took care of us both. She helped through the pregnancy, then, after Amber was born, she would babysit so I could work. I did anything – bar work, McDonald's. You can eat your dinner off the floors in McDonald's,' Faye said, suddenly smiling. 'I know, because I've scrubbed them. You wouldn't believe how fussed they are. Finally, when I got a proper job we moved here, to start again on Summer Street. There's something so hopeful about this place, isn't there? I felt it from the first.' She looked beseechingly at Maggie and Christie, wanting them to understand. 'I could begin again here, I could be someone new, someone Amber could be proud of. And I wanted her to be proud of me. The only other person who knows the whole story is my mother,' Faye added. 'Nobody else. I was too ashamed. My mother worked so hard all her life to put me and my brother through college and I paid her back like that,

187

thinking so little of myself that I let people use me. Mistaking sex for intimacy, thinking TJ's behaviour signified love and respect and affection. How dumb could I have been?' she said hoarsely.

'You were only a kid,' Christie said, feeling nothing but compassion for Faye. 'You did what so many women do: think sex is love, when it's not. You know now, and you must forgive yourself. You can't feel guilty for ever.'

'I should have told Amber,' said Faye blankly, as if she didn't hear Christie. Or, at least, couldn't hear the words 'forgive yourself' because she'd told herself so often that she had ruined her life. 'As a parent, you want your child to look up to you, to respect you and, as I don't respect myself for what I did, how could she? How could I tell her that her father was a low-life scumbag who had never cared?'

'Did he know about her?' Maggie asked.

'I brought her to see him at The Club when she was six months old.'

Faye thought she looked pretty good by then. A lot of the baby weight was gone and she could fit into her old jeans. Men still looked at her, admiring.

Amber was so cute, fluffy hair spilling out from under her crimson fleecy hat, wrapped up against the cold. Even then, her intelligence was apparent. She was so alert, watched everything with those huge magnetic eyes. How could anybody not love her, not want to be her father?

The Club hadn't changed an iota, even the people slumped at the bar in the early evening looked the same

'You can't bring a kid in here,' yelled the barman grumpily.

'Why not?' Faye said.

He shrugged. 'Don't come moaning to me about passive smoking, OK?'

'I'm looking for TJ.'

'He's in the back booth.'

She should have known. Why even ask? The back booth: their spiritual home.

Some of the faces round the table had changed. There was no sign of Jimi. She hoped he'd got out. He was like her too, a sweet guy in over his head.

Everyone at the table was clearly out of it, and holding court in the middle was TJ, the inevitable girl on his arm, not someone Faye knew. Except he was thinner now, and his face was even more gaunt.

'Hey, darlin'.' He smiled. 'You joining us?'

He didn't recognise her, Faye realised, and she was standing there with his child in her arms.

'TJ, it's me, Faye,' she said. His eyes remained distant, the thousand-yard stare of a joint-smoker.

Then, with a shock, she saw that the long, sinewy arm thrown around the girl had needle tracks in it. That was the one thing she had never known TJ do: shoot up. He could drink or smoke anyone under the table. He smoked dope and when he could get it, he was a hound for coke, but heroin had been off limits. Heroin was playing Russian roulette with a bullet in every chamber. Thank goodness she had got away.

'It's Silver!' said someone.

It was Jackie, older than TJ, one of the leaders of the crew, a man with a face like a gravel pit.

Jackie raised a glass to her. 'Hey, sweet kid you got there. She's not yours, is she?'

'Yeah, she's mine,' said Faye, holding Amber so tightly to her that the baby, who'd been drifting off to sleep, woke up and mewled with discomfort.

'What are you bringing a kid here for, Silver? It ruins the atmosphere. How can we party with a kid around? You up for a party?'

'I was supposed to meet someone,' Faye said, realising there would be no sign of recognition from TJ. 'But I guess they're not here.'

And without looking back, she walked out of The Club. Amber, her reason for living, snuggled in closer, happy, in her mother's arms.

'I never saw him again,' Faye told her audience. 'I never even tried to look for him. I told Amber her dad was from Scotland and died in a car crash soon after she was born. I said we'd never married, but we meant to, so it was like being a widow. I changed my name to my mother's maiden name but called myself Mrs so people wouldn't label us. And I said when he'd died, I'd lost touch with his family, that his parents were dead and he was an only child. More lies. It scared the hell out of me to wonder what would happen if Amber discovered the truth and tried to find TJ. He might still be a junkie.' She shivered. 'If he hasn't died of his habit – ninety per cent of heroin addicts do, you know. So that's the story. Memoirs of a woman from The We Screwed Up But Hey, We're Still Here Club, that's what I used to think it should be called.'

Maggie burst out laughing. 'Hey, can I join up?'

Faye looked at Christie, as if expecting the older woman's disapproval but there was nothing but sympathy and warmth in Christie's kind eyes.

'You deserve to be president of that club and get a medal,' she said. 'Amber's a beautiful girl, Faye. You have nothing to be ashamed of. You should be proud of the way you've brought her up on your own and she should be proud of you. But she deserves to know the truth, doesn't she?'

Christie stopped. The truth. It was easier to say it than to live it. She wasn't telling anyone her own truth, was she?

'We've all done things we thought we should hide,' she

said carefully. 'I've hidden stuff from the people I love and I wish to God I hadn't because it eats you up from the inside out.'

'How can I tell her any of this now?' Faye groaned. 'After all the lies I've told her.'

'You've reached the point where you can't do anything but tell her,' Christie said. 'She knows what a good person you are, because that's how you've brought her up. And the truth is it wasn't completely your fault, Faye. Stop imagining what other people will think and realise you were a scared, vulnerable young woman. Forgive yourself. Stop thinking of how everyone else would live your life in your shoes. You have to live it. You had to live it and you did your best. Tell her, face that truth.' Christie knew now she wasn't just talking to Faye, but also to herself.

Maggie, hanging on to every word, stared at Christie. Her hand unconsciously stroked the top of her thigh through her jeans, touching the scars that lay underneath, scars that would never go away.

So facing the truth made you stronger? She hadn't thought of that before. She'd certainly never faced any of the truths in her own life, she'd buried them instead, kept them from her family and friends, from everyone. But perhaps she had been wrong to do that.

'But what if Amber doesn't come back?' Faye asked.

Christie tried to push her mind into the future. It never worked that way, not usually. The future came to her, rather than the other way round. But now, in the face of Faye's raw, naked pain, she tried. And when the answer came to her in a flash, it was a mother's intuition rather than anything other-worldly.

'You've got to go and find her.'

# CHAPTER TWELVE

Amber had expected flowers and wine, well, even a few beers. After all, it was a horrible Monday morning and she'd just had the row from hell with her mother and had left home. It was like something out of one of those sweeping romantic epics on Saturday afternoon television.

Despite her misery, Amber's sense of the dramatic meant she could see herself in the role of tear-stained heroine fleeing from a tyrannical home to the arms of her lover.

Except that Karl clearly hadn't seen the same movies.

When he'd met her off the bus, he'd hugged her, taken the big suitcase from her and pulled it along, chatting all the while. There was no wild passion at what she'd given up for him, how he'd never forget her leaving her home to be by his side.

'What is it with women and all this stuff?' Karl grimaced, pretending he had put his back out hauling her case. 'How can one small woman own so much? Or is this just the make-up?'

Amber, still torn between tears and defiance, was not in the mood for jokes. She wanted passionate declarations of how he loved her and would take care of her.

But perhaps she mustn't be too clingy or needy.

'It's all my stuff from home,' she said shortly. 'Nearly eighteen years of belongings.' Including her four cuddly toys, although she'd stashed them in a pillowcase.

'Only slagging you, babe,' Karl said. 'Dunno where you'll put it all, though. The flat's a bit cramped.'

They reached Karl's front door. He manfully hauled her case into the rather smelly hallway and up two flights of stairs to a scuffed blue door that stood ajar.

'We're having a band meeting,' Karl said, as he kicked the door of the flat open with his foot.

He left her case in the hall, and pulled her into the cluttered living room that was testimony to a cleaning rota gone very wrong. Old papers and magazines, dirty dishes, empty take-away containers, ashtrays, items of clothing and dust covered every surface. Kenny T, Lew and Syd were sprawled on the room's couch and single armchair that were grouped around a coffee table that Amber had never seen without its coat of detritus. In turn, they all got up to hug and welcome her. To her shame, Amber burst into tears. After the huge row with her mother, it was so lovely to feel welcomed again and not a wayward child.

'There's no need to cry,' Karl said, hugging her.

'It's just I've never had a real row with my mother before,' she sobbed into his shoulder. 'We've been there for each other always. Her and me. But she's so square, she can't understand this and she never will. You didn't hear her, Karl: she hates me for this, hates me!'

'Your ma will get over it. My ma was the same,' Syd said easily. 'She never copped on that there's more to life than exams, you know. Saw me as a lawyer, she did. Jaysus, can you see me in court?'

'Only in the defence box,' cracked Lew.

'You'll be fine with us, Amber,' Kenny T added. 'You can

teach Karl how to wash his underpants. I've seen him using the cleanest ones off the floor.'

'No, I've seen you taking my cleanest ones off the floor, you skanger,' joked Karl in return.

Amber wiped her eyes and tried to join in the joking. She felt absurdly pleased to be welcomed in like one of the boys. Never mind that the place was a pit. She'd show them how to be tidy. It might be nice to be the mother figure for a change.

She'd show her mother that she could survive and be happy. There wasn't just one way to live your life, by the bloody boring book.

'Lew was just going to phone out for pizza,' Karl said to her. 'But now you're here, could you cook? We're mad for some lunch.'

'We've got chicken,' Lew said hopefully.

'It smells a bit,' Syd warned.

'Nuke it,' advised Karl. 'It'll be fine then, won't it?'

All eyes turned to Amber, who was a girl and, therefore, would know all about cooking chicken.

Cooking was her mother's department, Amber realised with a jolt. Hers was reheating or writing things on the list on the fridge, like *Out of muesli* or *Can you get me shampoo?*

'Sure, it'll be fine,' she said confidently. How hard could cooking be?

The fridge stank. Syd had been right about the chicken, although he should have just binned it, which was what Amber did.

Nothing else in there would have stretched to a meal for five without a bad dose of salmonella ensuing. There were lots of packets and cartons, but they were mostly empty, with the exception of a half-full orange juice carton which was curdled with age. The freezer box was jammed icily shut and

Amber couldn't prise it open. And the cupboards, stocked with crisps, cereal and lots of nearly empty bottles of booze, yielded nothing but a few stray bits of pasta and rice.

She marched into the band meeting.

'The chicken is an ex-chicken,' she announced. 'I'll go to the shops and get something for lunch but I need money.'

'Yes, ma'am,' said Karl and made a collection.

Amber smiled. She was in charge, what a nice feeling. Last week, she'd been a schoolgirl with a uniform and a childhood bedroom. Now she lived with a man, shared his bed, cooked his meals. How was that for progress?

But later that afternoon, she started to feel tearful again.

'I might call Gran,' sniffed Amber on the phone to Ella.

'Why?' Ella couldn't see the point in this. Any grandmother worth her salt would surely side with Faye's mother. There would be tears and shouting. 'Why don't you call your mother?' Ella said. 'She's the one you should be talking to, not your gran.'

'My mother will only go on about the bloody exams,' said Amber bitterly. 'There's more to life than exams. It's a stupid system to put people in little boxes based on how well they do on one particular day when asked one particular set of questions. How does that work out what sort of person you are and what you're capable of doing?'

For someone who'd been the poster girl for education for all her school life, Amber had honed her arguments against it pretty quickly. She didn't know how any of her new flatmates had got on in their final-year state exams, but Karl, who had passed his, was always saying that life was the real educator, not school books. She said this, not mentioning that it was Karl-speak.

Ella's lip curled. 'The hottest band on the planet all failed their exams, right?' she said succinctly.

'Karl is brilliant,' Amber snapped back.

'Yeah, well, did he stay in school to finish the year and his exams?'

Amber knew he had. After school, he'd gone to university for two years but had dropped out of his arts degree.

'But that's not important,' she said.

'Course it is. So he did pass them and now he's forcing you to skip your exams so you can be with him. Your mother's right, Amber. Why don't you finish school properly? It's only a few weeks away and you'd be wasting years of study for no reason. If Karl doesn't want to wait for you until the exams are over, then he doesn't deserve you.'

'He loves me,' said Amber, hurt and angry. 'I thought you were on my side.'

'I am. I'm only saying what I think.'

'Karl would love to wait for me but they've got to travel now.'

'And you can't stay here, do your exams and join him later?' Ella demanded. 'Or are you scared that if you're not with him, he'll find someone else to be his muse and keep his bed warm?'

The barb hit home. Amber was glad Ella wasn't there to see her blush. She knew it was stupid to feel so unsure of Karl after all he'd said to her, but doubt was a sneaky bedfellow and crept into her mind when she least wanted it. She could stay and make up with her mother, but what if Karl left and she never saw him again?

'We love each other,' she said coldly to her best friend. 'You wouldn't understand.'

'I understand plenty. I understand that you used to listen to me. We shared everything and now Karl's on the scene, I'm not important any more. That's a nice way to treat your closest friend, Amber.'

'Oh, grow up, Ella,' snapped Amber. 'You make it sound

like we're kids again, with nothing to worry about except which My Little Pony is our favourite.'

Ella had had enough. 'I liked you better then,' she said. 'You were still Amber Reid, my best friend ever, and not Amber the dizzy groupie who's forgotten everything she ever stood for. You were the clever one in school with the future and you're risking it all to behave like a *Ricki Lake Show* guest and cling to a loser guy. He'll dump you, you know. And you'll ask me why I didn't stop you. Just so you remember, I did my best. Bye, Amber, have a nice life.'

Amber hung up feeling lonelier than ever. Why didn't anyone understand?

Love changed you and made you a different person. What was wrong with that?

Why did everyone think she had to choose: them or Karl? Couldn't she have both?

# CHAPTER THIRTEEN

The card was nothing but a rectangle of fine cream paper, folded over, with a heart hand-drawn on the front, and on the inside written in Grey's unmistakable copperplate handwriting: *I love you. I miss you, please come home.*

Maggie reread the card yet again, then traced her fingers over the writing reverentially. A shop-bought one wouldn't have touched her but this, this gesture of love, made her ache with wanting to go back to Grey.

She'd been thinking about what Christie Devlin had said earlier, and then she'd come home from work to find this on the bundle of post on the hall table, a card from Grey wanting her back.

*Stop thinking of how everyone else would live your life in your shoes. You have to live it*, Christie had said to both her and Faye.

And she'd been right. Maggie hadn't been able to get the words out of her head.

She wanted to go back to Grey, that was all that mattered. Not what anyone else said. Not her pride or fear or lack of trust. It could all be worked through. What had happened had changed her, so their relationship wouldn't go back to the way it had been before: it would be better, stronger. Like her.

It was half seven in the evening and Grey would certainly be home from work. She desperately wanted to speak to him now.

She dialled the apartment but got their answering machine, still with its message saying that neither Grey nor Maggie could come to the phone right now. She hung up without leaving a message. This conversation had to be in person. Next, she dialled his mobile but it was switched off.

Damn. She felt so wound up. She wanted to talk to someone . . .

'Hi, how are you?' she said, when Shona answered the phone.

'Great,' said Shona breezily.

There was a lot of noise going on in Shona and Paul's flat. The noise of two people who knew how to enjoy themselves and weren't worried about bothering the neighbours by having the stereo turned up to This May Damage Your Hearing level.

'I just wanted to talk,' Maggie said.

'Serious talk?' asked Shona.

'No, not really.' She paused. 'Yeah, serious talk.'

'Turn the music down,' Shona yelled.

'So what happened?' demanded Shona, when the noise level dropped slightly. 'He turned up on your doorstep, confessed undying love and promised never to be a naughty boy again.'

'How did you know?' Maggie asked. She hadn't spoken to Shona since Grey had turned up to see her.

'You mean he did?' said Shona. 'Talk about Cliché City.'

'I didn't know he'd come,' Maggie said.

'Well,' said Shona, 'it's just the sort of thing a man like Grey would do. Bonk somebody else on your bed, not know how to say sorry properly, let you run away while he thought about it and then rush into your arms and bleat, "I'm sorry darling, it will never happen again", because he realises it's very boring doing your own washing and cleaning. And besides which, it's against faculty rules to screw your students and his college career would be finito if word leaked out. Not that myself or anyone in the library would say anything, no.' Shona sounded gleeful. 'Silent as the grave we are. Gossip never touches our lips – we spit it out so fast, it never gets to touch our lips.'

Maggie had felt cheerful a moment before but Shona's analysis of Grey's behaviour made it all sound so sordid and miserable. Not so much a great passion as a tawdry fling.

But Shona hadn't heard him speak, hadn't heard the tenderness in his voice.

'He said he missed me,' she protested, 'in public. And that he loves me. He means it, Shona. I know you think he doesn't, but if you'd seen him . . .'

'Oh, that's so Grey,' Shona said critically. 'He loves a scene, that boy, just loves it. I don't know why he's pretending he won't go into politics. If ever a man wanted to stand on a podium and have the party faithful worship at his feet, it's your ex. He's addicted to the applause, darling. That's why he likes bonking girl students.'

There was a sudden pause.

'What do you mean he likes bonking girl students?' Maggie asked fiercely. 'I knew he liked bonking one particular girl student but students plural . . . ? What have you heard?'

She could almost hear Shona running through escape scenarios in her head.

'The truth, Shona,' she insisted. 'Tell me the truth. I wish somebody had told me the truth a long time ago.'

'Oh sweetie,' sighed Shona, and Maggie knew it was bad news. 'Don't worry, I was going to tell you. You know me, tell all. I don't believe in that shoot the messenger crap. Well, like a good pal, I've been asking around ever since you caught Dr Grey Stanley sticking it to his cutesy, blonde student and it seems that she wasn't the only one getting some private tuition. Turns out, he's got quite a name for it.'

'Oh.' Maggie couldn't manage to say anything else. It was like thinking the world was round, and then finding out it was flat after all.

'Sorry, darling, but you had to know.'

If anybody else but Shona had told her this, Maggie realised, she would've wanted to shoot the messenger. But Shona was a true friend. She loved Maggie. It was comforting to think that somebody still did.

'I want to hear everything,' she said.

'Are you sure?'

'Yes,' she said firmly. 'Everything.'

'Paul,' called Shona. 'Turn off the music and make me a cocktail. This is going to be a long conversation.'

She could hear Paul reply: 'You're not telling her everything about that bastard, are you?'

'Somebody has to. The girl needs to see sense.'

There had been four women that Shona had been able to find out about, including the latest blonde. All students of Grey's, which was probably the worst thing about it. He was always such a stickler for ethics and doing the right thing, Maggie recalled.

Having sex with people whose papers he marked was breaking every rule of teaching.

'The good news is that none of them was long term,' Shona finished up. 'So you can console yourself with that, darling. I mean, he did love you in his own screw-around way. I had to dig deep to find it all out, so I honestly don't think he meant to humiliate you.'

'Doing it in our bed wasn't supposed to humiliate me?' Maggie shouted.

'Don't scream,' Shona screamed back. 'I'm clutching at straws here, trying to make you feel better. Yes, he's a class A shit but it's obvious that his brain is not his primary organ and he's clearly not as cerebral as he'd like us all to think.'

'Meaning he thinks with his dick,' Paul yelled in the background.

'He still didn't have to do it in our bed,' Maggie said, still reeling. 'Doesn't that say he wanted to be found out?'

'Oh I don't think he wanted to be found out,' said Shona. 'Come on, why would he? I think there was nowhere else to go, you were off at work, then you were doing your Pilates or whatever, the coast was clear.'

'He asked me to come back to him,' Maggie said, with a little laugh that held no humour.

Only minutes ago, she'd felt a little bit of hope warming her at the idea that it might all work out, she could have it all, again, only better this time. 'He wants us to be together. He said we should get married.' Her voice broke. 'And you tell me he's had four girlfriends in the past ... how many years, five? Why marry someone if all you want to do is sleep around?'

'It's the eternal question of life,' Shona sighed in a world-weary way.

She could hear Paul wanting to know what the eternal question of life was. Shona told him.

'I thought it was, was there life on other planets?' Paul could be heard saying, plaintively.

'No, that's the third eternal question, after why all the good ones already have boyfriends.'

Despite herself, Maggie managed a hoarse laugh.

'What a lovely sound.' Shona was pleased. 'Don't let Dr Dick ruin your life, Maggie,' she pleaded. 'You're an old romantic despite your best attempts to hide it. You want the fairytale, darling, and you're not going to get it with him, are you?'

'They say serial monogamy is the way forward,' Maggie said, not wanting to answer Shona's question. 'I wanted something longer and Grey obviously doesn't. Am I the old-fashioned one? Is everyone at it? Should I have been having an affair too?'

'No,' said Shona, 'joking aside, you shouldn't have been having an affair. You're too straight, it would kill you. When you love, it's with all your heart. He's different. If he'd gone to you and admitted about the other women, said he'd never do it again, well, there'd be some hope. But he didn't, did he? He just said sorry for Miss Bimbo. And by the way, her book-borrowing days are over. I'll have the word out in the library and that girl will never get another book out. She can try, but no matter what book she wants, it'll be unavailable or her card will be out of date. The library looks after its own!'

Maggie smiled.

'What am I going to do now, Shona?' she sighed. 'I was going to go back to him. I can't stay with Mum and Dad for ever, it's lovely and everything but . . .' She paused.

The shock hit her again. Damn Grey, damn him. Just when she'd begun to think there might be a future for them, his past had ruined it all again.

She'd begun to feel a little better the past day or so. Insulated in Summer Street. She'd even got used to her old bedroom again and the reassurance of looking at the same wallpaper she'd grown up with. It was easy to block out the pain of finding Grey in bed with another woman. The pain of feeling so stupid, so betrayed. And she liked the local library, it was a nice place to work. Maggie knew she was hiding, just a tiny bit, from the past and its power. But she didn't care. She wanted a little peace after everything that had happened.

And now Grey had knocked her right back to square one.

He'd reminded her why she was here, alone. What's more, he hadn't betrayed her with one woman, he'd betrayed her with four.

'Are you still there?' asked Shona gently.

'Yes,' Maggie said. 'Sorry. I don't know whether to stay here or go back to Galway. I don't know what to do about anything. I'm a mess.'

'Join the club, darling,' Shona said lightly. 'My roots need doing, my nails are like hooves and I haven't had a moment since you left, you know. The relief librarian they sent thinks the rota is set in stone and I'm having terrible trouble trying to swap shifts with her. Anyway, listen, sweetie, take your time, you don't need to make a decision quickly, you've got another week. You could come back and have nothing to do with Dr Grey or his nymphets. He's not in your life any more, you don't need him.'

Shona would say that, Maggie thought ruefully. Shona was strong and knew her own worth. She hadn't needed Paul to make her feel fulfilled. But Maggie wasn't so strong, she didn't know if she could go back and start again with all the memories of her and Grey everywhere she went.

But then, there were painful memories everywhere, even here, on Summer Street.

She wished she had told Shona about her school years, then maybe she'd understand why Maggie was so anxious about staying in Summer Street. But there had never been a right time to tell her. Shona knew the reinvented Maggie, the feisty person with a kooky personality, a soft heart and a clever word for every situation. It would be strange to tell her now. Talking about the bullying would make it all real and she would only have to confront it. Despite what Christie had said about facing the truth, it was far easier to keep the memories buried.

# CHAPTER FOURTEEN

If wishing could make a phone ring, Faye's mobile would have been blistering loudly all Tuesday morning. Her office phone rang every few minutes but her mobile, the number Amber always called her on, just sat there on the desk, silent. And despite being surrounded by all the other people in the office, Faye had never felt more alone.

It was a little over twenty-four hours since Amber had run off and changed Faye's world. There had been no phone call from her, nothing, just the blank emptiness of the house without Amber in it and Faye reliving her mistakes over and over again in her mind.

She'd spent hours the evening before with Ella and her mother, trying to work out where Amber might be, but Ella honestly didn't know.

'If I did, Mrs Reid, I'd tell you,' she said. 'I think she's crazy and you know she's my best friend. And I've told her I think she's crazy too,' she added, just in case anyone doubted her determination to make Amber see sense.

'I just don't understand,' said Trina, Ella's mother. 'She's always been such a good girl.'

Both mothers had talked before of how lucky they were

with their daughters. Amber and Ella had never given any trouble before, and their parents agreed that having tough rules about what was and wasn't allowed was certainly a factor.

'When she gets home, you should ground her for a month!' Trina insisted.

Ella and Faye looked at each other. They both knew it had gone far beyond that.

When Faye had left Ella's house that evening and returned home to Summer Street, she entered a house that felt like an empty shell. With Amber there, it had been a lively home; now it was cold and hard, all the life and the warmth gone. This was the rest of her life, Faye realised bleakly: being alone without the one person she loved most in the whole world. It was like the end of a love affair, except Faye knew she'd never have felt the loss of any man the way she felt the loss of her daughter.

Christie had phoned on Tuesday morning before Faye went to work.

'I wanted to see how you were,' she said, in her soothing way. 'To remind you that you're not on your own, that you've got people to talk to in this.'

'Thank you,' said Faye.

'Did you sleep?'

'If you call lying in bed crying, yes, I slept really well.'

'I'll bring you over some wonderful herbal tea later this evening,' Christie promised. 'I got it in a little shop in Camden Street and it's called Sleep Tea. It's very relaxing.'

'Do you have Instant Happiness Tea or Make Everything Better Tea?' Faye inquired.

'No,' sighed Christie. 'I wish I did. In fact, I'd also love a packet of the Make All the Old Secrets Disappear Tea but they were out of stock. Are you going into work?'

'Of course.'

The idea of doing anything else was ridiculous to Faye.

Work had been her saviour for many years. Work made you forget about humiliation and pain, and people who treated you like dirt. Work gave you confidence and courage and a tiny glimmer of self-respect.

Except not today. No matter what she tried, she couldn't concentrate.

She sat at her desk miserably. She had no idea how to get Amber back and all she could do was see the mistakes she had made and regret them. Faye had been so sure that she had brought Amber up in the right way, in a lovely cosy world, where education and faith in your own power were the most important things. She had been so sure that was right, and now it seemed, like mother, like daughter. Amber was merely repeating her mistakes. And Faye, who, she could see now, should have told Amber the truth, had let Amber grow up thinking her mother was a plaster saint.

She didn't tell anyone at work about Amber going. She couldn't. Keeping people at a distance was too firmly engrained in her. Yesterday, she'd let Christie and Maggie get closer to her than anyone had in years – she was still getting used to having done that.

Grace popped her head round the door at eleven. She didn't come in because she always felt it was really only a quick chat if she didn't stand entirely in a room.

'I've someone you've just got to meet, Faye. She's an image consultant and a life coach. You know, that's not even describing her properly, she changes people's lives. She has degrees coming out of her armpits and I thought it would be a brilliant idea to bring her into the business as part of our getting women back to work campaign.'

Faye had come up with the idea of a drive to recruit women coming back into the workplace after a few years of being at home taking care of their children and the campaign had become Grace's special project. Grace set up the interviews and had organised a whole retraining programme for mothers wanting to brush up on interview techniques and computer skills. It had been a huge success, with scores of brilliantly qualified women signing up, but the only problem, Grace said, was that some of the women coming back to work were terribly anxious about it all.

'No matter what top job they had before, they keep saying everyone's moved on and they've become mumsy and out of touch. You wouldn't credit the sort of superwomen who say they don't know what to wear or what to say because they've lost the knack. I tell them you never forget,' Grace added, 'but honestly, women's anxiety is terrible. Why do we do this to ourselves? I bet men don't obsess that they won't fit back in if they haven't been in the workplace for a few years? I mean, can you imagine Neil feeling like that?' she asked Faye.

As Faye felt that Neil didn't really work in the first place, she couldn't answer this accurately. But she nodded and said yes, she knew what Grace was getting at: the age-old problem of confidence had undermined many a woman.

'So your plan is to help people dress properly and do their hair and be full of enthusiasm?' Faye asked now.

'That's part of it.' Grace inserted her whole body into the room. 'It's giving women back their confidence more than anything. This life coach is just totally amazing. Her name's Ellen. You'll love her. She's in my office now and if you've some free time, come on in. She's going to do a consultation on me.'

A few days ago, Faye would have loved to meet this woman, but not today. She couldn't summon up the enthusiasm for life coaches or even her beloved business.

'Grace, you don't need a consultation. Nobody has more confidence than you and they don't do any better ball-busting office suits than the sort of things you wear. What help can she give you?'

'Well, I'd love to know if longer hair would suit me,' Grace said, thoughtfully, fingering her short, expertly high-lighted blonde hair. 'And Ellen has such an eye. You know, my hairdresser says he likes the way my hair is, but he would say that, wouldn't he? He cuts it. Come on, meet her.'

'Just for ten minutes,' countered Faye. 'I'll follow you down to your office.' She shouldn't have come into work at all – she should have phoned in sick. How could she make polite conversation in the midst of her grief?

She delayed following Grace, hoping that by the time she arrived in Grace's office, Ellen might have gone. No such luck.

'Hello,' Faye said. 'I've really only got a minute, Grace, because I've got to . . .'

'Hey, sit down,' interrupted Grace, in a voice that brooked no opposition.

Faye knew when she was beaten. Still, she could say hello, be charming and leave in five minutes.

'Meet Ellen.' Ellen was not the tall and exquisite creature that Faye expected. All the life coaches and stylists she had ever seen had exuded as much glamour as confidence. Ellen was remarkably normal-looking, around Faye's age and was simply but elegantly made up. She was beautifully dressed in a fitted skirt suit in a lovely pale grey that Faye wouldn't have looked at in a million years. Her eyes shone with a wealth of experience and innate self-confidence.

'Hello,' said Ellen. 'Nice to meet you, Faye.' Even her voice was elegant.

They talked about the business for a few moments, with Faye eager to be gone. This was Grace's area of expertise.

Grace liked nice clothes and high heels because she liked attracting attention, sexual allure was part of what made Grace tick. It was a part of Faye that she'd ruthlessly ripped out. She never wanted a man to fancy her again.

No man would ever call her honey or Silver or touch her again. Men were not on her agenda, ever.

'I've got to go,' she said finally, when she judged she could leave.

'It was nice to meet you,' said Ellen, and Faye could see the other woman's eyes on her, perhaps itching to do a makeover on her.

It was all so superficial – *style your hair, wear better suits, have a make-up lesson* – who cared? Faye thought, rage from somewhere deep inside her bubbling up. Who really cared what people looked like? The outside didn't matter. It was the inside that counted – didn't anybody understand that? Never mind that Faye's inside was a mess.

Five miles away, in the comfort of Karl's admittedly rather fusty-smelling bed, Amber stretched and luxuriated. It was eleven o'clock in the morning and she wasn't sitting in crappy old Irish class, bored out of her brain, thinking of the exams and what she was going to do for the summer. No, she was lying beside the man she loved, the man who was soon going to wake up and start kissing her gently, nibbling her neck and making love to her.

Then, maybe they'd get up and have a late, luxurious breakfast, padding around the flat together in their bare feet. She might wear one of his shirts: people did that in films, it was sort of cute. Then they could curl up on the couch and watch old movies and it would be blissful.

She and Mum used to love the afternoon movies when she was growing up, all those black-and-white classics. It was especially nice on winter weekends when the rain pelted down outside and they'd sit, cosy in their home, and . . .

Amber didn't want to think about Mum, because then she'd feel guilty. But it was all her mother's fault really. Her obsession with never upsetting the neighbours and having to always be whiter than white because 'you've got no dad and we don't want anyone looking down on the Reid family, making assumptions and remarks'.

What sort of assumptions would they make? It used to drive Amber mad.

If only Mum hadn't been so obsessed with all that crap she might have noticed Amber changing, or she might have understood why Amber had wanted to change.

None of it mattered any more anyway. She was with Karl and that was what mattered, as she'd told Mum. It had been horrible but it was over.

Amber had kept her mobile phone off since, afraid her mother would ring, demanding that she come home. Or worse, crying and looking devastated, as she'd been yesterday. It had been weird to see her like that, all sad and pleading. Not like the strong mother she knew.

'Hiya, baby,' murmured Karl, half awake. He rolled over in the bed, closed his eyes and appeared to sink back into sleep.

Amber stroked the back of his neck hopefully. She didn't want to lie here with her feelings for company: she wanted Karl to take her mind off them.

But Karl was asleep again.

Maybe she'd ring Gran, just to tell her to keep an eye on Mum, because knowing Mum she wouldn't tell anybody that Amber had left. That would be so her.

She'd ring Gran and explain, then Gran could explain to Mum, who'd get over it and perhaps, even fly out to New York to meet them when she and Karl were settled. Amber hoped the record company could sort out an apartment for them to stay in, something with a balcony, perhaps.

Or maybe a modern house, with huge glass windows that looked out on to the sea in the Hamptons. Now that would be major league. Ella could come and stay too, when they were back talking to each other again.

Time, Amber decided, was all it would take and everyone would get used to the idea. Stan answered the phone at Gran's house and he sounded as he always did, relaxed and laid-back, as if every day was a joy to be savoured, which indeed it was, according to Stan.

Ella and Amber thought Stan was a howl. The complete opposite to Gran, who fired on all cylinders and never stopped moving or talking. Stan could sit in his chair and listen, without saying anything for ages. He was a good step-granddad, Ella used to say, seeing as Amber couldn't really remember her real granddad.

'You don't have much luck with male relatives, do you?' Ella had said one day. 'I mean, your dad's dead, your granddad's dead, you don't know your dad's family, what's all that about?'

'Dad was Scottish and he was only working in Ireland, I told you that,' Amber said, annoyed at her friend's thoughtlessness. 'Oh, it's complicated.'

Ella was such a pain sometimes. Just because she had all her family around her with relatives coming out her ears, she thought everyone else should be the same.

'But it's romantic, isn't it?' said Ella, wistful now.

'Make up your mind,' Amber said crossly. 'One minute it's weird and strange, the next minute it's romantic, which is it?'

She'd often wondered about her dad, and what sort of father he'd be: strict and tough, or pretending to be strict, a bit like Ella's dad, who was a total softie under all that crosspatch, 'I'm your father and listen to me' stuff. Amber's mum didn't talk enough about Dad, she felt. She knew so little about him. Even Gran said practically nothing about him. She just knew he'd loved her. They hadn't known each other long when Mum got pregnant.

'We wanted to bring you up properly, together,' Mum had

said. And then Dad was killed in a car accident, and he'd only a few relatives left and they'd moved, so Amber and her mum had lost touch with them. She'd like to search for them sometime.

'Your gran's in the kitchen baking,' said Stan now to Amber. 'Yet another church event she's been asked to make cakes for.'

Just like Mum, thought Amber, another tinge of irritation hitting her. What was it with her mother and grandmother and all this church baking, holier than thou stuff?

'I'll get her for you,' said Stan.

'Hello, love,' said Gran cheerily after a long period when Amber could imagine her dusting off her floury hands and sitting down on the tapestry stool in the hall where the old-fashioned round-dial phone sat. 'I can't talk for long. I'm about to put my cakes in the oven and you know how cakes can flop if you hesitate. How are you, love? And why are you ringing me now? You should be at school – is something wrong?'

'No, I'm fine. The thing is, Gran,' said Amber, and suddenly it seemed quite hard to say this, 'I'm not at school because I've left home and . . .'

'You've left home?' The tone of her grandmother's voice didn't change, but something steely came into it.

'Yes,' said Amber. This was definitely more difficult than she'd thought. 'I've left home because I've fallen in love with somebody and Mum doesn't understand. I want to go to America with him. I just thought I'd tell you so that you'd keep an eye on Mum, because she's really upset.'

'Really upset, was she?' asked her grandmother, still steely, and Amber winced. 'That's not surprising if you told her you were leaving school to go to America with a man. When did all this happen?'

'Yesterday.'

213

'I meant,' Gran said, 'when did you fall in love with this man?'

'Over a month ago.' It seemed such a short length of time and yet, Amber felt as if she'd been with Karl for ever. Like Romeo and Juliet. Héloïse and Abelard. Kate Winslet and Leonardo DiCaprio in *Titanic*.

'His name is Karl. He's a musician, Gran, he's so talented. You'd love him, really you would. And he loves me. Oh, Gran, say you'll be on my side? Mum doesn't get it, you know what she's like. I told her yesterday and, well, we had a row.'

'Hold on and start from the beginning,' her grandmother instructed.

So Amber did, leaving out the bit about how she and Ella had got into the club illegally and leaving out the sex stuff, obviously, because she couldn't tell her grandmother that, but giving her the basics. How she and Karl were each other's futures, how he really wanted her to come to America with him because he wrote better songs when she was with him. It made so much sense. She could study art any time, that was a gift you never lost, wasn't it? She could paint in America just as well as she could paint in Ireland and, as for the exams, she didn't need a bit of paper to prove that she was going to be a doctor or a scientist or a teacher. She wanted to paint, it was simple, and she could do that anywhere.

Education was a fine thing in principle, but really what was the point of putting people in little boxes, so that you could decide what they were going to do for the rest of their lives, when you knew already what you wanted to do?

Amber finished this explanation in a rush and there was a pause. A long pause, that she found a bit uncomfortable.

'Are you still there, Gran?' she said, anxiously. 'You haven't gone off to put your cakes in the oven?'

'I'm still here,' her grandmother said with a certain coolness in her voice. 'The cakes have shifted down my list of priorities, Amber. I'm trying to work out why you can't be in love and be somebody's muse without finishing your exams first, or perhaps without telling your mother in such a way that the two of you ended up in a big fight.'

Amber flinched at the way Gran said 'muse', much the way people said 'door-to-door double-glazing salesmen'.

'That doesn't sound like you, Amber, and it certainly doesn't sound fair to your mother. You know how much she loves you.'

Amber did and this wasn't what she wanted to hear.

'Look, Gran, I'm not telling you this so that you can change my mind, I'm telling you so that you can keep an eye out for Mum. Obviously she doesn't want to talk to me right now.'

'I think that's highly unlikely. I'm quite sure she has been ringing you on the hour, every hour,' snapped her grandmother.

Amber flushed. She knew there were probably millions of messages on her phone but she didn't want to listen to them, didn't want to hear her mother's anxious, pleading voice. Everybody was blowing this whole thing out of all proportion: it was getting bigger and bigger, and it was going to be harder to sort out.

'Look, all I'm saying is that you can be a grown-up, live your own life and do what you want with the love of your life, but you can do it gently, in such a way that it doesn't break your mother's heart, Amber. And you can do your exams while you're at it. You've spent your whole school life working towards this moment. What's another month?'

'That's what everyone says,' Amber said furiously. 'It's my life, I can make the decision. Isn't that what you and Mum have always told me? *To be in charge, to make my own decisions, not to follow the crowd.*'

She knew that they hadn't wanted those same words and ideas turned against them.

Gran sighed.

'Without your father,' she said delicately, 'it was a very hard time for your mother.'

'Yeah, well, I didn't ask her to bury herself for me,' Amber insisted. 'That was her choice, Gran. She built her life around me, but I can't be responsible for that, so don't try to make me feel guilty, because I'm not.'

That was what Karl had said when he told her she shouldn't feel guilty. 'You're going off to have your life and she's got to get it together on her own.'

Except that she did feel guilty and nervous: everyone was furious with her. What had she started?

'Amber, why don't you come here and I'll ring Faye and get her to come here and we can all talk and get over this and maybe move on and . . .'

'No,' said Amber, thinking of Karl and how she couldn't risk not being with him. If she contacted her mother, Mum would stop her and she had to be with Karl, she had to. 'It was a mistake ringing you, Gran. I just wanted you to check up on Mum. I wanted you to know what had happened, that we'd had a row, but that's it. I'm going, OK?'

'Call your mother, please,' Gran begged. 'Does she even know where you are? If you give her a chance to talk to you, you might understand. You've got to see her side of the story, Amber, promise me you'll phone her.'

'Gran, I can't,' Amber blurted. She couldn't face her mother.

'Please, Amber. She tried so hard to give you everything because you didn't have a father, you owe her the chance to explain it all to you, why she was so protective . . .'

'Bye, Gran,' said Amber and pressed the end call button. She felt shaken. What was Gran harping on and on about? Get your mother to tell her, tell her what? Tell her how to make the perfect muffin, the perfect flapjack? What could Mum possibly teach her? If it was anything important she needed to tell Amber, she'd have told her by now, wouldn't she?

It was all just a ploy to get Amber to stay, but she wasn't going to stay, she was going on to her new life with Karl. Older people were so obsessed trying to tell you about the mistakes they'd made. You had to make all the mistakes yourself, didn't you? Besides, Mum had probably never made any bloody mistakes apart from being the over-protective mother from hell. She was always Mrs Perfect, wasn't she?

'Hey, baby, where are you?' called Karl.

'In here,' said Amber, trying to calm herself down.

Karl padded into the kitchen, sleep-fogged and beautiful.

'I was going to make some breakfast,' said Amber, trying to recover from the horrible conversation she'd just had.

'Breakfast, I could kill some breakfast,' said Karl. 'What are you going to make?' He sat down on one of the stools and looked at her patiently.

'I don't know,' said Amber. Cereal or toast was her limit. Her mother was the scrambled eggs expert. Amber gritted her teeth.

'Scrambled egg?' she said confidently.

'Yeah, sure,' he replied with a sleepy stretch.

Amber opened the fridge where one egg sat in glory in the box. She was sure there had been a few more last night.

'No eggs,' she informed him.

'Hey,' Karl said, 'maybe we'll go out.'

He reached and pulled Amber up against him, until she was resting between his legs, his arms around her waist. 'Or we can go back to bed and go out in another hour?'

Amber leaned into him, loving the feel of his skin against hers, this was so much better than Irish class.

'That sounds like a fabulous idea,' she said.

\*　　\*　　\*

217

After saying a polite goodbye to Ellen, Faye stuck it out at her desk for another half an hour. Her head throbbed. Her daughter had run away and not bothered to so much as phone to tell Faye where she was. It hurt so much.

She left her desk and went into the women's room. The women's room in Little Island was big, airy and full of light so that you could see to put your make-up on. It also boasted a small bench seat so that people could sit down during important searches of handbags or for tights-changing exercises.

'I've worked in far too many offices with appalling loos,' Grace had said when they were checking over the premises originally. 'This is a woman-oriented company, so let's have a woman-oriented loo!'

One of the stall doors was shut when Faye came in. She went over to the sink and splashed water on her face. She had painkillers in her bag, she'd take them too. Although the real ache wouldn't be lessened with aspirin.

Despite Grace's beautiful lighting, the face that stared back at Faye was grey and tired, with violet bags under the eyes. Even her skin looked grey.

The stall door banged. 'Hello again.'

Hell, it was Ellen, the super-duper life coach and life revamper looking appallingly marvellous beside her. Ellen washed her hands, but surprisingly she didn't have a bag of tricks to apply half a stone of lipstick or glue her hair into place. In fact, Ellen looked remarkably good without doing any of that. Her hair was dark, shoulder length and glossy. Simple but it suited her. She looked confident, happy, businesslike.

Beside her, Faye felt like a lost soul who kept all her belongings in a shopping trolley.

'Hello,' Faye answered automatically, as she searched her handbag for the aspirin.

Ellen didn't say anything for a minute. She appeared to be watching Faye in the mirror, thinking.

'How are you?'

'Fine,' snapped Faye, finding the elusive painkillers. 'Just a headache.'

'You don't look fine,' Ellen said candidly.

Faye was stunned by this honesty.

She thought that faking sincerity was top of the list for stylists and life coaches.

'Listen, I'm fine. I'm going through a bit of a personal crisis at the moment,' she said, 'that's all.'

Her eyes saw in the mirror what Ellen could see – her hair looked as if she'd slept on it badly instead of being smoothly under control as usual. She pulled the scrunchie from her ponytail, raked her fingers through it like a comb, then corralled it all back into the band again.

'I used to be just like you, Faye,' Ellen said suddenly. 'Invisible. I dressed down, wore no make-up, hid behind boring clothes and banished any vestige of attractiveness I had. It kept people at bay, you see. I used to think that if nobody saw me, it was safer.'

Faye's hands stilled on her ponytail.

'I'm not asking you what's going on in your life,' Ellen went on. 'I'm just saying I can recognise the signs, because that was me. Invisible and in pain. You're not doing yourself any favours by living like that.'

'Grace put you up to this, didn't she?' Faye said furiously.

'She didn't set me up to do anything,' Ellen said bluntly. 'I just recognise something in you that used to be in me. The same utter hopelessness. Someone helped me to move on and I did. I'd like to help you do the same, but you have to come to terms with it yourself.'

'So what if I don't care about clothes or having my hair done in a fancy place,' Faye said sharply. 'Big bloody deal. Those things don't matter.'

'It's not your clothes or your hair that tell me you think

you're invisible. It's in your eyes. Most people don't see it, only a woman who's been in that place too. You might as well have a sign around your neck saying keep away.'

Faye stared at her silently, her heart thumping as hard as her head.

'You know, I think you've got the wrong idea about what I do,' Ellen went on. 'I'm not here to make a fortune on the back of telling women to change their hair, wear red lipstick and high-heeled shoes and, wow, life will be suddenly better. That's not what it's about. It's about looking at your life, trying to change it and change it for the better. Taking back some power. You might be running the company here with Grace, but somewhere along the way you've lost some of your power. I did the same thing too, thanks to a bad marriage, and one day, I copped on and took my power back. Anyway,' she said brusquely, 'I didn't mean to insult you, just wanted to say I was like that too and I found out how to change. Right now, despite all the bad things that have happened in my life, and, trust me, there have been a few, I'm happier than I have ever been. And it doesn't involve a man, by the way, Faye, that's not what this is about. So if you ever want to talk, you know where to find me. Otherwise, I'll see you around. Bye.'

She swept out the door, leaving only a scent of jasmine and vanilla perfume behind. Faye slumped down on to the bench seat, stunned and angry. How dare she?

And yet, her words drifted back. Invisible, yes – Ellen hadn't got that one wrong.

Faye had tried very hard to be invisible, for a good reason, and she'd succeeded. People didn't notice her. They saw a business person, not even a woman.

And who had she done that for? She had believed she was doing it for Amber, but Amber was gone now, and, suddenly, she knew.

Standing in the bathroom, Faye faced one of her uncomfortable truths. Although Ellen had said that a man was not responsible for her becoming strong again, Faye realised that fear of being involved with a man again was the reason she, Faye, had made herself invisible. She'd spent years telling herself that men were not part of her plan for her and Amber's lives, that men only complicated things, that it wasn't fair on a child to bring boyfriends into the fold because they would inevitably leave. And how could she face Amber's hurt little face, wondering where the latest father figure she had come to trust had gone?

But that wasn't why she'd kept away from men, Faye knew.

She'd simply never wanted to go through the pain of being with a man again.

As Faye sat on the little bench in the women's room, thinking over the past, a sense of longing suddenly came over her. Amber might not need her mother at the moment, but Faye certainly needed hers.

She picked up her bag and hurried back to her office. She grabbed her jacket and her phone and ran downstairs, shouting over her shoulder to Jane on reception: 'Jane, I have to go. Family emergency. Tell Philippa to handle my calls.'

'Can I do anything to help?' asked Jane to Faye's retreating back.

'No, nothing, but thanks.'

Her mother's front door opened as soon as Faye rang the bell and before Faye could say anything, her mother put her arms round her.

'I know,' Josie said.

'You do?'

'She phoned a while ago.'

'And what's happening?' Faye almost wailed. 'Is she safe, is she coming home . . . ?'

'She's still going away with him,' said her mother. 'Come on in, we'll talk.'

When they'd shared all they knew, mother and daughter sat quietly at the kitchen table.

'Not hearing from her is the hardest thing,' Faye said.

'I think she's realised what she's done and she's scared to get in touch with us right now,' Josie said. 'But she'll change her mind. She'll miss you, you pair are so close. Don't worry, it'll work out.'

'What if it doesn't?' Faye demanded. 'I've got to do something.'

'Like what?'

'I'm going to go after her,' Faye said simply. 'Find her, tell her the truth and then, it's up to her.'

'You should have told her the truth a long time ago,' her mother said, although there was no criticism in her voice. It was just a statement of fact. Josie had always told Faye that she should tell the truth to Amber. She'd never wanted to lie to her granddaughter although she had, for Faye's sake.

'How did you feel, back then, when I was ruining my life and dropping out of college?' Faye asked. They hadn't had a conversation about this for so many years that she couldn't precisely remember it all. She knew her mother had tried her best to tell Faye that she was hanging around with people who'd hurt her. But Faye had refused to listen, just like Amber was doing now.

'I felt as if I'd failed as a mother,' Josie said. 'My friends said I couldn't live your life for you, but I kept thinking that if I'd been a good mother, you'd have been able to see that those people were bad for you and that you'd only get hurt.'

'You didn't fail,' Faye insisted, getting up to sit beside her mother. 'It wasn't you. I wanted excitement and thrills and romance, you couldn't have stopped me.'

222

'And you couldn't have stopped Amber,' Josie added.

The comparison was neatly done.

But in her guilt and self-contempt, Faye still refused to see it that way.

'It's different. You had always been truthful with me, had warned me about things. But I knew things I didn't tell Amber and I lied to her. If I had been more open with her, then she'd have known that men like this Karl are all smoke and mirrors . . .' Ella had not held back in her unflattering portrayal of Karl. He sounded like the worst sort of man – beautiful on the outside, vain and selfish on the inside. Men like him never thought of others.

'It's not different at all,' Josie interrupted. 'It just seems worse because you're so close.'

Faye nodded, tears in her eyes now. That was the awful thing, how she and Amber could share so much and that Amber could still leave. Christie had said something similar: that it was because of their very closeness that Amber had made the break this way.

*You have huge love and closeness, leaving you was like leaving a lover: to be done quickly, ripping the ties, before she'd have a chance to change her mind. She's only just eighteen after all. It's a time of passion, isn't it?*

As Faye sat in her mother's kitchen, she felt heartfelt gratitude to Christie again. It was comforting to interpret Amber's leaving that way, though it didn't make it hurt less.

'You know it wasn't your fault, don't you?' she asked her mother. 'About me.'

'I do now. I blamed myself for a long time. But blaming doesn't work. You can't beat yourself up about everything for evermore. I realised that you can't lay every problem at someone else's door, either. Your parents might do their worst, but then you're on your own and you can shape yourself the way you want and learn from what they did wrong. Stan taught me that,' she added, smiling. 'He says learn from the past and move on. I'm not saying your father wasn't a wonderful man, but he didn't think the way Stan did. Stan doesn't say much but when he talks, he makes sense. You can change up until your dying day, he says, so there's no point blaming the people who only had the moulding of you until you left home.'

'He's right,' Faye said, 'except he isn't accounting for parents who try to mould you too much. I didn't want Amber to have my past as a template. I wanted to give her a clean slate, not to have to learn from my poor example. I don't know why I never thought she'd rebel against that. Stupid really. She's my daughter, after all.'

'If you'd told her, she might have run off all the same.' Josie shrugged. 'You'll never know. But if you can sleep better at night having told her, then do. I don't worry about Amber so much as you do, love. I have great faith in her. You've brought her up well and she's a clever girl. She won't do anything really stupid, you'll see.'

But Faye, who thought of drink and drugs and what damage they could do to a clever girl's common sense, and of the people who take pleasure in destroying innocence and girlish dreams, did worry.

'Look at what happened to me,' she said.

Her mother laid a hand on Faye's and her eyes were shining with pride. 'Yes,' she said, 'look at you.'

# CHAPTER FIFTEEN

People's concepts of time were strange, Christie reflected. When you were six, a child of twelve was like a being from another planet. And when you were sixty, those six years meant nothing.

The six years between herself and her younger sister Ana had shortened over their lives so that they now spoke of 'people our age'.

But the maternal feeling Christie had for Ana had never quite gone away and she'd always looked out for her sister, trying to take care of her the way she had all those decades ago in Kilshandra, when their father raged and their mother tried to ignore it all.

Which was another reason why the thought of Carey Wolensky hurt so much. For when he'd come into their lives, Christie hadn't taken care of her darling little sister. And she simply couldn't forgive herself for that.

Ever since she'd seen his name in the paper, she had thought of little but Carey and the past, which was why she felt so jumpy and guilty when Ana phoned later that week and asked to meet her one afternoon.

'I want to talk about Rick's birthday surprise.'

Ana sounded breathless, as if she had a huge secret to impart.

'In the Summer Street Café at three?' Christie suggested.

By ten past, the two sisters were sitting at a window table with coffee and cake in front of them. At a table outside sat a group of girls from St Ursula's sixth year and they'd smiled at Christie. She grinned back, imagining them cursing her under their breath because they'd undoubtedly chosen that table so they could enjoy forbidden cigarettes – smoking while in uniform was supposed to be off limits. They were like glossy birds of paradise in the royal-blue uniform, with long colourful scarves wound round youthful necks and gorgeous long hair whipping around in the breeze, all looking far older than their years. Ella was there, and she looked diminished without Amber, her partner in crime. Where was Amber now? And how was poor Faye coping?

It was four days since Amber had gone and Christie and Maggie had dropped round to Faye's each evening, just for a chat and a cup of tea. Faye was travelling to the States the following morning even though she didn't know exactly where Amber was. Ella's information had been patchy. All she knew was that the band had talked about being produced by some company based in New York.

'That's not much to go on,' Maggie commented.

'If I'm in the same city, I'll find them,' Faye said firmly.

She'd spent the past few days sorting out things at work so she could take extended leave. She was being outwardly businesslike and calm, but inside, she was still broken-hearted. Each day, she sat on the bed in Amber's room, looked around, and wondered at how she'd managed to get it so badly wrong. Amber had left one message on the house phone:

'I'm fine, Mum. We're going to the US. I'll talk to you. I'm fine, really. Bye.'

If only she'd phoned on the mobile, Faye thought. But

Amber had undoubtedly not phoned Faye's mobile on purpose, and at least she knew Amber was all right.

'You'll get through it,' Christie had told her.

It was good to see Faye getting to grips with her situation, but Christie was beginning to feel like a fraud giving any advice. She had her own dark cloud hanging over her and she'd done nothing to address it. She didn't dare. She just longed for some peace in her head. Perhaps she'd never have peace again, or at least not until Carey Wolensky packed up his exhibition and left the country.

'I love it here,' sighed Ana, stirring her cappuccino happily and licking the spoon. 'It's so homey. You can just imagine this sort of place in Kilshandra when we were growing up, everyone knowing everyone else. Summer Street's great for that sense of community, it does remind me of home.'

Christie didn't agree but said nothing.

The difference was that she'd have hated people in a small café knowing her business in the home town of their youth because everyone would have looked at Christie and Ana MacKenzie with pity. Their father didn't confine his bullying and bad temper to his own home but spread it around liberally, so people knew what the MacKenzie children and poor Maura MacKenzie had to put up with.

'He's not an easy man, your father,' was about the kindest thing anybody had ever said of him.

The idea of drinking your tea in a public room where everybody pitied you was not Christie's idea of fun. The Summer Street Café was a haven for many reasons and the fact that she was happy with her own life meant she could appreciate it. Nobody had reason to feel sorry for Christie Devlin here.

'Actually, I don't want to talk about Rick's birthday,' said Ana. 'I've something to tell you. A secret. If I don't tell somebody I'll go mad.'

Christie felt herself go icy cold in spite of the warmth of the sun beating down on the window.

'You won't tell anyone, not even James? I know you tell him everything, so promise.'

'I promise,' said Christie, dread in her heart.

'It's Carey Wolensky. He's going to be here in Ireland for an exhibition, so I contacted his hotel and left a message for him. It's so strange,' Ana went on, looking flushed, 'an old boyfriend coming into your life. I haven't told Rick. Not that Rick would really mind. He knows it's all in the past and it was before I met him, so it's not as if he and Carey were rivals or anything.'

'No,' agreed Christie automatically. 'That might be hard for him.'

'Well, it could be, so I haven't told him and I feel awful about it. Not that I still have feelings for Carey or anything like that.'

Christie sat immobile and felt sick. This was the meaning of the great dark wing of fear in whose shadow she'd been ever since that morning at the end of April. This was the disaster she'd seen in the future, in *her* future.

'Besides, Carey's had women to beat the band since. I've followed his career; I know it's wrong,' Ana went on guiltily. 'But only out of interest, honestly. I love Rick. Me and Carey would never have made it as a couple. We were wrong together, I know that. He was too old for me, too sophisticated, too mad about art. He was much more your type, really. At least you and he could talk about art together. I didn't know a Picasso from a can of soup.

'But it's interesting when someone you were once in love with is famous and you can watch them. Of course, he's gone out with all these younger women. How is it men can do that? Imagine me with a thirty-year-old? Everyone would fall about laughing, but men can do it.'

Ana held up her knife to look closely at her reflection, squinting so that the lines around her eyes became more pronounced. She favoured their father's side of the family, with fair hair, pale eyes and sun-shy skin. Christie looked more like their mother and was the picture of her maternal grandmother, who'd died before she was born, a woman with the fine bones of Breton heritage, and slanting dark eyes like Christie's.

'Would Botox help?' sighed Ana. 'I have furrows like trenches everywhere and I don't care what they say about rubbing creams and serums in. I've done everything I was supposed to. I've cleansed, toned, moisturised and dabbed eye cream on with my ring finger. I haven't gone to bed once in my whole life with my make-up on and look at me: I'm a human Shar-Pei.'

In spite of the knot in her stomach, Christie laughed. 'You don't look a bit like a Shar-Pei,' she said. 'They are adorable, though. I wouldn't mind one, although the girls would go mental.'

The velvety Chinese emperor dogs with their heavily wrinkled skin were exquisite, but Christie knew that Tilly and Rocket would be devastated if another dog invaded their kingdom. Dogs were like children: fiercely territorial.

'You're still lovely, you big muppet,' Christie said, forgetting her shock to berate her sister in the way she'd been berating her for decades. Ana had gone through life thinking she was too fat, too fair, had bad ankles, and Christie had been the one who'd buoyed her up, told her they were needless worries.

'Was I wrong to phone his hotel?' Ana went on anxiously.

The thought that she was the biggest hypocrite ever danced in Christie's head.

'He might never get back to you,' she said, hoping. Please, please let Carey have forgotten the MacKenzie sisters.

'That's it, you see.' Ana bit her lip. 'I got a call from his assistant to say he'd love to meet up and talk about old times except that his schedule hasn't been finalised yet and she'd get back to me. But imagine, he'd love to meet up. He hasn't forgotten after all.'

When Ana had gone home, Christie sat in the garden and sipped a large glass of wine. James would be astonished to see her drinking at this hour of the afternoon. She'd tell him she just felt like a moment of hedonistic pleasure, sitting in the sun-drenched garden with chilled Chablis. Which was all complete rubbish. She'd simply wanted something to dull the spike of fear inside her. Carey Wolensky was back in her life. All those years of trying to forget it and her guilty secret had sneaked back into her life as easily as if it had all happened yesterday.

The months leading up to Christie's thirty-fifth birthday were endlessly busy. She'd started working part time at St Ursula's and in an attempt to make some extra money, was painting botanical watercolours which a dealer friend sold in markets at the weekend. James was working all the hours too, on a massive environmental study that meant late nights at the office and monosyllabic conversations when he did come home.

Christie could have coped with him working hard, but not with his withdrawal from the human race. It was as if he wasn't interested in her any more and the only bit of affection left in him was given to their sons.

'How was your day?' Christie would ask when he came home, trying to keep the lines of communication open.

'Fine,' he'd mutter, hugging the boys.

Once the children were in bed, James worked silently at the dining-room table.

Christie started to go to bed early to read, and was often

asleep when he came upstairs. If it hadn't been for Ethan and Shane, she'd have packed her bags and left.

She adored her sons, loved every moment of their hectic days, and sometimes felt overwhelmed by love for them: two small boys who did everything passionately, whether it was cycling tricycles hell bent around the garden or fighting to the death with toy soldiers.

'It's scary, loving them so much,' she told Ana on the phone one day. She hadn't talked about the crisis in her marriage with Ana: doing so would make it more real, more raw. Part of Christie hoped that eventually, when James's study was done, he'd come back to her. 'When I read about a disaster or an accident in the paper, I think what would I do if anything happened to the boys?' she told her sister. 'It's like a physical pain thinking about it.'

Ana, working in administration in a hospital and enjoying a series of relationships with hardworking doctors who didn't have the time to find girlfriends anywhere else, said she wished she knew what Christie meant.

'I'm never going to find a man to settle down with and have babies,' she said morosely. 'I worked it out the other night: in the past two years, I haven't gone out with anyone for longer than three months. I must have a "ninety-day limit" sticker on my forehead. Three months and zip, they're gone. I am so fed up of hearing "you're a wonderful woman, but . . ." I'm going to shoot the next man who says "but" to me. And I've had it with doctors. They're all obsessed with work. Girlfriends are just a mild diversion between shifts. Never again. I need to get out and meet different types of people.'

Christie felt guilty for being so insensitive and reminding Ana, who was wildly maternal, that she was still childless with no hope of a daddy for her children in sight. It was James's fault, she thought crossly. If he wasn't so tied up with

231

his work, so oblivious to her, she could have talked about her love for the boys with him, instead of upsetting poor Ana with it. What was the point of being married if the extent of your conversation was competitive exhaustion?

'I'm tired.'

'No, I'm tireder.'

'Of course you'll meet someone,' she said quickly to her sister. 'You're gorgeous, Ana, your time will come, I promise. You've been going out with the wrong sort of men, that's all. Get out and meet other people, go to museums, lectures, parties. Enjoy yourself and don't look for a man. When you're least expecting it, one will come along.'

How she was to regret that advice.

The day before Christie's birthday, she told James that they were going to a gallery to meet Ana's latest boyfriend – a Polish artist who was years older than her and sounded like he'd be another guy for the 'you're a wonderful woman *but* . . .' speech – and then on to dinner for a birthday celebration.

'I'm sorry, I forgot to organise anything for you, Christie,' James said matter-of-factly.

He wasn't even apologetic, Christie realised in fury. It was as if what he was doing was so important that everything else came a poor second, including her.

'What do you want?' he asked.

'A husband?' she said bitterly.

'Christie, don't be such a nag,' he snapped back. 'You know how busy I am.'

'I'm not nagging. I'm being honest. The boys and I never see you any more, James. You're obsessed with that bloody study. I cook, clean, work and take care of our sons, and the least I can expect is you to remember to buy me a birthday present. It's not rocket science. Even a card would be nice. I bet you haven't got a card for me for tomorrow either.'

He grimaced and said nothing.

Which meant no. 'Thank you, James. I'm touched by your thoughtfulness,' she said, hurt beyond belief. Not even a card. It was like her parents' marriage all over again. She must have been mad to get married. She should have just had kids and lived on her own. Men and women were utterly unsuited to being together for ever. It was the hunter-gatherer thing: men were warriors at heart, more suited to roaming, while women were better at taking care of their children and fighting their own battles.

They were on the bus from Summer Street into the city and they sat in silence for the next ten minutes.

'So,' said James, keen to end the cold war, 'tell me about this new bloke of Ana's.'

Christie, who had many friends in the art world, had heard that Carey Wolensky was a charming and wildly sexy genius with a brilliant future ahead of him and many dumped besotted women in his wake.

'He sounds like a nightmare,' she said to James. 'The more brilliant they are, the madder they are.'

'You're an artist and you're not mad,' said James equably.

He was obviously trying to make up to her for not remembering her birthday.

'I'm one of the practical ones and we're a rare breed in the art world,' she said. 'Besides, I haven't been able to earn much of a living painting, have I? I'm missing the mad gene. Thank God for teaching.'

'He might be as normal as you and me and turn out to be just the man for Ana.'

'I doubt it. If he messes with Ana, I'll throw turpentine on all his canvases, I swear,' she added grimly. She'd been protecting Ana all her life and she'd protect her from this maniac if it was the last thing she did. Then again, who was she to say what sort of man was right for Ana? She'd picked

James and he'd recently transformed himself into a grumpy chauvinist.

Word of Carey Wolensky's fame had certainly spread because there were bodies crushed all around the entrance to the Bamboo Gallery when they arrived, and people clutching catalogues emerged from the gallery itself, crying 'fabulous', 'marvellous', and 'such talent!'

They joined the crush and squashed their way inside, where walls of dark and brooding Wolenskys glared down at them. Christie loved art in all its forms, but she'd never been a fan of dark abstract work like this. Oils painted with masterly knife strokes, these pictures were like tornadoes caught on canvas, full of energy and power, and infinitely startling.

There were a few portraits in the collection, but the people in them were cold, harsh and angular, not warm and curved like the Gauguin women Christie loved.

But clearly she was the only one who didn't approve. There were lots of little red sold stickers stuck on the frames and it was clear that Wolensky would not need to teach at St Ursula's to pay the rent.

This was all wrong, Christie felt. This man with his dark sinister paintings was not the right sort of man to court her sister. Ana didn't know a sausage about art and didn't have a pretentious bone in her body.

The man who'd painted these pictures was fierce and utterly in control. She'd have to warn Ana off him. Christie didn't want another controlling man like their father to take her over.

'You got here! And you look wonderful, almost Birthday Girl!' Ana proclaimed, admiring her sister.

In honour of her birthday dinner, Christie had left her hair down and had stuck heated rollers in it, so it now tumbled darkly around shoulders gleaming in a plum velvet halter-neck dress that clung to her tall, womanly body.

'Really, you don't look like fifty at all,' Ana teased, and Christie threw back her head and laughed her rich, deep laugh. It felt lovely to be with her sister, someone who appreciated and loved her.

When she looked back at Ana, a man was standing beside her, and Christie felt something she didn't think she'd ever experienced before: a spark of tinder and a sensation that this was a person she'd known all her life.

Carey Wolensky wasn't any oil painting himself, Christie thought drily, but the same passion and vivacity that inhabited his work inhabited his person too. She was tall but he was at least six inches taller and lean, with rather wild dark hair and deep-set eyes that stared bird-of-prey-like at her over a broken boxer's nose, taking in every detail. He was around her age, maybe older, and looked as if he wanted to taste every emotion, touch every second of life, in case he missed anything. There were many people crowded around and yet Carey Wolensky had that rare ability to be the person every eye was drawn towards.

'Pleased to meet you,' said James, who seemed to be enjoying himself now he had relaxed with a couple of drinks.

Carey nodded and smiled, and the bleakness left his face.

More people gathered round him to say how much they admired his paintings, and Ana's friend Chloe announced that the gallery owner was having a huge party in his house, 'a mansion on Haddington Road, with a swimming pool in the basement!' and they were all invited.

'We're going out to dinner,' said Christie loudly. 'We can't come.' She didn't know why but she knew that staying here was a mistake.

'A party's exactly what we need,' James said, 'a wild, music-filled night to get you over the misery of being thirty-five.'

'I'm not miserable,' insisted Christie. 'I just don't want to go.'

'If Christie does not want to go, she does not have to go,' said a voice. It was the first time Carey had spoken and she thought his accent was like Lenkya's, the deep purr of drawn-out syllables. It was a voice used to the harsh rasp of Polish consonants and it growled over the softness of her language, making it a language of love.

They stared at each other, oblivious to everyone else. Christie could have drawn his face instantly, she knew it so well. He watched her as if he would touch the contours of her face, then move down to her body, unhooking the halter-neck dress to caress the skin beneath . . .

'Isn't he wonderful?' sighed Ana, taking Christie's arm. 'I think he's the one,' she whispered for Christie alone. 'Well, I hope he is. He says he's too old for me and that's sexy, isn't it? Reverse psychology. It makes me want him even more now.'

Carey still locked gazes with Christie and she knew she'd have to look away or it would be obvious to everyone around them, obvious that Carey Wolensky and Christie Devlin were experiencing a physical attraction hot enough to send the whole room up in flames.

'Wolensky, marvellous show.' A well-dressed and well-padded man with a cigar broke the spell by standing between them.

A rich collector, Christie surmised, exactly the sort of person to take Wolensky's attention. Only the greenest artist didn't know that the official language of art was hard currency.

Christie stood back and breathed deeply. She was married. This was her sister's boyfriend, her beloved Ana's man. There would be, could be, no electricity between them.

'Shall I take you round the exhibition?' asked Ana.

'Yes, take me round,' Christie said.

With James at one side and Ana at the other, they toured

the pictures, Ana explaining what each canvas was called and James standing back and raising his eyebrows occasionally. Normally, Christie would have teased him every time he did this, whispering that he was a philistine and the only picture he'd really adored was the one of the tennis player scratching her knickerless bum. Which would make James grin and say no, he liked the poster of the dogs playing poker best.

This time, James's lack of comprehension irritated Christie. Couldn't he see how amazing these paintings were, the energy and fire that burned out at the audience?

By the time Lenkya arrived at the gallery, Christie and James weren't talking to each other.

'Argument?' asked Lenkya, kissing Christie twice, European-style.

'Yes,' sighed Christie. 'What's new?'

Lenkya was with her partner, a sculptor, and they toured the exhibition quickly.

'We're going to dinner,' Lenkya said, putting an arm round her friend. 'You are sad, you should come with us. You and James will never make up your differences here in this noisy place.'

'No,' said Christie firmly, 'we're staying a little longer.' Another thing she regretted. For if she and James had left then, it might never have happened.

As the crowds milled around, Christie could feel Wolensky watching her, feel the intensity of his mind turned towards hers. She did all those things you did when you were being watched: stood up straighter, held herself even more gracefully, smiled more, wanting to look more beautiful in his eyes even though, as she did it, she knew it was wrong.

They went to the party on Haddington Road.

'It'll be a bit of craic,' James said. 'We said we'd be home by twelve and it's only half nine now. We can phone Fiona on the way to say we won't be in the restaurant but we won't be late, either.'

Fiona, who was babysitting, was a college student who lived on Summer Street with her parents. Her mother was a nurse, which gave Christie peace of mind that if anything did happen – please God it wouldn't – Fiona's mother would be at number 34 in a flash with the full breadth of her medical training.

'I don't know . . .' Christie began, feeling strangely edgy.

'Stop being a martyr!' exploded James. 'You're furious I didn't arrange a big birthday evening for you, and now we have a chance of a party where we'll have some fun, and you don't know if you want to do that either! You don't know what you want to do.'

Perhaps if they hadn't had the argument, perhaps if Christie hadn't felt so lonely and neglected for so long, perhaps if Ana hadn't started flirting with a young man with merry eyes, and perhaps if Christie hadn't felt pure admiration at Wolensky's stunning paintings, then none of it might have happened.

The house on Haddington Road was a large Victorian mansion with pale floorboards and walls, perfect for displaying art, and utterly unsuitable for a wildly boozy party. Christie felt old surrounded by Ana's friends, who'd soon located a stereo and a stack of records to organise an impromptu disco. Ana and a group of her girlfriends began to dance. The young man with the merry eyes joined in, and Christie watched as Ana laughingly held his hands, clearly not caring whether her supposed artist boyfriend saw them or not. He was nothing compared to Wolensky, Christie thought, mystified.

James was still barely talking to her and was ensconced on a deep window seat with a man who turned out to be one of his brother's old friends.

Christie felt alone and miserable, until a hand took hers and

238

led her out of the kitchen, into a small hallway and up three flights of stairs to a huge attic room hung with paintings.

'This is where he keeps the good stuff,' Carey said, not letting go of her hand. 'The paintings that are valuable. He has two of mine, see.'

They were alone, standing hip to hip, and even though her head told her it was wrong, her heart screamed that it was right.

She adored Ana, and she adored James. This should not be happening, she had to get out of there. Yet she felt as if she'd die if Carey didn't swing round and haul her into his arms, sinking into her soul and her body.

'You feel it too,' Carey said softly. He was looking down at her hand now, examining it, touching the palm as if he could see her whole life through the lines on her hand. 'What is between us. You feel it, I know.'

'No, I don't,' she lied. 'I'm married.' As if that was a talisman she could hold up like a crucifix to Dracula.

'So,' he said, still looking down at where her hand was trapped by both of his. 'Marriage severs the mind from the body, yes?'

'It does for Catholics,' Christie replied in an attempt at levity. 'It's in the ceremony. Forsaking all others.' She couldn't remember the rest of the vows, to her shame.

'Men who are not allowed to have women make up those rules,' Carey murmured. 'They cannot be expected to understand that such rules cannot always be followed.'

'I believe in those rules,' Christie said. 'And I love my husband.' This was true, utterly true. But she felt shaken still. For if she absolutely loved James, how could she feel so wildly attracted to this man? If he made just one move towards her, she'd offer herself to him, here on the floor with scores of people beneath them.

'Ah.'

239

He let go of her hand and Christie felt bereft. She hadn't been teasing. She'd meant every word she said, but having him touch her had been so tender.

'I will let you go,' he added, 'but can I touch your face, first, to remember?'

Her eyes, shining with excitement, must have said yes, because Carey stood inches away from her and with both hands cradled her face, rubbing his thumbs over the high planes of her cheekbones, down to the sweep of her jaw, and over the softness of her mouth.

When his thumb massaged her lower lip, slipping into the cavern of her mouth, she couldn't stop herself biting gently.

*Watch out*, said every instinct inside her. *This is not a game.*

'Not a unicorn after all but a lioness,' he said as her bite eased.

She made herself pull back from his touch.

'Married lioness,' she reminded him. 'And you're supposed to be going out with my sister.'

He shrugged. 'She is happy tonight,' he remarked. 'She has found the sort of young man she should be with. I told her so. I prefer' – he paused, looking at her – 'more complicated women.'

'I've got to go,' Christie said. 'Nice meeting you, Mr Wolensky.'

'Is that it?' he called as she almost ran down the stairs.

'That's it,' she replied over her shoulder.

In the kitchen, she filled a glass of cool water and drained it quickly, hoping it might douse the heat on her face and neck.

Back in the main part of the house, she searched for James. They had to go. He was still sitting on the window ledge laughing. Christie watched the man she curled up beside in bed, the man who'd held her hand through the births of two

240

children, the man she loved. Despite his current obsession with work, James was a good man. He was being blind, not seeing how he was hurting her, that was all. If she told him, sat down and said she was on the verge of walking out because of his behaviour, he'd be shocked and she knew he'd change in an instant.

And yet the image of James in her head was being crowded out by the dark brooding face of Carey Wolensky, who was all the things she'd ever dreamed of when she was young, and who'd come into her life when it was already full. Too late.

In the taxi on the way home, she held James's hand tightly. She would force Carey Wolensky out of her head. This was the man she loved, the father of her children.

James was exhausted and went to bed after politely walking Fiona, the babysitter, home. Christie stayed up and scrubbed the kitchen tiles with the small scrubbing brush. She made James's favourite apple cake, diligently and carefully, where normally, she flung ingredients in at high speed. She would push Carey out of her mind.

Ethan and Shane's little trousers hung on the clothes horse and she ironed them. Normally, she folded carefully, not bothering ironing garments that would be on and off within an hour.

She couldn't stop it: more than anything, she yearned to have Carey holding her in his arms, taking off her clothes, touching her breasts, lowering his head to kiss them, to feel his body covering hers, against hers, in hers.

Like the magic that came into her head unbidden and told her of the future, this longing was too powerful to push away.

Christie could no more resist Carey Wolensky than she could stop her mind from seeing what might happen.

# CHAPTER SIXTEEN

Faye and Maggie sat in Faye's garden listening to the exquisite tones of Julie London on full blast telling everyone about how she'd cried a river and now it was his turn.

They had a bottle of rosé between them and a giant box of Ferrero Rocher half gone, with scrunched-up gold foil wrappers littering the table. Christie had said she'd drop in but hadn't turned up.

It was four days since Amber had left and, the following day, Faye was going to the States to find Amber and she couldn't wait to be off.

At least if she was travelling, trying to find Amber, she'd be doing *something*. And that was preferable to being at home in the silent misery of number 18. Without Amber, the house was grave-like. Faye jumped every time the phone rang in case it was Amber; she checked her answering machine by remote access ten times a day, and in the morning, she ran to the letterbox when the postman came just in case there was a card, a letter, *anything* saying that Amber was all right.

'Should I turn the music down,' asked Maggie, 'in case the neighbours go mad?'

Faye's next-door neighbour was an irascible man who had

no animals, no wife, no children and no sense of humour – or at least, that's what Amber had always said. Faye used to hush her when she said this. 'He might hear!'

'Screw the neighbours,' Faye muttered. 'If Mr Dork next door has a problem, he can come in here and tell me face to face.'

'Fine by me,' said Maggie, who knew a woman gunning for a fight when she saw one.

Since Amber had gone, Faye had appeared defeated and sad. Today, something had clearly changed inside her and she was filled with fierce energy and rage.

Maggie suspected she was going through the phases of grief: she'd done disbelief, and hopelessness, and now was on to anger.

Maggie had been through that herself.

'Exercise helps me,' she volunteered. 'I do Pilates when . . . sorry,' she added. 'It's very boring to have people giving you advice all the time, isn't it?' She wished Christie were here. She felt singularly incapable of saying anything useful. Her boyfriend had been cheating on her for years and she hadn't had a clue about it, so both her skills of observation and her credentials as agony aunt were questionable.

Faye shot her a genuine, warm smile. 'Thanks,' she said. 'I appreciate that. Everyone else wants to tell me what to do.' Everyone else was Grace, whom she'd told about Amber's disappearance, and who was full of suggestions about what action Faye should take next.

'Grace at work has my head wrecked saying she's there if I need her and after all, Amber was going to leave eventually and all families fight, don't they? She's trying to help but she doesn't understand. She doesn't have kids . . . Well, perhaps that's not fair,' Faye amended. 'You don't need to have children to understand and I've only told her half the story. Me and my secrets. Perhaps I should have brazened it

243

out and told her the truth years ago. We've been through a lot together professionally, so in many ways we know each other well. But at first I was too ashamed, I thought she'd look down on me. Grace is so together, I couldn't imagine her doing anything she was ashamed of. And then, too much time had passed for me to suddenly say: hey, Grace, I'm not really a widow after all. I just say I am.'

'When you're ashamed, it's easy to build it up into a huge secret you dare not trust anyone with,' Maggie reflected, thinking of her own past.

Faye looked interested now, so Maggie had to go on.

'My problem was that when things went wrong for me, I felt I couldn't confide in my parents,' she said, amazed at her courage now. She'd never said that to anyone before.

'About Grey?' Faye was puzzled. Maggie had said her parents knew about her break-up, though not about Grey cheating on her.

'No, before that.'

'What . . . ?' began Faye, and stopped.

Maggie's eyes had filled with tears. Whatever her big secret was, it was too painful to touch.

'So, back to this cheating man of yours,' Faye said firmly, switching subjects. 'What has your dad threatened to do to him lately?'

Despite herself, Maggie laughed. 'They don't have a surgical name for it yet.'

'But it's performed without an anaesthetic?'

'With two bricks and a rusty razor blade,' said Maggie. Then sighed. 'Poor Dad has got it into his head that I left Grey because there was no sign of us getting married. He calls Grey "that bastard who felt he was too good to put a ring on my daughter's finger after five years".'

'That is a very dad thing to say,' Faye agreed. 'Luckily for Amber's father my poor old dad wasn't around by the time

I started getting into trouble with men. But what happened to you was pretty rough.'

'You don't seem that shocked actually,' Maggie said, surprised. 'Not that I've been broadcasting the information but so far, everyone I've told about what Grey did has been stunned.'

'They all live sheltered lives, I guess.' Faye grinned. 'I've heard of guys doing much worse and he did say sorry afterwards, although I know that's not the point. You were living together, he was your partner and it was way out of line. You're not taking him back, I hope.'

'I wanted to,' Maggie said. 'Isn't that pathetic? I thought he was right for me. I loved him and our life together.'

Faye interrupted: 'You just don't love coming home and seeing him bonking some blonde babe on your bed.'

'No,' agreed Maggie, 'that does sort of ruin things.'

'So you've got to dump him and start again.'

'I'm going to dump him all right.' Since Shona had told her about Grey's other women, she'd thought of practically nothing else. She felt so humiliated by the news. To think how he'd looked her straight in the eye and lied to her.

*It's never happened before.*

*I love you.*

To think of him offering to marry her while hiding the fact that he'd betrayed her in the past.

Grey had tried to phone her every day but she never answered when she saw his number appear on her phone screen. She wasn't ready for him yet. She'd cry if she spoke to him and she didn't want to do that: she wanted to build herself up to be strong and angry for that conversation.

'I'm not starting again with anybody ever,' Maggie said decisively. 'I can't go through all that dating, smiling and trying to be something you're not. Hoping they'll like you.' She shuddered, partly with remembered shame. She'd tried

245

so hard to be what Grey wanted and, in the process, had lost sight of who she was. The past had scared her and Grey had made her feel safe, so she'd never tried to work out who Maggie Maguire actually was and what she wanted from life.

'Hoping they'll like you sounds like me once,' reflected Faye. 'Trying to be something I wasn't instead of having the courage to be what I really was.'

There was silence. The CD had stopped playing and there was no noise at all, apart from the sound of somebody's lawn mower and a dog barking, far away in the distance.

'You have to tell Amber about the past when you see her,' Maggie said. 'All of it.'

Faye nodded. She had been thinking a lot about everything over the previous few days.

Ellen, the makeover lady, had been right when she said Faye tried to be invisible. Faye had tried to blend into the background, to make herself as asexual as possible, so nobody could connect her with the wild child she'd been. And she'd protected Amber like a crown princess, stifling her out of love, never telling her the truth. It kept coming back to secrets and lies.

'I'm going to tell Amber everything when I see her,' she told Maggie. 'It's just that I thought I was doing the right thing by inventing this person: Faye Reid, mum extraordinaire, conservative, decent, long-skirt-wearing person, pillar of the community, the sort of woman no one would ever imagine hanging out with dodgy men, having no respect for herself. I thought if I insulated Amber from the world, bad things would never touch her and she would grow up strong and confident. And if she ever met a man like her father, I thought by then that she would know better, that she would be stronger than I was. But I was fooling myself.'

'Me too,' said Maggie, thinking that she wasn't much

different from Faye after all. At least Faye had changed her life and begun to respect herself once she'd given birth to Amber.

While Maggie had always felt as if she wasn't worthy of Grey, that it was surprising someone like him loved her. She'd had to pretend to be the confident person to hide her insecurities. If that wasn't living a lie, what was?

'And the more you lie, the more you have to lie. The lies become bigger until there's no way out, apart from admitting that you're fabulous at being deceitful. What mother wants to say that to her daughter?' Faye asked.

'You thought you were protecting her,' Maggie said. 'She'll understand that, when you tell her.'

'But it's gone on for so long,' sighed Faye. 'Imagine if you have an adopted child and you never find the right time to tell them. Maybe, you miss that window of opportunity when they're two or three, when it should become part and parcel of their life – *You're adopted. Mummy and Daddy love you and picked you to be our baby, so our love is special* – and time moves on and you haven't told them. So you wait a bit longer and then you have to turn around when they're an adult and go, *Well, actually, by the way, we're not your parents, we adopted you*. It's like that with me and Amber. I should have told her in the beginning, but I didn't know how. It's gone on so long that telling her will destroy her and she'll hate me and I . . .' Faye paused. 'I don't know if I can face that. I love her so much, Maggie. Everything that I've achieved in my life this past eighteen years, has been for her. I couldn't bear for her to hate me.' Maggie got up and put her arms around Faye, holding her tightly.

And Faye, who longed for the comfort of another human being since Amber had stormed off, leaned against Maggie and began to sob.

'I just wish she'd come home, I wish she'd make contact,

anything. Just so I could tell her I love her and explain it all to her, that's all I want,' she said, as she sobbed. 'I'm sorry, Maggie, I'm sorry. You don't need this.'

'Don't be silly,' said Maggie, still holding Faye tightly, as the other woman's sobs subsided. 'Hey, you'll be doing this for me in a minute, when I tell you all my deep, dark secrets.'

'You mean you have deep, dark secrets too?' hiccupped Faye. 'Oh please, tell me, I don't want to feel like the only screw-up on Summer Street.'

Maggie laughed. 'There are lots of screw-ups on Summer Street,' she said. 'It's just we don't know about them, that's all. Do you think everyone hiding inside the pretty houses, with the coloured doors and the beautiful maple trees, lives a perfect life? Of course they don't. If you knew my mother, then you wouldn't think that. She knows everything that goes on around here.'

'Really?' asked Faye.

'Oh yes,' said Maggie, seeing that Faye looked cheered by this line of conversation. 'Mum is a fount of knowledge about everyone on Summer Street. It's the café, you see. She and dad go into the Summer Street Café at least once a day and Mum learns things, all the time. Not in a bad way: she's not a gossip, but she's interested in people's lives and she knows what goes on. Christie's the same, really,' she added thoughtfully. 'Christie seems to know about everyone.'

'She's a wise woman,' agreed Faye. 'I wish I'd known her properly before, instead of just nodding a distant hello in the street. That was another one of my obsessions,' she added. 'I thought if we kept ourselves to ourselves, nobody would get close enough to ask what exactly happened to Amber's father. But someone like Christie, she'd never ask you those sort of questions, would she? If I'd known her then, she might have been able to help me, stop me screwing everything up.'

248

'No,' insisted Maggie, 'we've got to help ourselves. I've got to fall out of love with my cheating boyfriend, a man who must think I'm the dumbest woman on the planet if I agree to marry him when he's had other women all the time we were going out.'

'You can't be the dumbest woman on the planet,' Faye joked. 'That's me.'

'No,' argued Maggie. 'It's me, I'm afraid.'

'Did you cut the arms off his suits and throw paint all over his car before you left?' Faye inquired.

'Don't be daft,' said Maggie. 'I'm a wimp. I went back to the apartment that night, talked to him like an adult and even considered – in my own head of course, I didn't say this out loud – letting him sleep in the bed with me because then he'd hug me and cuddle me and it'd all be all right.'

'Ouch,' said Faye.

'I know,' Maggie agreed, 'not just the world's dumbest woman, but the wimpiest too. But fortunately I stood firm and made him sleep on the couch. Then, the next morning, I packed and flew home to Summer Street. Cutting the arms off all his clothes might be fun though. He doesn't really wear suits, he's more of a casual jacket type of guy.'

'You could tell people he had some appalling venereal disease?'

'My friend, Shona, thought of that one too,' laughed Maggie. 'She works in the library with me and was all set to spread the rumours, but I said that sort of revenge would be beneath me.'

Faye grinned. 'It wouldn't be beneath me. Fight fire with fire. He slept with a student, so why don't you let that be known? He'd be sacked. The ultimate revenge.'

'True,' said Maggie, 'but I'm trying to put myself in that happy, Zen state where the only true revenge is living my own life well.'

'You're right,' Faye said gravely, 'that's exactly the right thing to do. Modern and very politically correct.' But she added wickedly, 'It would be great fun, wouldn't it?'

'Not as much fun as telling him I don't need him,' said Maggie firmly.

'Good for you. When are you going to do it?'

Maggie took the last chocolate. 'Tonight,' she said. 'I'll tell him tonight.'

'I've got some chocolate-covered biscuits in the kitchen,' Faye said. 'I quite fancy one of them. What do you think?'

'Good plan,' said Maggie. 'Men are nothing but trouble. We should stick to chocolate. It's safer.'

When she left Faye's house, Maggie walked across Summer Street to the park. Its cast-iron gates would close in half an hour but there were still plenty of people enjoying the summer evening. She headed for the pavilion and climbed the old wooden steps to sit on one of the built-in benches that overlooked the tiny fountain.

Birds sang to one another in the trees overhead, and there were giggles coming from the group of girls huddled on the benches beside the playground. Normal life went on no matter what personal disaster you were living through, she thought, taking out her mobile.

Grey answered the apartment phone quickly.

'Maggie, hello,' he said warmly.

'Hi, Grey,' she said, her voice flat. She still didn't feel angry. Her anger seemed to have deserted her and her main emotion was sadness at seeing how hollow her life with Grey had turned out to be. 'I don't want us to get back together, I'm afraid. It wouldn't work.'

'What?'

'It's over. I can't go back.'

'But Maggie, you want to, you know that. I love you and you love me. That's all that matters. We can get over what happened. We could have couples' therapy,' he volunteered, which made her smile wryly. Grey was proud of the workings of his own mind but would hate to have a third party probe it and question his beliefs.

'I don't want therapy,' Maggie stated. 'I want to sell the apartment and move on. You could buy me out, if you'd like. It's a good apartment and I don't want it. I'm not sure if I want to move back to Galway at all.'

She had friends there but a total break would help her more. The whole city was filled with memories of the past five years.

'We can start again, Maggie. We can move apartments, get married, do all the things I said.' He sounded earnest and Maggie's feeling of sadness grew. How easily he lied. And how easily she'd believed it all.

'I want to be with someone I can trust, Grey,' she said, 'and you're not that person. It's not easy doing this. I feel like I'm wasting five years of my life . . .'

'You are!' he cried. 'You can't give up on us that easily.'

'I'm not the one giving up,' Maggie replied. 'You are. Because you lied to me about how you'd never cheated before and now I know that's not true. There have been other women. Don't try to deny it. Shona told me. It's no secret apparently, except to me, that you've had other women.'

'Why does she have to interfere?' he growled.

'That's not interfering, that's telling a friend the truth,' Maggie said. 'I can't live that way any more, Grey. You've cheated on me, not with one woman, but with at least four – who knows how many? So you're the one who's ending our relationship. You made the choice to sleep with other women. Not me.'

There was silence on the other end of the phone. She wondered if he'd lie again or confess. What would the politician in him do?

'It was stupid,' he said finally. 'I have no excuse, Maggie. None whatsoever. But it will never happen again, I promise. Please come home. I love you.'

Maggie wiped her eyes but once the tears started to flow, she couldn't stop them running down her cheeks.

'You just don't love me enough, Grey,' she said. 'I won't accept second best. I'm sorry. I'll call again about the apartment but don't call me. It's over. Believe me. I won't change my mind.'

And without giving him a chance to beg, she hung up.

The birds singing in the trees didn't take any notice of the woman sobbing silently on the pavilion. Neither did the teenage girls chattering and texting furiously on the opposite side of the park.

They probably still believe in true love, Maggie reflected, watching them through blurry eyes.

She wished she could warn them, but there were some things you had to experience yourself.

Mum and Dad were in the kitchen watching a film when she got home. It was *National Lampoon's European Vacation* and the Griswold family were touring Europe, leaving mayhem and bewilderment in their wake.

'Sit down, Bean,' said Dad, wiping the tears from his eyes. 'This is hilarious. You used to love it.'

Maggie pulled up a chair, settled the cushion on it, and sat down.

'Did you have any dinner?' asked her mother.

'Yes,' fibbed Maggie. She'd had chocolate biscuits after all. She didn't feel up to eating anything else now and her mother would be bound to start fussing if Maggie had said no.

'I'll make us a pot of tea,' Dad said, patting her knee. 'Isn't this nice? It's like old times, isn't it, Una?'

252

'Yes,' sighed Mum happily.

Maggie looked at her parents with love. It wasn't what she'd planned to be doing when she was thirty – back living with her mum and dad, boyfriendless, and with her confidence shot to pieces. But it must have all happened for a reason. Faye wasn't letting circumstances stop her in her tracks: she was going to find Amber and try to make sense of the past. And that's what Maggie had to do too. If this was what a new life was all about, then she was going to give it her best shot.

# CHAPTER SEVENTEEN

On the plane, Faye sat in an aisle seat and watched her fellow passengers board. She had a fat magazine on her lap, but the scenes playing out in front of her were far more intriguing than anything else.

An older couple walked down the aisle slowly, resigned expressions on their faces at such a long flight ahead. A large group of teenage schoolgirls in some kind of sports strip arrived in a frenzy of excitement, already discussing swapping seats for maximum fun.

'Girls, you're supposed to sit in your correct seat,' said one of the harassed adults with them, either a teacher or a parent, already, Faye reckoned, realising that they'd bitten off more than they could chew.

'Oh, a baby, how cute!' one of the girls said, and the woman in the opposite row with an infant on her lap smiled weakly because at least she'd be surrounded by people who wouldn't object to the poor child's crying.

It had been years since Faye had been on a plane on her own. It was nice, she decided. Freeing. There was nobody to worry about but herself. Nobody could reach her on her mobile phone with bad news; nobody needed her.

For the first time since Amber had left, Faye felt a strange sense of acceptance at being alone. Amber would have left home inevitably and Faye would never have been ready for it. She could see that now. Her world was too tied up with her daughter, which hadn't, it turned out, been the right thing for either of them.

Faye ate the airline meal, watched the movie, then stuck in earplugs, pulled on a home-made lavender-filled eyemask Christie had given her for exactly that purpose and went to sleep.

The midtown hotel where her taxi pulled up was part of a budget chain and looked nothing like the adorable boutique hotels that the airline magazine had mentioned glowingly as places to stay in New York. Here, she reckoned the concierge wouldn't be able to whisk tickets for a Broadway show out of thin air. However, the marble lobby was clean and the whole place felt safe to Faye. Her room was a tiny twin on the seventh floor, with a microscopic bathroom and a mini kitchen that consisted of a kettle, toaster, microwave and sink, all cunningly concealed behind one cupboard.

Faye double-locked the door, stripped off and climbed into bed for another hour's rest.

It was mid-afternoon when she woke up and she stood at the window looking out over the city. She couldn't see much but other buildings, and directly below, she was staring at a grimy rooftop where somebody had once put a few wooden deckchairs, then forgotten about them.

But never mind the view, this was New York. She wasn't the victim any more, she was doing something, taking her power back, as Ellen, the makeover lady, had said. Ellen had a point, Faye realised. Somewhere along the way, she'd lost her power. Not any more.

In the lobby, she sat at a public phone and fed in her credit card. She couldn't afford the hotel-room charges, but down here, the price was pretty standard. It took seven calls to track down the production company who were supposed to be working on Karl's album with the band, Ceres. Then an interminable wait followed as a bored young guy searched for details of the band's schedule, saying all the time: 'I can't give you inside information, lady, this is only public domain stuff. If you're a stalker, I'm not taking the rap.'

'Do many unsigned bands have stalkers?' Faye demanded. 'I wouldn't have thought so. I told you, I'm Amber Reid's mother, she's Karl Evans's partner, and I have an urgent message for her.'

He didn't reply for a minute, then said: 'They did a gig at the O'Reilly Tavern recently, and that's all I have written down here because Sly was supposed to go to it. That's all I can help you with.'

'But they're recording an album and your company are producing it. I can leave a message for them, surely?' said Faye, who planned on just turning up and surprising them but wasn't going to tell this guy so.

'They were,' the guy said, and she could hear him flipping pages, 'but they're not down in the log any more. Doesn't say why.' More pages flipped. 'Not down for next month neither.'

'How could that be?' asked Faye, confused.

'Hey lady, it's all about dollars. If you can't pay, you can't stay. Guess whatever deal they had fell through. If they're good enough, Sly and Maxi will produce your album for a percentage deal. If you're not and nobody else is paying, it's *hasta la vista*.'

'Oh,' she said in horror, her only lead gone.

Her anxiety finally transmitted itself to the guy on the other end of the phone.

'All right. They were staying in the Arizona Fish Hotel

over beside the Port Authority,' he said. 'You didn't hear it from me, OK?'

'Bless you,' said Faye with gratitude.

It was the sight of the Arizona Fish Hotel that made Faye begin to feel really worried. Her own hotel was hardly a palace, but it was Trump Tower compared to this run-down place with its tawdry cloak of hip.

It might have boasted a lobby full of retro chic furniture and framed yellowing sheet music of hit songs allegedly penned in the penthouse suite, but Faye could see the seediness seeping from the walls.

No amount of trendy furniture or psychedelic prints on the walls, or even the neon sign for the hotel's own nightclub, A Fish, could hide the dirt.

It reminded her of The Club in her previous life: a dump dressed up as a cool hang-out by virtue of the fact that some band or other played there once, partying till the LSD or the heroin was gone. Not that she'd ever travelled anywhere with TJ, but she knew that if she had, she'd have loved the decayed glamour of the Arizona Fish. To a girl like Amber, raised in the quiet of Summer Street, hearing of the songs allegedly written in room seven, or the bed that had probably fallen through the roof in room eleven during an unbelievable party after a rock festival, would have made her feel a part of it all. This was excitement, this was life. And she was in the middle of it.

Faye knew exactly how excited Amber would be to be living this life, because she'd been just as excited twenty years ago to find herself in the world of The Club. But that life was like being in the eye of the storm. You thought you were safe, untouchable, when the storm was actually raging inches away. Then, nobody could have told Faye Reid that. She'd had to find it out for herself.

Faye wanted to get her daughter out of that storm before it hurt her. She wouldn't stop searching for Amber until she found her. And if she had to stay in New York for ever, she would. She'd get Amber back.

Amber looked at the cockroach and the cockroach looked back calmly. It wasn't as big as a rat, as some people claimed they were in this part of Utah, but she wouldn't have minded a rat. Furry was infinitely preferable to scuttling, crackly insects.

Breathing deeply, she backed out of the room, past Karl and the man with the dirty T-shirt, and stood in the hallway, feeling her skin crawl.

'I am not sleeping in there,' she said.

The man moved into the room, banged about a bit, and emerged smiling.

'He is gone, you can go in now.'

'Where is he gone?' demanded Amber, looking around the floor in the hallway with distaste. 'Into the corner he hides in with his eight million relatives until we're in bed asleep and he comes out to dance the Macarena?'

'No Macarena. He is gone,' the man repeated.

'It's all we can afford,' said Karl, sighing and hauling his stuff into the room. He'd stopped hauling Amber's stuff days ago.

It was hard to imagine that she'd once felt that the Arizona Fish Hotel was a bit on the grubby side, Amber thought wryly. The Arizona's dust balls and smeary windows were nothing to the squalor of this joint, a place where health inspectors clearly feared to tread.

Karl was right: it was all they could afford. The band were travelling across the country in a rent-a-wreck van, which was the cheapest way to get them all to LA, and staying in the most inexpensive motels around. This way, Karl had worked out, they'd have enough money to survive in LA for a few months in order to set up another production deal with somebody hot.

'Screw Stevie,' Syd muttered every day they climbed into the van and set off on the interstate. The suspension was not what it might have been and it took a while each day to get used to the bumpiness of the ride.

'Like a roller coaster,' said Lew the drummer happily.

'You must have a stomach of steel,' Syd replied in disgust.

When Demon had decided against producing the band's album, Stevie's big talk had dried up along with the meals out and the free-flowing booze.

Citing problems at home, Stevie had hopped on a plane back to Ireland, saying he'd work on a new deal for them and they'd talk when they were all back in Dublin.

'Crap,' said Syd succinctly. 'We'll never see him again.'

Stevie hadn't bothered with the last outstanding two days of their hotel bill, either, so when he left for JFK, reception were on the phone asking if the band were moving out or not, because with Stevie's credit card gone, they had to pay up or pack up.

Everyone had return flights home, a precondition of their entry visas, so following Stevie's yellow belly seemed like a sensible option.

'We can't go home with our tails between our legs,' Karl said furiously. 'I'm not anyway, I don't care what you guys want to do. This is my dream. I don't need guys like Stevie. I'll do it in spite of him.'

Amber waited for him to put his arms round her and say that the two of them would make it one way or the other, but he didn't. This was a band discussion, it seemed.

'I think I'll go for a walk,' Amber said abruptly. She grabbed the room card and was halfway to the lift when Karl caught up with her.

'Baby, don't go,' he said.

'You were talking as if I wasn't there,' she accused, tears stinging her eyes. She brushed them away with her sleeve. She would not cry.

'That was band stuff,' Karl said, pulling her into his arms. 'Course you're staying with me. Aren't you?'

And he'd looked worried, as if there really was any chance of her leaving him.

'I'm staying,' she said, leaning against him with relief. For one awful moment there, she'd thought she didn't mean anything to him. She'd given up so much too: home, Mum, Ella . . . so many things, really. If Karl went off without her, she'd have done it all for nothing.

'Let's go out on our own, to dinner and a club,' he murmured against her ear.

'Can we afford it?' asked Amber, ever practical.

'Anything for you, baby.'

That evening had been the last romantic moment they'd shared, Amber reflected now as she pulled her case into the now allegedly cockroach-free motel room in some truck-stop off the Utah interstate. They'd rented the van, left New York and were now driving hundreds of miles every day through the vastness of America. It should have been a dream trip, like the kooky road trips of teenage movies, but those movie-star kids had dollars to spare, while the band had none.

Their mobile phones didn't work here, even Syd's, which was a super-duper thing his girlfriend had bought him. He'd spent so long messing with it that it had locked itself and was now useless.

Karl was relentless in his quest to reach Los Angeles with the minimum number of nights spent in motels ('every night on the road is another few days in LA renting,' he insisted), so they couldn't dawdle in pretty towns off the interstates or take trips to places that caught their eye.

Karl was a man with a mission, and Amber and the band were following in his wake.

'I'm beat,' he said now, lying down on the bed cover. 'Three hundred and fifty miles today, it's got to be a record.'

Amber didn't reply. She was looking at the stains on the carpet and wondering what had made them. If only she had a vacuum cleaner and maybe some carpet stain remover, and cream cleaner . . . It could have been her mother talking.

*Look at the state of this place! Amber, get the antiseptic wipes out of my bag.*

They hadn't gone on many holidays: the money hadn't been there. But Mum had always packed cleaning materials so that if the place they stayed didn't come up to her standards, she'd clean it herself.

Amber felt a lump in her throat at the memory of the laughs they'd had in the places they'd stayed.

Turning to the bathroom, she went inside and shut the door. There was no tub, just a lived-in shower with a curtain beaded with other people's dirt. Amber sat down on the toilet seat and buried her face in her hands.

This was so not what she'd expected when she'd left home.

She'd thought she was running off to experience life and become a woman: instead, she was enduring life on the road with an obsessed boyfriend and staying in a series of dumps. She mightn't have minded if only Karl was obsessed with her but he wasn't.

He hadn't called her his muse in a very long time. We are not amused, she thought. And then she did cry.

# CHAPTER EIGHTEEN

The Monday after Faye had left the country, Christie came home from school to find a disturbing message on her answering machine.

'Hello, my name is Heidi Manton and I'm phoning on behalf of Carey Wolensky. He's trying to locate a Mrs Christie Devlin to invite her to the private viewing of his exhibition in Dublin in two weeks' time except he's not sure if she still lives at this address. If Mrs Devlin could phone me, I'd be most grateful. And if she's moved, any information on her whereabouts would be marvellous.'

The clipped tones of the woman recited a number in London and Christie allowed herself to take a deep breath. At least Carey wasn't in the country yet.

'From next week, you can contact myself or Mr Wolensky in Dublin at this number.'

The voice reeled off another number and Christie's relief evaporated.

He was coming here and he wanted to see her. It couldn't get any worse. What on earth was she going to do?

\* \* \*

While the maelstrom of Summer Street relationships whirled unnoticed around her, Una Maguire had taken it upon herself to set up the 'Save Our Pavilion' campaign.

'We can't let our lovely park be destroyed by those developers,' she said to Dennis and Maggie. 'Evil, that's what they are,' she added, as though the developers were in league with the devil and were ripping down the pavilion as part of some satanic bargain for making loads of money out of big ugly apartments.

'You don't want to overdo it,' said Dennis, attempting to be the voice of reason. 'Don't forget, darling, your leg is still broken and . . .'

'Oh fiddle faddle, my leg is fine,' said Una. 'Isn't it better to be doing something to help our community than sitting at home worrying about my old leg and thinking that I'll be ending up in a wheelchair before long?'

Maggie glanced over at her mother, but Una went on regardless.

'Somebody needs to stand up to those developers and I'm going to call a meeting of the residents of Summer Street and the streets all around. We don't want to use some hopeless new park three miles down the road when we have this lovely little jewel right here beside us. We will fight the council all the way!' and she waved her crutch menacingly in the air.

'Right, Mum,' said Maggie, alarmed her mother might take someone's eye out. It was easiest to humour her when she was in this mood. 'What do you want me to do?'

A printing firm would run off a hundred flyers for next to nothing if Maggie dropped by with details of the meeting. The only problem was that the firm's office wasn't on a direct bus route. The task would require the car.

'Your dad can drive,' Una said, then added, 'You won't be long, will you?'

She didn't like being left on her own these days, Maggie

263

had noticed, sure it was fear of falling and hurting herself again.

'Dad can stay with you. I'm sure I can remember how to drive,' Maggie said a little wearily. If she was going to become a stronger person, she had told herself, she would need to accept life's challenges, and trying to drive again would be the first. At least the fear of driving might take her mind off her own personal misery, the misery that kept her awake late at night, thinking about her and Grey.

'There's nothing to it, Bean,' said Dad, delighted.

'Of course there isn't,' she said cheerily. 'It's a long time since I've driven, that's all.'

'Any eejit can drive,' said her father. 'And you're so clever, it'll be nothing to you.'

With both parents smiling at her proudly, clearly believing that their only child was a cross between Stephen Hawking and Condoleezza Rice, Maggie had to smile back. They didn't have anything particularly to be proud of, but what was the point of telling them that? She'd managed to hide her misery pretty well. So well, in fact, that nobody at home appeared to see how sad she was underneath the smiling exterior.

The family car was a Volvo, like all the Maguire cars had been. Her father felt that Volvos could tackle the world head on and still win.

'Reliable,' her father insisted.

'You could hit a moose with one and there wouldn't even be a dent,' her mother would add. 'Extra hard side bars or something.'

Maggie sat in the driver's seat, looked at all the pedals, buttons and dials and hoped that the local moose population was safely off the road today.

The car started first thing and despite its general air of decrepitude because it was almost an antique, it moved forward smoothly when she let off the handbrake.

Indicator, check the road, off in first gear, smoothly into second. It was like riding a bike, Maggie thought triumphantly. She was driving. Nothing to it. Pity Grey couldn't see her now, the lying, cheating pig.

At a sedate twenty-five miles an hour, she made it to the printer's where they ran off her leaflets at high speed and she was back in the car within half an hour. Next, she stopped off at the supermarket and loaded up a trolley. The petrol tank was almost empty, she noticed as she pulled out of the supermarket car park on to the road.

Emboldened by her success at driving, she decided that a trip to the garage would round off her maiden voyage nicely.

A confident woman driver with a brave new life ahead of her would know how to pump her own petrol. Why had she never had a car before? The sense of freedom was heady.

She had to jiggle the pump nozzle a bit to fit it into the tank, and even then it leaked, but then the numbers clicked up on the pump counter in a most satisfying fashion, and when she reached twenty euros, Maggie pulled the pump out. She'd been thinking she'd make a gorgeous dinner for the three of them, nutritious, something out of a book perhaps, looking after her family and . . .

The little sticker on the petrol tank flap winked up at her. Diesel. Diesel.

With whiplash speed, she turned to the pump. Unleaded petrol. She'd just put unleaded petrol in a diesel car.

She stared at the car in shock. Trust her parents to have a diesel car and not tell her. No. Trust her not to notice. Shit.

She ran into the shop and stood at the back of the queue, thinking she might cry or maybe even laugh. She could feel her paper-thin happy face beginning to crack.

Anyone could do it, right? Someone could suck it out, couldn't they? Or something.

The man in front of her swivelled round and Maggie realised she'd spoken out loud.

'Anyone could put petrol in by mistake when it's a diesel,' she said, trying to put the whole 'they could suck it out' remark into context. 'It's my parents' car and I was doing them a favour and I didn't look at the tank. Thought it was petrol, not diesel. Could happen to a bishop.'

There, it was better to say it and surely he'd laugh. It had to happen all the time. There was probably a special queue for people who did it.

But the man gave her a glare that she instantly translated as All Women Are Idiots with a hint of We Should Never Have Given Them the Vote added in for good measure. 'Of all the thick things to do,' he grunted and turned his back on her.

'But the nozzle isn't supposed to be able to fit in,' pointed out the woman who'd just joined the queue behind her.

'Yeah, they're different, the diesel and the petrol ones,' someone else said unhelpfully.

'I thought I was doing it wrong, so I made it fit,' said Maggie forlornly, thinking of all the petrol she'd spilled on the ground. She hoped nobody lit a match out there or the whole place would go up.

Mr Stupid Woman Glare gave her another withering blast of it on his way past.

Maggie tried to ignore his contempt.

'You'll never believe what I've done,' she said to the impassive woman behind the counter, pleading with her eyes to be given a bit of female bonding.

The woman blinked slowly during the story, then jerked with her thumb.

'Out back. Ask for Ivan. Ivan Gregory. He owns the place. He's busy but he might help you.'

There was a queue waiting for the pump where the Volvo

was parked but Maggie ran past it to the back of the garage. Away from the shiny forecourt, she found a small workshop.

There were several cars in various states of disrepair suspended over pits or parked in small bays, and a radio tuned to a local station provided a backdrop to the noises of banging and welding.

The only person not working on a vehicle was a fresh-faced young man who was leaning against a desk with a mug in his hand.

'I'm looking for Ivan, the owner?' Maggie said.

'He's under there.'

She followed his gaze. A pair of overalled legs stuck out from under a large green Jeep, legs with big round-toed boots that a clown might wear. Were they hobnailed boots? she wondered irrelevantly.

'Hello,' she said, leaning down, 'are you Ivan? I was told you could help me. I've ...' God, she felt stupid. 'I've just put unleaded in my parents' car and it turns out, it runs on diesel. Wouldn't you know. I hoped there might be some gizmo to suck it out. Like a vacuum cleaner. Can you vacuum out all the unleaded?'

The legs seemed to shake a bit.

'Or drain it?' Maggie went on.

Yes, draining, that sounded like the business. They were always draining things in garages and doing stuff with stop-cocks, or was that cisterns? Whatever.

'I'm sure you're busy but I'd be really grateful if you could help me. My mother's sick and I've got all her shopping in the car and there's a big queue behind me ...' Maggie didn't say she thought she'd cry if anyone in the queue shouted at her for blocking the petrol pump. 'They're probably all going mental, saying they bet it's some stupid woman who's left her car there.'

One enormous oil-stained hand appeared from under the

Jeep, gripped the edge of the car and pulled. Maggie found herself staring down at a giant of a man who was looking up at her with undisguised mirth. He was filthy with dirt on his overalls, in his face, even in his hair, which was dark except for a few streaks of grey near his temples, and cut as close to his head as any marine's.

She was relieved to see that his face was nice, a bit square with a nose that looked as if he'd taken a few punches in the ring, and that his smile, because he was smiling broadly, was friendly.

He got to his feet lightly for such a huge man and stood towering over her. Good-looking, in an outdoorsy way, she thought absently, and probably Grey's age or thereabouts.

'You want to use the petrol-sucking vacuum?' he said evenly in a low gravelly voice. He wiped sweat off his brow with the back of his hand.

'If that's all right?' said Maggie. With any luck, she'd be home in no time and nobody would be any the wiser.

'Jack,' he called to the young guy. 'Where's the petrol-sucking machine?'

Jack had to bend over with a sudden spasm.

'You're telling me you don't know where it is?' inquired Ivan. 'What do I pay you guys for? Mick?'

A face appeared from under the bonnet of a Citroën. 'Yeah?'

'The petrol-sucking machine. You got it?'

Mick's gaze flickered over Maggie and knowledge began to dawn.

'Right,' she said, in a shaky voice. 'The joke's on me. There is no petrol-sucking machine.'

'Whaddya think this is? A milking parlour?' asked Mick, before succumbing to the same spasms as Jack and doubling up with laughter.

Ivan, the giant, looked at her with mischief in his face.

268

He had the deepest brown eyes she'd ever seen, and they positively glittered with humour. His mouth quivered at the edges, as he tried to stop himself grinning and failed.

It had been a horrible few days, in which her world had turned upside down, and Maggie felt that if one more person made her feel she was stupid, she was going to hit them, so help her. Her composure shattered.

'It's not funny!' she shrieked, reaching out and thumping the bonnet of the Jeep he'd been working on.

This was it, the last straw. All the pent-up fury at seeing Grey in bed with someone else, at running home to find her mother injured and herself appointed in charge, at discovering that Grey had a bloody harem and it had been happening under her nose, it all came flooding out. Thump, thump went her curled-up fist on the bonnet.

'I just wanted some help and nobody appreciates it. You jackasses think it's the biggest laugh ever to snigger at someone in trouble.' Thump, thump.

Ivan clamped her wrists in his steely hands and gently lowered them to her side.

'You'll hurt yourself and it was only a joke,' he said tenderly. 'I'm sorry, I thought you sounded so funny.'

'You thought you'd take the mickey out of me, well, I've had that done enough lately, thank you very much,' Maggie said, dry sobbing. She ran out of the workshop to the car, sat in the driver's seat and started it up. The engine turned over instantly, allowed her to drive a few yards then suddenly belched loudly and died like an elephant in great pain.

'Horrible, horrible car!' she said, crying on the steering wheel. She banged it hard, succeeding only in making her aware of how much she'd hurt her hand from bashing the Jeep in the garage. 'Ow!'

The driver's door was opened and Ivan squatted down beside her seat, apology written all over his face.

'It's better not to drive it,' he said. As kindly as if he was taking care of a tiny baby, he helped her out of the car and took the keys. 'I'll drive you and your shopping home, and I'll look after the car.'

'You will do no such thing, you jumped-up pump jockey,' she hissed. 'I'll bring my own bloody shopping home, thank you very much.'

Ivan looked into the back of the car which was piled with grocery bags.

'You sure?'

'I'm sure.'

She pulled every single bag out and dragged them to the kerb. 'I'll be back for the car tomorrow,' she said. 'Just bloody fix it, will you?'

Ivan nodded and went back into his workshop, whereupon Maggie got out her phone and dialled a taxi. So much for self-confidence.

Una was thrilled with the leaflet, which advertised a meeting at the park at eight o'clock in the evening in two days' time. And to Maggie's relief neither of her parents laughed or were angry when she explained, rather bashfully, what had happened to the car. 'I can't face going there to fetch it, I'm so embarrassed,' she said, 'but I suppose I must. Except I've got to work.'

'Don't worry, darling,' said her father, giving her a hug. 'The garage isn't far from the doctor's surgery and I must fetch a new prescription for your mother. It won't take me long to walk up there and I'll kill the two birds with the one stone.'

'Are you sure?' said Maggie, remembering that she was supposed to be strong and confident now, facing up to her mistakes. Except she just couldn't face those men in the garage again, especially the big one, Ivan. 'I could go after work,' she said.

'It'll do your dad good to get out,' said Una sternly, and so the burden was lifted.

In return, Maggie wasn't surprised to find that she was expected to be postie for the leaflets. She spent several hours late the following afternoon braving yappy dogs and pushing the leaflets through doors of the neighbouring streets and asking local shops to site them in their windows. One of the last places Maggie visited was the Summer Street Café, where Henry and Jane were thrilled to hear about Una's call to arms.

'That's fabulous, and so professional,' said Jane, reading the leaflet Maggie showed her and passing it to Xu, the shy Chinese waitress.

Xu smiled but said nothing. In all the time Maggie had spent in the café recently, she'd never heard Xu speak a word. But she smiled a lot, like she was doing now.

'Well done to your mother,' said Henry. 'She's a great woman. I can see where you got it from.'

'Oh,' said Maggie, pleased, and she flushed.

'It's very good of you to come home and look after her,' Henry went on. 'I know it has been difficult for you, but she's a good woman. Now, since you're doing so much for the community, would you like a latte on the house, or is it cappuccino you drink?'

'Plain old white coffee for me,' said Maggie, 'and thank you, that would be nice. It's weary work delivering all these.'

'That looks lovely,' said Maggie politely, when Xu brought her the coffee.

Xu bobbed her head in reply. She must be lonely, Maggie thought suddenly. The girl was young, probably only in her mid-twenties, half a world away from home. Maggie wondered whether she had any friends. Jane and Henry were sweet people but probably not sparkling company for a young girl.

\*　　\*　　\*

271

Word of the onslaught against the council quickly spread and the following night, at eight o'clock, the park was jammed with people from Summer Street and the surrounding streets all wanting to know what they could do to save it.

Maggie had been at work all day and so wasn't entirely sure what her mother's plan was. She was a bit disappointed to find out that all Una had thought of was a petition, signed by everybody and their granny, saying the evil developers shouldn't get their way and the council owed it to the people of Summer Street and the whole area to save their park. 'We need our voices to be heard!' said Una Maguire, standing at the front of the crowd, brandishing a crutch.

Maggie thought her mother had turned out to be surprisingly good at this rabble-rousing. Who'd have thought it?

'A petition is going to be no good,' a man down the back shouted dismissively, and privately Maggie had to agree with him. 'They don't take notice of petitions. We'll have to do something else, something more forceful.'

'Like what?' demanded Una. 'Come on, suggestions, please. If you're not part of the solution, you're part of the problem.'

This started a row with people shouting at the man down the back for trying to rain on their parade, while his supporters shouted that a petition was going to be no good whatsoever. What was needed was legal action or political involvement.

It was descending into chaos and even Una seemed to have run out of energy.

The man at the back got fed up and shouted, 'Who else can help? Anyone with friends on the council?'

Maggie looked around to see if there was somebody there who was up to leading the charge. Ideally somebody who knew how councils and businesses worked, she thought, and who could go through the proper channels. But she realised there were no volunteers. Everyone wanted the park saved, but, apart from Una, there wasn't anyone ready to stand up and do it.

It was the curse of the modern age, her mother often said, when it came to getting people to help out with charities and meals on wheels: everybody was too busy with their own lives to do much for anyone else.

'Well,' Maggie said, reluctantly, feeling she ought to help her mother out. 'I do work in the library and I suppose I would be able to research how we could go about this.'

She'd hardly got the words out of her mouth before people were saying, *Yes, good woman, fair play to you, brilliant idea*. Then the man who had heckled Una smiled broadly at the tall, slender redhead and called out, 'Chairwoman, let's have her for chairwoman.' And, without realising it, Maggie Maguire – who'd never so much as captained a friendly netball game in school – was elected chairwoman of the rapidly formed Save Our Pavilion committee.

'I'm so proud of you,' said her mother as they headed home, after several other people had been elected on to the committee, buoyed up by Maggie's supreme sacrifice and the hope that she'd do all the work. 'I knew you'd know what to do. I thought, if I started you off on the right path, you'd follow through. Didn't I say that, Dennis, didn't I?'

'Yes,' said Maggie's father happily. 'Your mother always says you're well able to run things. You can do anything, our Maggie can do anything.'

'And,' her mother went on, 'we should have a big party, in the park, when we get it all settled.'

'Hold on a minute,' said Maggie, 'nothing's settled yet. We might not win. Mum, be realistic.' Maggie was still shocked at how quickly it had all happened – shocked and horrified. *She* was chairwoman of the committee. Chair-women were tough, no-nonsense women like Shona, not wimpy people who had cheating ex-boyfriends and put petrol in diesel vehicles. If only there was a way out of it, but she knew there wasn't. What if she made a complete mess of the whole project?

'Ah now,' said her mother, confidence written all over her face. 'You'll have worked it out, I know well you will. There's nothing you can't do.'

'She's mad. Breaking her leg has affected her brain,' Maggie said on the phone to Elisabeth. She'd needed to get out of the house and had taken her mobile and walked slowly along Summer Street, thinking that Elisabeth might understand.

'Your mother was always mad,' said Elisabeth absently. Her office sounded noisy and busy.

'Not normal mad: thinking-I-can-do-everything mad. It's different,' Maggie went on.

'She always thought you could do everything,' Elisabeth said, surprised. 'It used to drive me nuts. Your mother never stopped talking about how clever you were and how marvellous your report cards were, which made my mother obsessed with my report cards being as good. The pressure.'

'Really?' Maggie couldn't quite remember that. All she could recall from school was the misery and how she'd never been able to tell anyone, apart from Elisabeth. 'If only I could do everything,' she added gloomily.

'Maggie, listen to me.' Elisabeth sounded stern, the way she spoke to teenage models on the phone, Maggie guessed. 'I'm up to my tonsils with work here and I'm irritable, which means I'm going to say something I've wanted to say for a long time, something I'll probably regret saying because you'll be hurt but I've got to do it: stop feeling sorry for yourself about what happened at school and get on with your life.'

Maggie gasped.

'I know you're going to hate me for saying this, but I've got to. You *are* clever and funny, you *can* do anything, and you should stop thinking otherwise. Now you've dumped that loser boyfriend of yours for good, go out and get a life. Auntie Una's right: you can do anything. You're the only person who doesn't believe it. Gotta go, bye.'

It took Maggie a full thirty seconds to take the phone away from her ear. Elisabeth had never spoken to her like that in her life. She was shocked. Elisabeth was the only one who'd known what had gone on in school, her only ally and now she had turned against her.

Maggie walked along in stunned silence, oblivious to where she was going. But finally something odd happened. In the midst of the shock and the self-pity, she began to feel a glimmer of self-worth. Everyone seemed to think she was capable of so much. They couldn't all be lying, could they?

Later that night, the gloom settled once more. It was sinking in that she'd somehow been elected as chairwoman of a committee with a tough job to do.

'I don't even know how to run a committee,' she moaned to Shona on the phone. 'I was never even on the debating team in college!'

'Oh, babes,' said Shona easily, 'it'll be no bother to you. You've seen plenty of university committees at work, you know how it goes. People sit around in rooms, have arguments, discuss things, discuss them even more, break for tea and biscuits and finally agree to disagree. At the end, they make arrangements to meet up at the same time next week where they'll go over all the same stuff again. Simple.'

'I know,' groaned Maggie. 'That's what I don't want. I want this committee to actually save the park, not talk about it until the cows come home – or until the developers whip a JCB in one night and pull the pavilion down, making the whole thing a fait accompli.'

'Right,' said Shona, thoughtfully. 'You mean this is a committee where you actually want to achieve something.

275

Mmm. University life doesn't prepare you for that. Paul,' she shouted, 'Maggie's chairwoman of a committee and they actually want to get something done. What should she do?'

Paul was one of the top research and development men in a computer software firm with dozens of people under him.

Maggie heard a rustling noise like the sound of a paper being folded. It was late and she could imagine Paul sitting on the cosy couch in his and Shona's apartment, the newspapers around him, with his feet up on the coffee table and the remote control on his lap.

'Hello, Maggie,' he said, taking over the phone. 'My advice is to write out what the aim of the committee is on a big sheet of paper, take it to your first meeting and stick it up on the wall. Explain that nobody is on the committee to make themselves popular or to give themselves something to brag about. They're there simply to achieve the aim you've written on the paper. What's the committee for, exactly?'

'We want to stop the council selling half of our park to a developer who's going to build apartments there.'

'Well, I guess you need to lodge a formal planning objection with the council, then talk to local politicians . . .'

'Talk to the newspapers,' said Shona in the background.

'Yes,' said Maggie excitedly, writing this down. She had an inspiration. 'What about finding out more about the park? They want to pull down this beautiful old pavilion. It's Victorian at least and it could be a meaningful historical site.'

'Exactly,' said Paul with satisfaction. 'Tie them up with surveys and formal objections and politicians complaining so that the whole thing's not worth their while. Or so that the bad press they'll get for it will scare the developers away. The key to committees, Maggie,' he said, 'is like amateur dramatics. Never let them see you're afraid.'

\*       \*       \*

The following night at eight, Summer Street Café was closed to everyone except the Save Our Pavilion committee. There were ten of them sitting around two tables pushed together, with Maggie seated at one end.

She'd gone out and purchased a businesslike navy jacket which she wore over her best dark denim jeans and a turquoise camisole. She'd tied her hair up into a chic knot, had a writing pad and pens in front of her, and was keeping all her anxiety firmly locked on the inside. The other committee members were all older than her and probably had miles more experience than she did, but she was still chairwoman and she was going to make this a success.

'The most important thing tonight,' she said, 'is our aims. None of us are here so we can boast that we're on a committee, or to have something to talk about or because we like arguments.'

One man opened and closed his mouth like a goldfish at this.

Paul had said there was always one person who joined up because they liked both the sound of their own voice and a good fight.

Maggie felt a wave of confidence hit her. Forewarned was forearmed.

She was ready for Mr Goldfish Face. 'We're here to save something very important to Summer Street. So this is not going to be one of those committees where everyone argues or grandstands or tries to get the better of anyone else. We're here to save the pavilion, that's it.'

The nine people facing her stared back, nodding, and Maggie thought how unbelievable it was that she was able to confront them and talk in such calm, measured tones, when inside, she really was quivering.

Luckily, nobody could see the inside.

'I've made up a list of what I think we should do and I'll

277

go through it. Then everyone else can come in with their suggestions until we've come up with a blueprint for what we're going to achieve over the next few days, right? I'm new to this and would appreciate ideas but we've got to work as a team, or we're going to go nowhere fast.'

The next hour and a half passed in a flash, but when Maggie wound up the meeting everyone had been allocated a useful task to perform before they reconvened. Maggie herself was to try to interest several politicians in their cause.

When everyone was gone, Maggie and Xu, who'd stayed behind to help and make coffee, tidied up.

'I hope you weren't bored out of your mind listening to that,' Maggie said to Xu.

Now that they were alone, she hoped Xu might talk to her.

'It was interesting,' Xu said. She had a low sweet voice and perfect English. 'We do not do this in my country. If the authorities want to pull down a building, they pull it down. It's very different.'

Maggie stopped collecting cups and sat down. 'Tell me,' she said. 'Tell me how you came here and what you'd like to do and what your country's like. I'd love to hear.'

She'd never seen Xu give anything other than a shy smile that was more defence mechanism than emotion, but now Xu really beamed at her.

'I never asked before because I was afraid I'd insult you or something,' Maggie admitted. 'You're very brave to come here on your own.'

'Brave is the only way in China,' Xu shrugged. 'My mother is much braver than me. This is nothing compared to what she suffered during the Cultural Revolution. I only had to get on an aeroplane and learn another language so I could go to college here. I can make choices in my life – she could make none.'

'Will your mother come here too?' asked Maggie, not wanting to upset Xu now she'd got her talking.

'Maybe. She loves China, it's her home. I'd like her to visit. But she doesn't speak English.'

'And will you go back?' asked Maggie.

'I don't know. I love China but I feel at home here. We are very alike, the Chinese and the Irish. We love our families.'

'Your English is fantastic. When did you start learning?'

'Nine months ago,' Xu said casually.

'Nine months ago! You're so fluent. I can't imagine being that good in such a short length of time.'

Xu laughed so loudly that her curtain of thick dark hair shimmered. 'Chinese people know how to work.' She grinned.

They sat talking for an hour, whereupon Xu said she ought to go home and Maggie said the same, because she knew her mother would be sitting up waiting for her to hear how the meeting went.

'Perhaps you'll come out with me sometimes?' Maggie asked Xu. 'To see a film or something?'

'I would like that very much indeed,' Xu replied.

On the way down Summer Street, Maggie reflected that if a girl from a small town in China could travel thousands of miles to a strange land where she knew nobody to start a new life, then she wasn't going to spend the rest of her life being afraid of what happened to her when she was a school-girl.


'Well, how did it go?' demanded Una, when Maggie got home. Her mother had been mad to go to the meeting, but since she wasn't on the committee, she couldn't.

'Marvellously,' said Maggie, still astonished at how she'd stood up in front of a room of strangers and handled it well. 'Everyone had loads of ideas and we've all got various jobs and I think we have a really good chance.'

'I'd like to be involved though,' said Una.

'Of course you're involved,' Maggie placated her. 'It was your idea in the first place, don't forget that. But you do need to rest.'

'Ah, rest, schmest,' muttered Una. 'I'm sick of resting. I want to do something.'

'Well, I need to make appointments to see three local politicians and you could come with me to see them,' Maggie said, thinking that she'd be braver with company.

'Marvellous,' Una said, satisfied. 'I better get my best suit out. Don't want to go stalking the corridors of power looking like some mad old dear in a bobbly cardigan, do I?'

# CHAPTER NINETEEN

The following morning, Christie phoned Maggie to ask her round for coffee.

'You can fill me in on the meeting,' Christie said. 'I couldn't make it, although the Summer Street grapevine has already broadcast the fact that you're in charge.'

Maggie laughed. 'The lunatics have taken over the asylum,' she said. 'But yes, I'm in charge. I'd love a coffee.'

When she arrived, Christie hugged her and rushed back into the kitchen to take scones out of the oven.

Maggie took the chance to stop and admire the paintings in Christie's hall, marvelling at the intricate watercolour strokes that brought delicate plants to life.

One wall was covered with lily paintings, interspersed with tiny Klimt prints in antique gold frames and black-and-white family photographs. On the other were displayed exquisite paintings of herbs, from the lacy froth of sweet cicely to the fire-red flowers of bergamot. There were herbs Maggie had never heard of, like comfrey, lovage and feverfew, alongside the soft purple of French lavender and sleek, slender chives, so well drawn she could almost smell their tangy scent.

'These are beautiful,' Maggie called into the kitchen where Christie was brewing coffee. 'You're so talented.'

'I love herbs and foliage,' Christie said. 'So many artists only want to paint flowers, but plants and the history behind them are fascinating. They have incredible medicinal uses and we've lost that, sadly. I try to put herbs from my own garden into my cooking. And if you haven't tasted proper fennel and lemon balm tea, you haven't lived.'

A lovely sense of warmth and comfort emanated from the Devlins' house. It was partly due to the scent of Christie's white tea roses with their tightly furled buds, and a burning candle that filled the downstairs with a citrus scent. But there was something more, more than the sum of its parts. It was a house of peace and security. Maggie felt as if nothing truly bad could ever happen as long as there were people like Christie in the world to make sense of everything and to offer her home as a refuge.

Finally, with the dogs scampering ahead, she wandered into the kitchen. Christie had laid coffee cups and the scones on a tray.

'You carry this into the garden,' Christie said, 'and I'll be out in a moment with the coffee.'

Christie had been thinking so much about Maggie and Faye lately that it was no surprise to wake up that morning with Maggie again in her mind. Only today, as Maggie stood there, holding out her arms for the tray, Christie had a moment of seeing exactly what had hurt the younger woman so much.

Sweet, tall, kind Maggie, who should have had lots of confidence, but didn't. Lovely Maggie, who'd been bullied when she was at school.

Lying in bed, listening to the birdsong and the rising and falling of James's breath the past came flooding back. Hers and Maggie's. It was easier to think about other people's problems than focus on her own. She'd tried to put Carey Wolensky out of her mind, but hadn't managed it. He loomed large in her fears.

So she made herself remember Maggie starting at St Ursula's almost twenty years before: shy and lanky, falling over her own feet all of the time. She was clever and good fun, so it was hard to work out why bullies had picked on her. Sister Aquinas, who had been headmistress at the time, had talked in the staff room one day about bullying in general and the fact that young Maggie Maguire appeared to have been targeted by a particular coterie of little madams in her year, led by a really nasty piece of work called Sandra Brody.

'We'll just keep an eye on it for the moment,' said Sister Aquinas, who was a great believer in not rushing into things. Girls needed more backbone, she felt. Sister Aquinas had spent twenty years in the field in Africa and was of the opinion that Irish girls could do with a little hardship because, compared to the children in the townships, they hadn't a clue about life.

Christie hadn't thought too much about it because Maggie hadn't been in one of her art classes, but she'd seen her sometimes at lunch. Maggie was so often on her own, reading, when everyone else was out playing tag or netball, or sitting in little groups discussing boys and the unfairness of life.

When Maggie went into the fifth year, the leader of the gang of bullies, Sandra Brody, left, although Christie couldn't recall why, and her gang fell apart without their natural leader.

But it seemed obvious now that the damage had already been done where Maggie Maguire was concerned. There were lots of naturally quiet, shy people in the world, but Christie now felt that Maggie hadn't been one of them when she'd arrived. It was as though she had found that keeping her mouth shut and blending into the background was the easiest way of survival.

Having taken the jug into the garden, Christie poured coffee into the cups and proffered scones.

'This is lovely here, a little oasis,' sighed Maggie, sitting back and looking around her. She wondered what Christie wanted to talk to her about. Perhaps she was going to help with the Save Our Pavilion campaign, which would be wonderful. Christie would be great at getting people to return her phone calls.

So it came as a total shock when Christie asked: 'Were you bullied at St Ursula's?'

Maggie's head shot up and the colour drained away from her face.

'What? How ... ?'

'I didn't know at the time,' Christie said apologetically. 'You weren't in any of my classes and I hardly knew more than your name then, but it suddenly made sense to me. It's your secret, isn't it? The thing that holds you back.'

Maggie could only nod silently.

'I'm so sorry. I was there and if I'd really been aware ...' Christie said. 'Your mum doesn't know, does she?'

This time, Maggie shook her head, biting her lip to make sure she didn't cry. This was so unexpected, like the ground being pulled away from her feet.

'I couldn't talk about it because –'

'– Because you thought she should know without you having to say it?'

'Yes, I suppose so.'

Tilly leaped up on to Maggie's lap, circling slowly on delicate paws, before lying against her. Maggie clung to this soft comfort, stroking the pansy-soft fur, grateful for a creature to hold. And she felt her shock subside slowly.

Christie leaned across the table and touched Maggie's hand gently, a touch that helped even more, filling her with peace.

'It's all right to talk about it,' Christie said. 'The people

284

we love often don't see our pain, and that's one of the hardest things in the world to cope with. We think they should see, they should *know*. If they don't, we feel as if they've failed us somehow and we have to deal with it all on our own.'

Maggie nodded. Mum hadn't seen what was going on and that had made Maggie lonelier than ever. Home hadn't been her refuge: it became a place where nobody understood her and what she was going through. Her parents' lovable idiosyncrasies had become irritating, their cheerful innocence annoying. If only they'd been more observant, they'd have *understood*.

'It's not their fault,' Christie said. 'It was St Ursula's fault. Bullying shouldn't have been tolerated. And it was Sandra's fault.' She noticed how Maggie winced at the mention of her tormentor's name. 'You were not to blame.'

'I thought I was,' blurted out Maggie. 'Something about me that was weak or odd.'

'Nothing I could see, though we all have weaknesses. But that's no excuse for their behaviour. You were just someone to pick on, nothing more.' Christie paused. 'Have you ever seen Sandra since?'

'No, although . . . I've been thinking about it a lot,' Maggie admitted. 'Since I met Faye and you, and Faye has had to face her own demons, I keep thinking I should face her. Stupid, I know. I haven't seen her for years.'

'Not stupid at all. You last saw her as a child. As an adult, you could put it all behind you, lay the secrets to rest.'

'Yeah, but who knows where she is.' Maggie couldn't even bring herself to say Sandra's name. 'What are the odds on her walking back into my life now?'

'You'd be surprised,' said Christie thoughtfully. 'You're thinking about her and talking about her. You're ready to meet her again. That's happened for a reason. Life is never random: I always find that, don't you?'

Maggie was on a late shift at work which meant she started at noon. As she walked towards the library, she went over what Christie had said to her.

Christie seemed to think that seeing Sandra Brody would allow the past to settle into the past, but it wasn't that easy, was it?

And Maggie had quite enough on her plate right now, anyway, what with being chairwoman of the campaign, getting over Grey and trying to get her life back on track.

She could face most things, but not Sandra Brody.

# CHAPTER TWENTY

That afternoon, Christie went into St Ursula's and found that overnight, almost the entire teaching population had plunged headfirst into exam anxiety. June was fast approaching and on the third of the month, the state exams would begin, the culmination of years of hard work distilled into a dozen two-and-a-half-hour exams spread out over three tortured weeks.

'It's like an incessant headache pounding away,' said Mr Sweetman, thinking of the third years' still-limited interest in *As You Like It* and how a small section of the English sixth-year class had still only half read *Pride and Prejudice* and were using one of the movie versions as their guide instead of the actual novel.

'*C'est vrai,*' sighed Mademoiselle Lennox, who was reciting Guy de Maupassant in her sleep because of how many times she'd read out passages to her beloved girls in 6 and 6A.

'We must be positive, for the girls' sake,' boomed Ms Ni Rathallaigh, the sports teacher, who didn't care much because the fifth-year netball team had won the league.

Everyone in the staff room glared at her.

Everyone except Christie, who was finding it hard to concentrate on worrying about the exams because of how much she was worrying over Carey Wolensky and his trying to track her down. She hadn't returned the strange phone call asking her to get in touch, and during the day, she left the answering machine off in case James came home early and heard another message on it. Nobody, she hoped, would phone in the evenings, would they?

In the meantime, mentions of Carey were everywhere. The arts section in one of the Saturday papers had carried a review of his work, accompanied by photographs of three of his paintings. Thank heavens there wasn't a picture of him, Christie thought with relief. She couldn't have coped with seeing his brooding eyes gazing out at her from a photograph.

Instead she had to look at one of his trademark wildly furious landscapes, and two of his rare – and infinitely more valuable – paintings of a dark-haired woman. In one, she was lying between the paws of a predatory stone tiger in a crumbling Greek temple, and in the other, she stood in the centre of a Turkish bath, where other women chattered and bathed, and she was alone, staring out, hair partly covering a face that was never completely shown in any painting.

'It is his uncanny ability to bring new meaning to traditional themes that makes Wolensky a master,' raved the article. 'His moody landscapes are imbued with energy, but it's his Dark Lady paintings that elevate him to another level. They are his masterpieces, but the identity of the lovely Dark Lady remains one of modern art's most fascinating secrets.'

Those words made Christie break out in a sweat. She'd spent long enough studying symbolism in art to understand that the dark-haired woman in Wolensky's paintings was always slightly beyond his reach, and by obscuring her face, he wanted her to be beyond everyone's reach. If he couldn't have her, nobody else could, either.

Her naked body was womanly, complete with the not-so-pert breasts and stretchmarks of childbirth. He'd painted his first Dark Lady some twenty-five years before and she was no figment of the imagination, the art critics reckoned.

Wolensky had lived in Ireland round about then, the article went on, and this was his first trip back with this triumphant exhibition. Christie thought of Carey Wolensky back in her city, living, breathing only miles away in some classy city centre hotel, and felt sick.

If only she could really see the future and know what was happening, then she could deal with it all. Tell James, if that's what it took. Face his pain. Whatever was required.

But the waiting and not knowing was killing her.

Ana hadn't mentioned Carey again, which was something, but still Christie couldn't think of anything else. How she'd betrayed James and Ana in one fell swoop.

Suddenly fed up with the stuffy staff room and everyone's moaning, she left early for her next class. At least she'd have a few moments of peace before the lesson started.

In the blue-painted corridor that led to the art room, a pile of papers lay scattered on the floor. Bending, she slowly gathered them up and as she did so a white feather fluttered out from underneath, lifting in the gentle draught, drifting away.

White feathers were a sign of angels passing by, her mother used to say.

Christie looked down at the papers. They were exam notes, several scrawled sheets of foolscap with a small bit of paper sandwiched in the middle. She pulled this out. It was a flyer for a market where stalls promised second-hand books, antiques at prices nobody would believe, plants, home-knitted sweaters, a coffee shop and there, at the bottom, almost as an afterthought, were the words, fortune-telling.

Things happened for a reason – wasn't that what she'd told Maggie only the other day? This flyer and the white

289

feather had come to her for a reason. She folded the flyer up and put it in her pocket. She'd think about it later.

That evening, she and James were supposed to go to a party at the house of some neighbours. The Hendersons had lived on Summer Street for fifteen years and they had been good friends with James and Christie for most of that time. Tommy Henderson, the husband, was a motorbike aficionado and while James had never had the funds for a bike, he loved standing in Tommy's garage watching him take apart the latest model, discussing the merits of the new BMW versus the classic Norton.

While James got on with Tommy, Christie found that she got on pretty well with Laurie Henderson. Tom and Laurie had three sons around Shane and Ethan's ages, and Laurie had worked outside the home for most of her life too, so she and Christie had reached the same stages in their lives together. Therefore, when Tommy Henderson hit sixty and a big party was to be held in the Hendersons' back garden, it was natural that the Devlins should be the first on the list.

'I'm not really in the mood to go,' said Christie as they pottered about their bedroom getting ready.

'You'll change your mind when you get there,' said James soothingly. 'It'll be fun. There'll be loads of people you'll know.'

'That's the problem,' said Christie, with irritation. 'I'm not in the mood to talk to the same old people.'

James stopped putting in his cuff links and began to massage her neck tenderly. For once, it didn't instantly relax her. 'You are tense, Christie,' he said. 'Is everything OK, darling? Do you have a headache?'

'No,' said Christie, slightly crossly. 'I don't, I'm just tired, that's all.'

Being tired was the ultimate excuse for everything, wasn't it? Any bad behaviour could be excused with 'I'm sorry, I was just tired.' *I'm sorry, your honour, I didn't mean to steal a million pounds, I was just tired. I'm sorry, darling, I didn't mean to cheat on you with another man, I was just tired.*

She turned to face James. 'I am sorry for moaning. I'll be fine.'

'Good,' said James, pleased. 'It'll be fun. You got flowers, didn't you?'

'Yes,' said Christie.

'I'll find a bottle of wine and we're all set.'

James finished getting ready, a job that took perhaps seven or eight minutes, and he was gone, leaving Christie sitting at her dressing table, staring at herself in the mirror, wondering if guilt was written all across her face.

They got there a bit late and the fun had obviously started.

'So you decided to grace us with your presence?' beamed Tommy Henderson, at the front door.

He threw an arm around James and Christie and pulled them together in a giant bear hug.

'So glad you could come,' he said.

'We only came for the free drink and the free food,' joked James.

'Free drink? You mean you didn't bring your own?' demanded Tommy. 'You lousers, I never had you down as mean, James Devlin.'

And the two men were off, joking, teasing, laughing, James asking what fabulous motorbike Tommy had got for his birthday from the family and Tommy jovially explaining that they hadn't got him a bike at all, but a girlfriend in a flat. 'That's what every man needs when he hits sixty,' he said. 'The wife thinks it's a brilliant idea too. No more messing about giving me my conjugals!'

The two men roared with laughter and Christie tried to join in, half-heartedly. She was so fond of Tommy and normally loved his palace jester persona, but not tonight.

The party was set up in the garden and it seemed as if half of Summer Street were there, talking, chattering animatedly, laughing, drinking, spearing bits of chicken into dip, discussing house prices, what their children were up to, what their children weren't up to and, of course, what the developers planned to do to the Summer Street park.

'I was at the meeting you know,' said one woman, 'and Una Maguire suggested a petition, but really a petition isn't the way to go. No council are going to be moved by a load of names on a list. Her daughter, Maggie, is taking it over, she's chairwoman. Clever girl, I always say, quiet though. I think there was some problem with her and the boyfriend, you know.'

Christie moved on, irritated by this gossipy attitude to Maggie. She must be growing old, she thought. So many things irritated her now. Some stranger, who barely knew Maggie, talking about her life and her pain, as if it didn't matter a bit. There was probably lots of gossip about Faye and Amber too. How the ultra-private and conservative Faye Reid hadn't a clue what was really going on in her house and what a wild one that Amber had turned out to be, for all her nice manners and the way her mother had tried to bring her up.

Christie moved over to where Laurie was holding court, wondering if in a few weeks the neighbours would be able to talk about her.

*Did you hear about Christie Devlin, the most incredible news ever. Split up with that lovely husband of hers, I always said he was too good for her. She was a bit wild and arty really, despite her airs and graces and reputation for wisdom. Hem, if she was that wise she might have seen this one coming. Imagine, some story about a Polish artist who painted her in the nude. He's filthy rich apparently. Disgraceful. Goes to show you don't know people, do you? You can live beside them for thirty years and you haven't a clue what's going on in their lives.*

'Christie, how lovely to see you.' Laurie moved away from the group of people she was talking to, reached out, and gave Christie a genuine, welcoming hug. There was nothing two-faced about Laurie. She wouldn't gossip about Christie, no matter what happened.

'Sorry we're late,' said Christie. 'I'm a bit tired and I couldn't get ready, to be truthful.'

'That's fine,' soothed Laurie. One of the many nice things about Laurie was that she wasn't the sort of person with whom you had to pretend. 'Come and let me introduce you to my sister-in-law, Beth. You met before I think? She's a teacher too, and a gardener, you'll have a lot to talk about.'

Christie smiled gratefully at Laurie.

Mercifully, Laurie's sister-in-law wasn't an art teacher, so there was no conversation about new, exciting exhibitions by enigmatic Polish artists who painted nude, dark-haired women over the past twenty-five years. She was an English teacher and they enjoyed a highly pleasurable hour talking about the difficulties of teaching, how hard the exams were on the students and how schools had changed so much over the past few decades.

'Oh, look,' said Beth.

Laurie had wheeled in a hostess trolley with an enormous cake on top. For pure fun, she hadn't gone for the one big candle saying happy sixtieth: she'd gone the whole hog with sixty single candles blazing with heat and possibly visible from space.

'There's a lot of candles there. Is it your ninetieth, did you say, Tommy?' said one wag.

'Call an ambulance, please,' said another. 'He'll need it by the time he's blown all them out.'

'Come on everybody,' insisted a third voice. 'We'll have

293

to help him. Poor Tommy doesn't have the energy for anything physical any more, apart from the mistress in the apartment that they're setting him up with.'

'Tommy!' came Laurie's voice furiously. 'That was a family joke, you didn't have to tell everyone! What will people think?'

'Ah, Laurie,' grinned Tommy happily, putting his arm around his wife and standing as close to his cake as the furnace of candles allowed. 'People know I adore you. You keep me busy enough, how would I have time for a mistress, tell me?'

Everyone laughed. From the other side of the garden, James smiled over at Christie. He motioned that she should come over and stand with him. But Christie shook her head, as if to imply that it was all too squashed to get there. She blew him a kiss, feeling like an absolute traitor. For the truth was that she didn't want to stand beside her darling husband and shriek happy birthday to one half of a happily married couple. Proximity to such a loyal marriage made her feel even more disloyal than ever. When Tommy closed his eyes to blow out his candles and wish, Christie Devlin closed her eyes too and wished with all her heart that she had never met Carey Wolensky. She knew that everyone did silly things in their youth, in their middle and old age too. But they moved on, made their peace and got on with life. Except, this was one thing she had never made her peace with and it had hung over her for years: Carey Wolensky and how he'd changed her life. It was the one big secret in her life and she was terrified, petrified, it was going to come out now and ruin everything.

A few days later Christie made a trip to the market advertised in the flyer she'd found on the floor of the corridor. The market itself was based in a big covered-in former flower market which had been taken over by stallholders who sold everything from dodgy antiques to velvet scarves, old leather-bound books and health food.

Christie walked through the market with a shopping bag slung over her shoulder. It was a perfectly reasonable place for her to be, she thought. She could buy some vitamins and perhaps some nice organic vegetables. Maybe think ahead and pick out some things for Christmas.

The reason she was trying to convince herself that this was a normal shopping jaunt was in case she met anyone she knew. In fact, the only excuse she needed was for her own conscience. For someone with a traditional Catholic upbringing like herself, going to see a fortune-teller was a big, slightly frightening step. Her gift of foresight was just that, a gift she had been born with. But deliberately consulting someone else who had that gift might well be frowned on by the Church, even in these more flexible times.

She circled the market once, purchasing some organic mushrooms, still fluffed with the earth they were pulled from, and some tea brack, darkly wet and honeyed-looking. James would love that for his tea. And then, she saw the fortune-telling stall. It wasn't the exotic spot she had been expecting. There were no velvet curtains or gold-sequined chiffon trailing all over the place. Just this small stall with a seating area of two chairs in front of a wall covered with old French posters, obviously from the stall next door. There was a little door, made of the same thin board as the wall, and presumably behind that lurked the fortune-teller. She looked about in case someone recognised her. There was no one. It was now or never.

She sat down in one of the chairs and waited. A few minutes passed and she was just about to get up and go, thinking that there was clearly nobody behind the door, when it creaked open and a woman appeared.

She was remarkably young, Christie thought, cross with

herself for expecting some wizened little old Romany woman, but this woman couldn't have been more than thirty. Pale and small with long dark-blonde hair tied back, the woman wore a decidedly plain blue blouse and dark trousers. Neatly put together, she could have been working behind the counter in any bank. Christie berated herself for stereotyping.

'Would you like to come in?' the woman said to Christie, her accent putting her from somewhere in the midland of the country.

'Yes, of course,' said Christie.

The little room boasted a table covered with a black velvet cloth, two chairs and was lined with heavy curtains.

'Sound-proofing,' the girl said matter-of-factly.

She tilted her head slightly. 'Why are you here?'

'What do you mean?' asked Christie, wrong-footed.

'Why do you want me to tell you things?' the girl said, sitting down and gesturing for Christie to do the same.

'Well, you're a fortune-teller,' Christie said.

'Yes,' said the girl, 'but so are you.'

Christie sat down, dropped her shopping and her handbag and leaned on the table. 'Sorry, what?' she asked.

'You can See, can't you?' the woman said, saying the word with a gravity that gave it capital letters. 'I can always tell.'

Whatever Christie had been expecting, it wasn't this. 'I'm Christie,' she said.

'I'm Rosalind,' said the girl. 'Nice to meet you.'

They shook hands across the table and it felt odd, this formality in such strange circumstances. Christie only hesitated a moment, she had come here not knowing what to expect, yet faced with Rosalind, who clearly could see that Christie had some sort of gift, she felt there was no point in hiding or prevaricating.

'You're right,' she said. 'I can see, I've always been able to see, but it's a strange gift. I've never been able to control it, it just comes to me sometimes. And I can never see anything for me.'

Rosalind nodded. 'That's often the way it is,' she said. 'There are plenty of people in my mother's family like you, they have a great gift, but they have never developed it. Not being able to see for yourself is common enough. Lots of people with the gift don't see for themselves or deliberately blank it out because they don't want to know. I try not to look into my children's lives,' she said with a shudder. 'I'd be afraid of what I would see.'

'So, what is your gift and how did you know about it?' asked Christie.

'I can see into the future, the probable future,' Rosalind said slowly. 'I'm a medium too, although I don't work as a medium very often because it drains me. It's exhausting.'

Christie shivered. 'I don't want to see a medium, I don't want to see people there beside me.'

'That's fine,' agreed Rosalind. 'A lot of people don't want that. Even as a child, I knew I had the gift. My mother has it too. It's a gift and a curse because there is no escaping it.'

'I know what you mean,' said Christie with feeling, thinking of the last month and the fear she'd felt. 'It comes when you don't want it to.'

'And you came here to me because you saw something you didn't want to?' Rosalind asked suddenly.

Christie nodded.

'I can never see for myself, I wouldn't want to, but I've just had these feelings of fear, of anxiety. Somebody has come into my life from the past and . . .'

'A man,' said Rosalind. She sounded a bit different now, more professional. 'A man once came into your life and you felt something for him but you were married and he went and you thought it was safe and now, a long time later, he's back making contact.'

'How did you know?' sighed Christie. It was a relief to hear somebody speak her fears aloud.

'The same way you've seen things before,' Rosalind said. 'I've learned how to develop my gift. You never did?'

'I wasn't brought up in that sort of home,' Christie explained. 'My father was religious and he would have gone mad. He didn't believe in seeing anything unless it was there in front of him or unless Father Flynn talked about it. I couldn't have told Dad.'

'But you know it must have come from somewhere?' Rosalind said. 'Would you like me to see where?'

Christie Devlin, possessor of a gift she had never understood, felt like crying. For the first time in her life she was able to talk about it to someone who understood. Why hadn't she done this years ago?

'You didn't know your grandmother, did you?' Rosalind asked and her voice was slower now, as if she was concentrating hard. 'Your mother's mother, I mean. I can feel that you didn't.'

Christie nodded. 'I never met her. She was a quarter French –'

'– And she died before you were born. She was from a large family and was the seventh daughter, and so was your mother. And you're the seventh child too, aren't you?'

Rosalind looked straight at Christie, who nodded again. She wasn't feeling shock or astonishment any more.

'Your grandmother had the gift,' Rosalind said. 'She could see things and if she'd been around she'd have told you what to do with it. She's here, you know. She's with us in the room.'

Christie gasped. 'I don't want to know that type of thing,' she said.

'Fine,' said Rosalind calmly. 'She's the one who had the gift and she's sorry that you had to grow up not knowing anything about it, but your father wasn't the sort of man to let you know. Your mother had the gift but when she married your father, he hated it so much, he forbade her to use it. She would have liked you to know that you might have it too, but your father told her never to talk about it, ever. She was very nervous of him, I think, he overpowered her.'

Christie smiled sadly, that was right for sure.

'There's nothing wrong with being able to see. Your grandmother was a good woman, she helped lots of people, she was kind, Christian, good. She said there was a lot of fear in her day. People thought that if you could see, you couldn't possibly be a good, true religious person. She says to tell you it's just another type of seeing, another type of wisdom, that's all. She'd have told you that, if she'd been alive.'

'I never wanted to see too much,' Christie said. 'It allowed me to be wise and I could help people and that was lovely, but I never wanted to be able to see for myself or see bad things coming or ... I suppose that's why I was frightened of coming to you, that you could see all the bad things.'

'Bad things happen whether you see them or not,' said Rosalind firmly, 'and anything I see for you in the future is the probable future. Nothing is set in stone, we can all affect our own destiny. If you read the cards and they tell you there is danger ahead, you will change your life: change what you do so that the danger doesn't affect you. Destiny is in our own hands. We all have choice and free will. Seeing the future is merely another type of wisdom.'

'Well, why are we so frightened of it?' Christie asked, thinking of her father. It all made sense now, how he hated the Gypsy fortune-tellers that used to come through Kilshandra occasionally. He hated them because he'd known that his wife's mother could have been one of them, and it frightened him. Maybe her grandmother had seen that her son-in-law was a bully and had warned her daughter against him.

'People don't like what they can't understand,' said Rosalind, shrugging. 'The reality is that there are people like you and me, who can see, for whatever reason. We'd be stupid to turn our back on it, because it's a gift, like any other gift, like being musical or having a lovely voice. As long as you are not seeing things to hurt people, as long as you're trying to help, well then, what's wrong with being a wise woman?'

'Yes, that's it,' said Christie, feeling a little peace enter her soul, 'a wise woman. People often say I'm a wise woman.'

'And you are.' Rosalind smiled. 'But even wise women need a little help sometimes. This man . . .' She reached out and touched Christie's hand. 'Why are you frightened of him coming back into your life?'

'Because if he came back and he told about what he meant to me, it would hurt the people I love most in the world. I don't want that to happen. I feel so powerless, that he's coming and I can't stop him and I've had this sense of fear for so long now that it never goes away.'

Rosalind nodded. 'I could read the cards for you,' she said, 'but I don't think I need to. I think you understand what you need to do. You're just afraid of doing it.'

'I don't understand at all,' said Christie.

'Yes, you do,' insisted Rosalind. 'Look in your heart. Close your eyes and think.'

For a moment, Christie thought of herself and Liz in the staff room in St Ursula's, when Liz had been worried about the man she loved and how he wanted to run out on her because it was all getting too serious. Christie had told her to close her eyes and think about what was in her heart. It was funny, she realised, she'd been using her gift just the way Rosalind did without any training or help. Perhaps she was a wise woman after all.

Closing her eyes now, she thought of Carey Wolensky and what he had meant to her. How his coming back could hurt so many people: Ana, Ethan and Shane, and James, most of all James. Because it really hadn't been his fault, it had been a series of coincidences and happenings that had led Carey to her.

She opened her eyes. The answer had come. 'I need to see him and tell him to leave my life, that he's not a part of it, that if he's kept a torch burning for me all these years he should let it go out. I've got to talk to James about it and tell him. Let him know, whatever the consequences.'

She shivered because she didn't know what those consequences would be, but she knew that's what she had to do.

Rosalind didn't comment on this. 'Maybe you'll come back and see me again some other time,' she said. 'I could read your cards.'

Christie smiled. She wasn't sure if she was ready for that. Better to get used to the information that the gift did run in her family and see where telling James about Carey Wolensky would lead her and then . . .

'Thank you,' she said. She opened her purse. 'How much do I owe you?'

'No.' Rosalind stilled her with the word. 'There's no fee. People who share the gift never charge other people who share it,' she said.

'You're sure?' asked Christie.

'I'm sure,' said Rosalind, 'and please, come and see me again.'

It was odd, Christie thought, as she walked back through the market, she felt a lightness in her heart that she hadn't felt in a long time, ever since the gloom had first appeared. She'd been so stupid really. For the past month, she'd let the memory of Carey Wolensky overshadow everything else in her life, all the wonderful things: James, her family, Janet's pregnancy, the good things she had. She'd let Carey over-shadow them all, because she'd allowed herself to be a victim.

She'd done something she'd been ashamed of and, instead of facing up to it, she'd been scared it would destroy her family. In doing so, she'd almost allowed it to destroy her family. Ironic that, she thought wryly. But she wouldn't be scared any more. Rosalind had just helped her to see what was in her heart and what she had to do.

She sat down on a bench near the market and made the call to Carey's hotel from her mobile phone. She was put on to Heidi, Carey's assistant, instantly.

'This is Mrs Christie Devlin,' she said coolly, although she was quivering with nerves. 'You've been trying to contact me with regard to Mr Wolensky's exhibition.'

'Yes, he'll be so thrilled you've got in touch,' said Heidi with obvious enthusiasm.

'I don't want to go to the private viewing. I'll be away,' Christie said, lying. 'But I'd like to meet with Mr Wolensky, if that's possible.'

'I'm sure it is. He was most keen to see you.'

Christie nearly hung up there and then, but she had to be strong. She had to do this.

'He's here next week from Wednesday on for ten days.'

'I can see him on the Monday morning,' Christie said, shocked that she'd have to wait that long to get this all over with. 'No other time, I'm afraid.'

'He's busy then but I can rearrange his appointments,' Heidi replied quickly. 'Eleven, here in the hotel?'

'Eleven would be fine. Thank you.'

Christie pushed the 'end call' button. She'd done it. She'd stopped running from the past. But she didn't feel any sense of relief – only pure panic. She could have just made the biggest mistake of her life.

# CHAPTER TWENTY-ONE

Thousands of miles away, sitting in the back of a beaten-up van with the band, Amber was wondering the same thing. Was this whole trip the biggest mistake of her life?

They hadn't expected a traffic jam in LA. Gridlock, a freeway nightmare. Cars jammed end to end, creeping along. That sort of stuff happened at home, not here, not in fabulous LA. But they still got stuck in it until finally, after three quarters of an hour in the heat – the air con didn't work very well in the rent-a-wreck – Syd took an off ramp and they ended up in a small, beat-up neighbourhood, with a couple of pool halls and what looked like a pub.

They all piled in. None of them really had enough cash to spend on drinks, but they were dying for something cool: cool beer, cool lemonade, cool anything. The bar was half full, but nobody even glanced at Amber, which made her feel even more miserable, although she knew she looked a sight. How was it that men ignoring her could be so depressing, when she and Ella had so often been dismissive of men who did notice them? Her skin was greasy and she'd got spots. She hadn't washed her hair for the last couple of days, she'd been so tired. How could you be tired getting up in the morning when you hadn't done anything all day except sit in the back of a van, bumping along?

They ambled over to the bar and ordered some drinks.

'You can drive from now on,' Syd said to Karl. 'I'm having some real liquor.'

'Hey, you're turning into an American,' laughed Lew.

'Yeah, right,' said Syd glumly.

The night before he'd confided in Amber that he was missing his girlfriend, Lola, so much. She was a make-up artist who worked for herself, often travelling around Ireland for jobs. There was no way she could have come on this crazy trek across America.

'It's impossible to get hold of her without my mobile,' he had grumbled to Amber, as they sat on the fire escape of last night's crummy hotel, Amber sipping a Coke, Syd chain-smoking.

'She wasn't worried that you were going away without her, was she?' asked Amber doubtfully, thinking that she'd been too nervous to let Karl go off on his own.

'No,' said Syd, with a laugh. 'We're too close for that.'

And then, she could see him realise what he had said, realise he knew exactly why she'd tagged along with the band to New York and now on the trek to LA: because she didn't trust Karl.

'But you know,' Syd said rapidly, 'people are different and she's busy. Plus, she's been to America a few times and she'll come out when we're settled. It's different for you and Karl, right?'

'Yeah, different,' said Amber, thinking of the exams her friends at St Ursula's were sitting now. Thinking of her seat in the big exam hall, near to Ella, and the grins and the glances and the anguished stares they'd have exchanged, had exchanged for every exam they'd sat through together since they'd met. Ella always had a supply of sweets and crunched them noisily. Amber was more a chewing gum sort of girl. She wondered who was sitting in her place now, what dreams and hopes they had.

Thinking of Ella made her think of Mum. The guilt about Mum was always there in the pit of her stomach. Mum had done nothing wrong except stifle Amber in an attempt to protect her, and look how Amber had repaid her.

She was a horrible daughter and her mother must hate her. Every time Amber thought longingly of home and of hearing her mother's voice, she reminded herself of her mother's hurt face that last day. She, Amber, had done that – hurt her mother as much as if she'd stabbed her. She didn't know how she'd ever say sorry for that. It was such a huge weight to carry that she didn't know how to try.

'It'll work out,' Syd said.

'What?' said Amber, half lost, not quite knowing what he was talking about. 'The band, you mean? You're all very talented, I'm sure it will work out.'

Syd looked at her silently, for a moment. 'Yeah,' he said, 'that's what I meant: the band. It'll work out, I'm sure of it.'

Now in the seedy bar in LA, Karl sloped off to phone Stevie in Dublin, just in case there was any news. Syd looked at Amber.

'What'll you have?' he said, gently.

Normally, Amber stuck to a couple of light beers, since she still wasn't the drinking sort of girl. Ella would laugh at that: to think they'd both been keen to have grown-up drinks in grown-up bars and now that she could, Amber had discovered she didn't like them that much.

'I don't know, Syd,' she said now. 'Something to cheer me up.'

Syd grinned. 'I know just what you need!'

By the third tequila shot, Amber was feeling no pain.

'It's great this stuff. Why did I never try it before?' She

was smiling happily, arranging and rearranging her shot glasses in different patterns.

'We never could afford it before,' Kenny T laughed.

'We can't now,' added Lew. 'Karl will go stark, staring mad when he comes back and finds that we've been spending the savings on tequila.'

'Well, Karl's not the boss, is he?' snapped Syd. 'Amber can have Cuevo Gold if she fucking well wants to. In fact, she'll have another one and so will I.'

When Karl came back from the phone a few moments later, Amber looked at him with eyes of love. She felt warm and hazy inside. It was all going to be wonderful. LA was a fabulous place, they'd live in a gorgeous house and go to amazing celebrity parties. Karl would be a world-famous musician, they'd have loads of money and people would look at her, envy her and think she had a fabulous life . . .

'Tequila?' said Karl, looking down at the empty shot glasses on the table.

'Hey, we felt like cheering ourselves up,' Syd said defensively.

Karl didn't look upset, though.

'You're not going to believe it,' he said, 'but Stevie came through.'

'Came through how?' asked Lew.

'Came through in that he's got us a meeting with a production company out here. It's a guy called Michael Levin and he's hot, Stevie says. He's one of the best producers around and he liked the stuff Stevie sent him. We're to meet him in his office tomorrow. Guys, it's going to be OK.'

The tequila-drinkers erupted in a cheer.

'That's incredible,' said Amber, getting up to throw her arms lazily around Karl's neck. 'You're incredible. Oh, I love you, I love you so much, that's wonderful. You're so talented and clever and . . .'

'Right,' he said, moving his face away from her boozy breath. 'You shouldn't drink tequila, Amber, it smells horrible.'

'We needed cheering up, you see,' she whispered. What he'd said hurt, but she was still insulated by the cosy fire of the alcohol.

'Yeah, yeah, whatever.' Karl settled her back in her seat. He sat down beside the band and began to plan with them. What they'd say to this producer, what they'd play for him, how they weren't going to be taken for some load of green young guys because now they'd been around.

Amber sat on the edge, sidelined again, but she didn't care. It was all working out, it was all going to be great. She knew it.

That night they stayed in another fleapit motel, the sort of place that was quite safe, mainly because there were two police cars parked outside the door most of the night. Sirens blared, people screamed and laughed and Amber barely slept a wink, partly because of the tequila hangover that had kicked in at about ten, and partly because of anxiety. She didn't like this town: it was scary. These constantly bright and busy streets weren't the palm-treed oases she'd imagined. There were no haciendas in this part of town, no nice cafés with movie stars sitting outside, no sense of Hollywood glamour: just dangerous guys driving big cars with music vibrating out from everywhere, and skinny girls in hotpants on the street corner opposite the hotel, watching every car that slowed down. Nobody smiled at anyone, nobody looked at anyone, as though eye contact was a threat.

However, in the California sunshine of the next morning, the streets didn't look menacing any more: just edgy and hip, like a scene from a video on MTV.

'Come back to bed,' murmured Karl, sitting up against the pillows, watching her looking out the window and admiring her body in the pink spotted G-string she'd slept in.

'Bed?' she said, doing her best call-girl voice. 'Can you afford me?'

She climbed on to the bed and began to crawl towards him, swinging her hair provocatively.

'I don't know,' Karl said, pulling her closer. 'I'm pretty broke now but I think there might be some money coming my way soon. Will you take an IOU?'

Amber straddled him. 'Only for you, my love,' she crooned before kissing him.

Within hours, their fortunes had changed. It took one trip to the producer's office. Michael Levin was a small, slim, dark-eyed guy who clearly liked the band's work. He said he'd work with them and that they needed to sort out some paperwork, as well as a lawyer to go over the small print. He recommended someone.

Amber raised her eyebrows at this: surely if the producer recommended a lawyer he knew, this was a conflict of interest? They should find their own lawyer to work out the percentages, etc, but nobody else looked askance at the suggestion.

Michael Levin was offering some money upfront and got them a deal in a lovely hotel near his office until they could sort out a house to rent.

Two hours after meeting him, they had four beautiful suites in the Santa Angelina Hotel, a hip little place with the requisite palm trees outside. Amber felt the bellboy looking at the five of them in faint disgust as he showed them up to their rooms. She was sure that they smelt of poverty, of life on the road in crappy motels where the toiletries ran to thin bars of soap and even thinner towels. She couldn't wait to get into that vast bath tub in the huge pale marble and mirrored bathroom and sink into all the bubbles that would be sure to emerge from the beautiful aquamarine glass jars.

'Wow, this is some place,' said Syd, admiring Karl and Amber's suite.

'I've never seen anything like it,' gasped Lew.

'Hey, relax, guys,' said Karl, trying to be cool. 'You've gotta get used to this.'

Amber felt a flash of impatience with him. Who did he think he was? They had just spent ten days on the road in cockroach-infested fleapits with no money, eating endless fast food until they were all spotty and lank-haired, and it seemed like sheer fluke that had brought them to this beautiful place. Now was not the time to be doing the 'we're so cool, we deserve this' act.

'Cop on, Karl,' she said sharply. 'We're lucky it's working out, let's not count our chickens. We did that the last time, remember? And then Stevie left and we were up shit creek without a paddle.'

Karl glared at her. 'I knew it would work, even if you didn't.'

He marched into their suite's second bathroom and slammed the door.

'Hey,' said Lew, grinning at Amber. 'Just as well you've got two bathrooms.'

Karl and Amber didn't talk to each other for the rest of the afternoon, although Amber didn't care. She was perfectly happy being in her own bathroom, lolling in a bubble-filled bath, scrubbing herself clean, rubbing scented body lotion into every inch of her body, washing her hair till it squeaked, feeling good about herself again.

They were being taken out to dinner tonight by Michael Levin, and as she rooted through her dirty, faded wardrobe, she realised she actually had nothing to wear and no money to buy anything. It was different for the guys, they could wear jeans and a T-shirt and still look fantastic, but girls needed something a bit more special.

She could have gone and asked Karl if there was any money to spare to buy something new but she didn't want to. Instead, she went over to Syd's suite.

'What's happenin', baby?' he said, opening the door, a fat cigar in one hand, the TV remote in the other and himself wrapped in a big, fat towelling robe. The huge TV blared a pay-per-view movie and a room service cart lay pushed to one side with the remains of a club sandwich and a bottle of champagne.

'You're fitting in around here very well, Syd,' Amber grinned.

It was funny, she got on better with Syd these days than she did with Karl.

'Yeah, I think I like this lifestyle, Amber. Better not get used to it, though, as you pointed out.'

'Sorry,' Amber apologised. 'I didn't mean that, I didn't mean that the band wouldn't make it. I was only trying to be realistic. We, sorry, *you* shouldn't count your chickens.'

'I know that,' Syd said, drawing her into the suite. 'You look all lovely and shiny.'

'I feel great,' said Amber. 'And clean! I thought I'd never feel clean again. There's only one problem, I have nothing to wear.'

Syd laughed. 'It must be a chromosome thing: women and shopping. Lola's just the same. Shop or die. I've got a few quid left.' He handed her over a hundred dollars. 'Sorry, it's not much, but it's all I can afford until we get some of the upfront signing money.'

'Oh, you're a star!' Amber said and threw her arms around him and gave him a big hug.

'Steady on,' laughed Syd, 'or you'll have Lola on the phone soon, giving out that I found me another woman.'

'Oh, sure,' teased Amber. She knew he was only kidding, he loved Lola to bits. 'Thanks, and don't mention this to Karl?'

'I won't,' said Syd. 'I understand.'

As Amber went downstairs in the lift, she pondered those last words. What did Syd understand? That she and Karl were breaking up in front of his eyes and that she couldn't go to Karl and ask him for a few dollars to buy a new outfit? Or that he wouldn't understand why she needed to in the first place?

Far away in New York, Faye Reid wondered if she should just go home and give up. She'd been in New York for two weeks now and she felt she was dying of loneliness. She missed Amber so much. And since that first phone call just after she'd left, Amber hadn't even phoned home again. Faye checked her Summer Street answering machine with a frequency that was verging on the obsessional.

Above all, she felt as if she'd failed her daughter spectacularly if Amber could run away and never contact home. What sort of a mother did that make her?

When her own mother phoned her to see how she was doing, Faye could barely speak from misery.

'I don't suppose Amber's been in touch with you, Mum?' she asked, ever hopeful.

'No,' said Josie. 'I suspect she feels so guilty and anxious that she's deliberately not phoning now. She knows I'd give her a piece of my mind for running off like that.'

'You're not to say a thing to her if she phones!' shrieked Faye. It might frighten Amber off and . . .

'Faye, listen to me!' said Josie calmly but firmly. 'If Amber phones, I will give her a piece of my mind because what she's done is unforgivable. I know she's only eighteen, she's in love and she's all upset, but that's no reason to treat your family this way. Yes, I'm sure she's afraid we'll be furious with her for what she's done, but that's no reason not to call again. I am furious with her and when you get over your fit of the guilts, you should be too. Yes, you lied to her.'

Faye winced.

'Yes, you made up a nice little fairytale about her father and you know I disagreed with you about that, but it was your choice. The bottom line, Faye, is that you've done everything you could for that girl, everything. You've given up your life for her. The Lord only knows I love her, but I am angry with her.'

'Oh, Mum . . .'

'Don't "Oh, Mum" me,' said Josie fiercely. 'If you don't make some progress in the next few days, then you've got to come home. Amber is a clever girl. She'll survive. She's got our blood running through her veins and we've survived, haven't we? So have some faith in her.'

'You really think she'll be all right?' Faye said, starting to cry.

'She might be wrapped up in young passion, but she's not stupid,' Josie said with a touch of pride. 'She's a strong girl. You've done a great job with her. Remember that.'

'I will,' sobbed Faye. 'I will.' But it was easier said than done.

Her mother was right: she'd have to go home soon. What was the point waiting here? Amber could have left New York days ago. She could be anywhere by now, and at least when she phoned home again – and she would, Faye was sure she would – Faye would be there to talk to her.

The fashion magazines were wrong, Amber thought crossly, after an hour and a half. They were always implying that Los Angeles thrift shops were full of exquisite vintage clothes: barely worn Schiaparelli gowns, original Dior suits, everything for next to nothing. In fact, she was finding an awful lot of very dull clothes and lots of jeans in teeny, tiny sizes. She *had* jeans. But jeans were not going to cut it in a town where people only wore jeans with half a million's worth of Harry Winston diamonds, accessorised with Manolo Blahnik shoes and a Judith Leiber clutch.

Then, finally, in a tiny little shop off Melrose, with rails so crammed full of clothes it hurt her arms to rifle through them, she found it. It looked like a 1930s nightie, which in fact it probably was: an emerald-green bias-cut silk-satin dress with spaghetti straps and a scalloped hem. It clung to her curves in all the right places and highlighted her creamy skin and her tawny mane. It was fabulous and, better still, only sixty dollars. With the rest of the money she bought an embroidered shawl with fringing, to throw over her shoulders, and a shiny lip gloss. There, she'd do.

Karl was sitting on the superking-sized bed putting on his watch when Amber emerged from her bathroom, all ready to go, a vision in shimmering green, her tiger's-eye pendant highlighting the silkiness of her slender throat.

'Wow, you look amazing,' he said in admiration. 'Come here.'

It was as if the row had never happened, as if there had never been any coolness between them on the road. He began to kiss her and suddenly Amber wasn't in such a rush for the dinner party after all. Karl's hands caressed her body and gently pulled the straps of her beautiful dress over her shoulders so it slithered like a skin to the floor.

'You're so beautiful,' he said, 'my muse. I couldn't have done this without you.'

As they made love, Amber thought that these were just

the words she wanted to hear. Karl loved her, adored her. That was what mattered, wasn't it?

They were late getting downstairs but the limo driver didn't seem to mind.

'What the hell were you pair doing?' grumbled Kenny T, who had been sitting in the back of the limo with Syd and Lew for ten minutes and was agitated, as if he wanted to get to this fabulous party soon.

'Nothing,' said Karl, with a grin that said quite plainly that he had just had mind-altering sex.

Syd said nothing, he just looked at Amber and smiled a small, knowing smile. She grinned back, feeling slightly treacherous for telling Syd she couldn't ask Karl for the money for the new dress. This was Syd's money she was wearing and she couldn't tell Karl. But couples had rows and arguments all the time, Syd must know that.

Los Angeles was a strange mix of dress up and dress down. The restaurant they went to looked as if half the clientele had come straight from the Oscars and the other half straight from doing their grocery shopping. There were willowy girls in jeans and socialites in Versace. Jewels gleamed on both men and women and everyone looked fabulously tanned and healthy.

In her second-hand finery, Amber felt she fitted in pretty well and she was with the most handsome man in the room, the superbly talented Karl Evans. Michael, the producer, thought so too, he spent the night talking about the band with Karl. They discussed different songs, what they'd rearrange, how they might bring in some other songwriters – people Michael worked with all the time – just to tweak, and perhaps to write a couple of new songs. Karl, who normally maintained that his work was not to be touched, and wouldn't even dream of singing anyone else's music, nodded vigorously to all this. He seemed fascinated by the talk of business.

314

There were ten people at the dinner table but Amber felt bored. Nobody was talking to her. It was as if, she realised sadly, she didn't quite exist.

She felt just the same as she had at the SnakePit that night when she'd had to hide at the side of the stage to watch the band play – a hanger-on. That's what Stevie had wanted her to feel, she was sure: that she was nothing but the girlfriend, and of course, the role of the girlfriend was to keep the lead singer/songwriter happy, as well as being attractive and sexually available. So much for feminism, Amber thought grimly and took another sip of wine.

The waiters, all staggeringly handsome out-of-work actors with cheekbones like cliff edges and bodies sculpted by hours in the gym, kept filling the wineglasses so stealthily and discreetly that it was hard for Amber to know how much she'd drunk. At first, as she toyed with her Caesar salad, she tried to keep a tab, but after a while she gave up. Karl was at the end of the table, separated from her by Michael and one of his assistants, who were talking to Karl at length about musicians they all admired and where Karl's inspiration had come from.

'It's got to be Robert Johnson, hasn't it?' Karl was saying intently. 'Oh, and Hendrix, naturally.'

'Well, you've got his gift too,' said the assistant, smiling, flattering.

Amber thought she was going to puke. Michael had seemed upfront and honest when they'd first met him, but tonight, he had changed: he was fawning on Karl, hyping up the band and their brilliance. What a fabulous team they'd all make. How they'd change the world. And Karl didn't seem to see.

Amber pushed her plate away, her appetite quite gone. She loved the climate in LA, adored the sense of freedom. But the insincerity was something else. Everything she saw or heard in this town was wrapped in a fleecy parcel of

315

bullshit. She almost longed for the straightforwardness of the places they'd stayed on the road: ordinary towns where people said what they meant. Or even miserable old Gretchen in the mini-market back home, who'd glare at you rudely if she was in the mood.

Or her mum. The mini-market made her think of Summer Street and of home. Could Mum ever forgive her? At that moment, Amber didn't feel as if she deserved forgiveness.

Karl didn't seem to notice her unhappiness. He didn't smile or even give her one of those 'are you OK, honey?' looks across the table. On her other side was a female producer. A slim, beautiful woman with olive skin, dressed in an exquisite coral wrap dress, she was talking intently to Syd and Kenny T.

Even Lew, who was never going to be a contestant on *Mastermind*, was busily being chatted up by yet another member of Michael's team on the other side of the table. But nobody was bothering with Amber. And she didn't like it. She was clever, she wasn't some bimbo girlfriend.

She lifted her wineglass and took another big sip and thought of her mum. Mum always said that beauty could only take you so far in life, while intelligence and self-belief could take you a lot further. Amber didn't allow herself to think about her mum much, although she fingered her tiger's-eye pendant thoughtfully. She wore it all the time and she did think of Mum when she put it on. It was her talisman of home. She hadn't rung since that first phone call, she knew she should have but the argument was all too raw, too painful. She'd been horrible, she knew that now. Not that she'd made a mistake, no, she'd done the right thing to go away with Karl.

But she still felt guilty when she thought of Mum's hurt face and what was it that Gran had said?

*You should let your mother tell you.*

She sometimes wondered exactly what her mother did have to tell her. Gran wouldn't have said it if she hadn't meant it, if there hadn't been some intelligent reason behind it. So what could her mum have to tell Amber that could possibly change the way she had decided to live her life?

'Was your salad OK for you?' asked the waiter.

'Yes, it was delicious,' said Amber, pathetically happy that at least someone was talking to her. 'It's just I wasn't hungry.'

The evening might have been endured if another party of people hadn't arrived when their table was drinking coffee. There was no dessert of course. God forbid that anyone in LA would actually eat dessert, apart from toying with some fresh fruit. Amber was cross because she felt like something sugary.

The party included a very beautiful woman with skin like ebony, the body of a supermodel and a face that Tyra Banks would envy. She came over to the table and kissed Michael Levin on both cheeks, a proper kiss, not just air kissing.

She was, Amber heard her neighbour whisper, the latest hot singing sensation with her first album just out, produced by Michael.

'She can sing too?' said Amber, staring at this vision of a woman. She was like an exquisite Somalian empress.

Wow, Amber thought, she'd be beautiful to paint: that face, that figure, that elegance.

'Yeah, she's going to make it really big,' said Amber's neighbour again. 'Everyone will know about Venetia, I promise you that. She's gonna be hotter than Beyoncé.'

Venetia. Even her name was beautiful, thought Amber mistily. And then, suddenly, she stopped feeling so friendly towards Venetia because Michael introduced her to Karl, not any of the other band members, just to Karl. A few more chairs were brought up and the exquisite Venetia snuggled in close between Karl and Michael, though slightly closer to

Karl than to anyone else. They were talking and laughing, and Amber couldn't hear what they were saying but she could see Venetia touching Karl on the shoulder and on the knee, as if she had known him for ever.

'She needs somebody to write some new songs for her,' said Amber's neighbour, catching Amber's fierce glare. 'Fabulous voice and she's written a few good tracks herself, but basically she needs songwriters and Michael thinks Karl has a few songs that just might suit her. He's a very talented songwriter.'

'Well, Karl doesn't write songs for anyone else,' Amber said heatedly. 'He doesn't believe in that type of thing, he only writes for himself.'

Her neighbour gave her a long, steady gaze.

'Karl seems like a pretty bright guy and if you want to get ahead in this business, you make your own music, you make music for other people, hey, whatever it takes. Venetia is going to go a long way, it mightn't be bad for him to be attached to her coat-tails.'

Amber was sick at the thought of Karl being attached to any part of Venetia.

She finished her wine with a flourish. She'd had enough of this. She was going back to the hotel and Karl was coming with her. They had been nice, charming, they had partied, you name it, but now they were going home to bed together and bloody Venetia had better get her hand off Karl's knee damn quick.

Amber got to her feet unsteadily. Her handbag was under the table, so she had to bend to pick it up and she banged her forehead on the table.

'Ouch.'

'You OK?' said Syd.

'Fine, fine,' said Amber with the unconcern of the very drunk. She swayed a little where she stood. 'I am perfectly fine, just think I'll go. Me and Karl, we're tired.'

'I'll take you home,' said Syd, pushing his chair back.

'No,' insisted Amber. 'There's no need. Karl will bring me home. I came with Karl, I'm going to go with Karl. He is my boyfriend, I am his muse,' she said loudly, so loudly that nobody at the table could have missed it. But Venetia, Karl and the producer didn't appear to have heard because they were all talking and laughing happily together.

Amber shoved her chair back and made it rather erratically around the table to Karl's side. She laid a hand on his shoulder. 'I want to go home, darling,' she said. 'Are you ready?'

Karl looked up at her. 'No, no, you go,' he said. 'I'm fine, baby. Don't wait up, whatever.'

Michael raised a hand and suddenly one of his team was escorting Amber outside.

'But I'm waiting for my boyfriend, for Karl,' she said. She could see Karl, but he wasn't watching her, although Venetia was looking at her with those exquisite cat-like eyes, her expression one of pity – not malice or jealousy or triumph, but plain, old-fashioned pity. It was the last thing Amber remembered as she was put in the back of the beautiful limo and whisked away to her exquisite, empty, hotel suite.

The next thing she knew there was so much daylight she could hardly open her eyes. She lay there, wondering where she was and then everything that had happened the night before flooded back. Karl. He hadn't come home with her. How dare he do that to her? She was going to give him a piece of her mind. She sat up in the bed, ignoring the murderous throbbing of her head, and turned to where he should have been, but she was alone. The bed was so big she'd only taken up a quarter of it. The other three quarters were pristine, unslept in. She threw back the covers and ran through the suite, but there was no sign of Karl.

Next, she phoned Syd and Lew in their respective suites.

319

'Gee, Amber, why are you ringing me at this hour?' groaned Lew.

'It's half eleven,' she snapped, 'hardly dawn.'

'We were out late, must have been six when we got in. Those people know how to party, one club after another.'

'You went clubbing?' she asked.

'Well, yeah, eventually. What a blast. You shouldn't have gone home so early, Amber. What was up with you anyway? Karl hates that sort of jealous stuff, you know.'

'I wasn't jealous,' said Amber, feeling wildly embarrassed that even Lew, who wasn't intuitive, had noticed.

'You were nearly spitting when you were going. I thought there might be a cat fight between you and Venetia. She's some babe. I'd pay to see that.'

'Thank you, Lew, you've been a great help,' hissed Amber and hung up.

Syd was more on the ball, but sounded just as hung-over.

'No, I do not know where Karl is,' he said and, to Amber's ears, his words sounded like a statement he'd been practising just in case she should call.

'Well, did he go off or did he come back with the rest of you? I mean he could have got another room here so he wouldn't wake me,' she said dubiously, knowing this was highly unlikely.

'Look, Amber, this is between you and Karl,' said Syd. 'OK? Just leave me out of it. You know what I feel.'

Amber didn't know what he felt, but she said thanks and bye and hung up anyway. Was Syd telling her that Karl had a thing going with Venetia, or that Karl was the sort of man that always had a thing going with some woman? Or was it something else? Syd was deep.

She went into her lovely bathroom and blasted herself under the shower, anything to get rid of this horrible old groggy dead feeling.

Next, she ordered breakfast. Not because she was hungry, more that she thought strong coffee and maybe fruit would jerk her out of her hangover. Afterwards, she sat outside on the balcony, which overlooked the pool and watched beautiful people having business meetings around the glistening water. There were also plenty of people sunbathing, women with beautiful bodies, tanned and oiled, in white bikinis or exotic designer ones in Pucci prints. There was so much money here. In their trip across the States they had seen the richest and the poorest. They had certainly stayed in the poorest places, and now they were in one of the wealthiest towns on the planet but Amber didn't feel happy or thrilled, the way she thought she'd feel.

Her dreams of it had been about her and Karl being happy together. The problem was, there was no togetherness. Here, Amber was even more alone than she had been before she met Karl, when she'd only been dreaming about what love might be. And now she had the guilt to carry for hurting her mother too.

Finally, she went out to the pool herself and lay there with a book, peeping over the corners of it, watching what was going on.

Eventually, the heat of the sun got to her and she fell into a dreamless sleep.

'So this is where you are,' said a voice. 'I've been looking everywhere for you.'

It was Karl, except he didn't look as if he'd had a wild night out in clubs. He looked like he'd had a very good night's sleep. There was that faint hint of stubble on his jaw, his hair was tousled. The look in his eyes gave it away though. It was a look Amber had come to recognise when he walked offstage: a look of triumph, of sheer, almost sexual, pleasure. The look said: *I've just stood in front of all these people and they all wanted me.*

'You can't have been looking too hard for me,' she said sarcastically. 'I've been here all day and all last night,' she added pointedly. 'Where were you?'

'Out,' he said, his gaze raking over her, as if he didn't like what he saw.

'Out?' demanded Amber, feeling her temper rise. 'Out with whom?' she added for effect.

'With Michael, doing what we came to LA to do, Amber, remember? Hook up with a big producer, make our names, you know. We're here to do more than just lie around the pool all day and work on our tans.'

'I'm only working on my tan because I have no money and I can't go anywhere and because I was waiting for you to come home,' she snapped back, stung. 'And I was worried, anything could have happened to you, anything.'

She could see his face soften at the thought that she'd been worried about him, and he smiled at her, became the old Karl again.

'Oh, baby, you shouldn't worry about me. Last night was so amazing, such a blast, talking about music all night long with someone like Michael.'

He sat down on the sun lounger beside her, leaned forward, his face boyishly excited.

'You wouldn't believe the people he's worked with, the bands, the names, people whose albums I have and he knows them, he's worked with them. Jesus, it's incredible. I can't believe we're here.'

'So that was it?' Amber asked hesitantly.

'That was it. Sorry, you're right, I should have called. I stayed over with Michael, he's got the most amazing house in the hills, you should see it, all glass and beautiful. Rebuilt after the mud slides, totally incredible. He said it was an amazing house before but now it's doubly amazing.'

322

'Somebody said he had lots of art as well, didn't they?' Amber asked. 'He's a collector.'

'Yeah, yeah,' said Karl. 'There were paintings and stuff, you know me, I'm not into that, I didn't really notice, but yeah, sure, lots of fantastic stuff. You'll see it. Listen, why don't you and me go out to dinner, just on our own, not the gang, somewhere nice?'

'How can we afford it?'

'It's OK, Michael's given us an advance against the advance, if you know what I mean.' Karl grinned. 'Money, we've got money, baby.'

'Somewhere casual,' said Amber hopefully, 'because I still don't really have anything to wear, except what I was wearing last night.'

'What was that you were wearing?' Karl said, furrowing his brow.

'The green dress?' Amber said. 'Remember, you took it off because you thought it looked so nice.'

'Oh, yeah, yeah. Wear that, it'll be cool.'

The concierge recommended a little crab restaurant out in Venice, and they got a cab, sitting in the back, holding hands like teenagers, pointing out the sights and looking at people, admiring this place that was so different from home. The cute little restaurant looked like a shack but with non-shack prices, Amber realised. That was the problem with staying in really cool hotels. When you told the concierge you wanted to go somewhere cheap and nice, he sent you to the cheapest place rich people went.

'This is so expensive, we better not have starters,' Amber whispered, scanning the menu.

'Hey, no problem, baby,' said Karl. 'I've got money, remember?'

It was lovely, Amber thought, to have some cash finally. At last she could buy some more clothes because her stuff from home wasn't suitable. Her flowery chain-store bikini, which looked really nice at home, looked sort of ordinary among all the little designer pieces the girls wore here.

'You'll have to give me some cash too,' she said, thinking of what she'd buy. 'For clothes and things.'

'Sure, should have thought of it before. Sorry.'

He took out his wallet, a new wallet, Amber realised, made of very soft suede leather. When had he been shopping? There was a nice fat wad of green notes in it, and Karl pulled out a few and handed them across to her at the precise moment that their waiter reappeared to take their order.

Amber grabbed the money and stuffed it into her purse, feeling hideously embarrassed. It was like she was a hooker and being paid in a restaurant. But neither Karl, nor the charming waiter, appeared to have thought so. The only person dying with embarrassment was Amber. Despite her happiness that things were working out for the band and that running away from home hadn't been in vain, and despite her joy that her relationship with Karl seemed to be back on track – even though he was a little different, and LA was working some magic on him – despite all the things she should have been grateful for, Amber was suddenly aware that something was wrong. She, Amber Reid, raised by her mother to believe in personal power and a woman's right to independence, had no job, no qualifications and was being handed 'pin money' by her boyfriend. That's what was wrong.

# CHAPTER TWENTY-TWO

Maggie always laughed when people imagined there was any faint glamour to the world of academia.

Nobody in academia ever had any money and the only glamour resided in the feverish dreams of brilliant students who longed to star on *University Challenge*.

However, she got caught in precisely the same trap when it came to politics, assuming that politicians worked in a corporate world of money and style. It took just one visit to a city councillor to realise that politics was as much a glamour-free zone as college.

The knowledge hit her as she and her mother waited in the office of Liz Glebe, their local councillor, who was having her afternoon surgery. The only person there before them, an elderly man who kept anxiously scanning a well-thumbed piece of paper, had gone in to see Ms Glebe, so they were alone. The waiting room and the office reminded Maggie of an old shop where someone had ripped out the shelf units, painted the walls a sickly yellow and stuffed political pamphlets and posters everywhere, claiming better futures, better Irelands, better everything.

'Pity they don't have better chairs,' muttered Una, as she shifted to get comfortable on the plastic chair.

Liz Glebe was the first politician Maggie had contacted and when they finally got in to see her, she looked nothing like the glamorous, heavily made-up woman in the election posters that hung in her waiting room.

She still had short blonde hair and a wide smile but there were dark bags under her eyes, and her very conservative jacket and shirt looked as if they'd been to the dry-cleaner's too many times.

'Now, what's the problem?' she said, barely looking up at them while she shifted through sheets of paper on her desk. 'Summer Street pavilion, right? I know the background, shouldn't have happened, I voted against it. I have young kids myself and I hate to see the community being ripped apart, but I was in the minority, I'm afraid. It's pretty straight-forward – the pavilion was never a part of the park proper. It's officially council property. I'm not sure what you can do at this point.'

'Don't the people who actually use the park get any choice in the matter?' demanded Una irritably.

'Well, the concept of politics is that you elect us in, and we make the decisions,' Liz said, the mask of politeness slipping.

'Ridiculous idea,' Una snapped.

Maggie shot her mother a warning look.

'I'm on your side about the park,' Liz said.

'That's what everybody says come election time,' Una said, eyes narrowed.

'If you're on our side,' Maggie interrupted gently, 'perhaps you'd give us some advice on what we should do.'

Liz Glebe looked from mother to daughter and sighed.

'Go to see Harrison Mitchell. He's the Green Party coun-cillor for the area and he's made his name preserving old buildings. If there's any history at all to your pavilion, he's your man. And he likes hopeless cases – he loves appearing in the papers as the champion of the underdog.'

'Meaning he loves appearing in the papers or meaning he likes being the champion of the underdog?' Maggie inquired sharply.

'Think media whore and you won't go far wrong,' Liz said. 'Good luck.'

Harrison Mitchell wasn't keen on meeting the members of the Save Our Pavilion campaign because he was busy fighting for a medieval castle that the government were trying to build a motorway over. In terms of column inches, fighting the government and the motorway was a much more interesting story than fighting over the fate of a little park on Summer Street.

'He's very busy at the moment,' said his constituency secretary on the third occasion Maggie phoned. 'I have put your proposal to him but I just don't think he has the time.'

Something in Maggie snapped. The night before, she and her dad had walked around Summer Street park, talking about life, the universe and everything, admiring the flowers and ruefully thinking that if the campaign wasn't successful it might all look so different in a few months. Maggie had decided there and then that she was not going to lose this fight. She had lost so many fights in her life. Things were going to change.

She'd got a book from the library on self-confidence and had read it twice. Practising affirmations in front of the mirror in the morning felt a bit silly at first, but it seemed to work. After all, if you said, 'I feel useless', it had an effect, so surely the opposite was also true.

Start believing in yourself and stop knocking yourself, the book said. So simple and so true. And it was working.

327

'Fine,' Maggie said to the constituency secretary in pleasant tones. She knew exactly what to say, having practised this argument in front of the mirror earlier. 'You can tell Mr Mitchell that I'm giving a newspaper interview tomorrow and one of the main points I will be bringing up is his complete lack of interest in our pavilion. I'm going to point out that Mr Mitchell is obviously only interested in projects that get his name in the paper and that he has refused to see us on three separate occasions.'

'Now there's no need to be like this,' interrupted the secretary.

'Oh, there's every need,' said Maggie. 'Watch me.' She hung up.

Within fifteen minutes, she had an appointment to see Mr Mitchell the next afternoon.

'I can't go with you,' wailed Una. 'I've a doctor's appointment. You really need someone to go with you. You can't go and see someone like that on your own.'

'Nonsense,' said Maggie, feeling a certain amount of renewed vigour. 'I'll be fine.'

Harrison Mitchell's office was much grander than Liz Glebe's and was in the basement of his imposing Georgian three-storey terraced house. Handy to be a councillor when you were independently rich, thought Maggie, as she went down the steps into the basement, admiring topiary box trees sitting in giant stone troughs with just the correct amount of lichen on them. The effect was very beautiful and very grand.

She doubted that Mr Mitchell's waiting room would be covered with awful, sick yellow paint. She was right. It was a tasteful light blue with white cornices and a flower arrangement on a stand in an alcove.

'Sorry about the delay in seeing you,' said a man opening the door to her. It was Councillor Mitchell himself. Maggie recognised him from the newspapers. He was tall, good-looking, charming, and the product of an expensive education that gave in-built confidence. Maggie drew herself up to her full height and gave him a half-smile.

'I'm sorry it's taken us so long too,' she said coolly. Start as you mean to go on.

Politely, charmingly, Harrison Mitchell did his best to get out of helping with the Summer Street park campaign.

'I think that local people working together on something they really believe in is very powerful,' he said finally, after half an hour of discussing vague plans for what the protesters could do for their cause.

Maggie had had enough.

'You're a bit of a snob when it comes to conservation, aren't you?' she said. 'You like projects with historical connections or fabulous architectural proportions and to hell with anything that's of use to the community but doesn't fit your criteria.'

'That's not true,' he snapped.

'Yes it is,' said Maggie, listing the last five projects he'd been involved in. Every one of them was a historical site, despite his political literature claiming he was interested in saving community landmarks irrespective of their age or architectural beauty. 'I work in the library,' Maggie went on. 'And research is my specialist subject. We need your help. We've a lot of press planned,' she said, which was more or less true. Lots of newspapers and radio stations had been contacted but nobody was very interested yet. 'This could be a wonderful campaign for you. At least it would stop critics from saying you're only interested in getting your name in the papers,' she added, thinking that a month ago she'd never have had the courage to say something that ballsy.

Mitchell narrowed his eyes and looked at the telegenic

redhead before him. She'd be stunning in front of any sort of camera and she had chutzpah too.

'All right,' he said. 'But let me deal with the press.'

'Sorry,' said Maggie calmly, 'we'll deal with it together. This is our campaign, remember.'

She saw a flicker of respect in his eyes.

'OK,' he said. 'It's your campaign, Ms Maguire. You're the boss.'

Yes, thought Maggie proudly, I'm the boss.

It was nearly half past seven when she walked up Summer Street from the park end, still running over the meeting in her mind. She was so engrossed in her triumph that she almost didn't notice the man getting out of a car outside her house.

'Coming home from your car maintenance class?' said a low, deep voice behind her. Maggie knew it instantly. Big bear of a man with absolutely no social skills, greasy overalls and dirt under his fingernails. The man with the petrol sucker-outer.

She turned and stared at him. She might have walked in her gate without recognising him if it hadn't been for that voice. The overalls were gone and he was dressed casually in jeans and a cotton jumper that stretched slightly across his huge shoulders.

He cleaned up well, she conceded. Without the patina of garage grease, he was really rather attractive with those sparkling dark eyes. Not her type obviously; she didn't go in for those big men who looked like they never went to the gym, just heaved trucks around the garage to keep their muscles in shape.

'No, I've given up car maintenance. I'm in training for the space programme,' she said gravely. 'We're working on a plan to ship mankind off Earth and leave womankind behind.'

'All men? Or just ones who work in garages and make stupid jokes?'

'All men,' she said firmly.

'Where are we being sent?' he asked. He really was tall. Beside him, she felt positively fragile, which was something Maggie wasn't used to feeling.

'Somewhere with no oxygen.'

She tried to glare at him, but it was hard, because he was smiling at her, a relaxed smile as if he felt utterly comfortable.

'I don't suppose you can tell me when we're being shipped off: mankind, I mean,' he said, and it even *sounded* as if he was smiling. Honestly, what was the point of trying to be clever with someone who glinted sexy eyes back at you and looked wildly amused. 'Except I came to apologise. Sorry, I should have done it the day afterwards but I thought you might be too angry to listen to me. I wanted to invite you out to say sorry. By the way, how much time has mankind left before being shipped off to this unoxygenated planet?'

'You came to apologise and ask me out?' Maggie repeated, wondering if this was another joke.

'Unless NASA has a non-fraternisation policy,' he added, 'and you can't. For reasons of international security.'

He *was* teasing her, but it was gentle and Maggie found she quite liked it.

'Only intelligent life forms are considered a threat to national security,' she pointed out with a hint of sarcasm, leaving him in no doubt that she figured he was in the non-intelligent life-form quotient.

'Well, then it'll be fine for you to go out with me,' he said evenly. 'Next Saturday at two. It's my cousin's wedding.'

'A wedding? You don't ask someone you've just met to a wedding,' she said suspiciously. 'I barely know you. I can't remember your name.'

'Ivan Gregory,' he said. 'We met at my garage.'

'I know where we met,' she said hastily. 'So, why are you here asking me out? Did your girlfriend dump you because of your awful practical jokes?' Even as she said it, she knew it was bitchy and not worthy of either her or poor Ivan. But he took it well.

'No,' he said, 'she dumped me because of the body odour. Every Christmas I got deodorant, aftershave, washing powder. I think finally she realised the message wasn't getting through.'

'All right,' said Maggie, grinning in spite of herself. 'Go on, what's the real reason? You don't turn up at your cousin's wedding with a woman no one in your family knows and nobody has ever heard of.'

'They're a bit mad in my family,' Ivan said, with a glint in his eyes. 'They won't mind. They'll be astonished that a jumped-up pump jockey has a date at all.'

Maggie flushed at that, remembering what she'd called him before. She'd better rethink her original evaluation. He was anything but stupid.

'Are we going to the whole wedding?' Maggie asked. 'The church, the dinner, the whole thing? Because if we are and it's fancy, I have to tell you, I don't do fancy. I'm more of a jeans woman.'

'I don't do fancy very well myself,' Ivan said gravely. 'Although I was going to make an exception in this case. Maybe buy a new pair of overalls. But the rock chick look would be fine.' He flicked an appreciative eye over her outfit, which was Maggie's standard look of jeans, cowboy boots and a peach-coloured T-shirt that clung to her slim body and showed off the rich russet of her trailing curls. Her new business jacket was slung over one shoulder. 'Be yourself,' he said.

Now Maggie really did laugh. 'Be yourself is one of those things people say when they don't really mean it and they don't know what else to say.'

'No,' said Ivan, with all seriousness. 'I mean it: be yourself. What else would you be?'

Maggie thought of all the different people she tried to be in her life. At school, she'd tried to blend in so nobody would notice her. Eventually, she tried to be tough, because invisible hadn't worked. Tough had been a good compromise. People left you alone if you were a bit tough.

She'd been working that whole 'don't mess with me' phase when she'd met Grey. She toned it down, then, becoming softer, letting her hair grow the way Grey loved. In other words, she'd been what she thought everyone wanted. And here was a man who wanted her to be herself.

Well, she might as well give it a try. After all, she had nothing very pressing to do.

'OK,' she said. 'I'll come with you. Not as a date, right?' The new improved Maggie, chairwoman of an important committee and worthy foil of politicians, said what she meant these days.

'No,' agreed Ivan easily, 'not as a date.'

Maggie didn't pursue why he needed somebody at such short notice. There was bound to be a story in it, but she'd find out later. 'You'll pick me up then on Saturday?'

'Your house at two?' he said.

'Done,' Maggie said, 'and I won't be wearing a hat.'

'A hat's not required.'

For a wedding she didn't want to go to, where she was going to meet lots of people she didn't know, Maggie found herself remarkably involved in trying to work out what to wear. On Friday evening, her mother sat on the bed and they went through all the various options.

'A little dress always works,' said Shona on the phone earlier when asked for advice, 'but then you don't have any little dresses, do you?'

'Shona, you know my wardrobe,' Maggie said. 'The last time there was a little dress in it, I was four. Although Mum probably still has the item in question stuffed up in the attic, I am unlikely to fit into it.'

'What about the bridesmaid's dress you wore to my wedding?'

'There is that,' Maggie conceded, 'but it's very glamorous and over the top for a man I don't know. I can't wear that.'

'Oh God, I don't know,' groaned Shona. 'Ring me when you're sorting through the clothes and I'll give advice.'

'Trinny and Susannah by phone?'

'Maybe not,' agreed Shona. 'Wear lots of lipstick, then. It'll detract from the jeans.'

'I have more than jeans, you know. I have other trousers too.'

'I know, but unless the trousers are part of a chic trouser suit with a matching jacket, then you're not going to be very weddingy, are you?'

'What do you think of this?' Maggie asked her mother, holding up a midnight-blue silk camisole, with sparkly, fake jewels sewn on the front. A thrift-shop purchase, it was a little worn around the edges but Maggie liked it.

'That's lovely,' sighed her mother. 'It's pretty. Now, what will you wear with it?'

There followed a big search through the piles of jeans, smaller pile of black trousers and Maggie's two skirts. One was a distressed velvet affair that had possibly once been brown and was now mottled and faded, in a way that was either fabulously beautiful or totally shabby, Maggie wasn't sure which.

'I don't know about that now,' said Una doubtfully. 'If it was fancy dress, that would be great but . . . Well, try it on anyway and we'll see.'

'Cinderella, before the transformation by the fairy godmother,' Maggie decided, when she'd pulled on the skirt.

'Oh, now, don't say that,' chided her mother. 'With a bit of make-up and if you curl your hair up, you'll be the belle of the ball.'

'Mum, I think that fall affected your brain,' teased Maggie, stripping off.

Her mother laughed. 'That's what your father says. How would he know, that's what I say! Now look at that lovely skirt.'

She pulled out Maggie's only other skirt, which Grey had once urged her to buy. A fitted pencil skirt that showed off her long, slim legs, she had worn it only once, for the purpose of Grey removing it.

'That'd look beautiful on you, Maggie. You never show off your legs.'

'I don't know,' said Maggie reluctantly, because there was a very good reason why she didn't show off her legs, which was that people would look at them. 'Anyway, I've no tights.' What would you need tights for if you didn't wear skirts?

'I'll get you some of mine,' volunteered her mother, hobbling off on her crutches at speed.

Finally, there were the beginnings of an outfit.

Maggie barely recognised this slim girl in the mirror with the long, long legs encased in sheer nylons and the sleek skirt clinging to her hips.

A memory came to her, a harsh, bullying voice telling her she was ugly, *a long streak of misery, like a boy*. Those taunts had had their effect: for years, Maggie had believed them. And yet now, she looked all right, didn't she?

'I suppose a white blouse maybe?' she said, unsure.

'You'll look like a waitress,' said her mother. 'No, it has to be colour. What's wrong with the midnight-blue camisole?'

'No,' said Maggie, thinking that she'd look totally unlike herself then with shoulders and throat on show as well as her legs. 'I wish I had someone to borrow something off.'

'Pity Elisabeth's in Seattle,' said her mother. 'She always has amazing clothes, all designer stuff too, you know. And if you had kept in touch with some of the girls from school, you'd be able to ring them up and borrow clothes off them too.'

'Yeah,' said Maggie shortly. She put the camisole back on.

'You look beautiful,' sighed her mother. 'I'll get out my marcasite earrings and necklace for you and Ivan won't be able to take his eyes off you.'

'He's only asking me because his date did a runner,' Maggie pointed out, not entirely correctly. It was what she'd said to her parents to explain how she'd happened to be invited to a wedding by a man none of them knew.

'Well, it'll get you out of the house and over that horrible old Grey,' said her mother, firmly. 'The louser. If your father ever gets his hands on Grey Stanley, well, let me tell you: we'll need bail money, that's all I'm saying.'

Saturday morning in the library flew by. They were incredibly busy and Maggie didn't have a moment to mull over her pleasure that she had a date for the rest of the afternoon. Still, it was nice to be able to answer, 'Yes, I'm going out to a wedding,' when people asked her what she was doing with her half-day off.

Better than saying, 'No, I'm going to sit at home and mope about my ex-boyfriend who bonked someone else.' Definitely, a social life made you feel more positive. She'd got up early and washed her hair and even put some of that curl separator stuff in, so that it was now lots of rippling, glossy waves, instead of the usual faintly frizzy curls.

'You look lovely,' said Tina as they rushed about behind the desk. 'Is your man from Galway coming back?'

'No, actually,' murmured Maggie. 'It's a different guy altogether.'

Tina looked impressed. 'I'm pleased for you. I mean he seemed lovely, your man, and everything, but . . .' she stopped.

'But what?' asked Maggie, fascinated.

'He was a bit too pleased with himself, wasn't he? Those gorgeous fellas always are. No one will ever love him quite as much as he loves himself.'

Maggie grinned. 'I think you hit the nail on the head there, Tina,' she said. 'It's one thing competing with other women, but you can't compete with the guy himself, can you?'

'You said it,' replied Tina, in a voice that said she knew what she was talking about.

Funny, thought Maggie, turning back to the desk, who would have thought that sedate Tina had a big history of men behind her? But you never knew. Everybody had secrets and dramas in their lives, they just didn't wear them on their faces.

Maggie had just come back from her coffee break and was making her way back to the library desk, when she realised with a shock that she recognised a woman who had just walked in. Billie Deegan, one of the bullying gang of girls who'd made Maggie's life hell.

Billie had never been as bad as the gang leader, Sandra Brody. But just seeing her made fifteen years drop away. Maggie felt the way she always had: her intestines literally churning with fear, her heart thumping, her hands clammy.

Billie was holding a small boy's hand and seemed totally and utterly oblivious of Maggie. Her hairstyle, her expression, were exactly the same as they'd been all those years ago when she'd swiped Maggie's school bag and tossed it to Sandra, laughing like a hyena as Sandra tipped the contents over the playground.

Unable to stop herself, Maggie ducked in behind a shelf, heart pounding, and listened.

'Now, love,' Billie said to the boy, 'we've got to be out of the library in five minutes. Come on, pick a book, will you? We can't be here all day, we're going to meet Daddy. He'll go mad if we're late, you know what he's like.' The boy stood looking lost. 'Oh, come on now! Hurry up!'

Leaning against a shelf, knowing it was ridiculous to feel the fear still, Maggie lived again those four years of hell. Even now, she couldn't quite explain how it made her feel, how frightened, how despairing. There was a brief time when Sandra's game was stealing and vandalising her possessions, when she'd wondered if killing herself was an option.

At least then she wouldn't be picked on. At least then she wouldn't wake up on a Monday morning with sheer dread in every atom of her being.

Sometimes now she read articles in the newspaper about bullying. The reporters who had written them had never been victims themselves, she could tell. They wrote about it as if it were a minor blip, something that occurred a couple of hours every day and then you'd move on to another part of your life. Those writers never realised that the bullying *became* your life, took hold of it, destroyed you.

'Maggie,' said Tina loudly, indicating the queue. 'We need you over here, sorry. I'm on the phone.'

Maggie took a deep breath and almost ran to the safety of the desk. Automatically, she stamped books, smiling at the children and their parents, saying things like 'The Narnia books are fabulous. I loved them when I was little, still reread them.'

And the children would grin and their parents would grin even more, glad to see their kids reading.

Tina was on the phone again, trying to tell some woman that the Jacqueline Wilson still hadn't come in. The queue was getting shorter, bringing Billie closer to Maggie.

Get off the phone, please, Tina, Maggie thought in anguish. Please get off the phone and deal with this woman. There were two more to go before Billie and her son now.

Peering up surreptitiously, Maggie watched her. Yes, Billie looked exactly the same, still hard and still with that dead-straight platinum-blonde haircut, probably not dyed at home any more, and the heavy eyeliner ringing her eyes into two cold slits of muddy blue. She and Sandra had been the eyeliner queens of St Ursula's, even when make-up was forbidden. They hadn't paid attention to the rules, naturally: rules were for other people.

Her clothes were remarkably normal: a long-sleeved top and pale trousers, none of them ripped or bearing a rude logo. That had been another of Billie and Sandra's idiosyncrasies. Outside school, they'd favoured tiny T-shirts, ripped leather jackets, tight pale-blue jeans and high-heeled boots. The punk slut look, Maggie's friend, Kitty, called it.

She and Maggie loved that name: being able to call the bullies something rude. It gave them a tiny, welcome sense of power. It was a shame when Kitty's family had moved away.

'Now, Jimmy, give the woman your book and we'll get out of here,' said Billie.

Maggie had no option. Keeping her eyes down, she scanned the book number, stamped it and handed it to the child, not saying one word.

'Thank you,' the woman said. 'Jimmy, say thank you.'

Maggie was gobsmacked. Thank you hadn't been in Billie's vocabulary when Maggie knew her.

'Thank you,' said Jimmy obediently.

He was eight or nine, Maggie reckoned, so Billie must have got pregnant soon enough after they'd left school. For a flicker of a moment, she wondered if Billie's life had been hard at that time, then dismissed it: Billie Deegan didn't need her pity.

'Come on, Jimmy, we'd better go,' and without exchanging one single glance with Maggie, Billie marched him out of the library.

There was a small stool behind the counter and Maggie sank on to it. Only days before, she'd spoken to Christie Devlin about laying her demons to rest and now, here was one of the bullies in her life. That bitch. Maggie hated her with a venom time hadn't diminished and, yet, Billie had strolled in happily, smiling, lively, as if she had no idea what she'd done, what she and her mocking pals had done to Maggie's life. How could she not know?

'Tina,' Maggie said urgently, 'I just feel sick, can I run to the loo for one minute?'

Tina, who had just replaced the phone, nodded. Maggie fled to the staff toilets where she locked herself in a cubicle, sat down on a seat and held her face in her hands. She could feel her cheeks burning and still, that familiar ache in her intestines. Sandra and her cronies had always been a cure for constipation. Rage, anger, impotence and fury flooded through Maggie. Laying your demons to rest was one thing but why now, why today?

Maggie had cleaned up the mascara that she had cried down her cheeks and reapplied more by the time Ivan arrived at the house to pick her up.

'Hello, Maggie,' he said, admiring her outfit. 'You look great.'

He looked pretty good too, all spruced up in a suit and tie.

'Thanks,' said Maggie shortly. She had read a book once about accepting compliments and apparently you had to say, 'Thank you, that's lovely,' instead of 'Oh, this old thing, I've had it for a hundred years,' or 'My boyfriend gave me this skirt and I never normally wear it.'

They got into Ivan's car, which was suitably Ivan, being a classic something or other. Maggie knew nothing about cars but it had to be old, what with the ancient dashboard and seats that looked like they came from a 1960s art installation.

He was playing classical music, Dvořák, if Maggie could remember anything from her music classes, a million years ago.

'That isn't the music I pictured you listening to,' she said.

'No?' he said good humouredly. 'What did you think? I'd be a Guns N' Roses sort of guy, one of those dudes who plays air guitar and dances with his legs spread apart, shaking his head.'

As this was an accurate assessment of what she'd thought of Ivan the first time she'd met him, she didn't reply to that but said: 'Lots of people aren't into classical music any more.'

'My mother taught piano,' he said. 'I grew up with music. It lifts me.'

'My dad's the same,' she replied. 'He went through a classical music phase. There were phases for everything. Phases for learning about stars and phases for learning about classical music. He's into opera too. I quite like it as well, but not played full blast, which is how Dad says you have to play it. His current phase is model-making. Planes and boats.'

'That sounds nice,' said Ivan. 'I like the idea of being a model-maker myself.'

He was easy company, Maggie thought. She didn't have to make an effort to be scintillating or funny. She just had to be. Sit there in the car and let the conversation roll on, or not, as the case may be. Ivan was quite happy to let the strains of Dvořák glide over them. Undemanding, that was it. Grey had been demanding, she realised suddenly.

She'd never had anything to compare him to but Ivan was so relaxed, the contrast showed Grey up.

'You're not quite yourself today,' Ivan said abruptly, putting the kibosh on the judgement.

'What do you mean?' she asked defensively.

'You've been crying.'

She flipped down the passenger visor and looked into the mirror. She'd cleaned away all the mascara, but her eyes were a teeny bit red.

'Most guys wouldn't have noticed,' she said.

'I'm not most guys,' he replied. 'Do you want to talk?'

'No,' she said firmly. 'I don't.'

But she couldn't stop thinking about her shock that morning. The worst thing about it was that she had been made to realise that she hadn't got over being bullied, not one little bit. And that made her conscious that the past would always imprison her unless she did something about it. But what?

It was a very modern wedding, although nobody seemed to have told the majority of the guests. The women, decked out in floral frocks, hats like galleons perched on their heads, with fluffy feather boas, dainty jewelled handbags and shoes in summery colours, all stared aghast at the bridal party who might have come straight out of Italian *Vogue* in their shades of cream and slate grey.

The bride wore a cream shift, so simple it looked as though Maggie herself could have run it up on her mother's old Singer machine, although it was so stylish the label undoubtedly proclaimed it as a piece of designer art from a Milanese atelier.

The groom wore a Nehru-collared suit in slate with his groomsmen similarly attired and the bridesmaids wore slate-grey shift dresses, with tiny posies of cream roses.

'Very hip and trendy,' Maggie said, trying to find the right thing to say.

'Where are the frills?' a woman in the pew beside her was wailing. 'What's the point in getting married if you can't have frills and flowers and . . . look at that for a bouquet, one hopeless flower. Desperate, that's what it is.'

The bride indeed carried only one flower, although Maggie wouldn't have called it hopeless, but she had never been a fan of those birds of paradise blooms. It looked like a plant that had somehow eaten a passing bird.

'Well, it's what they wanted, obviously,' she said to the woman beside her.

'You're very diplomatic,' said Ivan. 'I hate it.'

'I didn't think you had any interest in high fashion at all,' she teased him. 'I thought your only cosmetic interest would be in whatever miracle product you use to get the grease out of your hands after a day in the garage.'

'You mean after a day of honest, hard labour?' he said, holding up hands that were spotlessly clean.

Without thinking, Maggie took one of them to examine it. 'How do you manage that? If I do any painting or anything in the apartment, I'm filthy for days. You can't get stuff like that off your hands. What do you use?'

'Trade secret,' he murmured, 'but I might be prepared to reveal it to the right person.'

She dropped his hand quickly.

At the reception, they were at a table made up of various cousins, which included Ivan's brother, Leon, who looked a lot like Ivan, although Leon had more of a wolfish look to his face, as if he might pounce at any moment.

'Where has my big bro been hiding you?' he said to Maggie.

'Leave her alone,' said Ivan, good-naturedly. 'Leon's always wanted everything of mine,' he added to Maggie. 'Trains, toy soldiers, whatever.'

She was about to say, sharply, that she didn't belong to Ivan, therefore it was immaterial whether Leon wanted her or not, but for some reason she didn't. Instead, she talked to the cousin on the other side, a seventeen-year-old boy who'd brought along his girlfriend but who was clearly desperately shy, amidst all these idolised big cousins.

343

It was a wonderful day. Maggie normally enjoyed weddings about as much as she enjoyed twenty-four-hour migraines, but this one was different. Despite the bridal party stylefest, everyone else at the wedding was comfortingly ordinary. Most people were out to have fun – a few mad uncles throwing shapes on the dance floor, somebody grabbing the mike from the DJ to belt out 'Fever' off key and a gaggle of wildly sophisticated young girls, dancing together, looking horrified at the carryings-on of the older generation.

'Appalling!' Maggie heard one of them mutter. 'What will people think?'

'Were you like that once?' Ivan asked Maggie, watching her watching the girls dancing.

She was startled: she hadn't realised he was so close to her. People had moved seats after the meal and she'd turned hers so that she could look at the dance floor, which meant that she didn't really have to talk to anybody.

'No,' she said, caught off her guard. 'I was the ultimate uncool girl.'

'Really?' he said.

'Yeah, really,' she said.

'What about you?' she asked, just to shift the subject slightly.

'It seems so long ago, I can't remember,' he said thoughtfully, and Maggie figured out it had probably been great for him. People who didn't remember generally had enjoyed good school days. The awful stuff you didn't forget.

He added, 'I'm a few years older than you, thirty-seven next birthday.'

'Is your biological clock ticking then?' Maggie asked wickedly. 'Well, that's what thirty-six-year-old women get asked, it seems only fair to return the compliment.'

'I'm a mechanic,' Ivan said gravely. 'If anything starts ticking, I fix it, you know that.'

He persuaded her up to dance, but she only said yes because it was a fast dance, one where they could move without touching.

Not that there was something wrong with Ivan. In fact, there was absolutely nothing wrong with him from the top of his cropped dark head to his surprisingly elegant leather shoes. She was sure plenty of women longed to be in her place and she'd seen a few eyes cast enviously in their direction during the day. Well, they could have him, no matter how gorgeous he was. He wasn't for her. She didn't want any man.

'I hope you enjoyed yourself,' he said that night as he dropped her home.

They sat in the car outside her house, the engine growling while Maggie picked up her small handbag from the floor. 'Yes, I did. Thank you for asking me.'

'I wondered because you seemed to be in another place a lot of the time,' Ivan said gently. 'I hope everything's all right. If there is anything I can do to help . . .' His voice trailed off.

Maggie felt embarrassed that he'd noticed.

'I'm fine,' she said. 'Sorry, I didn't mean to spoil the party.'

'You didn't spoil it,' he said, smiling at her, those dark eyes glinting under the streetlights. 'You were lovely, they all liked you.'

'Who are they?' she asked.

The smile turned wolfish, like Leon's had been, and she could certainly see why the envious looks had been cast in their direction all day. When he smiled like that, sexily, Ivan was pretty irresistible.

'All my relatives. They were watching you surreptitiously. You didn't happen to see the big notice board in the hall with people giving you marks out of ten on performance, deportment, dressage –'

'Stop it,' she said, laughing. 'OK then, how did I score?'

He appeared to think about this. 'Pretty good from all I hear, although there was some talk about the fact that you didn't throw your arms around me or kiss me enough. Or that we didn't dance any slow dances together.'

Maggie felt embarrassed again, this time for a different reason. 'We weren't going as a couple,' she reminded him, although she felt strangely pleased that he might have wanted this.

'I know that,' he agreed, 'but you can't stop the relatives talking, can you? Any woman who appears on the horizon, they're hoping I'll slip a wedding ring on her finger. And don't forget, as you've pointed out yourself, my biological clock is ticking.'

'Oh, shut up, Ivan,' laughed Maggie and she leaned over and kissed him on the cheek, her lips brushing the faintest hint of stubble. 'I'll talk to you soon,' she said, and got out of the car.

He didn't drive off until she'd opened the door, stepped inside and waved at him from the lit hallway. He was a gentleman, he hadn't tried to pounce on her, he behaved exactly as he said he would behave, she thought. She liked Ivan and, as Faye said, she could do with a friend. But for the moment, she told herself firmly, as she got ready for bed, that was all.

# CHAPTER TWENTY-THREE

The night before she went to see Carey Wolensky, Christie cooked the most beautiful dinner for her husband she had ever cooked in her life. She put everything into it that he loved, along with herbs, carefully tended from her own garden, and thirty-five years of love, affection, kindness and gratefulness. As she cooked, Tilly wound herself around Christie's ankles, clearly in one of her 'pet me, pet me' moods, making little whimpering noises occasionally. Christie bent and stroked the dog's pansy-soft head many times. She adored Rocket but had to admit that Tilly was, ever so slightly, her favourite. Tilly loved Christie above everyone else in the world and there was something so very wonderful about any creature who loved you with that unconditional love.

She felt a little like a white witch cooking up a spell of love in her kitchen with her familiar, gorgeous Tilly, weaving in and out of her ankles, and her modern cooker in place of the kind white witch's fireplace. Was she cooking up a meal to ask forgiveness for what would happen afterwards or to ward off anything bad happening at all? Christie didn't know which.

'Wow, that all smells amazing,' said James, coming downstairs and dropping his report on the kitchen table. Going over to the cooker, he put his hands around Christie's waist and leaned over her shoulder, giving her a gentle kiss on the cheek, before peering down to see exactly what she was making.

'Is that roast vegetable soup?' he said. 'I love that, but you said it's such a pain to make.'

'No, I didn't,' said Christie, 'it's just a little time-consuming, that's all. I felt like making soup today.'

'Absolutely,' agreed James, leaning over a bit further so he could inhale the rich scent, 'and why not. It's a gloriously hot, sunny day and roasted vegetable soup is exactly the sort of thing I had on my mind tonight.'

'Brat,' she said, laughing. 'I cook you one of your favourite things and you don't appreciate it.'

'I'm teasing,' he said. He moved away, stifling a large yawn. 'I'm wrecked. If we don't get this report finished soon, I'll retire early, I'm telling you.'

He sat down in his usual seat at the kitchen table and picked up the newspaper which was folded at the crossword.

'I got most of it done earlier but I'm stuck on eleven down,' he said. 'I'm having a mental block – it's the name of that Nathaniel Hawthorne novel: Hawthorne's red message, the clue is . . .'

'*The Scarlet Letter*,' said Christie faintly, thinking of Hester Prynne forced to wear a big red A on her chest as a sign of her adultery.

'Ah, that's it!' James said. 'Thank God I married a clever wife.'

'Yes,' she said. How did people do it – conduct full-blown affairs without dying of pain and guilt and shame? It was beyond her.

She had set up a table outside in the garden and they ate on the terrace with the dogs at their feet, the scent of Christie's flowers mingling with the scent of the food. After the roasted vegetable soup came dressed crab, another of James's favourites and a rarity in the Devlin house because crab was expensive and Christie didn't like to buy it dressed, preferring to do it herself. It was cheaper but there was still a lot of palaver about it.

'You're not leaving me are you?' joked James, when pudding arrived and it turned out to be crème brûlé, his absolute, all-time favourite.

'No,' said Christie, managing a smile. She'd recovered her equilibrium somewhat thanks to two glasses of lovely wine. 'I just can't wait for the exams to be over and life can go back to normal.'

'So this is the almost-the-end-of-exams party?' James teased.

'Yes,' Christie replied, as if it had all been perfectly obvious. 'And can I not cook you a beautiful meal without there having to be a reason?' she demanded. 'Are you implying I am such a slatternly housekeeper that you have beans on toast every night, unless I'm running off with the milkman?' There, she'd made a joke about it.

'No darling, sorry,' James said. 'I didn't mean that at all. You're amazing, you know that? I always think you're an amazing woman, Christie, and I hope I say it often enough – after thirty-five years it's easy enough to forget to say it, but you are. It was a lucky day, the day I met you.'

'Oh, stop,' she said, afraid she might burst into tears.

'No, I mean it,' James said gravely.

When dinner was over, they sat in the garden for a while, talking, finishing the bottle of wine, watching dusk darken into night. Then they cleared up and went up to bed. Christie loved their bedroom. As a child, she and Ana had shared a cold hard little room with bare walls because their father hated nails knocked into the walls in case they damaged the plaster. So nothing could ever be hung to offset the pale-blue gloom. There had never been any money for furbelows, either, so the curtains were basic bits of cloth to keep the light out, and the furniture did nothing more than hold clothes. There was no beauty, no piece of art just for the sake of it, like a pretty vase or a picture.

By contrast, this room was a comfortable, beautiful room full of lovely pieces with no use whatsoever except to be looked at, like the driftwood Christie and James had found on a beach in Connemara thirty years ago and hung on one wall, or the vintage fan that dangled from the mantelpiece as if just left there by some elegant lady of the past.

Dominating this bower of lovely comforting things was a huge bed, where Christie had sat with her sons and James, all cuddled up in the mornings. It was where she'd lain with baby Shane and breast-fed him, Ethan sitting on the bed, playing with his toys, grumbling about not getting enough attention sometimes. Other times, he'd tried to cuddle up on top of Shane and Christie, making her laugh and making baby Shane squeal in outrage. And in this bed, she and James had made love countless times over the years.

James was very laid-back about decor and had always left it up to Christie, saying he hadn't minded whatever she did. Now, the room was full of rich autumnal colours, with a huge patchwork spread in rust, copper and old gold made up in satins and velvets swathing the bed. Tonight, they pulled back the covers, sank into the sheets and James pulled her into his arms. Christie had never, or rarely, felt like crying when she made love. Sometimes the intensity of the moment would make her eyes well up afterwards as they lay there and she thought of how wonderful it was, that perfect closeness from being with someone you loved. But tonight, every caress, every kiss, every erotic touch, made her long to cry with the meaning of it all. Because this might be the last time she and James ever made love.

When he traced a line down from her neck to the softness of her breasts – once so full and high and now, a lifetime and children later, lower, less firm, but just as beautiful in his eyes, or so he always said – she felt as if she would start to weep and not stop. As he kissed her, she felt the unbearable poignancy of doing something she loved and might lose. The last kiss, the last caress, the last time his familiar body entered hers. She knew the noises James made when he climaxed, the same way she knew her own face in the mirror, the same way she was sure he knew the small sounds she made in passion.

And then they held each other, and the tears came. She couldn't help herself, she couldn't hold them back. She'd been holding everything back all evening, thinking everything was the last time.

'Darling, are you all right?' asked James.

'I'm fine,' Christie said, her face against his shoulder, their bodies still joined. 'I'm fine, just, that was so beautiful.' And they lay there, holding each other until eventually she could hear her husband's breathing getting heavier and she knew he had fallen asleep.

She slipped away from him gently, so as not to wake him, and went into the bathroom to clean her face and wipe away the ravages of the tears. Looking in the mirror, she saw a woman who had everything and didn't deserve it. In that moment she hated herself.

Sometimes, the ordinary and the everyday was boring. When she was younger, Christie used to long for the extraordinary, something different to happen in Kilshandra, something to shake them all up and make life thrilling.

Yearning for excitement was definitely for young people, she decided, as she closed her door the next morning and looked out across Summer Street to the park. Once you had tasted extraordinary and the dangers it brought, you longed for the familiar and you thought how precious that was.

Today, she yearned for the mundane because today, she was going to see Carey Wolensky.

She walked more slowly up Summer Street than usual because she was wearing high heels. Against all her better judgement, she had decided to show off her still-good legs in high shoes and her figure in a wrap dress that clung in all the right places, with a necklace of larger-than-life pearls that hid the creeping at her throat. She wondered if he'd think her beautiful still or would he think that time had been very cruel.

'Hello, Christie, how are you?' yelled Una Maguire from her front garden where she was directing operations, with Dennis on his knees, weeding. Poor Dennis hadn't a clue about the garden, Christie knew. It was only sheer love of his wife that had him out there at all, poking around in the earth with all the vision of a mole.

'Where are you off to? Into town shopping?'

'Yes, shopping,' said Christie, because after all she was dressed very grandly for such an hour on a Monday. If it wasn't for the height of her heels and the silky sheerness of her stockings, a person might have thought she was on her way to see her bank manager, but no bank manager merited such a slinky outfit.

'How's your leg?' Christie paused outside Una's gate, not having the time to go in, but wanting to be sociable.

'Not so bad now. Before you know it, the cast will be off and I'll be a new woman.'

Would she? Christie wondered, getting that sense she had before of Una's bones as fragile and lacy, instead of strong and firm.

'You should take care of yourself, Una,' she said, sternly.

'Oh, I have Dennis to take care of me,' Una said happily. 'Don't I, love?'

Dennis nodded enthusiastically.

'How's Maggie?' asked Christie, because she knew that

352

Maggie was the person who did the real taking care of in that house.

'She's in good form, you know,' Una said. 'Very busy with the committee. You wouldn't believe all she's organised – publicity, an official complaint to the council and they're getting legal advice too. It's all go.'

Christie waved goodbye to the Maguires and headed past the café, which seemed unbearably comforting and homely this morning. Wouldn't it have been nice if it was a normal day, before all this had happened, when she could sit there, eating a scone, chatting with people, thinking about her nice, safe simple life ahead of her? Life before Carey had come back.

Christie did not frequent many of the city's grand hotels, but her very presence was commanding enough, so that when she walked into Carey's hotel, a stately block that overlooked the best square in Dublin, people looked up.

'May I help you, madam?' The young woman at the desk inclined her head graciously, like minor royalty greeting somebody.

'Yes, I have a meeting with Mr Wolensky,' Christie said coolly, hoping she looked like some important art dealer, rather than a woman with a past. 'Mrs Devlin,' she added, with a regal nod of her own. Christie didn't play games but she didn't suffer snubs either.

'Oh, yes, Mr Wolensky's waiting for you in the Maharajah Suite. Shall I get somebody to show you up?'

The receptionist's attitude had changed at the mention of Carey's name. Clearly he was just as good as he'd ever been at knocking pretension out of those around him, although he probably did it with money and power now, when once he'd done it with charisma and sheer animal presence.

'That would be good, thank you,' Christie said, as if every morning of her life involved being shown into the Maharajah Suite.

A young uniformed man escorted her up five floors in the lift and into an ornate corridor where they passed several doors bearing the names of long-dead dukes and countesses before arriving at the Maharajah Suite. A second young man opened the door and brought Christie into a huge drawing room, decorated in the eastern style.

'Tea, coffee or would you prefer something else?' he asked.

'Coffee please,' Christie said, thinking that this was getting even more bizarre.

She sat on the edge of a fat, bronze-coloured armchair with her coffee in her hand and looked around. It was an opulent room full of plump brocade cushions, rich dark splashes of fabric and vast creamy candles that had never been burned. It all screamed money, good taste and phenomenal success. What a different life Carey had led to hers.

And then, a door to the right opened and he was there in front of her.

'Hello, Christie,' he said and his voice was just the same, with the same power to thrill her, but his face was different.

He'd aged too. There was no Dorian Gray portrait in his attic. He was still tall and vibrantly alive, but now the dark hair was streaked like a magpie's with brilliant white and his face was craggy, with heavy lines where there had been smooth skin, and he had a sadness about him that spoke volumes.

'Hello, Carey,' said Christie, thinking how stupid it sounded. Twenty-five years of waiting and at least six weeks of having panic attacks about this very moment, and the best she could manage was 'Hello, Carey.'

'It's a beautiful room.' She got up and walked over to the window, to give herself something to do. She didn't really see the streets below her.

'You haven't changed,' he said. His accent was still the same: deep and dark, the Polish edge as strong and caressing as ever.

Christie turned around when she judged it was safe to do

so. 'Of course I've changed, Carey. I'm older and wiser and so are you, I hope. So tell me, tell me about your life.'

She sat down on one of the Louis XIV chairs as if they were ordinary old friends meeting up after many years to chat happily about acquaintances, times past and the fun they used to have. If she kept it at that level, then the conversation might stay there, might never stray into the terrifying territory of love, lust and passion.

'You're talking to me strangely,' he said, sitting down opposite her. 'What is this chatter? *How are you?*' he said, 'like we were strangers.'

'You know that was always one of the annoying things about you, Carey,' she said, 'you always refused to play the games, the games other people played.'

'You mean like pretending that we are just old friends, who mean nothing to one another?' he asked. 'You're right, I never played the games, and I still made it.'

'You made it because of your talent,' she retorted. 'It was nothing to do with your rudeness.'

'If speaking the truth is rude,' he said calmly, 'I'd prefer to live my life that way, not to lie, not to push the past away, like you're doing.'

'Well, that didn't take long,' Christie said and realised she'd spoken out loud. 'We're four minutes in each other's company and already all the façade is gone.' And she smiled at him, because it was impossible not to.

'That is one of the things I liked about you, Christie,' he said. 'You were not good at pretending either. You tried to be, but you were not good.'

'No,' she said quickly, 'I wasn't good at the pretence. Carey, why did you come back?' she said abruptly, and that was the right thing to say because it was what she'd wanted to know.

'I came to have an exhibition here, you know that.'

She searched his eyes for answers. Years ago, he'd been

good at hiding what he was feeling, but now Christie was older and wiser, she felt she'd be able to discern what he was really thinking.

'No, you didn't,' she said suddenly. 'Tell me the truth, why did you come?'

'I came to see you,' he said.

She'd known that was what he was going to say. She had never forgotten him and it seemed that he'd never forgotten her either.

'Oh, Carey, Carey,' she sighed, 'I told you a long time ago that you had to go away, for my sake, for both our sakes.'

'I just wanted to see you,' he said gently, 'to see what you looked like now, to see if you still had the power you had over me. And you do, it seems. You've seen the paintings?'

It was a question and she nodded.

'They're you, you know, all those paintings, my dark lady.'

'I'd worked that out,' Christie said carefully, 'and it frightened me, because I was afraid everyone would know and would guess it was me.'

'I never showed your face,' he said.

'I know, thank you. I was always grateful for that.'

'I could have, you know. I could have shown your face and broken up your marriage and you would have come to me.' There was real pain in his voice for the first time and Christie wanted to hold him and comfort him, but she knew she couldn't. She had never been able to touch him without feeling that flood of wild passion surge through her. It was a thing apart, a feeling she'd never been able to control. He was that other part of her, the fierce, wild side. And she'd had to give him up.

Now she picked up her coffee cup again. 'It would never have worked, you knew that. You didn't want a wife and two children tagging around behind you. That's not the life of an artist. And I had to think of my children first. I wanted my sons to know their father. If you and I had been together,

356

they wouldn't have known James, not properly, and they wouldn't have had you either. Quiet family life was never your destiny. Your only mistress is your art.'

Sadness flitted across his face.

'That was true once,' he admitted, 'but it wouldn't have been the case if I'd had you. I loved you more than art, I could have given it up for you.'

'And made yourself unhappy not doing the thing you loved just so you could be with me? How would that have felt after a few years? You'd have resented me for ever,' Christie said. 'There was only one solution, Carey, you must see that,' she begged.

There was a long pause, a pause filled with all the what-ifs that two people can contemplate over twenty-five years.

'Why did you come here this morning,' he said, 'if this is all you want to say to me?'

'I came,' Christie said, and it was hard to say now that she was here, but she had to bury the ghosts, 'I came because I wanted to end it fully, to say everything I never said before. I needed to make sure that you didn't have the power or the desire to hurt me or my family because of what happened a long time ago. That's why I'm here.'

'Do you want a drink?' he said, and got up to move to a sideboard behind them, where a full bar was laid out with proper crystal glass decanters.

Not your average minibar for him, Christie thought.

'No,' she said, 'thank you. I don't want anything.'

He fixed himself something dark and amber-coloured in a tumbler, then another for her and laid it in front of her without saying a word.

'You followed my career?' he asked.

'No,' she said, making a hopeless attempt at pretending she had never thought about him when there were times when he'd filled her thoughts to the exclusion of everything else.

'You're lying,' he said, sitting down opposite her again, leaning forward. 'I could always tell when you were lying. There's a faint flicker of one of your eyelids, it's a giveaway: a tell, they call it in poker. I play poker now, you know.'

'Is this your poker face?' Christie asked and it was like a fencing match, him parrying, she keeping him back.

'No, this is not my poker face, but you have followed my career, haven't you?'

'Yes, all right, I have. I teach art, you know that. I couldn't teach art, talk to my students about modern art without mentioning Carey Wolensky.'

'But,' he interrupted, 'you never talked to them about the dark lady and who she is?'

'Oh, for heaven's sake,' Christie said with irritation and, unthinkingly, picked up the glass of whiskey and downed half of it. It burned her throat as it went down. But there was something about that harsh violence hitting the back of her throat that brought her to her senses and stopped her playing a game with him. 'How do you think I'm going to tell schoolgirls I teach that I'm the dark lady, that the woman who stands there naked in every bloody picture was me? Do a lot for my teaching career, that would, not to mention what it would do for my marriage.'

'I like you better when you're angry,' he said, sitting back and smiling at her, looking relaxed for the first time. 'You're too passionate to hide it, Christie. We would have been so good together.'

'No, we wouldn't,' she said. 'I have too much and I couldn't give it up and you know that.'

'I'm sorry,' he said, and she knew he was sorry because of what might have been. 'I needed to see you again, just one last time. I wanted to talk to you, look at you, remember you. I have pictures you know, but pictures don't have warmth and their eyes don't shine. I had to rely on my memories to paint

358

you. And you must admit, my memories were good, the pictures look like you, don't they? Did your husband ever notice?'

'He never noticed,' she replied. 'He's not interested in art and I thank God for that, because I love him, I always loved him.'

'If you loved him,' Carey asked, 'then what happened with me?'

It was a question that always haunted her – how could she love James, adore Ethan and Shane and then risk all that to be with this enigmatic man in front of her? There was no answer to that question. It was like asking why did the rain fall, why did the sun shine? It just happened, and she'd been swept along in the moment, a moment she'd been paying for ever since.

'Women aren't supposed to be able to love two men,' she said, 'but that's not true. I loved James and I loved you. You were a door into another me, a Christie who was wild and had nothing to hold her back. Except I had two little boys and it wasn't a simple choice of you or James. I had to choose my family and I don't regret that. I'm not trying to hurt you, I'm explaining.'

She was determined to explain to him how hard it had been walking away from him but that it had been the right thing to do, and that she'd been so happy with James and her sons. Because the Christie who'd loved Carey was like a person from another world and she'd had to bury that person deep inside her and carry on with normal life.

She looked at Carey, remembering all they'd shared, remembering the passion he'd brought up in her, remembering how she'd touched his face in the past and thought she'd die if she didn't have enough of him. She had to put it all behind her now and move on.

'In another world, Carey, in another life, you and I could have been together,' she said.

She got up and sat beside him, not feeling any danger from the closeness now. He didn't have the power to hurt her. She had made her mind up to say what had to be said. She was older and wiser so that any magnetism, any passion that there had once been between them, was now gone. And she'd paid for that bliss a million times over.

She touched his hand and she was astonished to find that his skin wasn't the warm, vibrant thing she'd remembered, but felt old and papery and thin, like he was sickening, as though he was older even than he was in years. It confused her, but she couldn't see it properly. What was hiding there?

'I'm sorry, I never meant to hurt you, Carey,' she said. 'I never meant to lead you on, to make you think we had a future, when we didn't. That's why I came to meet you, not to look back and think weren't we fabulous and wonderful, because I felt guilty every day of my life for what happened. I paid for our time together. Adultery has a price and it's too high, believe me. I want to put it behind me. Can you understand that?'

His other hand reached up to touch her face and she closed her eyes as his fingers traced the bones, stroked her cheekbones, her jaw, the hollows of her eyes, the curve of her lips, the way he'd once touched her until she thought she'd scream with desire.

'You're still beautiful,' he murmured. 'No matter what age you are, you will always be beautiful because it's in your soul and I think that's what drew me to you, Christie: your soul, your goodness and your wisdom. I missed you all this time we were apart. There have been many women and they all look like you, strange, no? But none of them was you. So that's why I came. Yes, I have an exhibition here but they ask me to have exhibitions everywhere, I can say no, I have the power. But I wanted to come here, one last time, to see you.'

'Why do you keep saying "one last time"?' she asked.

There was portent behind his words and suddenly, with a shock, she knew.

'Can't you tell?' he said, half smiling. 'You have Gypsy sight after all. I'm sick. I shouldn't be drinking.' He laughed. 'I shouldn't be doing anything. I shouldn't be flying. The doctors didn't want me to. But I can keep going on and the drugs are good. Medicine has moved on so much.'

She didn't want to ask what was killing him. 'How long do you have?' she said, evenly.

'Months, they think months. I don't know, maybe not so long, but I want to make my peace before I go. That's why I had to see you. I didn't come to destroy your world, I came to say goodbye.'

'Oh, Carey,' she sighed, taking his hand from her face and holding it tightly. 'Were you happy? Did you have a good life?'

'Yes,' he said, 'I did. I didn't have you and for a long time you were all I thought about, but an artist needs something to drive him, doesn't he? And you inspired my best work. You gave me so many things, Christie.'

'You gave me things too,' she said. 'You made me see that I could still feel passion. You made me see how much I loved my husband and my children,' she added frankly, 'and I know it probably hurts you to hear that, but that's the truth. So you gave me a huge amount and I've never forgotten you.'

'It's good then that we had this chance to say goodbye,' he said, and, suddenly, he was formal again.

Christie put her arms around him. Now she could feel the frailness of his body, hidden under the beautifully cut jacket. He was dying, she could feel it, every part of her sensed it, and it might not be long. He didn't have months at all, and he knew it, knew she'd know it too.

'Don't pity me,' he said and he laid his lips against her forehead to give her a cool, dry kiss. 'Please don't pity me, I would prefer you remembered me the way we were.'

'I understand,' she said, and she did. She got up.

'I have a small present for you,' he said. 'It may be nothing you can ever show anyone but I wanted to leave it to you. A bequest, that is the word, isn't it?' He handed her an old cardboard box, large and unwieldy. 'Someone will help you out with it. Goodbye, Christie,' he said and he turned, but not before she could see the glitter of tears in his eyes. He left the room and shut the door behind him.

In the lift down, Christie stared at the box that the bellboy held carefully. She didn't want to open it here. She waited until she got into a taxi and the bellboy had placed the box reverentially on the back seat beside her. Then she carefully removed the lid. On top was a wrapped package that contained a small artist's sketchbook, like a writer's notebook, full of pencil drawings and charcoal sketches, cartoons for paintings, ideas, thoughts that had occurred to him. It must have been the sketchbook that Carey had used when they'd met.

The first few pages were full of his trademark drawings and then the pages were pictures of a woman, who could only have been Christie, her face obscured, her body the one Christie knew well. These were the sketches for his Dark Lady paintings. The masterpieces painted by a genius whom the world would mourn when he was gone.

She turned page after page, each more beautiful, interesting, alive than the rest. Some were just pencil, others charcoal, and yet more, coloured in with subtle pastels. It was an incredible gift. The second package was a small canvas, a scaled-down version of the most beautiful of all the Dark Lady paintings. The dark lady was again lying on a divan, in a painter's studio, but in this one her face was not hidden. Her face was alive with love and it was clear she was looking at the artist. Christie gazed at it, thought of Carey and what he meant to her and what was going to happen to him now, and she cried.

# CHAPTER TWENTY-FOUR

Maggie loved the silence of the library. Ever since she'd been a child, and her father had explained why libraries were special places where you had to whisper, she'd loved the fact that the only sounds to be heard were muted whispers and the gentle rustling of pages.

'It's quiet because all the books are sitting on the shelves, snoozing quietly as they wait to be picked,' Dad had said, 'because being picked by you is the start of an amazing adventure for them.'

She'd told that story to a small group of children only that morning, and they'd stared up at her, wide-eyed, just as enthralled as she'd been by the idea of silently waiting books.

'Spot was waiting for me?' asked one small girl with glasses and a mummy-cut hairdo, who sat holding one of the Spot books on her lap.

'Yes, Spot was waiting for you!' Maggie said, thrilled at being able to pass on the message to a new generation.

'Wow,' said the little girl in awe.

'Wow,' agreed the other children.

Maggie was sitting in the small staff room having her

morning coffee and talking to Shona on the phone about the children when another call came through on her mobile.

'Hold on a second, Shona,' she said. 'I'll be right back to you, OK?'

It was Ivan.

'How's it going?' he asked in his calm way.

'Not bad,' said Maggie. 'I'm at work, you know.'

'I know. You have your coffee break between half ten and a quarter to eleven, don't you?'

'I do,' she said, fascinated that he'd remembered.

'I wanted to ask if you'd come to the cinema with me tonight.'

'Tonight?'

'Yes, tonight,' Ivan repeated. 'I know that's probably bad form in the big book of women's dating techniques, and I'm supposed to give you a week's notice and you're supposed to come up with four other possible dates because you're washing your hair, having your legs waxed, going out with your girlfriends, seeing other men. But you know me, I'm simple. I thought it might be nice to go to the cinema tonight.'

Maggie had to laugh. 'You're unique, do you know that, Ivan?' she said.

'It has been said before,' he replied, 'although not always in a complimentary way. My grandmother says I speak as I find.'

'I hate that expression,' Maggie said. 'It's the sort of thing that horrible fathers in gothic novels say when they're alienating people left, right and centre. But sure, I'd love to go to the cinema tonight. I have no hair-washing or waxing plans. What will we go to?'

'I don't know,' he said. 'How about I pick you up at about seven and we'll decide then?'

'Great,' she said, pleased. 'See you then.'

'Sorry,' she said to Shona when she clicked back on to the first call. 'That was just Ivan asking me out to the cinema.'

364

'*Just Ivan asking you out to the cinema*?' said Shona. 'Is this the same big lug of a mechanic person with dirt under his fingernails who took the mickey out of you with the petrol-sucking machine and who made you so angry that you were keen to hire a contract killer to bury him with the fishes?'

'And who took me to the lovely wedding. That's exactly the guy,' Maggie said, laughing. 'I've cancelled the contract killer, by the way. They refused to do a two-for-the-price-of-one deal with Grey included, so I said no. Seriously, though, Ivan's nice when you get to know him. He's got a great sense of humour. It just happened to be working overtime the day I met him.'

'I'm teasing you,' Shona added. 'Go for it. Go out with this fabulous Ivan and bonk his brains out in the back of the cinema. Tell me, does he own the garage or does he work for someone else?'

'Shona, you are appalling,' Maggie said. 'I'm not interested in him that way, he's just a friend. And there's more to life than money, you know.'

'People who say that type of thing are generally not in full control of their senses,' Shona pointed out. 'Money may not be everything, but it sure helps, and if you're miserable, you can be miserable in comfort.'

'Besides,' Maggie interrupted, 'I'm not in the market for a man. And rebound relationships are always a mistake and never work out.'

'Dr Phil, right?'

'You're incorrigible,' laughed Maggie. 'No, that's Maggie Maguire advice.'

Maggie was on until half past six that evening, so she had to race home from work.

'Hi, Mum, hi, Dad,' she yelled, rushing in the door and

sprinting to her room to change out of her work clothes into her most comfortable jeans.

'Where are you going in such a tearing rush?' Dad yelled after her.

'Out to the cinema with Ivan, you don't mind do you?'

'Not at all,' said her father. 'Oh, the man arrived today with the posters about the park. Your mother has them, she's very proud of them. She keeps saying "to think I designed these myself". A very talented woman your mother.'

Maggie ran a comb through her hair and considered putting on some lip gloss, then thought better of it. There was no need, Ivan was only a friend. She spritzed on a bit of perfume and ran to the kitchen where her mother was indeed admiring the posters. Above a line drawing of the park gates, which Una had traced from a picture, were rousing words about saving Summer Street's heritage from the developers.

*'It's part of your community, help save it!'* ran the bottom line. They looked good. Nobody would be able to resist, Maggie thought.

Harrison Mitchell was actually being useful and had given her the contact numbers for a couple of journalists who were interested in campaigns like theirs. She was meeting one of them at lunchtime tomorrow in the park and they were bringing a photographer.

'Don't they look great?' said Una happily.

'Fantastic,' agreed Maggie. 'This will make the councillors sit up and take notice.'

'What film are you going to see?' asked Una.

'I don't know,' said Maggie, 'doesn't matter. It'll be nice to see a film. I haven't been to the movies for ages.'

'He's a nice fella, isn't he, Ivan?' said her mother idly.

'Now, Mother, don't start that,' warned Maggie. 'He's just a friend.'

'I know, love,' said her mother quickly. 'It's nice to see you happy.'

Ivan's stylish car drew up outside.

Maggie grinned, kissed her mother on the cheek, snagged a banana from the fruit bowl and gave her dad a hug as she ran out the door. It was true, she was happy. Odd that, when just a few weeks ago she'd felt as if her heart was breaking. Something was healing her, although she didn't know what.

'We could go to the multiplex, if you like,' said Ivan, as they stood in the foyer of the tiny local cinema where they had discovered that the three latest releases were fully booked. The only film with any seats available was a classic French film, with subtitles.

'Well, maybe we'll go to the French one, what do you think?' Maggie said, thinking that if she'd been with Grey, the French film would have been their original destination. Grey had no interest in films with popular appeal. The more populist they were, the less he'd like to see them. An old French film with subtitles would top his list.

'Whatever you like,' said Ivan easily.

That was the nice thing about having Ivan as a friend, he never tried to push her into anything. And he was so comfortable in his own skin that he didn't need to prove his intelligence by his movie choice.

'I don't have the energy to go into town. Let's try the French film,' suggested Maggie.

'If that's what Mademoiselle wants, then that's what she shall have.'

He went up to the counter to pay.

'No, let me,' insisted Maggie.

Ivan glared at her.

'Or at least let me pay half,' she pleaded.

'I asked you out, so I'm paying.'

The cinema was only half full and they found two seats right in the back row.

'I always love the back row,' whispered Maggie. 'You feel sort of naughty, as if you're going to get into trouble for sitting here when you should be down the front under the head nun's beady eye.'

'I still think you must have been a holy terror in school,' Ivan teased.

'I wish. Butter wouldn't have melted in my mouth,' said Maggie.

They were old-fashioned comfortable seats and somehow Maggie found herself leaning on the arm rest that separated her and Ivan, so that her shoulder was squashed against his. And finally, Ivan put his arm around her and pulled her closer into him, which felt absolutely natural. And Maggie, the person who kept insisting that they were just friends, found that she liked it very much.

Don't think about it, she told herself. Just enjoy it.

Then, somehow, when Ivan moved his other arm around to touch her face and turn it towards his, it seemed like kissing him was the most obvious thing to do and Maggie turned her face to his and their lips met. Suddenly they were kissing, passionately and hungrily, and who cared about the film? Who cared if anyone saw them in the darkened gloom of the cinema? They kissed wildly, Ivan's hand in her hair, sliding down to caress her neck, stroking her collarbone, reaching down to the softness of her shoulders and further, until finally, he said, 'I don't want to see this film, do you?'

'No,' she muttered, pulling her mouth away from him. 'Let's go.'

They held hands and ran to the car park. As he drove, Ivan steered with one hand and left the other big hand on Maggie's jean-clad leg, stroking gently, making her feel intensely excited. It was odd: until a few moments ago, she'd seen him as a friend, and now, in a flash, it was like a curtain being pulled down to reveal a totally different picture and he wasn't a friend any more. He was a man, a sexual, charismatic man and she wanted him. The intensity of the want frightened her.

The car pulled into a lane a few streets away from home and Ivan parked outside a small mews house. He took her hand again as they went inside and she barely had time to register what the inside of the house was like, noticing a giant fireplace with open brickwork and bare floorboards, before he had pulled her upstairs to a huge bedroom that seemed to take up the whole of the upper floor, an enormous low bed dominating it.

Then they were half sitting, half lying on the bed and Ivan was tearing her clothes off as she tore his off with fervour. His mouth found hers, as if he couldn't bear not to be kissing her.

And for the first time in her life, tall Maggie Maguire felt like a small fragile creature beside this giant of a man, who touched her lovingly, as if she might break. It was that, that and the tenderness and the love in everything he did to her, that made her melt.


Afterwards, they lay coiled together in bed and Ivan gently stroked the small scars at the top of her thigh.

'We should go to French films more often,' Maggie said lightly.

'Don't.' Ivan held a finger up to the softness of her lips. 'Don't make a joke about it,' he said. 'You do that when you're unsure?'

She nodded.

'I love that you're so funny,' he added, still holding her close to him. 'You make me laugh, but I don't want you to need your defence mechanism around me, I want you to be yourself, not to joke about the things that matter.'

369

'I'm sorry,' she said, turning around and propping herself up on her elbow, so that she could look down on him. She ran her fingers through his close-cropped hair lovingly. She didn't think she'd ever get enough of touching him. 'I can't help it. I always think that if you make people laugh they don't see what you're really thinking or they don't see that you could really be in pain.'

'I know,' he said. 'I saw that in you the first time I met you.'

'You did?'

'And I wanted you the first time I met you,' he added and the growl in his voice made her feel faint with longing again.

'But you teased me,' she protested, and he laughed then and pulled her close to kiss her on the lips.

'I'm sorry,' he said gently, his lips against her cheek. 'Seeing you gave me such a jolt, I wasn't thinking straight. All I know is that I wanted you from the moment you came into the garage. I knew I'd have to wait though.'

'What if I hadn't wanted you?' Maggie asked.

Ivan smoothed her hair back from her forehead. 'I'd have waited,' he said. 'I'd have waited a very long time for you, for ever in fact.'

It felt odd waking up in a strange bed in the morning, but only for a moment. Beside her lay Ivan: large, muscular and warm, one arm flung over her body. Even in sleep, he was holding her close. Maggie knew you shouldn't compare, but she couldn't help it: Grey liked to sleep in his own space, on his side of the bed, and she did the same. Except last night, she and Ivan had slept curled together, drawing comfort from each other. She wriggled against him, loving the feel of his warm, hard body against hers. And it was hard, definitely: a certain part *very* hard. She wriggled closer still.

'I wouldn't do that, unless you like making love in the morning,' came a low, sleepy voice.

Maggie moved a sliver closer, feeling herself grow warm inside, adoring the power she had over him. Just her touch seemed to inflame him.

'I warned you,' he murmured, and then, like a great bear rousing himself from sleep, he swiftly moved till he was pinning her down on the bed, grinning at her, his face covered in dark stubble, his eyes glinting.

Maggie reached up and pulled his face down to hers, eagerly. 'I thought you had someplace to be this morning?' she teased as he rested his weight on his elbows, the lower half of him holding her to the bed, hard evidence that they weren't going to be getting up for a while.

'It can wait,' Ivan said huskily and lowered his mouth on to hers.

Ivan's bathroom was typically male with cream tiles, a bath he clearly never used because he had the last word in power showers, and a mirrored cabinet that contained nothing but shampoo, shower gel, shaving foam, toothpaste and mouthwash.

'You've got no stuff in your cabinet,' teased Maggie, rooting through, trying to find something that might remove the remains of her mascara. There wasn't even any male moisturiser. Grey had as much in the moisturising and sunblock line as she had and borrowed hers if he'd run out of Clinique for Men.

'Would you prefer if I had a ton of women's stuff in here?' Ivan demanded.

'No, but you must have had other women here,' she added, trying to sound diffident, and failing utterly. 'Go on, tell me,' she said. 'We're modern adults, we need to know everything about each other. I've told you about Grey.'

'I'd quite like to hear more about Grey, actually,' Ivan said, a muscle tautening in his jaw.

'Oh no, you don't.' Maggie shook her head. Grey was the past, a never to be revisited place.

'Yes, I do,' Ivan said. He'd had his shower and wore only a small towel tied round his waist as he began shaving. He looked great, tautly muscular and just as wantable as he'd been minutes before.

Maggie wished women could look as effortlessly good as men the morning after. She had panda eyes and blotchy skin from not taking off her make-up and needed a shower cap before she could shower as she didn't have her hair paraphernalia there to stop the wild auburn frizz.

'Grey was a part of your life for a long time and I want to know it's over, properly over.'

'Of course it's over,' Maggie said quickly. She didn't want to talk about this, it was too soon for her two worlds to collide. The new improved Maggie and the old, stupid one.

'But Ivan, your past is a mystery to me. When you took me to your cousin's wedding in the first place, nobody mentioned any special person you were supposed to have taken,' she said. 'Did you train them all to keep their mouths shut, because I can't believe there's really been a drought on the girlfriend front lately.'

Once she'd admitted Ivan's fierce attractiveness to herself, it was obvious that he was the sort of man who'd appeal to women. However, Ivan was a hard man to get to know. He was quiet, intense and very private. Few women would get past his outward face, to see the man underneath. The kind, gentle man who was an incredible lover.

'There have been a few women in my life,' he said, 'but very few of them got to leave their toothbrushes over.'

'You don't like sharing your bathroom?' Maggie asked lightly.

'Up till now, no,' he said. 'I think I'm changing my mind about that.'

She grinned, took his toothbrush from the holder and began to brush her teeth.

'Nobody's ever used my toothbrush before,' he said, watching her.

'So this is a first,' she teased.

'Yes,' he said, 'this is a first.'

She'd wrapped a towel around herself and stripped it off to climb into the shower.

'Show me your thigh,' he commanded abruptly.

The night before, his fingers had touched one of the pale scars on the top of her left thigh and she'd muttered about the car crash – the same story she'd given Grey when he'd seen the marks. But this time, in the bright light of his bathroom, he looked at them more carefully.

'Sit down.'

Gently, he made her sit on the edge of the bath and knelt in front of her. Maggie wished she had something to hide her thighs but she had nothing. Her wounds were laid bare. They were ragged scars, not deep, not ever having required stitches, but they'd left their mark. There were many of them, uneven marks that would never fade, like a barcode scratched into her soft skin.

'It was a car accident,' she repeated.

Ivan's fingers traced the marks.

'These scars don't look like any accident,' he said. He looked up at her, his fingers still touching the scars. 'What really happened?'

'I don't want to talk about it,' she said, anxiety blooming.

Ivan put two strong arms around her waist and locked them behind her back, pulling her closer to him. 'I want to know all about you, Maggie Maguire,' he whispered, kissing her face, 'every inch of you, every inch of your head, so tell me the truth. Tell me, where did you really get those scars?'

\* \* \*

It had all started so innocently on her first day at St Ursula's, when she'd arrived full of excitement and enthusiasm at being in big school. She and the other first years had spent the morning being shown classrooms and meeting their new teachers. It was a busy and interesting day, learning where everything was, getting used to which lessons would be in which classrooms.

The group of girls were waiting to be told where to go next when it happened.

'Hey, lanky, what's your name?' asked a girl with fair hair, a little freckled face and eyes that made her look older than twelve.

'Maggie Maguire,' said Maggie eagerly, not seeing the word lanky as derogatory.

'Big Maggie, huh?' sneered the girl, and the small group surrounding her laughed.

Maggie had laughed too, half out of nervousness, half to show that she wasn't offended.

'Sandra, you're a panic,' laughed one of the gang. 'Big Maggie – that's classic.'

A teacher had arrived at that moment and corralled the first years into their classes.

The next morning, Maggie was in early, determined to be ready for this exciting new world.

She was sitting at the front of the class for English, her first lesson, shyly saying hello to other girls, when Sandra and her cohorts strolled in.

'Big Maggie's up the front of the class,' announced Sandra. 'You're a swot, are you, Big Maggie?'

Sandra walked past Maggie's desk and, in one swift move, shoved Maggie's neatly arranged textbooks on to the floor. 'Oops. Sorree,' she said insincerely, and the gang laughed.

Her face crimson and tears burning in the back of her eyes, Maggie bent to pick up her books, hoping somebody would stand up for her or flash her a sympathetic glance. But nobody did. Everyone was too scared.

Maggie wasn't the only one of Sandra's victims. There were several more, and as the years went on, the bullying ebbed and flowed. Maggie found if she got to class after Sandra, and ran out of the door before her, then Sandra didn't bother to follow her.

She became adept at rushing everywhere and trying to be invisible at times like lunch or break.

They even ruined netball for her. When she was alone, she loved the touch of the ball on her hand, the thought of springing it from long fingers into the hoop. But as soon as the bullies were in the background, taunting, teasing, making snide remarks, her hand–eye coordination fell apart. 'Oh yeah, look at No-Tit Maguire, screwed it up again,' Sandra would say.

Ever since she'd tried to make her flat chest look bigger, Sandra had swapped the Big Maggie name for No-Tit Maguire. Maggie pretended she didn't care and ignored her.

'You're nothing but a long streak of misery,' was another of Sandra's taunts.

In her more charitable moments, Maggie liked to think that maybe Sandra had lots of problems and that's what made her so hard and cross with the world. That was often what was wrong with people in the books Maggie read: when they were nasty, they were suffering really and they just took it out on the heroine, so that could be the answer.

But after a few years of unrelenting nastiness, she didn't want an excuse for Sandra or her gang any more, they were just bitches. Kitty, the nearest thing that Maggie had to a best friend in school, had no interest in the theory that Sandra's life was hard, which was why she took it out on other people.

'She's just a cow,' Kitty said, vehemently. Kitty was small, very clever, wore glasses and lived in the purdah of plumpness, which meant she was Sandra's ideal target.

Brains was the only obvious link between Maggie and Kitty but the two girls became united in terror. They had agreed there was no point telling anyone about it. The teachers knew what Sandra was like, they couldn't control her either, or the gang, so it wasn't as if people didn't know.

But nobody seemed able to do anything, not even that time in third year when it emerged that Sandra had been taking money from the first years. Nobody knew quite how that had been brushed under the carpet, but it had. Sandra had been off school for two days and then she was back and just as bad as ever, without even a flicker of remorse. In fact, she and her cronies seemed worse now, as if their leader had got into trouble and had walked free, so they felt they had nothing or nobody to fear.

The first and second years stayed out of their way. People in third year, Sandra's year, didn't have that option.

'Why do adults insist on that rubbish that your school days are the best days of your life?' Kitty said. 'They're not, they're horrible, I can't wait to get out of this place, away from those low-lifes.'

At least Kitty could talk about it at home. She had an older sister who was now at college and understood that being small, bespectacled and clever wasn't the route to popularity in school, and comforted her, but there was nobody Maggie could tell. Mum and Dad were so thrilled to see her fabulous reports.

'Look, five more As and an A+. You're amazing. Where did we get such a brilliant daughter, Dennis?' her mum would say delightedly, when the report cards arrived in Summer Street.

The reports always guardedly mentioned that Maggie was quite shy and needed to come out of her shell a bit too, but

Maggie knew that her parents couldn't quite see this because the Maggie they knew at home was funny and merry. She could see them working it out: this classroom version of their daughter was the one who worked so hard she got A+. That must be why only they saw the bright-eyed Maggie at home. In class, she was diligent, that was it.

She didn't know how to tell them that when she got home she merely felt weak with relief at having got school over for another day.

Telling them about Sandra, about how she didn't know if she could cope much longer, would have seemed such a failure. Sunday nights were the worst. From about four o'clock on, Maggie could feel her mood sink lower and lower.

Getting her bag ready for school, making sure she'd done all her homework, getting a clean uniform blouse ready, she felt like a French aristocrat climbing into the tumbrel.

She could never sleep on Sunday nights. She'd lie there in her bed, looking up at the stars on her ceiling, wondering if there was intelligent life on other planets and if there was, what did they do about bullying?

The production of *The Playboy of the Western World* in Maggie's fourth year brought matters to a head. At St Ursula's the fourth years – because they weren't doing state exams that year – put on a play in an attempt to help them understand the work of the great dramatists. There were sixty girls in Maggie's year and among the twenty-five or so with ambitions to be world-famous actresses, there was huge competition for the big parts in J.M. Synge's classic.

Maggie, who loved English and had adored the play the first time she'd read it, would rather have had an arm removed without an anaesthetic than get up on the stage and act. So she was able to stand back and watch the fights that went on in drama class. The play would be performed at Christmas with all the funds going towards a charitable concern.

'I want everyone to be involved,' insisted Miss O'Brien, the drama teacher, a woman who felt that public speaking was a great skill for any person and simply couldn't understand why everyone wasn't clamouring to be involved. 'It will be so much fun,' she said, her eyes shiny with emotion, 'the excitement, the glamour. Now, Maggie, you could be one of the people who help the actresses learn their lines, you're so good at English and you love this play. That'd be a fabulous job for you.'

'Oh, no,' said Maggie instantly, 'I couldn't.' Her school career had been spent trying to slip into the background and she'd learned that hiding was the best form of defence.

Finally, the enthusiastic Miss O'Brien persuaded Maggie and Kitty and a few of the other quieter members of their year to help with the scenery for the play. The stars of that year's art classes were going to paint the scenery, but a few more people were needed to put it together, hammer in nails and be general dogsbodies.

'Maggie, I thought you would want to be more involved,' said Miss O'Brien sadly when Maggie agreed to work on the scenery but not help anyone learn lines. 'A sense of community is vital. I'm disappointed in you.'

Maggie said nothing.

She liked Miss O'Brien. It would have been lovely to sit down and tell her the truth.

*Miss O'Brien, you don't understand. I'd love to be doing something with the play, but Kitty and I have safe places we can go to at break and lunchtime to hide from Sandra. We'd be sticking our necks out working with the actresses. Some of the gang are in the play and they would make our lives miserable.*

Instead she said none of this, she just looked steadily at

the teacher and Miss O'Brien studied the blank face that Maggie had perfected.

'Well, if you don't want to use your talents, that's your loss,' she said and sniffed to show her disapproval. 'You could do much more than be in the background.'

Working on the scenery proved to be quite enjoyable and there was a certain satisfaction to be had in cutting up the enormous cardboard boxes they had been given to help create the kitchen floor.

Kitty, Maggie and a few other girls had been provided with Stanley knives to do the work. As sharp as craft knives and much stronger, they ripped into the cardboard easily.

'Now, be careful,' Miss O'Brien warned. 'I don't want anyone cutting off a thumb or anything.'

'No, Miss,' said Kitty gravely. 'We'll be careful, we need our thumbs.'

The only person who hurt themselves was Maggie. She wasn't sure how she'd done it, but cutting towards herself, instead of away as they had all been taught, she'd managed to make a big swipe along her thigh. The knife cut right through her uniform skirt and made an indent, a bloody indent, into the skin of her thigh.

'Ouch,' she cried.

'Shit, what have you done?' yelped Kitty.

Maggie pulled up her ruined skirt. Her leg didn't look too bad. There was a sliver-thin stripe of red with beads of blood emerging, like a red crystal necklace, along the rip. And bizarrely, this intense physical pain was manageable. It hurt but she could see the hurt, not like the hurt inside her that nobody could see.

'I'll take you to the school nurse,' said Kitty.

'No, I'm fine, I'm fine,' said Maggie. 'It's OK, really. I'll put loo roll on it, it'll be OK.'

She ran off to the loo, still holding the Stanley knife. Sitting in a cubicle with the door locked, she hesitated before making another slice in her thigh. God, it hurt, but at the same time, it felt . . . good. She could control this pain. The fierce intensity of the physical hurt took away the pain in her head. This was centred on her leg. She was in control of it and that roar of control surging through her was like a blessed relief from all the hurt. She'd cut herself and let the hurt drip out. Who cared if she was marked or cut? Nobody cared. She'd do it again and feel the power of control over her life again.

Nobody noticed when the Stanley knife went missing. Nobody knew it was in Maggie Maguire's bedroom and that sometimes, not every night, because she couldn't do it every night, she cut small marks into her thigh. Over the months, there was a criss-cross of them: red raw and looking like she'd been flayed on one thigh. But nobody saw, she made sure of that. It was easy enough, who was going to see her with her clothes off?

Sometimes the wounds really hurt, stung her and she wondered whether they were infected. So she bought surgical spirit and doused her whole thigh in it, wanting to scream with the pain, and yet, that pain was good too, hurting her like everything else was hurting her. That knife became a symbol, the one bit of control she felt she had over her life.

The night of the dress rehearsal, Maggie and Kitty were waiting in one of the big rooms behind the stage when Sandra and her cronies came in. They were all allowed to wear ordinary clothes and Maggie was dressed in her favourite jeans and boots with a simple fleece. One of her legs was faintly bulkier than the other because it was bandaged up, though nobody else would have noticed. Her thigh throbbed all the time. There were so many cuts in it. But she didn't care, the pain made her feel stronger.

'Hello, No-Tit Maguire. Is this what you call fashion?' sneered Sandra, who was done up like a dog's dinner in the best schoolgirl hooker look money could buy. Her hair was platinum blonde now and her eyes were hard blue bullets in a ring of eyeliner black as hell.

Maggie's leg throbbed. She had her knife in the pocket of her fleece. Carrying it gave her a strange courage. She clenched her fingers around it now, feeling the rage well up. Then she felt herself fall over the edge.

'Fuck off, bitch,' she howled in feral tones and stood towering over Sandra, her face suffused with anger. She ripped the knife from her pocket and flicked the blade a few notches up so it glinted its dull metallic sheen.

Sandra's eyes widened.

'Don't come near me or Kitty again or I'll make you fucking sorry,' hissed the new Maggie.

And Sandra, confronted by someone who was no longer going to lie down and be kicked, backed off.

'Yeah, whatever,' she said.

'Not *whatever*, you fucking bitch!' Everyone heard the roar and watched, open-mouthed. Maggie advanced, rage burning in her head. 'Say it. Say it or I'll make you sorry. Say you'll never come near us again, never bully anyone here again,' hissed Maggie and there was no mistaking her determination.

'I'll keep away, right? Calm down, right?' And Sandra, who had enough cunning to know how to save her own skin, backed off for ever.

'Mad fucking bitch,' she muttered from a good way away.

The bullies left and there was utter silence in the room, before Kitty went up to Maggie and took the knife from her.

'You weren't acting, were you?' she asked, putting an arm round her friend and manoeuvring her into a chair.

'No,' said Maggie, weak now.

'You'd be up for an Oscar if you were,' Kitty remarked. She neatly reversed the knife so the blade was sheathed. 'I wouldn't blame you for carving Sandra up into little pieces but she's not worth the hassle. If one of you has to end up in jail, I'd prefer it to be her.'

Maggie managed to laugh. 'I can't believe I did that,' she said.

'But I'm glad you did.' Kitty laughed.

A voice from the corner of the room spoke up: 'I'm glad you did too. She's made my life hell for years.'

'And the meek shall inherit the earth, if that's all right with the rest of you,' joked Kitty.

Everyone laughed and the tension was broken.

Maggie looked up into Ivan's eyes. 'Do you think I'm a nutcase now?' she asked, anxiety flooding through her now that she'd actually told him the truth.

He smiled. 'I think you're the bravest woman ever,' he said. 'I'm so proud of you. That took huge courage.'

'Not really,' she said. 'It was more like madness, really. I just flipped.'

Ivan's hands touched her leg again. 'You don't do this any more?' he asked gently.

She shook her head. 'Without her hassling me, life was easier, better. I felt ashamed about cutting myself and I stopped it. I never told anyone, though. It seemed so stupid. I began to like school and she left at the end of that year. The relief! The gang of bitches were never the same without her. They were still nasty, but never to me or Kitty.'

'My warrior princess,' he said, hugging her. 'You vanquished your enemies.'

'I thought so,' she said, 'but the day of your cousin's wedding, one of Sandra's gang came into the library and I thought I was going to be physically sick. It all came back to me, Ivan, the fear, the terror. It was like being a kid again.' Her voice wobbled and his embrace tightened.

'They're the fear I haven't exorcised,' she went on. 'Like my leg, they're scars that won't go away.'

'They'll go away with time,' Ivan reassured her.

'No, I have to face them. Christie Devlin says I probably have to face Sandra to get her out of my head. She's right, you know.'

Ivan pulled her to her feet and looked stern. 'If you go near those women, I'm going to be with you,' he said. 'Let them try and bully you with me there.'

Maggie hugged him, burying her head in his chest. 'Thank you, but no. I have to do this on my own.'

Gossip central on Summer Street was the mini-market where the surly owner, Gretchen, ruled supreme. Gretchen's daughter Lorraine, the one who was married to the rich French pilot, and had been at school with Maggie, had been in Sandra Brody's gang. If anybody knew of Sandra's whereabouts, it would be Gretchen.

So that evening, for the first time ever, Maggie went to Gretchen's checkout on purpose. She might not have had the courage to do it had it not been for the afterglow of a successful meeting with the reporters.

'Hello, Maggie,' Gretchen said, with the air of a cat who had a mouse's tail trapped between her paws. 'How are you?'

'Great,' said Maggie cheerfully. She was ready for tough nuts like Gretchen now.

'How's Lorraine?' she asked idly.

'Fabulous,' said Gretchen, seeming slightly surprised that Maggie would ask after Lorraine.

'And does she still see Sandra Brody?' Maggie continued.

'Sandra McNamara, you mean? Not really, I mean you know Lorraine is living in the South of France now . . .'

'Yes,' interrupted Maggie, not wanting to hear Gretchen's

boasting all over again. 'But they were such great friends in school. Their gang did everything together, didn't they?'

Gretchen looked shifty for a moment. 'Well, Sandra was a bit wild really, wasn't she?'

'Wild?' said Maggie, acting surprised. 'In what way was she wild?'

Gretchen looked even more uncomfortable. 'Oh, you know, she was a bit of a bad influence, we were all glad when she left St Ursula's.'

'What sort of a bad influence?' went on Maggie, feeling as if the tables were turned and she was the grand inquisitor.

'You know, leading girls on, getting them into trouble. My Lorraine was always a good girl, but when she was with Sandra, well, you never knew what they'd get up to.'

Maggie looked Gretchen straight in the eye.

'Actually,' she said coldly, 'I do know what they got up to and you're right, it wasn't very nice at all. Does Sandra live around here now?'

'She comes in from time to time,' Gretchen stammered and for once it seemed as if she didn't want to talk. She began scanning Maggie's groceries with an unaccustomed speed.

'And has she changed, do you think?' Maggie asked. 'Is she still *wild*?'

'She has children of her own and she's settled down, wouldn't that change anyone?' Gretchen said, whisking through the groceries.

'So she's different?'

'You might say that.'

'What does she do?'

'I don't think she works. She's got small children and the husband has a good job, I hear. That'll be seventeen euros and eighty cents.'

Maggie counted out the money. 'Do say hello to Lorraine

for me, won't you?' she added. 'I'm sure she'll remember me.'

'Eh, yeah, yes, yes, of course,' said Gretchen.

Maggie walked down Summer Street towards her house with her shopping in two bags. She'd made progress. She'd found out that Sandra's reign of terror hadn't been a big secret, that people had known about it. Maggie had spent so many years wondering whether she had been paranoid, exaggerated the whole thing to herself, that she felt vindicated now to find out that Sandra Brody's actions hadn't gone unnoticed, that other people had seen what she was. It was just that nobody had done anything to help the people like Maggie. This knowledge didn't make her feel even more upset or betrayed, it made her feel stronger. Having horrible old Gretchen admit that Sandra had once been a vicious little bully had given Maggie the key to her own freedom. She hadn't been at fault, Sandra had been, and now, she was going to confront Sandra about it. The past was not going to keep Maggie Maguire in its stranglehold any more.

The phone book had the answer.

Tony and Sandra McNamara lived a few miles away on a new housing estate.

Maggie wondered what Sandra McNamara was like now. Could she still reduce people to quivering wrecks with one nasty look? Did she still smoke and flick her ash at other people? She'd burned Maggie a couple of times with a cigarette, always pretending that it was accidental. Once on her leg, once on her knuckle, there was still a faint mark from that. At least those scars were surface ones. The marks on her thigh were Sandra's marks, hers as if she'd made them herself, with her own penknife. Maggie would carry those scars till the day she died. But it was time to heal the scars on the inside.

'I'm going out, Mum,' Maggie called to her mother. 'If Ivan phones, say I'll be back soon.'

'Fine,' came her mother's voice from the kitchen.

Maggie hopped on the bus that would take her past the McNamaras' road. Sandra and Tony McNamara lived at number 13 and when Maggie walked up to the gate with her head held high, she noticed there were two cars parked in the driveway. One, a standard people carrier with a baby seat in the back.

Children. Imagine Sandra having children of her own! Imagine if they were there when Maggie confronted her. There was no way she wanted to hurt the kids – it wasn't their fault their mother was a cow. Maggie faltered at this proof that Sandra Brody was more than an evil presence from her past. She was a person after all.

She stood on the pavement outside, trying to summon up the courage to go to the wooden door, when it opened and a man appeared. Instantly, Maggie turned and fled up the street, her heart thumping.

She didn't want confrontation with anyone else. A husband who might have no idea what his wife had once been like. Her heart pounding, she walked home, feeling ashamed.

That night, Maggie lay in her childhood bed in the house on Summer Street and stared up at the ceiling. The events of the past couple of months ran through her head. Betrayal and misery had taunted her, yet she'd got through it. Incredibly, she hadn't been flattened by it all. If anything, she felt stronger and happier now because she'd taken back control of her life.

It seemed very obvious to her now: she'd been stuck in victim mode for so long that she'd forgotten how to take control. Being a victim was easier as you could blame everything on other people. Taking control was frightening as it meant things might go wrong and you mightn't be able to handle them. But then things went wrong anyway. So why not face the fear, and take control?

The following morning, Maggie sat in her parents' car on the road outside Sandra McNamara's house and waited until Sandra returned from the school run. She'd left twenty minutes ago with three children, and now she had just one small boy with her. Maggie walked over to where Sandra was taking the child out of his car seat.

'Hi, Sandra, remember me?' said Maggie pleasantly.

Sandra turned. She was still blonde but her hair was shorter now, and the heavy eyeliner was absent. She wore no make-up, and looked pale and plain in an unflattering sweatshirt and jeans.

'No,' she said. 'Sorry.'

It was uncanny how she sounded the same. She looked different, but she sounded just the same.

'You honestly don't remember me, do you?' Maggie said.

'Remember you, should I?'

'We were in school together, St Ursula's, until you left after fourth year.'

There was no crash of cymbals as realisation hit Sandra's face, no triumphant chorus as she stared at Maggie in dismay. Her expression was blank.

'Sorry.' She shrugged. 'I don't remember.'

And she meant it. She really had no idea who Maggie was. When the crash of cymbals hit, the noise was inside Maggie's head instead. The girl who had tormented her and made her life hell had no recollection of it. Which meant that people often did horrible things randomly and didn't remember them.

'Do you live round here?' asked Sandra politely.

'I live on Summer Street,' Maggie said. 'I've been away for a few years and I'm back now. I'm trying to catch up on old friends, and people like you. I was one of the quiet ones at school and you were the leader of the bullies.'

Maggie could see the dawning of comprehension in Sandra's eyes.

'We were all a bit crazy then, you know, teenagers,' Sandra said.

'No,' insisted Maggie. 'It wasn't just a bit crazy, it was nasty and horrible.'

'I mean we all went through phases where we weren't very nice, teenagers can be little bitches,' protested Sandra.

'I wasn't,' Maggie said. 'I wasn't a little bitch, but you were so horrible to me I hated going to school. I used to feel sick thinking about it. No, that's not right – it's not that I hated going to school, it's that I was frightened of going to school. You made my life a misery for years. Do you have any idea what that feels like?'

Sandra shut the car door, leaving the little boy in his seat.

'Listen, lady, I don't remember you, right, so go.'

'Maggie Maguire, that's who I am.'

'Oh.'

Maggie could see Sandra staring at her in horrified recognition. Maggie knew she looked so different nowadays. Everyone said she was beautiful. Today, she allowed herself to feel it and stood tall in front of this woman.

'I knew you'd remember,' she said. 'No-Tit Maguire, you called me. It's funny you not recognising me when I'll remember you for ever. You made me feel so scared of going to school, which is something so normal you're supposed to do it every day of your life without bother. But you ruined it for me. Your nastiness affected every part of my life, did you know that?'

She didn't want an answer. In a way, she wasn't even talking to Sandra any more, she was finally voicing how she felt all those years ago. Sandra just happened to be there: an ordinary, fraught woman who was the one looking trapped now.

Maggie realised that meeting your demons head-on meant you could see they weren't the huge, dark monsters of your nightmares, but just stupid, pathetic people who'd had power at the time and had used it against you.

'I'm sorry, OK?' Sandra said. 'I know I was a bit of a pain when I was in school, I had lots of problems and I took it out on other people, but please, I'm sorry, I'm sorry for whatever I did. Now, just go. I don't want anyone overhearing this.' She looked around at her neighbours' windows, clearly anxious that someone might witness this strange meeting.

Maggie smiled inside, thinking that Sandra must have calmed down if she wanted to fit in with the crowd.

'Worried what the neighbours will think? You never worried in the past. Have you reinvented yourself as a nice person now? Do you go to coffee mornings and pretend to be an ordinary mum?'

Sandra flushed.

'Guess I hit the nail on the head,' Maggie said, looking Sandra coolly in the eye. 'I've one question: how can you say sorry to me, if you don't remember what you did to me?'

Sandra remembered, Maggie was sure of it.

'What would you do now if somebody bullied your children?' she went on. 'How would you react if they came home from school and said they were terrified because someone was picking on them?'

'I wouldn't stand for it,' growled Sandra with a hint of her old menace.

'Oh, you wouldn't stand for it?' interrupted Maggie. 'You'd march into the head teacher's office to complain, would you? That'd be pretty hypocritical, given how many people you bullied in school. Would that make you realise how much you hurt me and all the other kids you bullied, if you had to watch it happen to your child? That should be the punishment for bullies, seeing their own families getting bullied.'

'Look, I can't talk now,' said Sandra, looking harassed. 'Can I make it up to you? Can we meet for a cup of coffee and talk and . . .'

'I don't think so,' said Maggie. 'I've said what I wanted to say. I guess I'm lucky enough to have the courage to stand up to you. I'm sorry I never had the courage when I was at school, except that one time.'

'I'm sorry, just go, go!' Sandra said. She wrenched open the car door and fumbled with her little boy's car seat straps.

'Bye, Sandra,' said Maggie coldly. There was no need for her to stay. She'd said what she wanted to, had given Sandra McNamara something to think about. Maybe she'd toss and turn in bed at night from now on, remembering the people she'd hurt.

Then again, maybe she didn't have the ability to see how much damage she'd done. Incredibly, her only worry was what if the neighbours overheard.

Maggie walked back to her car. She'd never been the sort of person who liked confrontation but nineteen years of bottling something up did strange things to a person. She'd faced Sandra. She'd had the courage to coolly say all the things she'd wanted to say for years. And it felt good.

Maggie drove out of the estate and headed for home. At the bottom of Summer Street, she parked and took out her mobile phone.

She dialled Ivan's number, thinking that only a few weeks ago, the person she would have wanted to ring was Grey. Except that if she was still with Grey, if her whole life hadn't come tumbling down, she'd never have reached this moment in the first place.

Besides, Grey hadn't known about her past. In five years,

she'd never been able to tell him the secret Ivan had instinctively known was there in a few weeks.

Ivan was busy, she could tell from his voice when he answered his phone. But when he realised it was her, his voice softened.

'Hello, Maggie,' he said.

He didn't call her babe or honey or any of the things Grey called her. Ivan used her name.

'What's up?'

'Just wanted to say hello,' she said. Then, 'You'll never guess who I just met.'

There was a beat.

'Not Grey?' said Ivan, strangely uptight.

'No, no,' said Maggie. 'Sandra, the girl at school, the girl I told you about.'

'And did you say anything to her?' he asked softly.

'Yes,' Maggie said and she felt proud of herself, proud for standing up for herself. 'I did.'

When she hung up, Maggie thought back to her school days. Except, today, it all felt different. Resolved. She'd faced Sandra Brody with courage and learned two lessons. First, she hadn't been the perfect victim – she'd just been in the wrong place at the wrong time. And secondly, the past could only ruin your life if you let it.

Sandra wasn't important any more. Maggie had faced her and won. The real challenge was letting the past go.

# CHAPTER TWENTY-FIVE

Could you ever truly know somebody you loved? Could you ever know what went on in their minds when they lay in the dark beside you under the covers?

Those questions filled Christie's thoughts in the hours following her last, emotionally charged meeting with Carey.

As a child growing up, she'd watched her parents' marriage and known that she'd wanted exactly the opposite of what they had. There had been no real closeness between her mother and father, no knowledge of each other's inner thoughts and dreams.

Her father bullied his way through life and treated his children like bonded servants, there to do his bidding.

Christie's mother lived inside her head, not coming out for any of them. It was her survival technique and while Christie could understand it, her mother's mental retreat had made life lonely for her children.

So Christie had watched them, utterly separate and yet bolted together in marriage. She knew that she wanted something different.

That's what had made her marriage to James so special – closeness, respect, honesty. She shaved her legs and bleached her upper lip in front of James, let him know when menstrual cramps used to plague her and let him rub her knotted belly. She'd put her arms round his shoulders when he had the vomiting bugs he was prone to catch, steadying him as he threw up, wiping his face with a cool face cloth.

He'd seen her give birth to their two sons, and it hadn't diminished his desire for her, as some of the books said it might. He'd seen her cry a thousand times and knew which scenes in films and books made her upset and knew that she loved white roses above all other flowers.

Yet despite her craving for utter honesty, there were parts of her mind that she kept to herself: the parts that related to Carey Wolensky.

She'd tried so hard over the years to forget, hoping that eventually the memory would fade like writing on old parchment. If nobody could see it, it was no longer there. Except it was.

Now she could see it in full oil on canvas, hard evidence of a secret she'd tried so hard to forget.

She'd hidden Carey's gifts in Shane's old bedroom and found herself flicking through the sketchbook as a kind of punishment. There were cartoons of many of his most famous pictures here, rough sketches of paintings much prized amongst collectors. And the exquisite drawings that would become his Dark Lady series, each painting worth hundreds of thousands.

But it was the painting that revealed her secret.

She knew now what she had to do.

The day after her thirty-fifth birthday, Carey Wolensky phoned her at home, having found the number in Ana's address book.

Christie, who'd known instinctively that he'd contact her, knew what she ought to say. She'd practised it in fact. 'It was lovely to meet you, but no thank you, I don't want to see you again.'

However, knowing what you should say, and saying it, were two very different things. When she heard that low, husky voice, a voice that she'd dreamed of, she found herself saying yes.

She'd just meet him, she decided, to get this crazy bug out of her system. It would all be different in the cool daylight, when she wasn't annoyed with James or when she wasn't overwhelmed by the sight of Carey's stunning paintings.

She would be able to see that the rush of fierce sexual excitement had all been in her mind, a fantasy, a little break from the real world.

It was the perfect justification for meeting him. Despite the churning guilt in her stomach, she convinced herself that agreeing to meet Carey in his studio was a wise move. There, nobody would see them.

There would be no witnesses to what would inevitably be an embarrassing moment when she apologised but explained that she was married, he was going out with her sister, and they should forget all about that inexplicable moment in the attic gallery the other night.

In the end, her meeting with Carey took little planning. She dropped the boys off to school and playgroup respectively, organising with her friend Antoinette to pick them up afterwards, in case she was delayed, in case coffee went on longer. You had to be practical, Christie reasoned.

The moment Carey opened the scuffed door that led to the huge loft studio, practicality went out the window. He was everything that she remembered, everything and more. Towering, darkly brooding, danger emanating from every pore. The electricity was still there, strong enough to power a city.

'I didn't know if you'd come,' he said, his eyes intense on her face.

'I said I would and I don't lie,' Christie said and then winced, thinking that she'd lied to be here.

'I want to paint you,' Carey said, which was what he'd said on the phone, but Christie knew that was just an excuse – flattering, but just an excuse.

'My studio is up the stairs,' he added, moving back to make room for her.

She climbed the wooden stairs, conscious of him close behind her, his presence at once thrilling and scary. The studio was like all the artists' studios that Christie had ever been in: devoid of glamour and warmth. It was a big barn of a place with huge windows for the light, a paint-stained floor and canvases stacked in a corner. There was a table littered with dirty crockery in a small kitchen area. None of it surprised her. She could imagine that when Carey painted, he didn't think of boring things like cleaning up.

'Do you like my work?' he asked as she walked over to look at the canvases, something she wouldn't normally have done unless she knew the artist very well. Strangely, she felt she did know him very well.

'I think it's wonderful,' she said truthfully. 'What I don't understand is why you want to paint me. I didn't think you liked painting portraits.' She was calling his bluff as there had been portraits at his exhibition.

She turned to face him and realised he'd moved to stand right in front of her. He moved so silently, like a big cat. That's what he was like: a predator, fierce, wild, taking what he wanted. Excitement rushed through her body, making her nerves stand on end with the sheer charge of sexual tension.

'I have painted portraits before,' he growled, the accent husky as his eyes roamed over her face.

He wasn't touching her, but he was standing so close she could almost feel him tracing the fine bones of her face with his long-fingered artist's hands. She had left her hair loose again today, conscious that it had been that way when she'd met him first.

'I didn't say I would pose for you,' she said, taking a step back.

'But you're here, aren't you?' he replied.

'I came to see what sort of picture you wanted to paint.'

'A nude,' he said, as if it was the most obvious thing in the world.

Christie didn't answer.

Against one wall was an old ormolu day bed, piled with cushions and swathed in a piece of crimson velvet. Artists loved velvet: painting the textured folds was a life's work in itself. To one side of the day bed was a screen over which hung a faded silk print dressing gown.

'You can change behind the screen,' Carey said, watching her.

Christie looked at the day bed and thought of herself lying naked upon it with him watching. The very thought made her feel unlike herself and enhanced the sensation that this wasn't happening to Christie Devlin, married mother of two. This was an adventure occurring to her other self. Christie wouldn't do this but the wild, fey woman she might have been would.

She went behind the screen, undressed and pulled the dressing gown on. With huge sleeves like a kimono and an oriental print, it made her feel like a geisha.

'What do you want me to do?' she asked when she emerged from behind the screen.

'Lie with your head on the pillows, one arm along your side,' he said absently.

He'd already moved an easel so he was facing the day bed and it was as if he'd forgotten all about her except as his model. Shrugging, Christie slipped off the kimono and lay down.

'No, move your hand, further, there, that's right. And your hair . . .'

He strode over to her and every inch of her flesh tensed, but Carey was not seeing her naked in front of him. He arranged a tendril of hair to brush her breast and his hand touched her nipple, making it tauten into a hard nub, yet he still didn't react.

'Better,' he said, standing back and assessing her like a horse breeder looking at a mare. 'Better.'

She lay there for three quarters of an hour until her muscles ached holding the pose. After art college, she knew that an artist absorbed in his work might selfishly want a model to pose for ever, but she couldn't hold it any longer.

She stretched, no longer feeling conscious of her nudity, got to her feet, and pulled on the kimono.

Carey grunted and went back to his canvas.

'I'll take fifteen minutes,' she said, walking stiffly into the kitchen section to make herself a hot drink.

After fifteen minutes of silence, she went back to her pose. Half an hour later, she moved again. It was time for her to leave.

'I have to go,' she said, standing. She desperately wanted to see the painting but knew better than to look. He would ask her to look if he wanted her to.

'Fine,' he said, engrossed in his work. 'Let yourself out. You can be here tomorrow, yes?'

She didn't reply but she knew that she'd be back. She couldn't help herself.

The brisk chill of autumn gave way to winter while Carey painted Christie Devlin and the studio, no doubt a beautiful place in high summer, became cold, bringing up goose pimples on Christie's naked skin. She was used to the pose now, had sat for Carey several days a week for two months and even lying on the couch at home in the evening, she unconsciously found herself sitting the way he'd positioned her that first day.

She hadn't told James or Ana that she was posing for Carey. There was no need: it was all totally innocent, she convinced herself. Carey barely spoke to her and never touched her, not after that first day. She wasn't doing anything wrong. And yet she knew that lying there naked while this incredible man took in every millimetre of her skin was not quite as straightforward as it sounded. She knew that when she lay there on the day bed, with crimson velvet caressing her body, she really wanted Carey Wolensky caressing her body. But nothing had happened, and nothing was going to happen. As November began, she knew it was time to end it. She had to because the guilt was driving her insane. The only time she didn't feel it was when she was with Carey: every other moment of her life, guilt over the people she was betraying racked her.

It was James's birthday in November and he had been talking about a long weekend away. Christie knew that if she and James were alone together, without the children, then the crystal-clear guilt of betraying him by not telling him would hit her.

Then there was Ana, little Ana whom she'd been like a mother to. She adored her sister, and even though Ana was less enamoured of Carey these days – 'He's obsessed with painting, Christie. He's not interested in going out with me. We're too different for it to work. I don't want to hurt him but remember that man from the night of the party in Haddington Road, I've seen him a few times. He's gorgeous. I know it's wrong, but . . .'

It was small comfort to Christie that Ana wasn't interested in Carey any more. It would still devastate Ana to discover her sister's involvement with him.

Finally, Christie knew she had to end it because she knew she was powerless against Carey if he raised one little finger to her. The magnetism between them was so great she would run into his arms and Christie knew if she did that, she would never forgive herself.

So, one cool November morning, she decided that this was the last day she'd pose in his studio.

Surely, he must have seen all he needed, he must have tilted his head at an angle enough times, looking at her, analysing her skin tone, her shape, the movement of her muscles and her skin. He had drunk her in for long enough and she was going to finish it.

She waited until her break, when, as usual, she went into the kitchen and made herself some tea. The weather had grown colder and the thin robe was insubstantial. She shivered, clutching the mug of tea close to her chest, with her arms wrapped around herself.

'I'm sorry, Carey, but I can't come here any more,' she said, looking out from the studio windows over the roof tops of the surrounding artisan cottages. There, she'd said it. She felt herself tremble.

'Why?' he said, and incredibly, he was behind her in an instant, his hands on her shoulders, his strong embrace filling her with warmth. She hadn't heard him approach, he moved so silently and with such animal grace.

'You know I've got to stop,' she said, determined not to relax back against him. His hands slid further down her arms, pulling her back against him, making her feel the warmth of his body. She closed her eyes and leaned back.

'Carey, you must see that?'

'I don't see that at all,' he said. 'I see that you inspire me.

I see what I feel for you and what you feel for me. Why should we stop that?'

Her eyes still closed, she sighed.

'Because it's wrong. I love my husband, my children, and Ana. I shouldn't be here. You have no idea how much I torture myself over you, Carey. I think endlessly of the people I'm betraying by coming to see you. If they knew, imagine if James and Ana knew about this.'

She knew Ana was no longer interested in Carey but that excuse wouldn't work with her husband.

'Ana is a lovely girl but she's not for me,' Carey said. 'She knows that. I told her I was wrong for her in the beginning. She's stubborn. She went out with me to prove me wrong. I have told her she should find a nice quiet man to settle down with. I am not a nice quiet man.'

'Like my husband, you mean?' Christie asked, sensing the criticism of James. 'He's a nice man and he doesn't deserve this. It's wrong, all wrong, what you and I feel for each other.'

'How can it be wrong to feel like this?' he asked, holding her even more tightly. 'I have been so cautious, Christie, I haven't touched you, even though I want to every moment you're here, every moment you're not here. But I've given you the distance you need, you deserve. I let you make all the decisions and now you say you won't come any more?'

He turned her around gently and she stared into those dark, dark eyes. She'd never felt anything like the connection between them, the feeling that she'd known him for ever, in another life.

She'd heard some say that there were people destined to meet again and again in many lives, to search each other out until some scene had been played and their spirits could rest. Was Carey Wolensky from her past? The faith she'd been brought up in didn't countenance such things but there had to be some reason for the intensity of her feelings for him, the sense that he was another part of her.

Then, he took the mug from her hands, put it down on the table, cupped her face between his long, sensitive fingers and kissed her. And Christie knew she was lost.

# CHAPTER TWENTY-SIX

Her thoughts still with the distant past, Christie shut the front door quietly.

There was no noise in the house, but Christie knew James was there. She knew it because the dogs didn't come rushing frantically to greet her the way they did when she was the first person to arrive home.

James's shoes were in the hall, along with his briefcase and his jacket left on the stairpost.

Everything looked normal: except it wasn't. It was only a day since Christie had been to see Carey, and already, everything had changed.

She walked into the kitchen and the dogs bounced happily at seeing her.

James didn't say hello or get up to hug her. He was sitting at the table with Carey's sketchbook spread in front of him and the small oil painting propped up against the fruit bowl.

'I never knew,' he said, still staring fixedly at the woman in the picture.

Christie could see the real scene in her mind's eye: the artist's studio dirty, grubby and in no way romantic. The smell of turpentine and dust in the air, old paint-smeared rags thrown on the ground, and there was the divan, just as musty and dusty but with a piece of beautiful crimson velvet cloth thrown over it. Only the best painters could make velvet look beautiful with the warmth almost of living flesh. And her lying on it, naked, smiling, feeling beautiful.

'Did you sleep with him?' James asked, never taking his eyes off the painting. 'I have to know, Christie. Did you sleep with him?'

Christie hesitated, thinking. She'd thought about that for years. Which was the bigger betrayal – the act of sex, the intimacy of feeling another person's body inside yours, skin on skin, flesh to flesh? Or was it worse being close to them, talking to them, learning their most intimate thoughts, laughing to hear their voice, sharing a secret from the world? Was that a far greater crime than actually sleeping with somebody?

If their places had been reversed, if James had gone off with another woman – like dear, sweet Veronica from his office, who was shy and adored James, but would never, ever make the move on him – and shared moments of quiet time together, *that* would have broken Christie's heart. Not the fact that he'd brought Veronica to a hotel somewhere, stripped her clothes off and made love to her, the way he'd made love to Christie.

No, the intimacy, the kindness, the shared secret: that would have been the most painful thing to deal with. Not the sex.

She had to explain before she answered.

'That's not the most important thing . . .' she said.

'It is,' snapped back James. 'Did you sleep with him?'

The truth was the only answer. 'Yes,' she said quietly. 'I'm telling you because I don't want there to be any more secrets between us.' She sat down at the table beside him.

James looked haunted, aged, not the man who had left the house this morning.

'I'm so sorry,' she said, the words sounding useless. Sorry was too small a word to cover the huge regret for having hurt him.

'I should have told you years ago, but you know what they say, there is no point telling about an affair if the only thing you do is salve your conscience.'

'Then why did you leave this here for me to find?' he asked hoarsely. 'To salve your conscience by admitting you'd slept with another man or to hurt me by showing me his pictures of you.'

Even as she'd left the sketchbook and the painting there for him to find only hours before, Christie had agonised. But she knew she had to do it. James would be home by seven, so she'd put Carey's work on the kitchen table where he would see it, and she'd gone to sit in the Summer Street Café, staring blankly into an untouched coffee until it was time to go home and face him.

It was one of the hardest things she'd ever done but the truth had to be laid bare now. There could be no more secrets. 'I didn't want to keep this from you,' she said. 'And,' she paused, 'I was always scared you'd find out and it would destroy us. I couldn't bear that possibility.'

'You kept your dirty little secret well. I hadn't a clue,' he replied, with fingers clutching the sketchbook tightly as if at any minute he might fling it across the room, regardless of its worth. 'Ana – does she know what her beloved sister did? And why did you tell me now?'

Christie didn't know why – she only knew that she'd felt this intense compulsion to tell the truth to her husband. Beyond that, she hadn't thought rationally. Once she'd told him, he could do what he wanted with the information and she would have to take the consequences. 'It's different with Ana,' she said, thinking aloud. 'She didn't really love him. She was fed up with all those doctors, remember? They had no lives outside the hospital and they just wanted someone to date occasionally.'

'I remember,' James said grimly. 'You were the one who urged her to get a new life, to meet new people and she met him.' He snarled the word and Christie had no doubt that if Carey Wolensky had been in the room at that moment, James would have killed him.

'You said he was the wrong sort of guy for her, controlling, crazy, remember that too?' James demanded.

'I remember,' Christie replied. 'He was all of those things and he was wrong for her.'

'But not wrong for you?' James snapped.

'He was wrong for me too,' Christie said evenly.

She'd never seen James like this before, but then she had never admitted adultery to him before.

'She didn't really love him,' Christie said, and she was pretty certain of that.

When Carey had left Ireland abruptly, Ana hadn't really cared. Soon afterwards, she'd met Rick, the great love of her life.

'Are you going to tell *her* what happened?' James asked.

'No, I don't think she needs to know.' That guilt would have to live with her for ever.

'But I did?' He sounded so angry, was clearly barely holding on to his fury and pain.

'Yes, you did,' she said. 'If Ana knew, it wouldn't destroy our relationship. We'd go on. But the secret would destroy you and me. I heard he was coming back to Ireland for an exhibition and I was crucified with doubt and fear. I had to have the secret out, to tell you.'

'To tell me what?' James said. 'That he's here and you're running off with him, to the land of millionaires? Is that it?'

He looked angrier than she'd ever seen him before and

405

Christie felt humbled by his love for her, destroyed by her betrayal of this good, decent man. But she had to continue her explanation, so James could understand.

'I went to see him yesterday,' she said, 'and that's when he gave me the sketchbook and the picture. I'm not leaving you for him, there was never any question of that, James.'

'Well, that's good to know,' he said sarcastically.

This wasn't going the way Christie had planned.

'James, I wanted you to know about the past and that's all it is: the past, not the present. I've been so anxious about it and I realise that a secret like this can't be hidden, it's always going to be there and it would be better for us to get it out in the open, for me to tell you.'

'Why?' James demanded. 'To make me realise that thirty-something years of marriage have all been a sham?'

'No, they haven't,' Christie replied. 'There's nothing sham about our marriage, there never was. It was a moment of madness, stupidity.' She threw up her hands. 'I can't explain.'

It was impossible to explain that Carey had stood for the wild passion of art that she'd loved, something she'd had to suppress inside herself in order to live the life she had. Perhaps if she hadn't met James and married him and had two small children, perhaps then she could have lived happily in Carey's bohemian world. But James, Shane and Ethan meant that that path could never be for her.

'I love you, James, I've always loved you. What I had with Carey was just stupid and crazy and I knew it at the time and . . .'

'And you posed for him, naked,' James spat out, looking back at the picture. 'This is you. I looked it up on the internet just now. He's famous for these mysterious Dark Lady paintings. You knew I wouldn't know about them. Art doesn't interest me, so you were pretty safe with your secret. You knew I was never going to notice a painting by this man and

406

realise, that's my wife lying there naked, because I would have recognised you anywhere.'

'I know,' she said soberly, 'it made it easier that you weren't interested in art. It must mean something to you now that I am telling you, that I trust you enough to say all these things to you.'

'Trust?' he said. 'What's trust, Christie? I thought we had trust, but I was wrong. What was wrong with me? Was I too safe, too boring, too dependable, with my government job? Did you really want another life with someone else? Have you been waiting for bloody Wolensky to come and claim you all these years? Were there secret phone calls and trysts? Tell me!'

'No,' she shouted. 'I haven't seen or heard from him in twenty-five years. I wasn't waiting for him. If I'd wanted a life with someone else, I would have left to be with him when he asked me, but I didn't.'

'Oh, so you gave up the chance to run away with the great artist, for me and our dull life?' said James coldly. He got up abruptly, stared at her, as if she was a stranger. 'I don't know what to say to you, Christie. I've been looking at that book for what seems like hours, looking at pictures of you from every conceivable angle. Drawings by a man who looked at you in the way only I was supposed to look at you. Maybe at our age you're not supposed to care, maybe you're supposed to be beyond all that jealousy. But you know what, I do care. I care so much it hurts here.' He struck his chest fiercely. 'I don't know if I can forgive you or him. Where is he anyway?'

'No, don't go near him,' Christie said. 'That's how I have the sketchbook and the picture. He wanted to give them to me, he's dying.' She said it quickly, in case James rushed out into the city, searching for Carey Wolensky with a view to killing him.

'He's terminally ill, James. He wanted to find me and say goodbye, that's all. I knew he was coming, that's why I've been so anxious lately. Anxious that he'd come and ruin our lives. That's when I realised I had to tell you myself because I couldn't live with the fear, the fear of losing you.'

'Well, there's a pity,' said James with uncharacteristic harshness, 'because you've lost me anyway. I'll leave you with your lover's grubby little pictures. Wolensky can come here any time he wants now, because I won't be here. Isn't that what you want? Oh yes, you can talk to our sons and tell them what happened.'

'James, we don't need to bring Ethan and Shane into this,' Christie begged. 'This is not about them, this is about us. Please don't let's involve them.'

She couldn't bear it if her two sons learned of this. She couldn't bear them to look at her with disgust and anger, to think of what she'd done to their beloved father. She thought of Faye: how she'd been terrified of letting Amber know the truth about her past life, and Christie understood it completely. Could there be anything worse than having your darling children stare at you with disgust, where once they had looked at you with pride?

'Please don't say anything to them,' she begged.

'I'm not saying anything to anyone,' James snapped. 'I need some time to myself. I'll be on my mobile phone. I might go fishing.'

He hadn't gone fishing for years. She couldn't imagine where his fishing boxes and tackle were. Suddenly, she realised that that was hardly a problem and that James probably wasn't going fishing anyway. He just needed to get away, to be anywhere, except near her.

'I understand,' she said humbly, 'and I'm sorry. That's all I wanted to say, I'm sorry. It was a huge mistake and there is nothing else I can say except I love you. It was a mistake.

He was a mistake. But I didn't go with him when he asked me to, I stayed here with you.'

'And I'm supposed to be grateful for that fact?' James said. 'Because right now, I don't feel very grateful. I just feel very angry.'

'Will you phone me tonight so that I know wherever you're going, you got there safely?' Christie asked, not wanting to think of him driving recklessly.

'No,' he said. 'I don't want to talk to you, Christie. I can't, I have to think.'

'I don't want our marriage to be over,' she pleaded.

'I can't tell you that either,' James said.

He stormed out of the room, but for once the dogs didn't get up to follow him halfway up the stairs, torn between the humans they loved most. Instead, they lay on the floor, noses on their paws, big dark eyes looking soulfully and worriedly up at Christie.

'I know, babies,' she said. 'Daddy's upset. But it'll be OK.' She talked to them like she'd talked to her children when they were small. You always told children that things would be OK even if they weren't going to be. Christie didn't know how this would all pan out. Her gift of vision was blank. She wished she could look into a crystal ball and see James coming home, forgiving her, throwing his arms around her, saying it was all in the past and they could forget it. But that might never happen. She'd done what she thought was the right thing, because she couldn't live under the fear for ever. But now the fear that James would one day find out about her infidelity had been replaced with an entirely different type of fear. The fear that James would leave her for ever. Had she done the wrong thing after all?

# CHAPTER TWENTY-SEVEN

Faye, too, felt lost and alone, waiting in New York for news of Amber. She'd meant to go home sooner: she'd been there nearly a month and it was costing her a fortune. But leaving would be like giving up on Amber and she just couldn't do it.

She rang Ella each evening, hoping that Amber might have rung her friend with details of where she was, but no such luck. It was as if Amber had fallen off the face of the earth. Now that she'd made her choice, she was going to stick with it, not talking to friends, family, anyone, she'd cut them all off. Like mother, like daughter, Faye thought endlessly, remembering how single-minded she'd been all those years ago, before she'd become pregnant with Amber. Then, she wouldn't listen to anyone. She should have known that Amber would have inherited that trait too.

Alone in New York, she had plenty of time to think. She wasn't a shopper, so she bypassed the stores that would have left Grace in paroxysms of delight. Instead, she forced herself around the sights.

She visited Ground Zero one day, and stood there silently and felt ashamed of herself. She might not know where Amber was, but she was pretty sure she was alive. She'd simply chosen not to have contact with her mother any more. Whereas the people who had died here were gone for ever. She could and would see Amber again. The Ground Zero families were not so lucky.

Faye left with a new sense of determination. There had to be something else she could do to find Amber: that was the first thing on her list. And the second was to move on. She hadn't had so much time on her own in years, time to look at herself. She found she didn't like what she saw.

Getting back to her comfortably familiar hotel room, she phoned Grace's office answering machine and left a message.

'Grace, this is Faye, I need your help. When you get this, will you ring me at the hotel? We can talk and I'll give you all the details.'

Grace phoned at eight p.m. Irish time.

'You're in late,' said Faye.

'Well, my fabulous partner and second-in-command is on leave,' retorted Grace, 'so somebody has to keep the home fires burning. But you don't want to hear my problems. How's the search going?'

'Not well,' Faye replied. 'Whatever deal the band had going is off, so God knows where they are. I imagine they'll be looking for another production company. Amber's friend, Ella, says that Karl Evans – he's the guy Amber's fallen for – is very determined to succeed, so it's unlikely they'd just give up . . . But it's a whole other world here and I can't get much information. I thought maybe you could ask around at home, see who knows of the band or their manager?'

Grace knew everybody, senior policemen, politicians, business movers and shakers. If anybody could track down Ceres and Karl, it was Grace.

'Give me all the details,' Grace insisted, businesslike. 'I'll see what I can do.'

Faye felt a weight lift off her shoulders; she wished she'd asked for Grace's help ages ago.

Three hours later she rang again. 'I think I've found them,' she said.

'Do you know what day it is?' Amber asked Karl.

They were sitting by the pool at a small table enjoying breakfast. The rest of the band were around them, all looking bright and energetic even though it was half past eight in the morning. There was no drinking or carousing now. Life had turned serious. They were working on their album, had been for the last three days. Amber had never doubted Karl's ability but she had never seen him so focused, so dedicated. And so happy. But she was finding it hard to see the person she loved filled with a joy that had absolutely nothing to do with her. It made her feel lost and alone.

'What day it is?' he echoed genially. He had a Californian tan now. His skin was naturally dark and even though the band had spent a lot of time in the studio, he had a fabulous glow about him. He looked different. It was as though he was moving away from her, thought Amber, with growing despondency.

'Yeah, do you know what day it is?' she repeated.

'No.' He shrugged. 'The fourth day of the rest of our lives?' Karl had said recording an album was like starting a new life, the one he'd been dreaming about since he could dream. 'I don't know, what day is it?'

'It's the day the exams end,' Amber said.

Right now, she knew Ella was probably still asleep. Back home it was late afternoon and the gang at St Ursula's would already be planning to go out partying to celebrate the end of school and the end of exams. How many times had she and Ella thought about that moment, imagining what it would be like, especially in the dark days of winter when they trudged home, school bags heavy with books, their hearts weighed down with the thought of all the study.

'I know what I'm going to do when it's all over,' Ella would say dreamily, 'I'm going to go home, get into bed and lie there and turn my TV on and read magazines. And paint my nails and have a bath, oh, and do my hair and put on my make-up and dance around and go out!'

'Sounds perfect to me,' sighed Amber, although she didn't have a TV in her bedroom. Her mum disapproved of televisions in bedrooms. But she'd put on her CD player and dance around and do nothing, have absolutely nothing hanging over her.

And now, here she was thousands of miles away in beautiful sunshine surrounded by arguably some of the most beautiful people on the planet, doing nothing and it should have been wonderful. Except that it wasn't. The boys were going off into the studio soon and she'd be alone again.

She'd never been so much on her own in her whole life. She'd always been with people: Ella, girls from school, Mum, yet now here she had vast tracts of time to herself and not really anywhere to be or anything to do. It was odd. Doing nothing wasn't as much fun when there was nothing else you should be doing. The fact that she felt so out of place here added to her sense of sadness.

'Bet you're glad you missed all that exam crap,' Karl said, taking another bran and cranberry muffin from the pile. 'What's the point of all that kind of bourgeois garbage? Exams didn't get us where we are today, did they?' he said, with a touch of the smugness that was creeping into everything he said these days. The band were going to make it, they were going to be on the cover of *Billboard*. He didn't say these things quietly to Amber in the privacy of their own suite as they lay in each other's arms and shared dreams. She wouldn't

413

have minded that. But no, this unshakeable self-belief was said publicly and without a shred of embarrassment. Even Syd, who was the voice of reason, was affected by it and grinned when Karl went on about how big the band were going to be.

'I keep thinking,' Amber blurted out suddenly, 'I should have stayed at home to do the exams after all. I feel guilty now. I mean, it wouldn't have made any difference if I'd come late. I could have got on a plane tonight and been here tomorrow.'

'But you'd have missed all the fun,' said Kenny T.

'Exactly,' said Lew, who was stuffing his face with an omelette, a full egg one, a fact which had astonished the waitress.

'Not an egg white one?' she'd said, because nobody here ever ate full egg omelettes. Think of the cholesterol, the fat?

'No, the whole egg, the yellow bit and all,' said Lew happily. Lew planned on never learning how to spell cholesterol. If he couldn't spell it, it couldn't get him.

'I mean, think of the fun we had on the road, the adventures,' he said now.

Amber looked at Lew. He'd rewritten the road trip in his mind. She remembered it exactly as it had been: miserable, scary, cockroach-ridden. Being totally broke was not a nice way to travel through a foreign country where you knew nobody.

'You'd have missed being part of the adventure,' Kenny T added. 'You wouldn't have been part of our history, the history of the band.'

'You see, when they write about us in *Rolling Stone*,' Syd said, with a sly grin in Karl's direction, 'we'll be able to talk about how the five of us trekked across America with only a dream in our hearts and you'll have been a part of that.'

A part of the trip, thought Amber. But not a part of what

414

had happened afterwards. Having survived the travails of the road didn't make her a member of the band. Instead, she was a hanger-on, the girl with the band.

Thinking of this, she glanced at Karl, hoping he'd say the right thing and make her feel that her presence was still important to him. She wanted to hear him say that it wouldn't have been the same without her, that her presence – as his muse – had made it all work.

But he wasn't even listening and was flicking through the papers again.

A helicopter buzzed overhead, breaking up the perfect sky for an instant before disappearing. Amber looked up to see the glint of the chopper between the fronds of the palm tree shading their table. This really was a slice of paradise. Except it wasn't her paradise. She wasn't here on her dime: she was here on someone else's. Karl didn't really care whether she was here or not.

She'd been stupid to think he had. It had been fun while it lasted, but she'd given up so much for him and he neither understood nor appreciated her sacrifice. That realisation was crystal clear.

The boys sat there eating, and talking, all openly admiring an extremely attractive, very skinny blonde who sashayed past in a sliver of a dress hardly covering the most phenomenal breasts Amber had ever seen. They were clearly not real, but the boys didn't seem to realise that, or they didn't care. They just stared anyway, watching her skinny flanks appreciatively, even Karl.

Amber found that she didn't mind very much, whereas, once, she'd have been outraged at Karl ogling another woman so openly. Was this her Damascene conversion, she wondered, and then grinned, thinking that at least Sister Patricia would be pleased that Amber had been paying attention at some point in religious education at St Ursula's.

She got up from the table. 'I'll see you guys later, right?'

'Yeah, sure, right,' they all said.

'Bye, babe.'

'Yeah, see ya,' said Karl absently.

Amber walked back to their suite. She shouldn't have given up her life for Karl and the realisation didn't make her feel stupid, it just made her feel sad.

She'd burned a lot of bridges for him. Even her eighteenth birthday had turned into pretty much another day with Karl.

Instead of Ella and her friends organising a night out after the exams, Amber's birthday had been celebrated in a pub in Dublin just before they left when Karl had given her a silver bangle which was now tarnished, proof of how cheap it had been. She thought of the lovely portfolio her mother had bought for her and wanted to cry.

She'd been so blind to his faults, she realised. At least she was wiser now.

That night, while she was still working out what she was going to do, Michael took them to another party. There were parties every night but nobody stayed out late. Nobody got drunk either. LA was, as Michael reminded the band, a working town. Going to parties was a public relations exercise, not an excuse for wild behaviour.

Tonight's party was in the Hollywood hills and Amber, who'd worked out in the hotel's gym and then swum lengths in the pool, felt physically tired as she got ready in her bathroom. She was wearing her green thrift shop dress and pendant again. It looked lovely and she did have a faint tan too, not Hollywood gold but certainly something she'd have considered mahogany in Dublin.

The house they were driven to in the requisite convoy of Jeep Grand Cherokees was hotel-sized, appeared to be mainly made of glass and sat perched on a hillside with an intricate terrace and a gently curving pool filled with Japanese carp. Walking in the door was like walking into an interiors magazine.

Not that it was ostentatious – quite the opposite. Painted a warm vanilla, with dark floors, creamy upholstery, and carefully placed modern lighting, the effect was of simple elegance, like the guests. The music was muted jazz, the drinks were clear cocktails, champagne and plenty of juice, and the band loved it.

Within half an hour of arriving, Karl had left Amber's side and when she saw him a few minutes later, he was talking to Venetia, who looked as exquisite as the first time Amber had seen her, white linen pants and a white silk halter top emphasising both her figure and the rich colour of her skin.

Amber didn't feel threatened by Venetia tonight, although she couldn't have explained why, if anyone had asked her. Venetia was so beautiful, she was in another dimension of beauty. Normal people like Amber could never compete with Venetia's exquisite ebony limbs, those dark, flashing eyes and lips that were full of promise.

Lew wandered up to Amber and put an arm round her.

'How's it going, babe?' he said, then, when she didn't reply, he followed her gaze and saw Karl sitting with Venetia.

'She is one amazing-looking woman,' he said with the sigh of someone who knew Venetia was way out of his league. 'No offence, Amber, I mean you look pretty good too.'

Amber smiled wryly. 'None taken, Lew.'

At first the evening was fun, seeing people who looked vaguely familiar, people from the music industry, people whose albums Amber had bought. But it wasn't always easy to join the groups of people who already knew each other and eventually, she and the band, minus Karl, ended up relaxing in a split level part of the house in front of a huge stone fireplace where vast expensive candles burned in the grate.

Syd was holding forth on the parties they'd been to, insisting that the people with the entourages and bodyguards were faking it, despite the bling.

'The quiet ones in jeans with those discreet watches you've never seen in any normal jewellery store, they're the multi-billionaires,' he pointed out shrewdly. 'The bling, blings aren't that bling at all. Take away the diamonds and the bulked-up bodyguards and there's nothing left.'

Amber laughed. She liked hanging around with Syd. He had a sense of humour similar to Ella's.

She'd thought about calling Ella earlier, having had one of those moments when she'd longed to hear her friend's voice, to hear someone say 'How nice to hear from you' and really mean it.

Nobody here needed her like the people back home did. Kenny T and Lew were sweet guys, while Syd was a genuinely kind, good man, terribly in love with his Lola. They liked Amber, were fond of her, probably in the same way you'd be fond of a puppy or a kitten that clambered on to your lap and wanted to be petted. Nothing more. And Karl? Karl had moved on.

She'd chickened out of ringing Ella. So much time had gone by. In their whole friendship it had never ever been weeks since they'd talked. Even when Ella's family had gone to Italy to visit relatives, they'd kept in touch, Ella facing the wrath of her mother for making so many international calls.

But it had been worth it because they were best friends, weren't they? And now, weeks had gone by without hearing Ella's laugh or hearing her joke or moan about her grandmother. It was funny the things you missed.

She sighed and tried to stop thinking about back home in case she cried. She forced herself to observe the party and the Hollywood hierarchy. In some subliminal way people from lower down the celebrity power chain ignored each other as they tried to attach themselves to upper groups.

Amber wasn't part of any of the groups, but she didn't care. It would all make a wonderful painting, she thought suddenly, her artist's eye trying to imagine how she would sketch it out. She could see it in her head and itched to record what she'd seen. Paper and a pencil, that's what she needed.

In the kitchen, in clear contrast to the cool calm of the rest of the house, the catering staff ran around frantically. They didn't notice her in the bustle when she appropriated a pad and a pen lying on a table. She went back to the lounge, leaned against the fireplace and began to sketch. It felt great to be drawing again. Energy burned within her with each deft stroke of her pen. As she drew the room and outlines of the people in it, quickly, speedily, because they were moving all the time, she felt that buzz she'd always felt when she had a pen in her hand. That was how she saw the world: through her eyes directly into her hands and on to the page. Maybe that's why she screwed up so much with Karl. She'd seen him only with her eyes, she'd never made the connection and put him down on paper. If she had, then she might have seen that he was insubstantial, not what she'd first thought.

A tall man, dressed in a simple white shirt and khaki combats, walked over to her with a glass of wine in his hand.

'I've been watching you,' he said. 'Are you drawing us?'

He stood beside her and looked down at the picture.

'That's really good,' he said, in both shock and astonishment, 'really good.'

He looked at her again, this time with renewed respect. 'You're an artist?'

Amber turned her amazing grey eyes with their copper flecks upon him.

'Yes,' she said, feeling a surge of self. 'I'm an artist. I'm

419

not really sure what I'm doing here, hanging out with a band and a man.'

'Which band is that?' asked the man. He was probably in his forties, way old, sort of a bit like Ella's dad actually.

'Ceres,' she said, pointing over to where Karl was sitting on a low couch with Michael and Venetia. She hadn't sketched them in her picture yet, she'd been working on the people around them.

'He's the band? Or is he your boyfriend?' asked the man.

'Both,' said Amber grimly.

The man said nothing, just assimilated the information.

'Who are you?' she asked.

'I'm Saul, this is my house, my party.'

'Pleased to meet you,' Amber said. 'Where I come from, you generally know the people whose party you're going to and, if you don't, as soon as you get there you're introduced and you say thank you so much for inviting us. It's different here.'

'You're Irish, right? Land of saints and scholars and maidens dancing at the crossroads.'

'Exactly,' said Amber, with mock sincerity, 'in the same way that Los Angeles is a glorious city where dreams come true and there are beautiful women on every corner.' She gave him a hard look.

'Touché,' he said.

'Do I look like a maiden who dances at the crossroads to you?' she asked.

'Not in that dress.'

'Good,' said Amber. 'I wouldn't want to be, any more than I'd want to be the LA version. This city does seem to suck the individuality out of people and make them different, but all in the same way.'

He laughed this time, showing beautiful dental work.

'And you have lovely teeth,' she added. 'Everyone here

420

has lovely teeth. When people smile, it's like being in a toothpaste advert.'

'You have pretty nice teeth yourself,' he countered. 'You ought to be a writer instead of an artist. You've certainly got the bite.'

'I prefer painting,' Amber said. 'That's my first love.'

'I thought the guy from the band was your first love?' Saul motioned to where Venetia and Karl sat together.

'Touché to you,' she replied. 'The truth is I'm a total moron, following a group of guys around, watching them fulfil their dream, having dumped my own dream by the wayside.'

'A common movie theme.' Saul nodded. 'Boy meets girl, boy tells girl he loves her, boy drags girl on long trek and pretty much ignores her, boy loses girl. Boy realises what he's lost and runs after her. Cue credits. Are you at the boy loses girl part yet?'

Amber looked over to where Karl and Venetia were locked in their own world. Karl had that look on his face, the look he had all the time these days, the look of blazing triumph and excitement. The power of his talent made him sexier than ever. He was like a supernova.

'Yeah,' Amber said to Saul. 'I think we're at that stage.'

She didn't think they'd ever get to the part of the movie where Karl realised what he'd lost and ran after her. Movies and real life ran on different paths.

'And you're not going to race over to throw your drink over them?' Saul asked.

Amber smiled.

'What would be the point of that?' Amber asked. 'Apart from creating a nice little scene for everyone to laugh at. I'm with the band, you know. Girlfriends are supposed to understand that musicians don't have the faithful gene. Playing lead guitar removes it.'

Saul grinned. 'As long as you know your place,' he dead-panned. 'That's very important in this town. Everyone is trying to get up to a higher place, but you need to know where you are to start with.'

'Oh, I know,' Amber said. 'I know. That is to say, I didn't know when I got here, but I've worked it out.'

'You're pretty smart,' Saul reflected.

'My mother wanted me to know stuff,' Amber revealed. 'She wanted me to understand the world, my place in it, what I could do and what I couldn't do and never to follow the crowd and . . .'

'That's why you're here, with the band?' Saul said.

'Precisely. I had to do exactly the opposite of what my mother taught me.'

'I work on the belief that you've got to learn by other people's mistakes, because you never live long enough to make them all yourself,' Saul remarked.

'I'm the opposite,' said Amber. 'I have to make all the mistakes myself.'

'Will you stay in LA? It's a nice place to be an artist, the light is pretty fabulous in the hills.'

'I don't know,' Amber said, shrugging. 'I don't know what I'm going to do.'

'I guess you're not going to stay with the band, are you?'

Amber glanced over to Venetia and Karl. Venetia was so close to Karl that she was almost sitting on his knee, a position Amber remembered being in the first time she'd met Karl back home. It seemed a million years ago. Which of them had been shallow and stupid, she or Karl, she wasn't sure.

'I don't know,' she said to Saul now. 'I don't know what I'm going to do.' But she knew she couldn't just go home alone, could she?

Amber didn't bother telling Karl she was leaving the party.

She hitched a ride in somebody's Humvee back to the hotel and she wasn't surprised when she woke the next morning to find herself alone. It seemed he and Venetia were now an item, except he hadn't had the courage to tell her. Never mind, Amber thought, she had enough courage for both of them. She was going to move out, she wasn't going to hang around where she wasn't wanted.

When reception rang to say there was a delivery of flowers for her downstairs, Amber wondered what it could be. Flowers with a goodbye note from Karl? She almost laughed at the thought. That's probably how he'd do it, with roses and a card that said, 'Bye and won't be seeing you soon, Karl.'

She pulled on her jeans, a T-shirt and some flip-flops and made her way down to the lobby. She was just about to approach the concierge desk when, out of the corner of her eye, she saw a movement that was instantly familiar. She turned, and there, halfway out of her seat, was her mother. Comforting, familiar and utterly welcome.

'Amber,' said Faye, and there was no escaping the pure joy on her face. 'Amber, it's so good to see you.'

Amber's first instinct was to run and hug her mother, so that was exactly what she did. It was wonderful to touch her mother, to feel loved, safe and secure again.

'Mum,' she said, burying her head in her mother's shoulder.

'Darling, it's so wonderful to see you,' said Faye shakily.

'You too, Mum. I'm sorry, I'm really sorry, how it all happened,' Amber muttered, holding tight.

'Hush,' said her mother. 'Hush. It's OK now. I've missed you so much.'

'I've missed you too, Mum,' Amber said. 'Come on, come back to the room. We'll talk and we can have breakfast,' she added eagerly. 'I just have to pick up a delivery.'

Faye grinned.

'The delivery was from me,' she said. 'I said they had to be given to you personally, which is why they rang up to your room.'

She gestured behind her to the table beside the armchair where she'd been sitting. A small posy of wildflowers sat in a basket on the table.

'They're beautiful.' Amber felt teary again. She loved wildflowers.

'I wasn't sure if you'd want to see me,' Faye went on and Amber felt the weight of guilt. How awful that her mother had had to adopt such a ruse.

'I'm sorry,' she said. She ran over and picked up the flowers, then ran back, linked her arm through her mother's and said: 'Come on, we'll have breakfast and we'll talk.'

They might as well have one last big blowout on Karl, she thought, leading her mum back up to the room.

They sat on the small balcony with coffee, pancakes and fresh fruit salad in front of them and barely touched anything in their eagerness to talk. Faye wanted to hear everything that had happened and Amber was amazed to find her tongue rushing away with her, as she described the hotels they'd stayed in, the misery when the band's deal had fallen through and how everything had turned up trumps in Los Angeles. She didn't mention a word about her and Karl though. Not one sentence about how they'd moved so far apart that you could drive a car between them. She was too proud for that.

'This is a beautiful hotel,' Faye said, when she'd recounted her fear at seeing the awful Arizona Fish Hotel and realising that Amber had had to stay there. 'I've been so worried about you. You couldn't imagine all the scenarios that came up in my head. I just kept thinking of all the . . .' she paused, 'all the trouble I'd got into when I was your age and in love.'

Amber looked at her curiously. What trouble had her mother got into?

Faye could see the question forming in her daughter's eyes. Amber looked so well, she thought, with that faint tan. Her daughter really was beautiful. Beautiful, clever, intelligent and a grown-up. She should have told her the truth a long time ago.

Ever since Grace had phoned with news of where the band were staying in LA, thanks to locating their manager, Faye had been practising what she was going to say to her daughter. She'd had a month to think about it but it was only when she knew for sure where Amber was that she allowed herself to have that mental conversation.

In her mind, she'd thought maybe they would drive to the beach, walk on the sand and talk there. Amber had always loved the sea and maybe if they walked side by side and let the wind ripple through their hair and the waves crash in beside them, she could tell her story and Amber would understand.

But now, sitting on a small, sheltered balcony overlooking a beautiful pool, unable to do anything except drink cup after cup of coffee, Faye knew that it didn't matter where she told Amber the truth.

'I want to apologise,' she said first. 'That's what I came here to do, not to drag you home, which is what you probably think I am here to do.'

'You're not here for that?' Amber said, startled.

'No,' Faye said. 'You're an adult, you're right, I'm sorry. I've treated you like a child for so long I didn't know how to treat you any other way. I can understand that when you wanted to leave you thought you had to do it brutally, because I wouldn't understand it any other way. That's only part of what I'm apologising over. Remember one of the things I said before you went?'

That last row was engrained in her memory, but she wasn't sure if Amber would remember.

'I said I knew because I'd been there and you didn't believe me.'

Her daughter nodded. At the time, she'd thought it was a stupid statement, just another ploy to get her to stay because how could her mother have any clue what real life was like?

Faye took a very deep breath.

'I lied to you about your dad. We weren't desperately in love and he didn't die in a car crash,' she said bluntly. 'He was just some guy in a bar from a horrible life I lived and I didn't want you to ever know about it.'

Amber stared at her mother.

'I know it's awful to hear this after eighteen years of hearing a different story about your father. I just didn't know how to tell you without you hating me.'

'I'd never hate you,' Amber said weakly, trying to process this new information.

'You could hate me because I lied to you about your birth, your father and my life before you were born.' Faye stopped.

That was the hardest thing to say: that she'd lied to Amber about everything.

'I tried to bring you up to be truthful and honest, yet I spent your whole life lying to you. I hate myself for that.'

'What really happened, then?'

Faye poured more coffee she didn't want and began to talk.

Amber sat opposite her and didn't flinch as her mother's story unfolded. It was incredible to hear all this for the first time. It was as if her mother was another woman, a woman she'd never known.

'I didn't value myself or respect myself,' Faye said finally. 'I ran with the pack, I did things because other people did them, I didn't stand up for myself. I tried to fit in. You see, all the things I spent years telling you not to do, I did every single one of them. Are you shocked?'

'No.' It was a lie. Amber had never been so shocked in her life. Her mother didn't look like her mother any more. She was still the same: the neatly tied back hair, the plain loosely cut T-shirt, the slick of lip balm the only sign of make-up. But her eyes, they were different. Her expression was different.

'I . . . I can't imagine you like that, you're so strong now,' Amber said. 'I can't imagine you letting anyone walk on you.'

'Walk on me! They walked all over me,' Faye said sadly, 'and I let them, because I didn't know who I was or what I was and that's what I was ashamed of.'

Amber tried to keep her expression neutral. All these years her mother had convinced her she was the epitome of the conservative, working mum. And now, here she was, telling Amber that she was just the opposite.

'I never told you the truth because I didn't want you to grow up being ashamed of me and I didn't want you growing up being the same sort of person I was. So I thought that if I invented this new me who didn't let anybody near, then you would grow up like that. I'm really sorry, Amber,' Faye said, and she began to cry. 'I've let you down, I'm so sorry about your dad, so sorry. All these years lying to you, telling you we were in love and . . .'

It was all too much to take in.

'Did he even know about me?' Amber interrupted.

'No,' said Faye. She might as well tell the whole truth while she was at it. 'I went to see him once, when you were a baby, but he was out of it, on drugs, and I never went back. He was on heroin. I couldn't cope with that, it wasn't what I wanted for you.'

'Wow, heroin. Right, so he could be alive or dead, you don't know,' said Amber. It didn't feel like her mother was talking about her. She felt remarkably distant from the whole thing. She'd grown up without a father, so she'd never felt the loss of one. But now there was the possibility of a father after all, a man she might have known, and her mother had kept him from her.

In the background, Amber heard a click, the click of the door opening.

She turned to see Karl coming into the suite. She leaped to her feet and ran over to him. 'Hi, darling,' she said brightly and loudly.

Karl looked at her in astonishment. They'd been co-existing in the suite for the past couple of days and she hadn't run to welcome him for a long time.

'My mother is here,' she whispered, her mouth close to his. 'Try to pretend we are still together, for me, will you do that for me? Just for today and then we can go our separate ways.'

'What do you mean "separate ways"?' he said, his face going suitably blank.

'Get real, Karl,' she snapped back at him. 'Do you think I'm blind as well as stupid? I saw you and Venetia last night. I know what's going on. I'm getting out of your hair tomorrow, but I want my mother to go home thinking it's OK between us. You can do this for me, I've given up a lot for you.'

'Sure, OK. Is she angry with me?' Karl asked anxiously.

'She should be,' Amber whispered, 'but she's not. Lucky you. I'm bloody furious with you but that's a discussion for another time, you bastard.'

She turned around, smiling.

'Mum, meet Karl.'

He was every bit as good-looking as Faye had imagined: handsome, sexy, charismatic. She could imagine Amber falling in love with this gorgeous man, wrapped up in his talent, watching him on stage.

'Hello, Karl,' said Faye, trying to be civil although it was incredibly difficult not to yell at this man who'd stolen her daughter and put her through hell for the past month. She'd do it for Amber's sake and she just hoped that Karl Evans would treat her daughter with love and respect, because if he didn't, he would have Faye to answer to. 'Nice to meet you, at last.'

When Karl had showered and gone off again at high speed, Amber took her mother down to sit in one of the cabanas by the pool.

In her white T-shirt and a pair of cream chinos that did nothing for her figure, Faye was aware that she probably stood out like a sore thumb amid all this LA glamour, but she didn't really care. She was with Amber, that was all that mattered.

They talked about Summer Street and home. How Faye had spoken to Ella, who was delirious that the exams were over.

'She sends her love,' Faye said, 'and wants you to phone her soon, or email her.'

'I will,' said Amber, guiltily. 'I just felt so bad when such a long time had gone by and I hadn't talked to her. Do you think she'll forgive me?'

'Of course she will,' her mother said. Faye went on to explain how she'd made friends with Christie Devlin and Maggie Maguire and the plans to demolish the pavilion and put up an apartment block.

'They can't do that!' Amber said, outraged. She didn't want bits of home being ripped up while she was away. But she changed the subject quickly, because she didn't want to talk about her going back to Summer Street, repeating her exams or going to college.

Her mother never mentioned these things either. It was as if they'd tacitly agreed that their rapprochement depended on avoiding the question of Amber's future.

It was only when evening arrived, and they walked down the street to a little trattoria, that Faye had the courage to bring up Amber's return.

'Are you going to stay here long?' she asked. 'Or are the band coming home soon?'

Amber had been holding it together all day. She felt like a boat on stormy seas, rocked by both Karl's defection and the story that her mother had hidden for so long. She'd tried to be calm and non-judgemental, but her composure finally shattered under the weight of the two blows.

Karl had cared for her, but not enough. She'd been the one to make all the sacrifices for him. He wasn't what she'd thought he was and neither, it seemed, was her mother.

She wanted to lash out at someone in hurt.

'Mum, I'm doing my own thing now, OK!' she shrieked. 'I don't know when I'll be home. I'll stay in touch but there's no point hanging around here waiting for me. I don't need that. I can make my own decisions!'

It was said as much for Karl as for her mother, except that Karl wasn't there and Faye took the brunt of Amber's anger and shock.

'I'm sorry,' she said, chastened. She should have known that she couldn't tell Amber her history and expect her daughter not to be hurt. 'I'm not going to hang around. I'll fly home but I've got some money for you.' She dug out the envelope filled with dollars and handed it to Amber. 'I know you don't want hand-outs but I worry about you. Please stay in touch.'

Amber nodded, clutching the envelope.

'Mum, dinner's a bad idea. You should go. The band have an event to go to and I have to go too.' She hadn't planned on going but it made a good excuse. Right now, she needed to be alone to think.

They stopped on the street and stood awkwardly, at arm's length.

'I love you, Amber,' Faye said, reaching out to touch her daughter tentatively. Amber looked as if she was about to break down and Faye wanted to hug her, but didn't know if this new Amber would allow that. Things were different now: the time apart and all that had happened had changed them both. 'Don't forget that. I'm sorry I lied. Our home is always there for you, please remember that. It'll always be our house, not mine. Never be afraid to come home or to call me if you need me.'

'Thanks,' said Amber. She kissed her mother quickly on the cheek because if they hugged, she might break down and tell Mum everything. And she couldn't. There were too many lies around, too many people not telling her the truth. She felt so hurt, raw.

'I have to go, Mum. I'm sorry. I need to think,' she added shakily before turning and running back down the street to the hotel.

She was more like her mother than Faye knew, but Amber couldn't say that now.

Behind her, Faye watched until her daughter was out of sight. She felt as if her heart was being ripped out of her chest and jumped on. This was almost worse than the time Amber had run off because then, she hadn't known all the facts. Now she did.

This was Faye's punishment for all the years of lying: Amber couldn't forgive her. She had to give Amber space, even though she wanted to forcibly drag her on to a plane and fly her home to Summer Street. Walking away was the hardest thing she'd ever done, but she had to do it.

# CHAPTER TWENTY-EIGHT

Shona threw open the door to her Galway apartment and dragged Maggie in with a giant hug.

'Maggie, I've missed you!' she yelled happily.

Maggie hugged her back. 'Me too,' she said. She dumped her small holdall on the floor and looked around Shona's apartment where she'd once spent so many happy hours. 'New curtains?' she asked, instantly spotting the thick creamy ones that had replaced the old beige paisley drapes. 'And new cushions, too.' She picked up a fluffy fake-angora cushion. 'I love these cushions,' she sighed.

'Shows how long since you've been here,' Shona said, excitedly. 'Wait till you see the kitchen. Paul painted the units and Ross and I picked the cutest china handles for the doors.'

Shona hadn't changed in the weeks Maggie had been away, she thought fondly. Her friend was still as effervescent as ever and had squealed down the phone when Maggie had rung to say she was coming to Galway to take the rest of her stuff from the apartment.

'You'll stay with us,' she insisted.

'Thanks,' Maggie had said. She couldn't bear to stay in

her old apartment with Grey, not even for one night. It represented the past and the person she used to be. And she was still close enough to that person to want to distance herself.

When Maggie had admired the new-look kitchen, they sat at the tiny breakfast bar having tea and Maggie filled Shona in on Ivan, her job in the children's library, and how she'd talked to a lawyer about selling her share of the Galway apartment to Grey.

'I want to do it now,' Maggie said. 'The apartment's the last bit of that life and I want it removed, surgically.'

'I'll miss you, though,' Shona reminded her. 'It's not the same in work without you and it'll always be different now with you living in Dublin and us here.'

'I know,' Maggie said apologetically. 'I'll miss you too, but it's not as if I'm emigrating to the moon or anything. We have email, the phone and cheap flights to Dublin.'

Shona nodded, looking as if she was about to say something else, but had thought better of it.

'Come on, let's go out and liven up this town,' Shona said. 'I fancy a French pastry in Delaney's, or maybe a slice of double chocolate cake.'

They took the stairs. pausing briefly by Ross's door on the floor below. Loud music could be heard through the door.

'Is that "I Will Survive"?' Maggie asked. Ross had had so many break-ups, it was his anthem.

''Fraid so,' said Shona. 'He's very cut up about it, says he's going to emigrate to somewhere where men are allowed to wear pink velvet and kiss on the streets.'

'You mean San Francisco?' grinned Maggie.

'He's got his heart set on Edinburgh. I know, I've told him Edinburgh isn't known for men wearing pink velvet or kissing each other wildly on Princes Street, but he says he looks so much better in winter clothes that Edinburgh's got to be the place.'

They both pondered the workings of Ross's mind.

'The end of a love affair does strange things to a person,' Shona went on. 'I said I couldn't bear to lose him too. What will I do if both you and Ross are gone?'

'He'd never leave Nureyev,' Maggie pointed out. 'Can rabbits get a pet passport?'

'That's the only sticking point, but if Nureyev can't go, Paul and I are going to adopt him.'

'We will be hearing the patter of tiny feet around your apartment!' teased Maggie.

Shona didn't respond to the joke.

'Tiny feet, get it?' said Maggie.

'Mmm, funny,' muttered Shona.

'Have I put my foot in it?' Maggie asked quickly, alarm bells ringing. The day Shona didn't laugh like a drain at even the feeblest joke, you knew there was something wrong.

The phone and emails were great for keeping in touch but there were some things that you had to be present to feel – what if Shona had received bad news about the possibility of her having children?

'I didn't mean to upset you,' Maggie said earnestly.

'You didn't, you big nelly,' said Shona. 'I was waiting to get you sitting down in Delaney's to tell you. I'm pregnant. Paul and I are going to be parents! A baby and possibly a rabbit too! We're thrilled.'

'That's wonderful,' Maggie said, giving her friend another hug, then pulling away anxiously in case she squashed Shona's belly.

They both looked down there.

'It's still flat,' Shona said, patting her waistband. 'I've been into a maternity clothes shop where they have a cushion you stick up your jumper to envisage being five months pregnant so you can buy your clothes in advance. Actually, I keep going in. I can't afford to buy the clothes but the cushion is so realistically baby-like, I genuinely look pregnant with it and I love looking at it under my jumper. They're sick of the sight of me there.'

'Let's go there!' insisted Maggie. 'I want to see what you look like five months pregnant too.'

She held Shona's hand as they went down the last flight of stairs and out on to the street.

'I didn't know how to tell you though,' Shona admitted. 'You know, it's like we're so happy and Paul is nearly doing a dance of joy, while Grey is up for bastard of the year award and I feel so bad for you.'

'Bastard of the year award? I love the sound of that,' Maggie said. 'Really, I don't know if anyone will approve, but I think it adds something to college life.'

'You're not upset, though?' Shona asked as they crossed the street and arrived at Delaney's café.

'Shona, I am thrilled for you both. This is the most incredible bit of news ever. Why would it upset me?'

'Well . . .' Shona paused, while they waved hi to the waitress and squashed on to a little table to one side of the door. 'You were going through so much. I felt so sorry for you and I didn't want to land my joy on top of you. You know, when you're feeling bad, it can be hard to take other people getting everything they ever wanted.'

Maggie digested this bit of information. In all the years she'd known Shona, Shona had never implied that she wanted kids or even thought about it; in fact, Shona and Paul seemed like two kids themselves, happy to lurch along in their lovable way, having fun, throwing parties, buying rollerblades, going to Euro Disney on their own.

'I'm thrilled,' she repeated. 'Absolutely thrilled. How could you ever think I'd be otherwise? Just don't feng shui me out of your life when junior comes along. I'm your friend and I want to keep on being your friend. I've done plenty of babysitting in my time. I can be a good auntie.'

'Thank you,' said Shona tearfully. 'I am so happy. Paul is so happy. It was a surprise, I can tell you. We weren't trying, we don't know how it happened.' Maggie opened her mouth to explain but Shona got there first. 'No, well, we know how it happened but, you know, really happened.

'Then I felt guilty because Paul said he'd love us to have a baby and I kept thinking of you and Grey, how you never seemed to think about kids either and I thought my being pregnant would remind you of that.'

Maggie shook her head.

'Stop feeling guilty,' she said. The issue of children was one of those great unmentioned subjects between her and Grey and surely if you loved someone and they were the one, you'd have the conversation, wouldn't you? But there had been times as she'd neared thirty that she'd begun to think about children.

'Grey and I never talked about it,' she said, bluntly.

'I didn't think so,' Shona said sadly, 'so I never talked to you about kids or even the thought of having them because it might . . .'

She stopped.

Maggie filled in the rest of the sentence. '. . . Because it might make me realise the difference between you and Paul and me and Grey. You thought he was wrong for me when we were going out, didn't you?' she said, not wanting to hear that Shona, whom she felt so close to, had thought he was the wrong person for Maggie.

'Hey, I loved Grey,' Shona insisted. 'Honestly. He's sexy, funny and charming, what's not to like? Paul, well, he was never really into him. I just told him to shut up. You were our friend and we couldn't hurt you.'

Maggie thought of all the nights they had spent together as a foursome and cringed.

'It's not that he's wise after the event and realised that Grey was a two-timer under all the gloss,' Shona went on quickly. 'They just didn't gel. Paul thought that Grey was a bit, you know, pompous, intellectual, trying to prove how smart he was and you know Paul hates that sort of stuff. He thinks Simone de Beauvoir was a French singer and Nietzsche was an astronaut.'

Maggie burst out laughing. 'It's good to be back,' she said. 'Let's cut to the chase, Shona, and order something full of cream.'

The next morning, Maggie left Shona and Paul's apartment a little after nine and walked a couple of blocks to the book-shop-cum-coffee shop where Grey liked to sit reading the paper and enjoying his breakfast of double espresso. During term time, it was a favoured hang-out of the political students and would-be intellectuals, a spot where many an admiring student had sidled up to Grey and Maggie as they enjoyed coffee and said a shy 'hi' to Dr Stanley.

She hadn't wanted to visit him in their apartment and neither had she wanted to phone him. She didn't want him prepared for this meeting with ready arguments all laid out. Instead, she had an armful of legal documents from her newly hired lawyer relating to selling their jointly owned apartment.

She pushed open the door of the bookshop and made her way upstairs to the tiny coffee shop. He was there, lounging elegantly on a chair, coffee cup held in long artistic fingers, gazing at the paper earnestly.

'Hello, Grey,' said Maggie.

He looked up from his newspaper and she could see that he was astonished. 'Maggie!' he said, delight in his voice. 'How wonderful to see you.'

The way his eyes roamed over her made her sure he was pleased to see her. She had made an enormous effort with what she was wearing, and had abandoned her jeans for a long cotton skirt with slits up the side that showed off her legs and a soft aqua shirt that tied neatly around her slim stomach. She looked good, better than good, she looked great.

The morning affirmations and the book of self-confidence – which she'd read for a third time – were working. After all, there was no point in being the only person who thought she looked like Quasimodo's younger sister.

'Can I sit down?' she said.

'Please do,' Grey said suavely, taking the rest of his morning pile of papers off the other chair.

Maggie sat, feeling strangely relaxed, but Grey didn't look relaxed at all. He glanced nervously at his watch as if he was worried about the time. Was he waiting for another woman maybe? Maggie tested to see how much that would hurt, Grey waiting for another woman. She bounced the idea around in her head and found that she didn't care. It hadn't been that long, she knew, since they had split up, but so much had happened. She'd got over him, she thought. She'd tried so hard to keep him by being what he wanted that she wondered if the real Maggie had loved him at all or he her.

'I didn't expect to see you here,' Grey said. 'I didn't think you were coming back to Galway.'

'And how was I going to move the rest of my stuff out of the apartment then?' Maggie asked calmly.

'I thought maybe Shona would do it.'

'You mean you thought I couldn't face coming back,' she said.

'That too,' he said. 'I'm sorry, Maggie,' he began.

'Let's stop all this "I'm sorry", Grey. We've gone through it so often it's becoming boring. It's over between us, it was over the first time you lied to me, except I don't know exactly when that was.'

'The only thing Shona wasn't able to find out,' he said, bitterly. 'That woman should work for Interpol, she's so good at ferreting around for information.'

'It's called keeping an eye out for your friends,' Maggie said evenly. 'Shona understands that I wouldn't want to be married to a man who could cheat on me, and lie about it. We might have had some chance if you'd been honest but . . .' She thought about it. 'Actually, no,' she said. 'Strike that. We wouldn't have had a chance whether you'd told me about the other women or not, Grey. I'd never trust you again. And I couldn't respect a man who'd make love to me, and still manage to screw other women without feeling in the slightest bit guilty. So no, it wouldn't have worked out. But I'd have appreciated the honesty, I'd have respected you more.'

'There's no going back, then?'

She shook her head.

'Are you coming back to Galway to live?'

'I don't think so, I've made a new life for myself, I'm busy.'

'I noticed. I saw you in the paper, you and your mother, the heroines of Summer Street.'

Maggie grinned, where once she would have been embarrassed at the thought of such publicity.

'They used that picture of us on the steps of the pavilion because you're gorgeous and I'm not too bad for an old bird!' her mother had said proudly at the time and Maggie had stared at her in astonishment. Her mother was saying she was gorgeous. Maggie didn't remember anyone saying that when she was growing up, but maybe they had and she just hadn't noticed. Her own insecurities and the emotional pain of the bullying had stopped her hearing the words. She'd been loved and adored; of course they would have told her she was beautiful.

'There was a stunning photo of the pair of you on the steps of that old building,' Grey went on.

'My mother loves that picture – she says we're gorgeous in it,' Maggie said proudly. She was able to say such a thing without wincing and was almost beginning to believe it. Men didn't look at her in the street because she had her jeans on backwards or her hair was stuck to her head, they looked at her because they thought she was attractive.

'Beauty sells,' agreed Grey morosely, staring at her. 'Are you going out with anybody?' he asked. 'It's just you seem happier, happier than you were with me.'

'I am, as a matter of fact,' Maggie said, unable to hide the broad smile that lit up her face at the thought of Ivan. 'He's a good man. Kind, handsome, very sexy.' She couldn't resist adding that, just to show Grey that he wasn't the only one who could hook up with members of the opposite sex. 'And he's older than me, by a few years,' she added.

'Not a twenty-year-old student, you mean,' Grey snapped.

'Exactly.'

'He makes you happy?' He looked as if he would prefer to hear that this man didn't make Maggie happy.

'He makes me very happy,' she said softly. 'I can be myself with him.'

'You were yourself with me,' Grey insisted.

'No, I wasn't,' Maggie said, determined to say what had to be said. 'I was what I thought you wanted me to be. We did things you wanted to do, because I wanted you to be happy. Not things I wanted to do. Not that it was all your fault, I had my own issues,' she said, 'but you didn't help. You wanted a certain type of person as your girlfriend and I was pliable enough to fit perfectly into the role.'

'I loved you,' Grey said defensively.

'Loved me enough to have four affairs while we were together?' Maggie asked sharply. 'That's not love, Grey. That's selfishness masquerading as love. If you'd really loved me, you wouldn't have needed anyone else.'

'What a cliché,' he said in irritation. 'I don't know why women buy into all that romantic bullshit. All the same, all wanting fairytale marriages and white dresses and happy-ever-after. Life isn't like that.'

'It can be,' Maggie stated. 'It can be if you want it to be, and I want it to be. And if the man I'm with is unfaithful to me, then I'll leave him too. Do you understand?' she said. 'I don't want happy-ever-after romance. I want real love and respect and I'd prefer to be on my own than be with someone and without it.'

Grey wasn't listening. He was staring, like a goldfish, at someone approaching from behind her.

Maggie turned to see a slender young blonde girl, mid-twenties at the most, standing awkwardly a few metres away from their table.

'Er . . . well . . .' stammered Grey, no doubt anticipating seeing the remains of his coffee landing on his clothes.

'Relax,' Maggie said. 'You're a free agent, Grey. See who you like.'

She got to her feet, handed him the sheaf of papers and held out her hand for him to shake it. 'Let's sort this out as soon as possible,' she said.

He took her hand and shook it.

Then she turned to face the blonde woman.

'Hi,' Maggie said. 'I'm just leaving. He's all yours.'

Then she walked down the bookshop stairs, head held high.

For old times' sake, she took the bus out to Salthill and walked along the beach. The vastness of the Altantic always awed her. She'd loved walking here when she'd first come to Galway, loved the knowledge that centuries of women had walked along here, thinking about their lives and loves when there were no amusement arcades in the background, just the stretch of the bay encircling them.

She'd like to share this place with Ivan. But perhaps not just yet.

As she walked, Maggie realised that she didn't want to make any big decisions yet about her and Ivan. She'd tried to get other people to fix what was wrong with her. And it hadn't worked; it couldn't. Only she had been able to fix herself. She didn't want to make that mistake with Ivan.

If they ended up together, it would be for all the right reasons, she promised herself that. Smiling, she turned and headed back along the beach.

# CHAPTER TWENTY-NINE

The office looked exactly the same as when Faye had left it. The 'Flipper Does Dallas' painting still dominating the reception area, the arrangements of flowers on the tables in reception looking unchanged, and Grace's stilettos still crackling as she ran across the reception floor.

In a stunning cream suit with a nipped-in waist and buttons like golden golfballs, she was the epitome of the corporate madam.

'Welcome back!' Grace said delightedly. 'I love your hair!'

Faye laughed and kissed Grace on the cheek.

'I've been away for a month, I've gone through all sorts of torments and the first thing you mention to me is my hair?' she demanded in mock disgust.

It was very different. The brown ponytail was gone, to be replaced by a jaw-length feathery bob which really suited her.

'It's only a haircut, Grace,' she added, although she knew it was more than that. Asking for a new look hadn't just been chopping off a lot of hair. It was making an effort, albeit a small effort, to step back into the world.

'It's fabulous though,' said Grace, giving Faye's hair a

professional once-over. 'All you need is for Ellen to come in and maybe do something about your clothes.'

'Grace!' warned Faye as they stepped into the lift. 'I like my clothes and it's only because you're an old friend that I allow you even to mention them and my lack of interest in them without killing you.'

'Sorry,' said Grace unsubdued. 'It's just, you have had that suit quite a long time and there is a sale on in Debenhams.'

'Point taken.'

'Fine.' Grace put up her hands in resignation. 'It's lovely to have you back, even if . . .' She stopped herself.

'Even if Amber isn't with me?' Faye said.

'Sorry, I don't know what to say. I wish I knew how to console you but I suppose there is no making it better. At least you found her and talked to her.' Grace wasn't entirely sure if Amber had any plans to come back because she hadn't wanted to ask Faye such a tough question, but whatever had gone on in California between the two of them, Faye was actually looking better than she had for years. It wasn't just the hair. That was only a surface thing, Grace knew.

But Faye genuinely looked different – not content exactly, because Grace knew that Faye could never be content when Amber was away from her – but strangely more comfortable, less uptight, as if a weight had been lifted from her shoulders.

'The whole office has missed you.' Grace changed the subject. 'Personally and professionally. Little Island can't cope when you're gone. You better not have any holidays again,' she said, teasing.

'No, not ever again,' agreed Faye. 'Although I'm thinking of taking a month in September to visit Amber.'

She hadn't discussed this with Amber, not sure how her daughter would react to the news that her mother was going to fly out to LA to spend a month there. Faye realised that if Mohammed wouldn't go to the mountain, then the mountain would have to go to Mohammed.

'The month of September, that's fine,' Grace said evenly. 'Are you free for lunch? We've a lot to talk about. Neil has been driving me mad, driving Philippa mad too. You know what he's like when he gets involved in the business.'

Faye did know. Grace's husband, Neil, was not one of life's instinctive people managers. He could start an argument in an empty room.

'Of course I'm free for lunch,' she said.

When Grace had gone, Faye had sat down and glanced around at her office, thinking it was odd to find it looking the same as ever when so much had changed within herself. Her desk looked exactly as she always left it, with the phone and the stapler precisely at right angles to the top of the desk; even the cleaners knew to leave it that way, because Mrs Reid insisted upon everything just so.

God, she was anal, Faye realised ruefully. She reached over and moved the phone, the stapler and the lamp. There, just a little bit of chaos, a smidgen of unpredictability. It was probably better that way. She didn't know what she was going to do next with her life – that was unpredictable, too, but as she mulled this over she decided it could be rather exciting. She'd muted herself for so long in order to be the perfect mother and, instead, had turned into a controlling person who'd lost sight of the real Faye.

Now it was time to work out who the real Faye was and to enjoy life again. She'd punished herself enough for the past.

Amber looked around her new home, a tiny studio apartment in west Hollywood, and grimaced. Compared to the hotel – where she'd been staying in one of the cheapest rooms after moving out of Karl's suite – it was nothing much to look at

445

and definitely needed some serious cleaning products. Her mother's weak bleach solution might do the trick. Still, it was furnished, in a reasonably safe building with security doors, an intercom system and she was on the second floor rather than the ground.

Number 2F contained a kitchenette, a tray-sized balcony overlooking the apartment block next door's pool and a minute shower room. It hadn't taken her long to move in. All she had were a lot of clothes, some nice hotel toiletries and that was it. She made a list of all the stuff she needed, like groceries, cleaning products, washing powder, some plants to brighten the place up, and headed off to find a shop.

It was Syd who had helped her find her new home when she'd told him she was leaving Karl.

'You can't –'

'– Leave?' said Amber. 'Syd, you know I have to. I can't hang on to Karl's coat-tails for ever, not when he doesn't want me. I have some pride, you know.'

'I know,' he'd replied.

So Syd had talked to Michael Levin about Amber and asked for his help in getting her a job and a place to live.

Karl, on the other hand, had done nothing.

He'd barely spoken to her since the day after her mum left.

He'd come home in the morning as usual to find Amber packing up her stuff.

'You're going,' he said flatly.

'There's nothing for me to stay for.' Amber shrugged, still packing.

'What will you do?'

'There's a street corner on Sunset Boulevard for me,' she replied sarcastically. 'Since you've been treating me like little more than a prostitute, I might as well go the whole hog and make money from it. Hopefully, Richard Gere will see this Pretty Woman and rescue her, although I forgot – you already rescued me from my boring life. Nobody would be so lucky to have it happen to them twice.'

'Amber, don't talk that way,' Karl said. 'It wasn't meant to happen like this, but it sorta did. I've got to think of the band . . .'

'You're thinking of Karl,' Amber shot back, 'as usual. Number one. Nobody else gets in the way. I was useful when I was your muse but as soon as another muse came along, I was history. I hope somebody tells Venetia that you run through girlfriends pretty quickly. Although she'll probably last longer than me. She's more useful.'

'It's not like that,' he said. 'Don't be bitter, Amber. You had a blast. Nobody forced you to come.'

She glared at him. 'You did.'

'Did I hold a gun to your head and make you get on the plane at Dublin airport? No. So don't go all "you made me, Karl"! Right?'

There was no point talking to him.

'You're right, Karl. It was all my fault. I should have known better. I will in future,' she said.

She was quickly running through the money her mother had given her, and for the past few days had been working as a receptionist in a hairdressing salon close to the Beverly Center, although she guessed that her entire wages were less than the tips some of the stylists got from their wealthy clients. Because she was working illegally, she'd been lucky to find such a job. Most illegals ended up chambermaiding and cleaning but Amber's Irish accent had touched a chord with the salon owner and he'd hired her on the spot.

The salon staff were friendly and Syd seemed determined to keep in touch every day, inviting her to parties and gigs so that she felt as if she had some social life in LA. He'd also given her some more money.

'I can't take this!' she said. 'It's the band's money.'

'You were a part of the band, Amber,' Syd said sadly. 'I feel bad about the way Karl's treated you. I've known him a long time, I should have warned you. I thought it was different with you because you're not his usual type, you're smart.'

'That's something.' She grinned.

'I told him not to make you leave Ireland in such a hurry, but you know Karl, once he sets his mind on something, he does it.'

'You said that to him?' she asked.

'It's important to think things through,' Syd muttered.

'I wish you'd said it to me,' Amber replied. 'But I wouldn't have listened, would I?'

She thought about home a lot: her mother, Ella, Gran, the life she'd left behind. The longer she was away from home, the more she wanted to go back.

But after the way she'd run off, nobody would want her there, would they?

And then Saul came back into her life.

He'd simply turned up at the salon one day as they were closing, and said, 'Hello, Amber.'

She stared at him in shock, remembering that it was at his beautiful house, at his party, that she'd finally realised Karl didn't love her after all.

'We're closing, sorry,' she said. 'Do you want to make an appointment?' Pen poised like the professional she was, she smiled at him.

'I don't want an appointment. I wanted to talk to you, Amber. Syd told me you were here,' Saul said. 'I've a proposition for you.'

It took ten minutes before Saul managed to convince Amber that he wasn't a sleazy guy trying to take advantage of her now that she was penniless and alone. They sat in a health food café nursing smoothies while Saul explained.

'You know I'm an art collector and I think you have great talent,' he said. 'I'd like to invest in your talent. No strings attached,' he'd added for what had to be the tenth time. 'You know I'm a collector: you saw the paintings in my house. I'm interested in your talent as an artist. If you spent a year out here or in New Mexico, just think of the work you'd produce. I've still got the picture you drew in my house. You left it behind that night. It's only a sketch but it's more vital and alive than a lot of the work that's going for thousands of dollars in local galleries. So, what do you think?'

Amber was speechless.

'You still want to paint, right?' Saul asked. 'You don't have to go to art college to do that. You could make a damn good living right now.'

Still, she said nothing.

'You could go home and do the art college thing too, and then come back,' Saul went on. 'We'd have to hire a lawyer to sort out your immigration status first, though. There's nothing stopping you from making it. You've certainly got the talent.'

In her head, Amber repeated his words 'there's nothing stopping you'.

There was nothing stopping her – except her pride and fear of facing the people she'd hurt. What she really wanted to do was go home, be with the people she loved and go to art college. And she could do that. All she needed was her plane ticket.

'Thank you for the vote of confidence,' said Amber earnestly, 'but I'm going to learn my trade first. You need to learn how to paint an apple straight before you can paint it abstract. I want to go home. Then, I'll be able to paint.'

James had been gone over a week and Christie, who'd often thought that her beloved dogs were the best companions in the world, found that Tilly and Rocket's adoration didn't mean quite as much when James wasn't around.

She tried hard to be her old self, but it was almost impossible. Her hands shook sometimes for no reason, as if her body was trying to express the shock she was desperately trying to suppress. She felt exhausted every evening and fell into bed early, drifting into a heavy sleep and then waking in panic in the middle of the night. She could never go back to sleep and lay alone in the big bed she and James had shared for so long, her whole chest aching with sadness as the dawn rose. She couldn't even cry. Tears weren't enough to express what she felt.

During their married life they had spent so little time apart.

James had gone off on a few fishing trips and she'd gone away on school trips a couple of times, but all added up together, it wouldn't account for more than a few months apart, over thirty-five years. She told nobody what had happened, she felt too ashamed and embarrassed.

Shane and Ethan still knew nothing, for which she was eternally grateful. At least James hadn't decided to destroy her totally by telling their sons how she'd cheated on him with another man. But Christie knew that if James never came home, the boys would have to learn someday. Which was the scariest thought – James never coming home or Ethan and Shane learning about Carey Wolensky?

Ana had dropped in unexpectedly one day, smiling as usual, full of chat about what she and Rick were up to.

Christie hugged her longer than was necessary, feeling the familiar remorse at how she'd betrayed her sister. If Ana ever found out ... Christie paled at the thought of that. She'd lost her husband, please let her not lose her sister too.

Citing James's working too hard and ignoring her was not a valid excuse for what she'd done to Ana. She hoped she would never have to tell her. Living with the guilt of it was punishment enough.

'Rick says we should downsize,' Ana was saying as they walked up to the Summer Street Café. Ana was mad on the new lemon muffins there. 'The house is big and so's the garden, but it's got character. Not as much as your house, but still, I don't fancy moving into something characterless, even if we made money on the move.'

Christie ordered coffee and cake, although her mouth was so dry she might as well have been eating ashes.

'Did you ever go ahead with seeing Carey Wolensky?' she asked finally.

Ana gave the irrepressible grin that reminded Christie of what she'd been like as a child, with her fair hair tied in pigtails, a dimple on either cheek.

'No,' admitted Ana. 'It was wishful thinking really. It's not as if we ever had anything to say to each other when we were going out, so what would we say now, twenty-five years down the line? And I saw a photo of him in the papers. He looks about a hundred now, you know. I suppose you always have a thing for the ones who dumped you.' Ana took another bite of her muffin and looked thoughtful. 'And he gave me a great bit of advice.'

'What did he say?' asked Christie lightly.

'That I should stop going out with men like my father, tough, controlling ones, and find a decent, nice man who'd appreciate me.' Ana beamed. 'He hit the nail on the head there – that's what you used to say to me too. But you were both right. So I went off and before long I met Rick, who turned out to be the love of my life and still is. And there aren't many people my age who can say that, now, are there? Well,' Ana added, 'apart from you and James, obviously.'

\* \* \*

With an absence of anyone to talk to and with no work, now that school was closed for the summer, Christie did the only thing she could do under the circumstances. She set up her easel on the terrace where the pergola gave her shade and began to paint. She'd planned to do one of her botanical pictures, the detailed representations of irises and orchids she had always loved to draw, but found she couldn't concentrate on them. Perhaps she could only work on them when she was happy. So she gave up and began painting a portrait instead.

For her, painting was like therapy: as she painted, she thought of the mistakes that had brought her to this point.

She and Carey had had two days of a love affair. Two days of pure, joyful pleasure when they made love on the day bed, and curled up afterwards talking, Carey smoking the unfiltered cigarettes he adored, the ones Christie hated.

It was like being in a dream, one where none of her actions could hurt either herself or anyone else. A lovely dream from which she would awaken with a pleasurable memory and no guilt.

'If I were your husband, I would wonder where you were every day,' Carey murmured in the late afternoon of that second, glorious day.

'My husband hasn't even noticed I'm not at home every day,' Christie said bitterly. 'It's as if I don't exist for him. Right now, he's only interested in his work. I'm just someone to look after his children and cook dinner each night.'

'Is that why you did this? To get back at him?' Carey asked, like a scientist probing a rat in an experiment.

'No,' said Christie. 'That's not why. He never notices me these days, but you do. That's why I wanted to be with you . . .' Saying it out loud make the words sound feeble. Her husband was busy so she'd betrayed him.

It was more than that, wasn't it?

'We need to talk,' Carey said. 'I am going to London next month. I have an important commission, it could make me rich. Christie, leave, come with me. Bring your little boys. I can love them too. I love their mother.'

It was talking of the future that made Christie's daydream crumble. The future. Life without James, life ferrying her beloved children back and forth between them. Anger, hurt, betrayal. Ana hating her. James hating her more.

The dream shattered and she felt the iron grasp of guilt around her soul. What had she done? She must have been mad.

'No, Carey,' she said, getting up. She was naked, and she found her clothes where he'd thrown them on the floor after ripping them from her in the heat of desire.

'I can't. This was a mistake. I have to go. I can't see you again, sorry, but it has to be that way.'

Shoes, where were her shoes? She couldn't see them for tears.

'You don't mean this?' he demanded, uncurling his body from the day bed and grabbing her by both arms. 'You have to come with me. We were meant for each other, you know that. This is not tawdry sex between an artist and his model, this is real love, true passion. I've never felt this way about a woman before,' he said, almost in wonderment. 'You can't go.'

'I can,' said Christie wildly. 'I've got to. I'd lose so much, I'd lose all the people I love if I go with you. I'm sorry.'

She found her shoes, put them on, flung her coat over her shoulder and went to the door. She made herself take one last look at him standing there, looking bewildered and hurt, and so devastatingly attractive. 'I'm sorry,' she said again.

'You'll be back,' he snapped.

'I won't,' she said.

\*　　\*　　\*

453

When she'd emptied her head of all the tumbling thoughts, Christie painted quickly and furiously.

The next day, she was outside, standing putting the finishing touches to her painting when she heard footsteps in the hall, moving into the kitchen. The dogs, who'd never been much good in the watchdog department, leaped to their feet, yapping happily and ran into the house. She could hear a man's voice, James's.

She could imagine him bending down, petting Tilly's ears, rubbing Rocket's soft belly. But Christie stayed where she was. He mightn't want to see her, he might have just come to pick up more things.

'Christie?' came his voice.

'I'm in the garden,' she called, not knowing what to expect. She put her brush down and sat down on the chair. She thought she might need to be sitting for this. James walked over towards her, then hesitated. The easel stood between them.

'How are you?' she said tremulously, her eyes glued to his face. He looked tired, pale.

James gazed back at her steadily, and Christie wished she knew what was in his heart. Please, she prayed, please.

'I've been thinking,' he said.

'Me too,' she answered quickly.

'Thinking about our lives then. How hard I was working, how hard you were working. It must have been difficult, with me so busy and you coping with the children and work and everything at home. We had no time together, no time at all. I wasn't the best husband ever at that point.'

Christie held her breath. He hadn't said, *Goodbye, I've come to pick up my stuff*. There was some hope.

'I don't know if I can ever forget what happened between you and him.'

Again, he didn't say Carey's name and Christie felt her spirits sink at his words.

454

'But,' James went on, 'I could try.'

'You could try?' Christie asked. 'Try to forget? Try again?'

He nodded. 'I love you, Christie. You're my whole life, you always have been, ever since I met you. That's what hurts, to think that there was a time when I wasn't your whole life, to think that we've been living a lie.'

'But we weren't,' Christie pleaded. 'It only happened for a short time, it was stupid, and then it was over. It didn't rewrite our history, it doesn't negate everything we had, our love, our children, our life together.'

'I know that,' James said. 'Doesn't make it any easier to handle, though. I kept imagining you and him –' He stopped. 'I can't bear to think of that, Christie. And then, when you left the pictures for me to see, I was so angry and hurt. All I could think was you were trying to show me how much he loved you, because he'd been able to paint you. I don't understand art, that's your world and I was never a part of it. But I felt bad because I'd never tried to be a part of it and, at the same time, furious with you for having him, having that other life.'

He was being so honest and it was so heartbreaking that Christie wanted nothing more than to get up and to put her arms around him. But she couldn't. She had to let him speak his piece. That was his right. She'd done what she thought was right, now it was his turn.

'When you showed me the pictures,' he went on, 'I thought you'd done it for a reason: that you wanted to be with him again. When you said it wasn't that, that he was dying and that he wanted to see you one last time, I don't think I believed you. I still thought you must be trying to hurt me.'

'I'd never hurt you, not intentionally,' she said. 'Although I have hurt you, I didn't mean to.'

'I didn't go fishing,' he said. 'I took some time off to think. I stayed in the B & B beside the lake, but I just walked and

455

walked every day. I couldn't bring myself to actually fish,' he said ruefully. 'And I realised I couldn't let the past destroy us. We're stronger than that. You're an honest person and that's why you told me, I know that now. You could have left me in the dark and I would never have known and some day, a hundred years from now, someone would put two and two together. You'd be named as the dark lady and I'd be the fool, the cuckold, the man who never knew. I don't want to be the man who never knew, that's not what I married you for. I can't say I'm glad you told me, but now that you have, it's not going to end our marriage.'

'Oh, James,' said Christie and she ran to him.

He held out his arms and pulled her into his embrace.

'Thank you,' she sobbed, 'thank you. I couldn't ring you or try to get in touch with you, I knew you had to do this on your own. I never meant to hurt you, not twenty-five years ago, not last week, not ever, you know that. I just don't want there to be any more secrets. I've lived my life frightened that this would come out and destroy what we had. I just couldn't live with that any more.'

He held her close, saying nothing, stroking her hair, her head burrowed into his shoulder.

'I missed you,' he said. 'That's what made me come back. Thinking of a life without you, what it would be like to live on my own. We'd sell this place, split the money and both of us live out lives of quiet misery because of my pride, because of something that happened twenty-five years ago. And no, I didn't want to do that,' he said. 'Carey Wolensky nearly took so much away from me, he wasn't going to take you away again.'

And Christie stood in his embrace and prayed thank you to whoever was watching over them. They stood there for a while, until the dogs got tired of sniffing around their feet and lay down and fell asleep. It was nice just to stand there and be held by the man she loved most in the whole world.

'What are you painting?' asked James, eventually.

Christie moved back and wiped her eyes with her hand.

'I started doing one of my flower pictures,' she said with a sniffle, reaching into her cardigan pocket for a tissue. She wiped her eyes and blew her nose. 'But I couldn't concentrate on it, couldn't concentrate on anything really, I was just waiting for you. And then, I found this old photo and it came to me that's what I should be painting.' She led James around the other side of the easel and stood while he stared at the picture. In her own style, she'd copied an old family photograph of when the boys were young. Shane and Ethan sat on a couch and behind them, leaning over the back of the couch, smiling, arms around each other, were James and Christie. It was a beautiful family shot, hidden in an album for far too long, and she'd captured the joy on their faces perfectly.

'It's a family portrait,' James said.

'Because my family is what's important to me,' Christie said. 'You're what's important to me.'

He put an arm around her waist and squeezed.

'I know,' he said.

# CHAPTER THIRTY

Autumn on Summer Street came very slowly. The gently curved road was a sheltered place and, by September, the leaves of the maples that lined the pavements were only tinged with the most delicate hint of gold. The Japanese maple in Una Maguire's front garden, however, had turned a startling dark crimson attracting admiring glances from passers-by. Christie Devlin's soft white blousy roses were losing their petals daily, except for the creamy climbing rose that crept up over the wall and wrapped tendrils around the ever-open gate. That still bloomed, sending a heady rose scent on to the breeze and making people talk of an Indian summer.

But in spite of the good weather, the summer indolence of barbecues and sitting out sunbathing on front steps was over.

There was a sense of business about the whole street, the feeling of a new start. Holidays were over and the new school term had arrived.

At the Summer Street Café, Henry took in all but two of the little tables that stood on the pavement. His customers were drifting indoors now, preferring their coffees looking out over Summer Street. He liked autumn with its sense of renewal; it reminded him of being a kid going back to school with a bagful of clean new copy books, ready to be filled with wisdom.

'I think you were always a wise man,' teased Xu. She'd really come out of her shell, Henry thought proudly, feeling a certain responsibility for that. He and Jane had done their best to welcome her warmly, and her growing friendship with Maggie Maguire had helped integrate her into their community too.

Xu was a lot different from the shy woman who'd come to work for them at the start of the year. She was a big part of Summer Street.

Xu herself was excited that her mother was coming from China to visit her.

Henry and Jane had insisted that Xu's mother stay in their spare room.

'You've only got a tiny bedsit,' Jane pointed out. 'There won't be room to swing a cat there.'

'She doesn't have a cat,' Xu said gravely, then laughed. She loved being able to make jokes in English now. Everyone assumed her to be so sober and serious that they didn't expect her to make jokes.

'We've taught you too well,' smiled Jane. 'You'll be as bad as Henry soon with the jokes.'

'I told you the Irish and Chinese were similar,' said Xu. 'We have the same sense of humour, except it's more hidden in my people.'

'It's not hidden now,' said Jane cheerfully. 'Come on, you pair, let's get those chairs in or the customers will be tripping over them.'

At number 34, Christie Devlin was getting ready for another teaching year, her last, she'd decided.

'Are you sure you want to do this?' James said to her the night before school started. 'Don't do it just because of me.'

'I'm ready to retire,' said Christie. 'Think of all the places we can go then, the things we can do together.'

Although James could stay another two years before retirement, he'd decided to go early. He'd stop working when Christie did the following summer. They had already amassed a collection of brochures about long holidays abroad for the adventuresome spirit. Christie particularly liked the sound of the trip around India, although Ethan and Shane had been a bit anxious when they had seen the brochure.

'A month?' said Shane, the brochure opened to the fares page. 'For this price, you're hardly going to be staying in old maharajahs' palaces,' he said doubtfully. 'And what about the food, what if one of you gets sick?'

James and Christie looked at each other and laughed.

'If we get sick, we get sick!' James said cheerily. 'We'll bring plenty of medicine to bung us up from each end. We're grown-ups, you know,' he added, 'we're not ready for the nursing home yet.'

'That's not what I meant,' Shane explained.

'I know, I know,' said his father.

'But why now?' said Ethan. 'Why did you never go on these sorts of holidays years ago? You could have taken the time off.'

Christie and James exchanged another look, a private look.

'This is time for us now,' she said. 'You're all settled, you've got your own lives, your own families, it's time for us to be selfish.'

'Yeah, but what if we need you, with the baby and everything?' Shane said, sounding briefly like a child and not like an adult with a wife and a first child on the way.

'The baby will be fine,' Christie said, and she knew he would be.

She'd seen a healthy little boy in the future, to be followed, hopefully, by two more. She and James had given Shane and Janet some money for their new arrival and to help them buy a house.

'We promise we'll do double babysitting duties when we

get back,' she added. 'You can always email us, we have a hotmail account.'

'I don't know,' joked Ethan, 'parents these days: they're crazy and want to travel the world and don't care about anyone else.'

The whole family laughed at this.

'You're right,' James said. 'It's like we're in our second childhoods.'

At number 48, Una Maguire was back on her feet and had taken up yoga.

'Flexibility is the key to taking care of yourself,' she told everyone who'd listen. 'If I'd done yoga years ago, who knows, I mightn't have broken my leg after all. Your father and I have a bet on about the lotus position. I said I'll be in it by Christmas and he says never. I'm going to win that tenner from you, Dennis.'

Maggie laughed at her mother. It was brilliant to see her on such good form. Una Maguire was one of life's strong people. No matter what life threw at her, she threw it right back with her own peculiar topspin. Maggie had stopped obsessing about how she'd turned out so different from her mother and had begun to appreciate her differences.

She was a bit more like her dad really. Quiet and shy, but with enough of her mother's strength and fire, if required. The developers involved in trying to destroy the Summer Street pavilion had certainly learned that to their cost.

The holiday season had meant that both the plan to knock down the pavilion and the campaign to save it were at a standstill. But the fact that no bulldozer had entered the park in the dead of night and ripped the pavilion to pieces was down to Maggie's work. She'd given so many interviews with newspapers and radio stations about the pavilion that she could recite her points in her sleep. And it seemed newspapers liked using her picture too.

'The pavilion may be crumbling and need a fortune to restore it, but it's a beautiful building,' Ivan said, looking at the picture everyone liked best, the full-colour one of Maggie and her mum sitting on the pavilion steps: two radiant redheads, smiling at the cameras with the Save Our Pavilion posters in the background. 'But having two beautiful women in the picture certainly helps,' Ivan went on.

'That's the type of thing Shona would say,' Maggie teased him, but she didn't contradict him either.

He said she was beautiful ten times a day, and he meant it. What was more, Maggie was beginning to appreciate her own worth. When there was nobody else around, she'd examined her photo in the paper, trying to be objective about her own face, and realised that people hadn't been lying to her when they said she was beautiful.

She didn't think she would ever totally see it herself. There'd always be that core of self-doubting somewhere, the doubt that made Maggie so lovable and vulnerable. But she was growing stronger and more confident every day. She had become slightly more adventurous when it came to clothes and had just purchased several new bikinis for the holiday she and Ivan were going on in November. They planned to tour Croatia and then spend one week in Dubrovnik mixing culture and the seaside all in one glorious package.

Going on holiday with Ivan wasn't the only momentous event in Maggie's life. He'd asked her to move in with him. Actually, he'd asked her to marry him, but she'd said it was too soon to think of all that.

'It's a wonderful idea and I'm honoured you've asked me,' she said, sitting on his lap, her arms around his neck. 'I just don't want to rush into anything, Ivan.'

'It wouldn't be rushing,' he said. 'But OK, I understand. I won't push you.'

'Thank you for that,' she said. 'You know I'm crazy about you.'

'How crazy?' he asked.

'Oh, this crazy,' she said, leaning forward and hungrily catching his mouth with hers.

At number 18, Faye Reid had decided that there was no point letting her savings sit miserably in the bank for ever and had employed a landscape gardener to transform her back garden.

'I love sitting in yours so much,' she'd said to Christie. 'It's so peaceful and lovely with the pergola and the scent of all those roses, and I thought why am I killing myself trying to make my little square of grass look attractive? I don't know anything about plants and, without professional help, it'll always be a disaster of a bit of lawn, loads of weeds and a few hardy shrubs that can survive my hopeless horticultural skills.'

'Brilliant idea,' Christie said. 'You need a little haven.'

With Christie's help, Faye had come up with the template for her own garden and although the flowers and plants would need a good year to settle in properly, it was a different place already. Now, down the bottom of the garden, she had a new shed which would take her gardening equipment.

'You have to actually do some gardening now,' Christie teased. 'But I promise to help.'

In front of the shed was a bed filled with large rambling plants that screened the shed, then a path that curved in an S shape around the tiny lawn, a lawn that was now sinuously rounded at the edges with beds of flowers cut into it. There were plants clustered amid rocks, beautiful grasses lazing in a raised bed filled with gravel and a cluster of pots with herbs brimming out over the top. Closer to the house was a trellised wall and a pergola, with honeysuckle and fledgling roses planted at the base waiting to spread. Finally, there was a small terracotta paved terrace graced by the new garden furniture she'd bought.

'This is a perfect place to relax,' Christie said when she saw the finished product. She sat down with a glass of wine to admire the handiwork.

'Who needs to go on holiday to get the sun?' added Maggie, sitting back on a lounger with her eyes closed and a glass of wine in one hand.

The evening sun filled the terraced corner.

'I love it,' said Faye proudly. 'I don't know why I didn't do it years ago, but I was always saving money for Amber.'

She talked about Amber all the time now with Maggie and Christie. At first she'd found it hard to mention her daughter's name to others in case she cried. Amber hadn't come home. And although the lines of communication were firmly open and Amber – who had her own US cell phone now – rang frequently but only ever briefly, there was always a sense of sadness and failure in Faye's heart. But she had to move on. Sitting still waiting for Amber was not how she was going to live her life.

It wasn't fair to herself and it wasn't fair to Amber, because one day if, God willing, Amber did come home, she wouldn't want it to be to a mother who sat anxiously watching her every move, balancing her own hopes on Amber's slender shoulders, expecting Amber to be everything to her. That was wrong. The realisation that this was what she'd done before had shocked her.

She was determined to be different. And she'd phoned Grace's makeover friend, Ellen, for that reason. She knew that Ellen didn't want to transform her with red lipstick, blonde streaks and high heels – she hoped she'd gain some of Ellen's wisdom about life and about not being invisible any more. It was time to trade in the Faye Reid who'd hidden herself for eighteen years.

464

'Amber would love this,' Faye said now to Christie and Maggie, looking out over the beautiful garden. 'She always used to wonder why I wouldn't spend money on things and I told her we were broke, that work didn't pay me that much and, in fact, I was just saving it for her future. Crazy really, obsessively saving so that she'd have everything and I didn't see that wasn't what she wanted.'

Christie reached over and held Faye's hand gently.

'She'll come home one day, Faye: I'm sure of it.'

'I hope so,' Faye said sadly. 'I hope so.'

A mile away, Amber sat in a small traffic jam and half listened to the taxi driver telling her all the news since she'd been away. He was very informative and clearly listened to talk radio at length, because once she'd mentioned that she'd been away from Ireland for over three months, he went into great detail to fill her in on the goings-on in the corridors of power.

'That's terrible,' Amber muttered at intervals, glad of his conversation because at least then she didn't need to think about reaching Summer Street and what sort of reception she'd get.

It was all she could think of since she'd decided to come home. Would her mother hug her the way she'd hugged her that day in the hotel in LA? Or would she feel that Amber had pushed her too far by staying away so long, and that by so doing, had sliced a division between them that could never be healed?

If that was the case, she'd say she had come home because American immigration was very efficient and she could easily be deported. But if her mum hugged her, then Amber would admit the truth: she missed her mother more than she could say.

It was all very well being wild and carefree when you had one special person to share that dream with. But when that person turned out to be nothing like you'd imagined, then the dream turned sour pretty quickly. She was working illegally in the US, relying on her tips, while the so-called love of her life was with another woman.

Amber thought back to the day she and Saul had sat in the health food café and talked about her career as an artist.

She remembered that feeling of freedom she'd experienced when she'd realised that the only thing stopping her going home was herself.

She could go home if she wanted to.

'If you want to go back to Ireland, that's great,' Saul said. 'But keep in touch, right? I still want to invest in your talent.'

He'd been about to leave and had casually said that he thought her family must be proud of her.

After spending so long pretending that everything was fine, all the pent-up misery had come tumbling out and Amber had burst into tears.

'My mum and my gran are my family and they were proud of me, and I threw it back in their faces,' she sobbed. 'I didn't understand how much Mum loved me, I just hated the fact that she expected so much of me.'

'That's parents for you,' Saul pointed out. He sat back down at the table and gazed at her seriously. 'Only they don't stop being proud of you.'

'You think so?' Amber asked. The tears kept pouring out. She'd suppressed her sadness for so long. She couldn't be miserable or tearful at work: the glossy LA women came to the salon for pampering, not to stare at the red eyes of a young receptionist who had life problems. Glossy LA women didn't do problems.

'Hey, Amber, get real here. It could have all turned really bad for you,' Saul said. 'Your ex is no prince, that's a fact, and this isn't a city where you want to be broke and alone. But it didn't turn out bad because you're a strong woman, and clever enough to walk away at the right time. You could have hung on with Karl and you didn't. I admire that.'

Amber nodded and dried her eyes with her sleeve.

'I don't know your mom, but I'd say she taught you well and I'd also say she'd be proud of you if she knew.'

Amber thought about it all. 'You're right,' she said, suddenly pleased with herself. 'I am a strong woman. And my mum did teach me well. I'm just like her, in fact.'

The taxi driver dropped Amber and her bags outside number 18 Summer Street.

'Thanks,' he said, when she paid him and gave him a decent tip.

At least she had money now, Amber reflected. She hadn't spent much of her earnings and she had refilled the envelope of cash her mother had given her. Mum was getting that back. The rest could go towards household expenses. If she was going to repeat her final year in school to do her exams, then she was going to be a paying member of the household.

She took a minute to fluff up her hair – even more tawny blonde now thanks to free mesh highlights at work – fix the collar on her sleeveless shirt, and adjust the tiger's-eye pendant around her neck. Her hand stilled around it, caressing the smooth stone. How many times had she touched this and thought of her mother? How many times had it felt like a talisman of her past life?

And now it was going to be part of her future, she decided, shaking back her mane of hair.

Dragging her bags to the front door she stood listening. There were sounds of music and laughter coming from around the back of the house. As the end of the terrace, number 18 had a tiny side passage, and Amber left her bags and walked curiously along it, pushing open the gate at the end and walking into a garden she definitely didn't recognise.

It was so pretty, full of plants and curves and . . . there

was a terrace with sun loungers and sitting on them were her mum, Mrs Devlin and a beautiful red-haired woman that Amber thought might be Mrs Maguire's daughter.

Nobody noticed her approach. They were too busy talking and laughing, and the music – Mum's adored Billie Holiday – was playing loudly. Mum's hair was different too – short and flicky, lovely. She looked so happy, so content.

Amber felt tears well up. Everything was different. What if her mum didn't want her back, what if she'd found other people she wanted to be with?

'Amber?' Faye stood up. She couldn't quite believe it. It had to be a mirage, but it wasn't: it really was her beloved Amber standing awkwardly at one side of the garden, watching.

'Amber!' she roared.

Christie and Maggie watched the two women embrace so hard it must have crushed their bones.

'Mum!'

'Amber!'

They were both sobbing and hugging, and saying sorry at the same time.

Christie got to her feet. 'I think I'll go home,' she whispered to Maggie.

'Me too,' agreed Maggie.

They both slipped out of the side gate, leaving mother and daughter in their own little world.

It was a beautiful evening and the sun was low in the sky now, with a hint of deep pink soaring up from the horizon, bathing Summer Street in its rosy glow. Across the road, children played in the park, dog owners walked slowly as their pets danced along happily, and a teenage boy and girl sat on the pavilion steps talking quietly, their arms around each other.

Christie walked home slowly, thanking all the stars in heaven that she lived in such a special place.

# ACKNOWLEDGEMENTS

There are so many people to say thank you to but first on the list are the three men in my life who are simply the loves of my life: John, Murray and Dylan.

There's nothing nicer in the world than being 'Mummy Cathy', as Murray calls me, in our family. I love you three guys.

Very little would be possible without the help of Mum, who can still make me roar laughing in the middle of a crisis. An enormous, grateful thank you to my darlings Lucy and Francis, amazing and talented people who are always there for me; thanks to Anne for being an inspiring mum, and a big hug to Laura, Naomi and Emer, to whom this book is dedicated. Thanks to Sarah for so many things, and to Lisa for inspiring phone calls.

Thanks also to Annabel, David, Justine, Andrew, Jessica, Luke, Adam, Emily and John for our friendship.

Thanks to Margaret for kindness and for cool unflappability in every crisis; thanks to Marta for being a warm, funny and inspirational person; thanks to the kind and enviably long-legged angel Brenda Doody without whom this book wouldn't have been even started, and no, do not buy me a

KitKat, Brenda, my body is a temple . . . Oh well, OK. You go, girl! And huge thanks to Liz for all your kindnesses.

Heartfelt thanks to Marian Keyes for being there when it mattered; to Kate Thompson for being one of those people who shine like a bright light in your life; to Kate Holmquist for an incredible friendship that was meant to be; to Lisamarie Redmond for being the funniest person I know; to Fiona O'Brien, a beautiful kindred spirit with talent in abundance; to Cathy Barry for endless encouragement; thanks to Susan Zaidan and Barbara Stack, my fellow twin mummies who agree that we're blessed,

To Tricia Scanlan who is an angel herself; to Sheila O'Flanagan, the sharpest, wittiest woman in books. Thanks to my friend, the amazingly wise Maureen Hassett (without whom this book really wouldn't have been finished); to Beccy Cameron for the incredible yoga advice when I needed it; thanks to the gorgeous Amanda Cahill for the fun on Wednesdays; thanks to SuzyMcMullan for hilarious emails; to Ber Kelleher-Nolan for great fun on nights out; to fellow writers Colette Caddle and Suzanne Higgins for the laughs; and to Angela Velden for being such an inspiration.

Enormous thanks and hugs to the marathon-running genius, the kind and lovely Jonathan Lloyd at Curtis Brown. Huge thanks to all the Curtis Brown team, especially the always kind Camilla Goslett, Diana Mackay, Carol Jackson and Sarah Thursby for the exquisite hand-knits that will be family heirlooms. Thanks to Louise Page for utter professionalism in every moment of hilarious panic, and for her marvellous sense of humour. And much thanks to lovely Deborah Schneider for everything she does, all accomplished with style and charm.

Thanks (and really, thanks begins to stop sounding like a useful word and becomes hopeless as it doesn't say enough)

to my family at HarperCollins. When I get into Fulham Palace Road, I want hours to rush around, meet everyone and hear all your news.

First, a huge thanks to the always exquisite Lynne Drew who is simply a marvellous friend and is as wise as she's wonderful; thanks to the über-talented writer and editor Rachel Hore who has such vision that I can hear her voice in my head when I'm doing something daft, and who's taught me how to self-edit; an enormous thanks to Amanda Ridout for being dynamic and making it clear that us small women are a force to be reckoned with. And I'm sure I'm taller . . .

Thanks to the elegant Victoria Barnsley; thanks to Maxine Hitchcock for being an utter darling; thanks to Alice Russell, Fiona McIntosh, Lee Motley, Anne O'Brien, Damon Greeney, Wendy Neale, Clive Kintoff, Lucy Vanderbilt, Katie Espiner, the whole incredible sales and marketing team, all the gang in Glasgow (never let me into the book room again!), gorgeous Anita who lights up the reception, and everyone else in the HC family.

Last but certainly not least, especial thanks to the Irish superheroes: Moira Reilly and Tony Purdue.

Thanks to HarperCollins Australia and New Zealand, who make tours such a joy. (I say tours, but really, we have fun and go to restaurants and manage to shop. Can I live in Alannah Hill's shop?) For all of that, thanks to supermom Mel Caine, my dear friend Karen-Maree Griffiths, Christine Farmer, Louisa Dear, Jim and Pandi Demetriou, Lorraine Steele, Tony Fisk, Anne Simpson and Chris Casey. Thanks also for the welcome to Shaunagh O'Connor and Bron Sibree.

Thanks to my US family at Simon & Schuster: the ever kind Lauren McKenna, Megan McKeever and Anne Dowling (good luck, Anne).

Thanks to my fantastic worldwide family, particularly Anna Bajars at Gummerus and all the lovely team there, and thanks to everyone at Random House, Kontinents, gorgeous Empiria, Presses de la Cité, Sonia Draga, Eksmo and The House of Books and forgive me if I leave anyone out.

Thanks to Mary O'Reilly for sterling work and telling me she was enjoying it as she went, which matters a great deal; thanks to Carol Flynn of Nanny Solutions for giving me information on recruitment firms (naturally, my fictional creations are entirely from my own mind) and who will definitely be entrepreneur of the year any moment now.

Thanks to Jenny Turner, boutique-owner extraordinaire in Enniskerry, for giving me such helpful advice for *Always & Forever*, not to mention showing me lovely clothes to admire when I drop down to the village for a litre of milk ...

Thanks to Helen, Ming and Ethan Xu who are so brave and clever and a wonderful inspiration to me; thanks to Erin Estrich (beautiful inside and out) who will always have a special place in our hearts; thanks to Mary Walsh; to Jill Ross; to Carmel Ruttle; to darling Camilla Carruth; and thanks to one of the most spiritual people I've ever met and who's an amazing mum, Jana. I can't wait to see darling Lili.

Thanks to the lovely person in Dundrum Town Centre who found my Sony digital tape recorder and handed it in with all my notes in it.

A thanks that could go on forever to all the wonderful readers who make sense of what I do. Thanks for all your letters and emails: without you guys, none of it would work.

Thanks to my lovely friends in the bookselling world who are such fun to be with and love book gossip just as much as I do and who are the other vital part of what I do.

Finally, thank you to UNICEF Ireland for giving me the chance to become part of their team. I feel so privileged to be one of their ambassadors and for the chance to go into the field to meet wonderful people who, simply because of where they're born, don't have access to the same education, civil rights and medical help we do. My first trip to Mozambique was both humbling and life-changing. You can't see the work UNICEF do in conjunction with local people and not be changed for life. Remember: these people want a hand up, not a hand out.

So thanks to the UNICEF team: Maura Quinn, Thora Mackey, Grace Kelly, Julianne Savage, Ann Marie Foran, everyone in the UNICEF Ireland office and the incredibly hard-working committee who all work so hard to make a difference. Thanks also to Stephen Rea for being a brilliant travelling companion.

For a television interview once, we worked out how many children would have developed HIV in the time the interview took. Julianne did the maths for this book and the numbers are scary: if it takes you four days to read this book, then 5,700 children will have died from AIDS in that time and 7,014 children under 15 will have become infected with HIV.

The overwhelming majority of these children will have been infected through their mothers at birth. It would have cost around $5 for drugs to cut this infection rate by 50% but these mothers, like so many women in impoverished countries, wouldn't have access to either the drugs or the information about them. That's what UNICEF is about: changing lives for the better.

# Keep up to date with Cathy

## Log onto www.cathykelly.com
## for the latest news, reviews and photographs

You'll also find details on all Cathy's books –
including sample chapters and what happened
next to your favourite characters– plus sign up
to Cathy's Newsletter